3

TREASURED DREAMS

Book Three in the Treasure Hunter Series

KENDALL TALBOT

D1569583

Published 2018

Treasured Dreams

© 2018 by Kendall Talbot

ISBN: 9781072447245

This is a work of fiction. Names, characters, places, and incidents are either the product of the author's imagination or are used fictitiously, and any resemblance to actual persons, living or dead, business establishments, events, or locales is entirely coincidental.

❀ Created with Vellum

About the Author

Kendall Talbot is a thrill seeker, hopeless romantic, virtual killer, and award-winning author of stories that'll have your heart thumping from the action-packed suspense in exotic locations and the swoon-worthy romance.

Kendall has sought thrills in all 46 countries she's visited. She's abseiled down freezing waterfalls, catapulted out of a white-water raft, jumped off a mountain with a man who spoke little English, and got way too close to a sixteen-foot shark. When she isn't writing heart-thumping suspense in exotic locations, she's enjoying wine and cheese with her crazy friends, and planning her next thrilling international escape.

She lives in Brisbane, Australia with her very own hero and a fluffy little dog who specializes in hijacking her writing time. Meanwhile, Kendall's two sons are off making their own adventures – look out world.

Kendall's book, *Lost in Kakadu* won the acclaimed title of Romantic Book of the Year 2014, and her books have also been finalists for Best Romantic Suspense, Best Crime Novel, Best Continuing Series, and Best New Author.

I love to hear from my readers!

Find my books and chat with me via any of the contacts below:

- www.kendalltalbot.com

- Email: kendall@universe.com.au
- Kendall Talbot Facebook page

Or you can follow me on any of the following channels:

- Amazon
- Bookbub
- Goodreads

Books by Kendall Talbot

Maximum Exposure Series

(These books are stand-alone and can be read in any order):

Extreme Limit

Deadly Twist

Zero Escape

Other Stand-Alone books:

Jagged Edge

Lost in Kakadu

Double Take

Waves of Fate Series

First Fate

Feral Fate

Final Fate

Treasure Hunter Series:

Treasured Secrets

Treasured Lies

Treasured Dreams

If you sign up to my newsletter you can help with fun things like naming characters and giving characters quirky traits and interesting jobs. You'll also get my book, Breathless Encounters which is exclusive to my newsletter followers only, for free.

Here's my newsletter signup link if you're interested:

http://www.kendalltalbot.com.au/newsletter.html

Chapter One

Rosalina didn't want to look at the bruises on her leg, but she couldn't help it. With each passing day the swelling had subsided, but the dark cloud still stained her skin from her toes to her knee. She was lucky though. Considering half a helicopter had landed upon her, it was a miracle she hadn't broken both her legs. It was impossible not to think about all the injuries she'd sustained since she'd started hunting for treasure with her fiancé. This one was by far the worst. At night, when she closed her eyes, her dreams were filled with a scrambled concoction of glistening treasure and crazy mad men trying to steal it from them.

Archer took the crutches from her, rested them against *Evangeline's* chrome railing and helped her lift her other leg onto the plush sun lounge. The plaster cast that ran from below her knee to the edge of her toes was heavy and she was sick of lugging it around. She'd painted her toenails that poked out of the cast in bright pink. At the time, she'd thought it would cheer her up.

It hadn't.

Three more weeks until the cast came off, and it couldn't come soon enough.

"How's that?" Archer knelt at her side and lifted her chin with his finger, drawing her eyes to his. "Better?"

She nodded. "It's good." Her blood pounded against her swollen skin, throbbing out a painful pulse that was her constant companion. Now that her legs were elevated though, the agony should subside.

Archer tilted his head at her. It was one of her fiancé's signature moves and the angle he chose captured the sunlight in a way that had the golden halo of flecks circling his dark irises positively dancing. It was one of the first things that'd attracted her to him. His eyes had a personality of their own. He ran his thumb over her chin and when he touched her lips, she kissed his thumb.

Five weeks ago, while she'd lain on the dive deck below with half a mangled helicopter pinning her to the teak timber, she'd thought she'd lost him. He'd plummeted from the helicopter into the black water and vanished. With each ticking second, as black smoke had poured over her and she'd waited for Archer to resurface, her heart had crumbled to a thousand pieces and drifted away with the smoke-filled air.

Since that gut-wrenching moment, when she'd thought her new fiancé had died, she'd been gripped with melancholy. Archer, on the other hand, had been stretching his creativeness to try to cheer her up. Bringing her back to *Evangeline* was another one of his attempts to help snap her out of it. She hadn't been back here since that night. Yet it was one of her favorite places in the world, so maybe he was right.

"You stay right here," he said. "I'll grab a few things and be right back."

She nodded. He leaned forward, kissed her lips, then walked away. He was spectacular to watch. Light and shade alternated off his broad shoulders as he strode across the sunlit deck, and his perfectly toned bottom glided up and down with every step. He soon disappeared down the steps.

To avoid looking at her legs again, Rosalina flicked her long skirt over them. It took several attempts to cover them completely, and it was only once that was done that she looked around.

Over her left shoulder she had a perfect view across other magnificent yachts in Italy's Marina Di San Vencenzo. Most marinas could barely accommodate Archer's yacht, but here in Livorno's prestigious new yacht club, *Evangeline* was like a toy in comparison to the magnificent vessels they were moored up alongside.

The morning sun hanging high in the sky, dripped dazzling stars onto all the shiny chrome surfaces on the surrounding vessels. The sparkle made Rosalina wish she'd remembered her sunglasses. Normally she'd never forget something like that, but ever since the helicopter crash a dark fog had shrouded her mind. She let out a slow breath as she turned her attention to the damaged part of the sun deck.

Jimmy and Alessandro had been working tirelessly to clear away as much of the crash remnants as they could, but the police forensics team had restricted their access. The image of the body covered by a white cloth flashed into her mind. Thankfully, Ignatius Montpellier was the only person who'd died in that fiery crash.

She felt no remorse for him.

The damage from the crash was extensive. Most of the helicopter pad, which was one level up, had been crushed into the deck she was now sitting on. The narrow steps that had led up to the helipad were a tangle of metal and plastic. One of the helicopter's blades must've struck the deck before ricocheting into the ocean, because a long-jagged gash in the teak decking looked as if a great monster had sliced through the polished wood with a broadsword.

Jimmy's deep, hearty belly laugh had her smiling.

Their laughter grew louder and soon they stepped onto the sun deck. As usual, Jimmy wore no shirt, and the sun captured the graying chest hairs covering his leathery skin. With a smile on his face and a six-pack of beer clutched in his hand, he strode towards Rosalina with his signature prize-fighter swagger. He was light on his feet for such a solid man.

"Heya Rosa." Jimmy's chin was a rough abrasion on her skin as he leaned over to brush his lips to her cheek.

"Ciao, Jimmy, how are you?"

"Couldn't be better. How about you? Getting used to those crutches yet?"

Rosa huffed. "No. I don't think I ever will."

He placed an antipasti platter on the table at her side, and as she eyed off the lovely selection of cured meats, cheeses and olives, a champagne cork popped.

"What's going on?" She suppressed a grin as she nodded at the champagne Archer had just opened. They usually didn't have a drink until at least midday.

"Actually quite a few things." Archer topped up the five crystal champagne glasses that he'd brought up with him.

"Not all of us have been lazing around on our ass since Dickhead crashed his helicopter into us." Jimmy's grin was getting ridiculous now. They were both itching to tell her something.

She refrained from pointing out that she would rather be doing anything but sitting around on her bottom. Archer held a glass towards her and she sat up to reach for it. "Okay, I'm ready. What is it?"

Archer eyeballed Jimmy. "Should we wait till Alessandro and Ginger get here?"

Jimmy opened a bottle of Peroni. "That'd be the right thing to do." He took a swig of beer and his lip quivered as he attempted to keep a straight face.

"Okay then." She could play this game too. "Who made the antipasti platter? It looks good."

"I did." Archer bit into a slice of cured meat that she guessed to be Bresaola. As he tugged it from his teeth, he turned to Jimmy. "Maybe we could tell Rosa some of the news."

Jimmy's eyes switched from the salami he was about to devour to Archer, and he nodded with over-exaggerated emphasis.

Archer rubbed his hands together and then picked up a champagne glass for himself. "The police have finished combing over this area so we're right to go ahead with the renovations." Archer strode from her and stopped near the center of the sun deck. "Jimmy has suggested we put a Jacuzzi right here." He indicated to his right. "And he was thinking a rooftop bar over this side."

She glanced at Jimmy who was grinning like a drunken teenager. "Sounds like you boys have thought this through."

"Not me." Archer palmed his chest, feigning horror at her suggestion. "I'm thinking something much more sophisticated would be appropriate."

"Really?" She said it sarcastically.

Archer always enjoyed a drink after a day of scuba diving. It was a wonder they hadn't thought to put a bar on the top deck before.

Rosalina hadn't put any thought into what they could do with the sundeck. Now that it was almost completely destroyed, they had an opportunity to do anything they wanted. Maybe this was exactly the distraction she needed. "You know what we could do? We could set up one of those amazing outdoor kitchens. With a teppanyaki barbeque or something similar."

Archer snapped his fingers. "Great idea. It could go here, right alongside the bar."

"We could have a nice table setting up here too so we can eat outside for a change." She could already picture it brimming with food.

"We'll need a decent beer fridge." Jimmy added, in all seriousness.

She laughed. "Of course we will."

"Hey guys."

Rosalina couldn't see her yet, but Ginger's Australian accent was unmistakable. The younger woman stepped into view. Her tiny white shorts showed off her long, tanned legs as she strode towards Rosalina.

"Buongiorno. How is everyone?" Alessandro strode across the sundeck behind Ginger, carrying a manila folder.

Archer's eyes shot to the folder and by the excitement glimmering in his eyes, Rosalina figured half of his excitement was because of whatever it contained. Ginger clutched her blonde braid in her hand and bent down to kiss Rosalina's cheek.

Alessandro placed the folder on the sun lounge at Rosalina's left and then he too kissed both her cheeks. For the first time since she'd met Alessandro, he seemed to be wearing a different aftershave. Ginger would've been the influence behind that.

"*Come ti senti?*" His eyes were the picture of concern.

"I'm okay, just sick of these crutches. And tired of sitting on my bottom, despite what Archer and Jimmy think."

All of them gathered around her and she felt both the weight of their concern and the prickle of anticipation. Their concern probably wasn't about her injuries. They would heal. It was because she hadn't been herself lately. Nearly losing the man she loved had consumed every waking thought and some of her dreams, as did nearly being killed herself. It'd been five weeks and she really was struggling to snap out of the gloom that gripped her.

Whatever was in the folder had both Archer and Jimmy falling over each other with excitement, and knowing them, it probably had something to do with ancient relics. She prepared herself, because she wasn't sure she could handle anything to do with treasure hunting yet.

"Did they tell you what I found?" Alessandro indicated at Archer and Jimmy.

"No. They wanted to wait till you were here."

Alessandro nodded. "*Grazie, signori.*" The sun bounced off his slicked black hair as he bent over to open the folder and reached in. Archer sat on the edge of Rosalina's sun lounge and carefully lifted her legs onto his. His eyes, however, remained on the paperwork Alessandro lifted out.

"Ginger and I made five copies." As a university professor, Alessandro was accustomed to making presentations to large crowds, but as he bounced from one foot to the other, Rosalina couldn't decide if he was excited or nervous.

The pages were held together with gold clips, and Alessandro handed one set to each of them, starting with Rosalina.

"I've done some digging on the Awa Maru. Because it's been some time since we've discussed it, I took the liberty of summarizing what we already knew about her."

Rosalina scanned down the list as Alessandro read out their findings so far.

"As we all know, the Awa Maru was a passenger ship that was requisitioned by the Japanese during the war, and in 1945 she was deployed by the Red Cross to carry supplies to American and allied prisoners of war held in Japanese custody. After delivering those supplies to Singapore, she was boarded with stranded marines, military personnel, and civilians."

"And treasure." Jimmy's voice was that of an excited child.

"Yes. Treasure." The word treasure was highlighted and underlined on the page. "Billions of dollars apparently."

"Apparently." Rosalina emphasized, and shrugged her shoulder when Archer glanced her way.

Alessandro cleared his throat. "She is also rumored to have carried the priceless Peking Man skulls."

Rosalina couldn't fathom what someone would do with the 500,000-year-old skulls. Yes, they were priceless, but how someone could ever expect to sell them without revealing their identity was a mystery she couldn't piece together either.

"Near midnight on the last day of March 1945," Alessandro

continued, "the Awa Maru was torpedoed by an American submarine."

"And there was only one survivor," Ginger said.

"Yes," Alessandro agreed. "The captain's steward, who is reported to have been the sole survivor of three torpedoed ships."

"That's one lucky bastard." Jimmy shook his head.

"Or unlucky," Archer said, "depending on which way you look at it."

Jimmy screwed up his face. "True."

"In 1980, China located the wreck of the Awa Maru, but no treasure was found." Alessandro folded a slice of Culatello cured meat around a semi-ripened tomato, popped the appetizer in his mouth and watched Ginger scroll her finger down the page as she read. He waited until she was near the bottom before he spoke again. "You all knew this up to this point."

Ginger looked at him and grinned a silly, childish grin. Sometimes Rosalina forgot Ginger was only twenty-one years old.

Alessandro rubbed his hands together. "I've spent *significativo* time with my associates in the war museum, and I'm quite *certo* I have something."

"Spit it out, numb-nuts." Jimmy was an impatient man.

Ginger slapped Jimmy in the arm as Alessandro reached back into the folder and removed an A4-sized black-and-white photo.

The photo was of ten Japanese men. They were in uniform and positioned in two rows with the men at the front seated and the five men at the back standing behind them. None of them smiled. The man centered at the front held what looked like a Japanese samurai sword. A banner to the left of the picture had Japanese writing on it.

"Are you going to tell us what it means, or should we start guessing?" Jimmy scowled at Alessandro.

Jimmy and Alessandro were both as bad as each other and had made it practically a hobby to needle each other at every opportunity. Before he'd taken up the offer to come treasure hunting with her and Archer, Alessandro was a professor of ancient history and architecture at Accadamia di Belle Arti in Florence and had spent a significant portion of his day lecturing to disinterested students in a packed auditorium. Out here, he only had one naughty student to contend with. . . Jimmy. As usual, though, Alessandro appeared to take it in his stride.

"This photo was taken in the Solomon Islands on a small island called Munda," Alessandro said.

Rosalina examined the background of the photo and noticed dense jungle behind the men, and possibly a wooden hut with a thatched roof hiding within the vegetation.

"These men were World War Two Pacific soldiers. See this *signore?*" Alessandro pointed at the man seated at the far left. "That's Kimoda Yukimura."

Archer snapped his fingers. "The only guy to survive the sinking of the Awa Maru."

"*Correcto*. See this *signore?*" Alessandro pointed at the man standing directly behind Kimoda Yukimura. "That's Hiro Yukimura. Kimoda's identical twin brother."

Chapter Two

For five weeks, Nox had tried to make his way back to where it had all begun. It hadn't been easy with no money, food or clothing, and no idea where he was to start with. Every day, hell, nearly every hour, had presented him with another problem. But finally, he'd arrived outside the church he'd lived in from the age of twelve until the day he'd killed his father and ran off in search of the Calimala treasure.

He didn't have a plan. Nothing he did seemed planned these days. He only had a mission. The same mission he'd had since he discovered the ancient scroll hidden in the trumpet statue when he was ten years old. His mission was to find the Calimala treasure that had been stolen from the Church of St Apostoli seven hundred years ago.

That treasure was his.

His death would be the only thing that would stop him from succeeding. They'd tried. In the last year, he'd nearly died several times.

And yet here he was . . . a dead man walking.

He stood at the edge of the Piazza Del Limbo. The large concrete expanse did little to respect the hundreds of babies buried beneath it centuries ago. Nox had always thought it a little ironic given that the priests he grew up with were constantly worshipping the dead.

The church at the far edge of the plaza looked vacant, but then, it always had. Unlike all the other magnificent churches in Florence, the

Church of St Apostoli was insignificant in grandeur. It stood amongst rows of homes that had been built and rebuilt continually over the centuries to the point where a cursory glance made it impossible to establish what era they belonged to.

Nox scanned the area. Nobody was around. He didn't expect anyone to be. At this time of night, most people were filling their bellies with food. That thought made his stomach growl. He couldn't remember the last time he'd eaten a decent meal. Over the last couple of weeks, he'd had to fight for nearly every feed. He'd stolen food from gardens, stalls, and the odd café table when no one was looking. He'd rummaged through garbage bins, hoping for something of substance. He'd begged for food from complete strangers and he'd feasted on oranges that he'd plucked from an overburdened tree until he threw up.

Standing outside the church, aromas of garlic and herbs wafting from the abundant cafés nearby made his stomach twist with hunger. He needed to eat.

The back kitchen in the church's underground was where he'd cooked his last meal. It was also the room where he'd killed his father. He suddenly wondered whether Father Benedici's death had been recorded as an accident as he'd planned, or was Nox's name at the top of the suspect list?

He didn't care. They wouldn't catch him. Everyone thought he was dead.

He ran his hand over his hair and for the hundredth time was surprised at its length. For decades, he'd been shaving his head. The last time he'd set foot in this church he'd been bald and overweight. Now his hair was shoulder-length and he was thin. Very thin. The chances of anyone recognizing him were minuscule.

This epiphany had Nox conclude that returning to his old bedroom was going to be much easier than he'd anticipated.

Riding that confidence, he strode towards the front door of the church, stepped over the landing and entered the peaceful space. A quick glance around confirmed he was alone. Nox walked up the black-and-white tiled mosaic floor and went straight for the statue of the woman with the eagle on her arm. Behind her, hidden beneath a heavy black drape, was a small door. His only hope was that it was unlocked. It usually was.

His wish was granted and Nox ducked his head as he entered the darkened space.

Nox had been crawling the tunnels of this church for decades. He knew every passage, every secret doorway, every room. He even knew where he could stand that allowed sounds to travel from a significant distance away. It was one of these very spots that had blessed him with the information about the treasure. For that he would be forever grateful.

Nox didn't have too many things to be grateful for.

He pushed off from the wall, glided down the steps and navigated the tunnels to his bedroom without running into a single soul. Nox pushed open his bedroom door, stepped in, and closed the door behind him.

The smell of disinfectant invaded his nostrils. The room had been cleaned. He clenched his fist at that.

One of the things about this room he'd loved was the musty old smell of the mushrooms he'd grown in there. That pungent scent had almost masked his own distinct body odor. Almost. Having lived with Trimethylaminuria all his life, Nox rarely smelled his apparently offensive stench. Fish Odor syndrome was something he'd learned to live with.

The disease had helped shape him into the man he was today. A man he was proud to be. He was a survivor. He'd survived a spear through his belly, near drowning, falling from a lighthouse, starvation and dehydration. He was stronger than he ever been in his whole life.

His bed was still there, but the mattress was gone. He suspected the tapes he'd hidden in the base of the bed were gone too. He lifted one of the wooden slats on the bed and peered inside. Empty. His mind flicked over the numerous people who had featured on the tapes as he contemplated who could've found them.

What did they do with all the incriminating evidence I'd collated on them?

Probably nothing.

Whoever found the tapes most likely featured on one or two of them. Nox had gathered evidence for years, recording anything he could use as blackmail.

Not too many people had remained unscathed.

The only other thing, the one crucial thing he'd returned to this room for, was hidden behind a brick in the wall.

He rolled his shoulders, trying to manipulate the tension mounted there as he stepped up to the head of the bed and sat on the wooden slats. Every brick looked the same. He hoped that would be his salvation. Without any prior knowledge of his hiding hole, it would be impossible for others to know where to look. He let his breath out slowly as he wriggled the brick from its place in the wall. Inch by inch, the brick eased towards him, then finally, with his fingers on either side, he tugged it free.

He sighed with relief. His scroll, the seven-hundred-year-old leather parchment, was still there. He plucked it from its hiding place and, resisting the urge to unroll it, he slipped the scroll into his pocket. Although the words upon it had already been committed to his memory, just having the ancient letter in his possession made the treasure hunt seem more real. Knowing he was the only person alive to ever have seen the ancient vow filled him with divine power.

As Nox shoved the brick back into place, a furry creature weaved between his legs.

He gasped. "Shadow!"

Nox reached down and scooped the feline into his arms. The silver-gray Chartreus purred as Nox hugged the cat to his chest.

"How are you, my boy? I knew you'd survive without me."

The cat licked the back of his hand.

"I'm sorry, I don't have anything for you." Nox sighed as Shadow purred under his caress. "They took my tanks away."

"Did they give the mice to you, my *bellissimo* boy?" One of Nox's greatest joys had been watching Shadow devour the rodents whenever the stray slinked into his room. For nearly a decade, Shadow had frequented his bedside via the small air tunnel at the back. It was the only visitor Nox ever looked forward to.

"Come on, I'm hungry too. Let's see what we can find."

Nox hooked his arm under the cat's belly and clutched him to his chest as he opened the door and listened. Nothing but stone-cold silence. He didn't expect anything else. Unless someone had moved into Father Benedici's room after Nox had killed him, then he didn't think anyone would be living in this wing of the church anymore.

He navigated the passages to the kitchen. This was just one of the three kitchens in the church and orphanage complex. The main one that serviced the orphanage was a full industrial kitchen designed to feed the hundreds of orphans whose parents had passed away, or had abandoned them, such as in Nox's case. The second kitchen was up in the youngest building in the church. Most of the brothers lived up there. The kitchen Nox headed towards had once been used by the staff. It was small, basic and rarely frequented by anyone else.

This was where Nox had eaten most of his meals. It was also where he'd cooked up the poisonous mushroom risotto that'd killed his father.

Chapter Three

Rosalina watched her grandmother's frail hands as she peeled the skin from the red onion. Nonna's bulbous knuckles were white with the motion, and yet she handled the knife with ease.

Rosalina was relegated to the kitchen table, and Nonna was insistent that she elevate her legs. It made cooking so much harder when she couldn't stand.

Together, they'd been preparing meals all morning. But Rosalina wasn't complaining. . . she loved every minute in this old kitchen with her Nonna.

Villa Pandolfini, with its twelve bedrooms and sprawling vineyards, was her home. But this kitchen was where she'd grown up under the feet of her wonderful grandmother, learning everything there was to learn about food and cooking the traditional Italian way. Cooking was at the heart of her family.

She'd missed this place while she was abroad. The seven-hundred-year-old villa had so much character and history. Four generations of her family had lived here. Tears threatened as she reflected on how much she'd missed them all, and particularly her Nonna. Her grandmother wouldn't be around for much longer, and just the thought of it produced a lump in her throat that was impossible to swallow.

Rosalina wondered, as she often had, how different her life

would've been had her mother lived. She'd been just seven years old when her mother died. Although she had a few wonderful memories of her mother, none of them were in this kitchen, or any kitchen for that matter. Maybe her mother hadn't liked cooking, which was hard to believe, because all the other Calucci women in her family were fabulous cooks.

"Glide it across." Nonna clutched her fingers around Rosalina's hand and curled the rubber spatula from one side of the fine sieve to the other, forcing the mashed sweet potato through the small holes. "*Come questo.*"

"Yes, Nonna."

"Make it easier. *Comprendere?*"

"*Sì*, Nonna."

Rosalina's grandmother was not one to argue with. Nonna chose to ignore the fact that Rosalina had spent two years in one of Italy's finest culinary schools. Rosalina didn't mind, though. Any chance to refine her skills under her grandmother's expertise was golden.

Nonna plucked a cork board from the cluttered duchess shelf and placed it on the counter next to the stove. She then opened the oven door, and the delicious aroma of roasted garlic wafted about the kitchen. Nonna placed the steaming tray of parmesan puffs onto the cork mat.

The temptation to eat one of the pastries would've been impossible to resist had Rosalina been able to reach them. Having the leg cast removed couldn't come soon enough.

She glanced at the clock over the fireplace. Two more hours until Nonna's friends arrived for their monthly gathering. They'd originally taken turns when it came to who'd host the afternoon tea, but it wasn't long before Nonna's amazing cooking and her dominating personality overrode their plans, and the venue had been permanently fixed at Nonna's villa for as long as Rosalina could remember.

Preparing for these afternoons filled with food, laughter and the occasional tear from one of the ladies, produced some of Rosalina's fondest memories of growing up in this kitchen. Nonna was blessed to have such a wonderful group of ladies to grow old with, and they'd certainly shared some significant ups and downs together. Nonna became a widow in her early fifties, but with the abundance of

Calucci family and her life-long friends surrounding her, she was rarely alone.

Rosalina plucked fresh herbs from the ceramic pots Nonna had moved from the windowsill to the table for her. She finely chopped the chives and parsley and folded them into the sweet potato and mashed ricotta cheese with a little sea salt. Then she added half the flour and folded it in with a spoon.

Once again, Nonna showed her how to mix by guiding her hand, and despite Nonna's petite fingers, the old lady had a strong grip.

The last big feast Rosalina prepared had been for her own engagement party. She'd set the long table up in the vineyards that stretched from the back of the villa right up to the lowest row of grapevines.

It had been a magical afternoon. And night, too. Her heart ached with the weight of what had happened after that wonderful evening though. It was hard to believe that was five weeks ago. She sighed as she recalled Archer whisking her around the dance floor like a professional ballroom dancer.

Rosalina suddenly remembered a moment at her engagement party that'd slipped from her mind. In light of everything that had happened since then. . . the helicopter crash, the treasure stolen from the yacht, her broken leg and Archer's broken ribs, it wasn't surprising she'd forgotten.

But now it came back to her as if she were reliving the moment.

Rosalina had been wearing a bracelet. It was a silver chain with only one small pendant dangling from it. The chain had been given to her by her mother the very last time Rosalina had seen her.

When Nonna had seen her wearing the bracelet at the engagement party, a look of horror had swept across her face, then she'd raced out of the room.

Rosalina hadn't had a chance to chase her, and after all that'd happened, she hadn't thought any more of the bracelet or Nonna's odd reaction to it.

Until now.

Rosalina's stomach rolled. She had to ask Nonna. There was no way she could leave it undiscussed. As much as she didn't want to upset Nonna, she had to know why the bracelet had affected her that way.

Rosalina removed the sweet potato gnocchi dough from the bowl, placed it onto the lightly floured tabletop, and divided it into four portions. Nonna sat at her side, and together they rolled the gnocchi into a thick log. Nonna was quick, working with expert skill as she cut the log into bite-sized pieces and pressed a fork into each one to make corrugated indentations. Within a matter of seconds, Nonna had prepared a whole plateful.

Before Nonna could stand up again, Rosalina seized the opportunity. She placed her flour-dusted hand on her grandmother's wrist.

"Nonna," she said.

It may've been the way she said it, or maybe Nonna had been dreading this very conversation, but when Nonna looked up at her she had fear in her eyes.

"At my engagement party, I wore a silver bracelet. When you saw it, you. . . you looked horrified. What was it, Nonna?"

Nonna turned to her hands and stared at them, rubbing them together to dust off some of the flour. It was a long time before she seemed ready to speak, and this was unusual. Nonna loved to talk.

Finally, she looked up at Rosalina with tears pooling in her eyes. "That bracelet was *la madre di.*"

"I know, Nonna. . . Mom gave it to me."

Nonna frowned and her eyes searched Rosalina's, maybe seeking the truth.

"*Madre* was leaving for hospital to have the baby. I was scared for her, and she gave me the bracelet to look after until she came home with my new brother or sister."

Nonna blinked up at her. "Your *padre* looked everywhere for that bracelet. Did you know?"

Rosalina nodded. "I didn't want to give it to him. It was the last thing Mom gave me, so I hid it in the back of that picture frame on my nightstand."

"With the photo of *Padre*?"

She nodded again. That photo was the only photo Rosalina had of her father smiling. He'd never smiled again after her mother died.

"Is that why you reacted the way you did, Nonna?"

Her grandmother pursed her lips. She looked frozen in that moment, and Rosalina knew there was more. "Tell me, Nonna. If it's about my mom, I want to know." Acid pooled in Rosalina's stomach.

Nonna stood and walked to the stove, her back to Rosalina. "It was long time ago, Rosalina. It not *necessario* to bring up such dreadful things."

"What dreadful things?" Rosalina struggled to her feet, and without the crutches, waddled to her grandmother. She placed her hand on Nonna's bony shoulder and squeezed. "Nonna. Tell me."

Nonna cupped her own cheeks as if horrified by what she was being asked to do. There was a long pause before she met Rosalina's gaze. Tears threatened to spill over, and Rosalina resisted the powerful urge to clutch her grandmother to her chest. She needed to be strong. She needed to know what happened.

"Sit." Nonna motioned with her hands for Rosalina to return to her chair, then Nonna sat at her side, clutching her own hands as if trying to stop them from trembling.

"Your *padre* was always busy busy with the vines, *la raccolta, la semina, nutrimento*. Then there was the grapes and the wine-making. He rarely came home. Here. Your *madre* was very overwhelmed with six *bambini*." Nonna slowly ran her hand through the flour on the table. "She missed him so."

At the emotion quavering in her grandmother's voice, Rosalina knew not to interrupt.

"But after many years she stopped missing him. Soon he was no longer *importante*. You, your sisters were everything. It was like your *padre* was just guest who *visitato* from time to time. Once you started school, your mother, she have more time on her hands and she found herself work at the florist in town. She loved it. All day she would design *bellis-simo fiori* for men wanting to romance their lovers. She blossomed. . . just like the flowers she arrange. And men flocked to her like bees to the sweet flower nectar."

Rosalina had a feeling she knew where this was going and wasn't sure she wanted to hear any more. But how could she stop it? She'd begged Nonna to tell her the story; now she had to listen.

"At first, your mother she laugh at the *attenzione*. She could not believe that any man was interested in a woman with six children. But they were. Many were. Your mother was *bellissimo*, confident, sensual. Yet hollow. She needed more than what she had at home. Especially as you children were growing."

Icy fear built in Rosalina's as she dreaded what secret Nonna was about to reveal. "Nonna, you don't need to go on."

"Yes I do." Her eyes, blazing with fire, snapped to Rosalina. "I have started now. You will hear it all."

Rosalina could barely swallow. "Shall I fetch a glass of water? Or tea maybe?"

"Wine. We will have a wine."

Rosalina hesitated, unsure if Nonna was serious, but before she could decide, Nonna stood and reached for the bottle in the cupboard at her right. She plucked two wine glasses from the hanging rack, splashed a generous quantity into each glass and handed one to Rosalina. Before Nonna sat back down, she took a large sip.

Nonna rolled her tongue over her bottom lip as she returned to her seat. She wrapped both flour-caked hands around her glass, then she let out a long, slow breath. "Your mother met another man. She never told anyone his name. It just a little fun, nothing serious, she told me. And it was." Nonna paused, took another sip of wine, and swallowed hard. "Until she fall pregnant."

Rosalina cupped her mouth. A wave of fire flooded her body as she watched Nonna swallow another large gulp of wine. She too had a sip, hoping the wine would settle her churning stomach.

"Filippo?" It was a question, although it need not be. Rosalina already knew the answer.

Nonna rocked ever so slightly back and forward for a long moment. "When your mother pass away during childbirth, your *padre* was forced to look after a child that was not his own flesh and blood."

Chapter Four

Nox casually strolled his way to the kitchen, pleased that he'd gone undetected. He pushed open the door and nearly walked straight into Brother Linchin.

"*Scusami,*" Brother Linchin said as he placed a large ceramic bowl of creamy pasta on the table and stepped back.

The bald man had put on significant weight since Nox had last seen him. Nox waited, watching his eyes for a flicker of recognition, but there wasn't one.

"*Scusate un po perso.*" Nox pretended to be lost. Then, he realized his mistake. Shadow, his beautiful gray cat, was going to ruin his disguise. Nobody had been able to even get near Shadow other than Nox.

Linchin blinked, lowered his eyes and backed up farther. When sweat beaded on Linchin's upper lip, Nox was certain his ruse was over.

"Still sneaking food I see, Linchin."

Linchin's lips quivered. "Don't hurt me."

"Why would I hurt you? We're just having a conversation." But Linchin's words proved that Nox had been identified as a murderer. *But which murder?* There'd been a few.

"I thought you were--"

"Dead." Nox finished his sentence. "You can't believe everything you see in the media." Nox laughed as he put Shadow on the table. The cat slinked towards Linchin's bowl of steaming pasta.

Linchin's backed up against the counter, his hands up. "I … I didn't …"

A little beat of curiosity pulsed through Nox's brain as he raised his eyebrows. "What are they saying about me?"

The fat man's chins trembled. "They say you tried to. . . to kill some people in Greece. I thought you'd been shot."

"*Si.*" Nox nodded. "That's all true. I did try to kill them. And yes, I was shot with a spear gun." Nox winced at the memory. "I drifted for days at sea until a couple of complete fools found me and held me captive on their island for God knows how long."

Nox was babbling like a madman, but he had so much to say. An extraordinary number of things had happened to him since he'd last left this room. Nobody knew what he'd been through. If he told them, nobody would believe him. Nor would they care.

Shadow made loud smacking noises as he helped himself to dinner.

Linchin blinked at Nox. Fear riddled his eyes as he inched sideways.

A big pot was sitting on the stove. The very same pot he'd used to make the poisonous mushroom risotto he'd fed to his father. He was surprised it hadn't been taken away as evidence in the murder.

"So, you did try to kill those people?" Linchin's eyes were as big as Shadow's.

"Yeah," Nox said flippantly. "They had my treasure."

"Oh no!" Linchin's body trembled. His eyes darted from Nox to the door. Suddenly, he made a run for it. His rotund belly bounced off the table as he tried to round it.

Nox dodged to the front of the table, blocking his escape, and Linchin halted, trapped. A blaze of red flooded his cheeks. Sweat trickled from his temples.

Sweat dribbled from Nox's armpits. It would only be a matter of seconds before his pungent fish odor filled the room. A large kitchen knife was on the counter. He snatched it up and waved the blade at Linchin. Linchin skidded to a halt.

Nox had never killed with a knife before. He imagined blood gushing from the fat man's neck, and the thought made him cringe in disgust. There were many other ways to kill, without getting messy.

Linchin's lip quivered. "Don't. Please. I won't tell anyone I saw you. I can keep a secret."

"Like the secret about Sofia. You remember her, don't you?"

A flicker of recognition crossed the fat coward's eyes.

"You were the only one who knew how I felt about her," Nox persisted, softening his voice. "I told you in confidence. You were supposed to be my friend." He enjoyed watching the fat man squirm. "You set me up."

Red spider veins crawled across Linchin's bulging eyes.

"She was a pretty girl," Nox continued, merciless. "She didn't look so pretty on her deathbed, though."

Shadow finished licking the bowl and began purring as he cleaned his whiskers with his front paw.

Nox waved the knife. The kitchen lights glinted off the blade. "Humiliation is a powerful motivator."

Linchin lunged for the fork on the table, and Shadow arched his back, bristling his hairs.

"I'm sorry." The fat man aimed the utensil at Nox like a weapon.

"You don't look sorry."

Shadow was up on his haunches, hissing at Linchin.

"Good boy," Nox said to his feline friend. His only friend.

Nox's body odor flooded the room. He usually didn't smell his own pungent scent. Times of excitement or fear heightened his stench, and in this moment, excitement was dominating.

"I. . . I p-promise I won't tell anyone." Linchin's body odor soured the room too.

"I know you won't." Nox chuckled.

A gasp released from Linchin's throat and he lunged for the door. Nox slashed with the knife and a bloody wound opened up on Linchin's arm. The fat man screamed and backed away, glaring at the red gash.

Linchin's incessant high-pitched squeals echoed off the ancient stone walls.

"Shut up, you fool." Nox hissed though clenched teeth.

But he didn't. Spittle foamed at the corners of Linchin's mouth, the white of his eyes blazed and his knuckles bulged as he clutched at the counter he'd backed up to.

Nox raged with adrenaline as he grabbed the big steel pot off the counter. He crossed the distance between them in a flash, and as he stared into Linchin's startled eyes, he smashed the pot over fat man's head. A handful of the creamy pasta escaped the pot and splattered up the wall.

Linchin dropped so hard and fast his head hit the stone floor with a loud crack. Nox clenched his jaw and whacked Linchin over the head again.

Nox backed away, and with the room silent again, he grew conscious of his cat purring.

He wiped the sweat from his brow. Then he used a spoon to scrape the remains of the pasta from the pot and dished out another feed to share with Shadow.

Chapter Five

Archer and Jimmy worked quickly, stripping back the damaged curved lounge, reducing the area to its shell. Jimmy yanked at the loose bits and pieces with his bare hands.

For a fifty-year-old, Jimmy had bounced back remarkably well after being shot by Nox. But Archer certainly didn't need him ruining his recovery by acting out his anger. "Calm down, big fella, you'll hurt yourself." Archer rested his hand on the corded muscle running over his mate's shoulder.

"You know our treasure is going to end up on the black market somewhere." Jimmy tossed a large wooden splinter into the growing pile of rubbish.

"I know."

"That's our treasure." Jimmy's squared out jaw and steely eyes underscored his rage.

Archer bit back the temptation to share his anger with Jimmy. It was a pointless waste of energy. "We found it. But it doesn't mean it's ours."

"Bullshit! Don't give me that crap; you had every intention of laying claim to that treasure." Jimmy clenched his jaw, forcing the muscles in his chin to bulge.

Measured control was nearly impossible. "Agreed, but then we were handing it over to Alessandro's museum for safekeeping."

"Right, so you were going to claim it first." The tendons in Jimmy's neck were cables of steel. "Like I said. It was our treasure."

Archer wiped his brow. Having the treasure stolen from them while they were celebrating his engagement to Rosalina was what hurt the most. Not only did it ruin their special night, it also meant Ignatius Montpellier had been listening in to their conversations for some time. There was no other way to explain how he'd known exactly when they would be off the yacht and for how long.

Although the thieving bastard had burned to a crisp in that helicopter crash, the precious pieces he'd stolen were never found. Someone had helped him, and that pissed-off Archer even more.

"I hope you're planning on going after the Awa Maru treasure, boss." This was as close as Jimmy would get to pleading. Ever since Jimmy had put his hands on that first piece of gold, he'd been hooked on the obsession that'd been in Archer's veins since he was a little boy.

"I've thought about it."

"And?"

"We still need to be careful."

"What for? Nox is dead. Ignatius is dead. It's just us and that treasure now."

"I saw that boat scooting away from *Evangeline* right before the helicopter crashed. We know Iggy was working with others. We've got no idea who stole the treasure or what they know about us."

"They don't know everything. Alessandro only just found out about the Solomon Islands thing. They'd have no idea we were heading there. We'll have that treasure on board *Evangeline* before they even get their shit together."

"You know it's never that easy, Jimmy."

"It's been easy so far. Look how much we found at Anafi."

"And look how dangerous that was."

"Nobody died."

Archer cocked his head at his buddy. "Four people died."

"Only the bad guys, and they don't count."

Archer chuckled. "We'll have a tough time convincing Rosalina; she's certain this treasure is cursed."

Jimmy waggled his finger at Archer. "No. No. She said the Cali-mala treasure was cursed. Not the Awa Maru treasure."

"True." A piece of melted leather that he'd been working on for a while finally broke free, and Archer flung it aside.

His thoughts drifted to Alessandro's discovery that Kimoda had an identical twin brother. It was a long shot that the two of them would've had the opportunity to steal the treasure during the war, but it was an angle worth following. Archer couldn't believe how lucky they were to have Alessandro on board. His research skills were priceless. "Do you think Alex is onto something with this identical twin brother thing?"

"Shit yeah. But figuring out that Kimoda Yukimura had a twin brother wouldn't have been too hard." Jimmy screwed up his face. "Why hasn't anyone gone down that road before?"

Archer shrugged. "Maybe they have."

"But the brother was near where the Awa Maru went down. Wouldn't that have put up some red flags?"

"Possibly."

"Possibly! Maybe!" Jimmy threw his hands in the air. "Put your balls out there. Tell me what you think."

Archer blinked at his best mate. "Calm down. What's wrong with you? You've been pissed-off all morning. I thought helping me fix *Evangeline* would be a good thing for you."

"I want to go after that treasure." Jimmy tossed an unrecognizable piece of wreckage away.

"And we will."

"When?"

"I don't know when."

"And that's the problem. We've been sitting around here for five weeks doing jack shit when we could be on our way to the Solomons."

"We've had no choice. The police have been crawling all over the place, and Rosalina has a broken leg. Not to mention my broken ribs. What else could we do? We're getting there, Jimmy. I promise."

"Not soon enough." Jimmy whacked at the shattered lounge with a sledgehammer.

Chapter Six

Nox was covered in sweat by the time he'd dragged Linchin's body to his old bedroom. But it was the best option. The chances of anyone going in there had to be minimal.

He returned to the kitchen and wiped his fingerprints off everything he'd touched. A surge of satisfaction coursed through him as he hugged Shadow to his chest and smoothed down the cat's fur. He was good at revenge, and there were still many more sinners on his list. Maybe he could tick off a few more while he was here.

Sadly, there was no time. He had to get to that bastard Archer before they headed off after the treasure again. For all he knew, they may have already gone.

This next part of his plan he'd mapped out, but in order to capture Rosalina again he needed a weapon. And he knew exactly where to start.

Over the years, Nox had been to the nurse's office on many occasions. Usually he snuck in there while no one was looking. The drugs had come in handy. Morphine, in particular, was one of his favorites, and it was what he sought this time, too. He felt completely at home as he traveled the underground church labyrinth towards the nurse's office near the orphanage. With each silent step, he felt more confident that his visit would go unnoticed.

Nurse Isabella was a stick-thin waif of a woman who was a jittery rattle of nerves. Nox always wondered if she'd been taking her own concoction of drugs to put her in that state, but if not, maybe she ought to.

Isabella's job had been a busy one. With more than one hundred boys in the orphanage, there was always some incident or illness that had needed tending to. Nox had had his share of bloody injuries, most at the hands of his regular tormentors. They were incidents that everyone, including Nurse Isabella, had neglected to report. Nobody had wanted to cast a shadow over the orphanage, especially after the first orphanage he went to had been shut down because of illicit activity.

If he ran into Isabella, he'd have no qualms about smacking an apology out of her, too.

Nox paused at the edge of a poorly lit tunnel and listened. This was one of the places that cast voices from afar. Now though, there wasn't even a whisper of noise. The entire establishment was holding its breath, or so it seemed. He stepped from the shadows and walked with a measured pace towards the nurse's office. At the door, he didn't bother knocking; he pulled down the handle and pushed. It was locked.

"Damn it."

Nox didn't contemplate breaking through. The door would be at least three inches of solid wood.

The nurse's office was manned twenty-four hours a day, so that meant the nurse was out, tending to someone. All Nox had to do was wait. He thought about going back to his old bedroom, but with Linchin's lifeless body lying inside, that wasn't an option. Instead, he decided to head towards the Esagonale room. It was his other favorite room in the ancient building.

Nox stepped up to the door and listened. As he expected, he heard nothing, so he opened it and entered the hexagonal-shaped room, closed the door behind him, and flicked on the light switch.

Everything was as he'd left it. Of course, it would be. This room was rarely used and had probably looked the same for hundreds of years. The chunky wooden table accompanied with the just as solid and elaborately decorated wooden chairs were all centuries old, as was the wax encumbered candelabrum dangling from the ceiling. Nox tugged out one of the heavy seats and sat on the cold wood.

He twisted his antique ring around his finger. The three red stones dominating the ring glimmered in the dim light. He took that as a sign. . . a glimmer of hope that he was nearing the end. Thirty years was long enough, and he was so close he could almost taste the gold on his tongue. Although he'd been closer before. He'd literally had his hands on his precious pieces. Before the bitch speared him, that was.

Nox heard laughter and jumped up to switch off the light. Plunged into darkness, he edged back against the wall as the laughter grew louder. A man and a woman. His heart launched to his throat when the door swung open.

They stepped into the room. They shut the door.

Seconds later there was heavy breathing mingled with lip sucking.

They were kissing. It was disgusting.

His brain ticked over his options. He could let them go on and hope they simply left once they were finished. Or he could attack them in the dark, and they'd have no idea what hit them.

"Oh, Isabella. You smell so beautiful tonight."

Isabella! The scrawny nurse. Nox couldn't believe his ears.

Chairs scraped back. His blood boiled.

They're going to have sex on the table. My table!

"And you taste lovely," she whispered.

Nox had had enough. He searched the wall in the darkness, looking for a weapon. Dozens of times he'd been in the room, and yet he couldn't recall seeing anything other than the table and chairs.

Their breathing became fervid, their moaning deeper, longer. A zipper glided, and Nox gritted his teeth in revulsion.

"What's that?" The woman had fear etched into her voice.

"What?"

"That. . . that smell."

Nox froze. His damn body odor was his enemy. He had to act now.

At that very moment, his foot touched something on the floor, and he knew exactly what it was. The small cast-iron statue had probably been used as a door stop for centuries, though at some point in its history it had most likely held a much more glorious posting. Nox picked it up from the floor and admired its significant weight. The little statue was about to make history.

The element of surprise was in his favor. Nox strode forward and swung blindly in the darkness at the table. The statue thumped into something solid. It wasn't wood. There was another loud moan, not one of sexual arousal, either.

"Niccolò, are you okay?"

A body flopped to the floor.

Nox stepped towards her voice. "No, he's not."

She screamed. He slammed down the statue.

Her scream died and he hit her again. And again.

Silence returned to the room.

Nox let out the breath he'd been holding and when he inhaled again, he sucked in the metallic scent of blood mingled with his own fishy odor.

It was time to get the keys to the nurse's station, and as much as he didn't want to, he had to turn on the light. Inhaling a deep breath to calm himself, he raised the statue above his head in case either of his victims moved, then flicked the switch.

Blood and mangled bits of flesh splattered his table.

His stomach buckled.

He held his breath and cringed while feeling along the woman's body. It was an eternity before he located the jingling keys in her coat. With the keys secured in his pocket, Nox wiped his fingerprints off the little statue and returned it to the floor. Then he flicked off the light with his knuckle, left the Esagonale room and closed the door, and using Isabella's keys, he locked it.

The nurse's station was only a short walk, and once there he tried six keys before he unlocked the door. He shut the door behind him and turned on the light.

Nox went straight for the drug cabinet and again fiddled with the keys until he located the right one to open the door. He stuffed a couple of syringes into his pocket, along with bottles of morphine, and a few other bottles with names he couldn't pronounce.

He took a moment to go through then desk drawers in the hope of finding cash. In the bottom drawer, he found something that was so much better.

A gun.

Nox drew the small weapon out from beneath the paperwork and turned it over in his hands. He would never have guessed a woman like

Isabella would obtain a weapon. Then again, he would never have imagined her having sex on the ancient table in the Esagonale room either.

Checking through the other drawers, he found a chocolate bar, but nothing else of interest. He stood to leave, and that was when he noticed a handbag hanging on a hook on the back of the door. Upending it, he spilled the contents onto the table and rummaged through the purse. Nox smiled at the one hundred and sixty euro slotted into the side. It was more cash than he'd held in months.

Nox put the gun, money, drugs, syringes and his scroll into the bag. Then he took off his coat and slung the bag over his shoulder and put his coat back on. Now all his worldly possessions were tucked up nicely near his armpit and away from view. For the third time that night, Nox wiped down the surfaces he'd touched and left the room.

With multiple weapons in his possession, the only thing left to do was kidnap Rosalina. For months he'd stewed over a suitable place to keep her captive once he'd kidnapped her. The answer had come to him one afternoon a couple of weeks ago while he'd been sitting in a sun-drenched Rome street begging for food. An old man and little boy had approached him to toss a few coins into his lap. When Nox had glanced up to thank them, he'd looked into the eyes of a man who had ruined many young boy's lives.

Father Domenico Zanobi. The name had frozen on his lips at the sight of the pedophile.

Nox had gone unnoticed. Of course, he had. It was more than thirty years since Zanobi had laid eyes on him. But Nox could remember it like it was yesterday. Zanobi had had a penchant for glaring down at the orphaned boys from the curved balcony that hovered over their dormitory beds. Most of the children would be asleep when Zanobi scanned from one sleeping child to the next.

Nox had wanted to be chosen. He'd wanted to spend time with Zanobi, as most of the other boys had done. When Zanobi's eyes fell on Nox, his childish breath would catch in his throat as he waited for his turn. But Zanobi would sneer at Nox and move onto the next bed.

When Zanobi had tossed those coins into his lap in Rome, Nox had glanced at the young boy holding the old man's hand. The child had looked blissfully happy.

Nox had never had that pleasure.

He'd followed Zanobi that day in Rome. Watched him hold the little boy's hand as he led him through the cobbled streets. When the old predator went along a narrow alley and disappeared up a set of ancient stairs, Nox had followed him up there. Nox had gone into Zanobi's room and after Nox had let the young boy leave with a new pair of white shoes, Nox had reacquainted himself with the old bastard.

Zanobi would never choose another boy again.

That freak encounter in the stifling afternoon sun in Rome had been another sign of destiny. It had helped Nox work out where he would take Rosalina once he kidnapped her.

The old orphanage.

The one that had been abandoned in a hurry one sunny morning thirty years ago. Until that day in Rome, he'd forgotten all about it. He just hoped they hadn't demolished it.

Nox felt for the gun in the bag beneath his armpit as he ate the chocolate bar and worked his way along the tunnels beneath the church. He would have no hesitation using the weapon if he needed to. Rosalina had turned out to be a strong one. She'd nearly strangled him the last time he'd captured her. She would not get that opportunity again.

Ever since Rosalina had shot him with that spear, she'd hit the top of his revenge list. Once he'd finished using her, he was looking forward to watching her die a slow and agonizing death.

Chapter Seven

Rosalina dragged her eyes away from the twinkling lights on the neighboring yacht outside *Evangeline*'s window to stir the garlic and butter with her wooden spoon. The aromas were just beginning to release when she tossed in the onion and stirred.

"That smells great." Ginger sidled up beside her. She had already learned so much from Rosalina about cooking, and yet she never seemed to tire of it.

"Tip the rice in," Rosalina instructed.

Ginger poured in the Arborio rice as Rosalina continued to stir. "We coat all the grains in the butter first and stir until they become a little translucent."

"Okay." Ginger rose up on her toes to look into the pot.

"The trick with a good risotto is to allow the grains of rice to absorb all the moisture before you add any more liquid," Rosalina said.

In another pot on the stove she had her homemade duck stock already simmering. The duck meat was resting beneath foil on a plate in the oven.

"Now we increase the heat and pour in the red wine."

Rosalina took a quick sip first. She couldn't help herself. Made from Villa Pandolfini's own grapes, the wine had a deep pomegranate color and offered subtle aromas of oak and raspberry. She would never tire of its exquisite taste.

"How are *le mie belle signore* going in the kitchen?" Alessandro swanned up to them, draped his arms over both Rosalina's and Ginger's shoulders, and kissed each of them on the cheek. His long lashes lowered and his chocolate-colored eyes softened as he turned his attention to Ginger.

"Rosa's teaching me how to make duck risotto." Ginger cast Alessandro a sparkling glance and a crimson tide colored her creamy skin. Rosalina turned away, grinning.

"Oh *delizioso*. I'm so hungry." Alessandro loved his food, which had always made him the perfect guinea pig for Rosalina's creations.

"How are you boys going?" Rosalina glanced at him over her shoulder. "Solved all the problems of the world?"

"Some. . . yes. Some not quite yet." He laughed as he reached for the bottle of wine at her side and brought it to his nose. "Mmmm." The sound of appreciation tumbled from his throat as he poured a good splash into a glass he'd plucked off the kitchen counter.

"Here, Ginger, see how all the wine has evaporated from the rice?" Rosalina pointed at the grains in the pot.

"Yes."

"Now we add the duck stock, one ladleful at a time. But we must keep stirring, otherwise the grains will burn. Here, you take over."

The ladies swapped places, and Rosalina hobbled to the counter and sat on one of the bar stools.

"Alessandro, how about you set the table? Ginger and I will have dinner ready in about twenty minutes. It's all in here." Rosalina had a basket ready with cutlery, bread plates, pasta bowls, butter, and a fresh sourdough, wrapped in a dish towel that she'd taken out of the oven just ten minutes earlier.

"Oh sure." He gave Ginger a kiss on the cheek then, juggling the basket and his wine, he headed towards the stairs.

"I think this is ready for more stock," Ginger said.

"Okay. Put in another ladle."

"You don't want to check?"

"No." Rosalina offered Ginger a reassuring smile.

Ginger scooped the duck stock from the saucepan and tipped it over the rice. Once she'd stirred it a couple of times, she looked over at Rosalina, and the corners of her lips curled to a smile. "This smells so yummy."

"Wait till you taste it. Would you mind getting the duck meat out of the oven for me? I might as well shred it while I'm sitting here."

"Sure." Ginger reached for an oven mitt and opened the door, releasing the earthy sweet aroma of the roasted duck.

When Rosalina had made the stock earlier, she'd removed the meat from the bones but left the pieces whole as much as possible so they wouldn't dry out. Now, as she shredded the meat with two forks, it fell apart beautifully.

"That's all the stock into the rice now, Rosa."

"Okay, so add the peas. And then we'll add the duck and parmesan, and it'll be ready."

"Is that it?" Ginger's finely plucked brows raised on her forehead.

"Sure is, I told you it was easy." She rose to her feet, hopped to the crockery cupboard, and searched for a serving bowl large enough for the risotto. She fished out a large white dish with gold-trimmed edges.

"Here. . . use this dish for the risotto."

"Sure. Let me grab it." Ginger placed the bowl next to the hotplates, and Rosalina hopped back to the counter. "I can finish this if you like. Why don't you head on upstairs? I'll bring this up in a sec."

"Okay. Thanks." Rosalina reached for her crutches and made her way to the stairway and hopped up the stairs.

The men were seated at the new bar. Discreet blue lighting filtered from beneath the marble top, accentuating the decorative pattern in the stainless-steel sheeting. It was the first time Rosalina had seen it at night, and she was delighted with her choices.

Archer swiveled on his chair and jumped off to greet her.

"Hey babe." He kissed her cheek, and then pulled out a chair at the head of their new dining table. He lifted the crutches from her and leaned them against the railing. From where she sat, she could take in almost all the deck as well as the marina that was lit up like a pretty Christmas parade.

Within seconds, Jimmy placed a glass of red wine in front of her. "Here you go, baby cakes."

It'd been a while since Jimmy had called her that nickname, and right now it felt so normal.

"Thanks, Jimmy. It's lovely up here." The renovations were almost complete, and it looked like the bar and jacuzzi had always been there.

"We should've done this a long time ago." Archer read her own thoughts as he slipped onto his bar stool and spun towards the back of the yacht.

Rosalina admired the three polished timber steps leading up to the new jacuzzi that was still empty. The high polish on the teak timber reflected the blue lighting. "They've done such a good job in just two weeks."

"That's what you get when you pay bucket-loads of money," Alessandro said, and the way he'd said it made Rosalina glance at him. Neither of them had grown up with the opulent lifestyle they were living on *Evangeline,* and for the first time she wondered if Alessandro was jealous of Archer's wealth. Alessandro was prone to jealousy from time to time.

"Jimmy and I've been helping, too." Archer raised his glass at Jimmy.

"Too right. The sooner we get this done, the sooner we get moving again."

Rosalina cocked her head at Archer. "Moving? Where are we going?"

Archer glared at his mate, and Jimmy mouthed, 'what'?

Archer clenched his jaw and cleared his throat. "We were going to discuss it after dinner," Archer said. "Is it nearly ready?"

She nodded, but her mind was already chewing over what Jimmy and Archer had been planning. "Ginger should be up in a moment."

As if on cue, Ginger announced her arrival. "Who's hungry?"

Rosalina had her back to Ginger, but she could hear the smile in her voice.

No sooner had Ginger placed the risotto in the center of the timber tabletop than the three men had slotted into chairs around it. Archer slipped into the booth seat at Rosalina's right-hand side, and his hand found her leg. He leaned over and kissed her cheek, and she could tell he was trying to smooth over Jimmy's gaff.

It seemed the boys had a plan, and Jimmy had already blown it.

"Is Helen joining us?" Rosalina asked.

Archer's mother rarely joined them for dinner. Although she was gradually improving, she was still a long way from escaping the tortured mind that had trapped her for decades.

Archer squeezed Rosalina's knee. "Not tonight. She was sleeping when I checked in on her."

Rosalina wasn't surprised, but she was always worried about Helen eating enough; the elderly woman was still very thin.

"Alex, can you please slice up the sourdough?" Ginger asked.

"Sure, *il mio dolce*."

Alessandro reached for the bread and removed it from the dish towel.

Rosalina admired her own baking. The five decorative slices she'd made in the dough before she'd put it in the oven looked perfectly measured in the golden crust. Sourdough had a lovely depth of flavor, which was why she believed it went so well with risotto, especially with a slathering of butter. Real butter, not that ghastly margarine spread.

Alessandro cut the loaf into thick slices and juggled a steaming piece onto her bread plate. Rosalina quickly buttered it while it was still warm and licked her lips as the butter melted.

She decided to open the conversation as Ginger spooned the risotto into their bowls. "Okay, fellas. How about you tell me what's going on?"

Both Jimmy and Alessandro looked in Archer's direction, and he in turn bit into the sourdough poised at his lips and hastily swallowed the mouthful. "Okay. We've been going through my dad's scrapbooks, trying to decipher his scrambled notes."

Rosalina nodded. So far, the notebooks, which potentially had important clues to finding treasure, had remained allusive.

"Do you remember how each notebook had four countries listed inside the front cover?" Archer said.

Rosalina placed a spoonful of risotto in her mouth, nodding as she enjoyed the delicious roasted duck meat mixed with creamy rice.

"Okay. We started by looking for any references to Singapore in the books. We only did this because we know for a fact that the Awa Maru was docked there. Alessandro, how about you carry on?"

Archer practically tossed the conversation to Alessandro, and by the look on his face, the Italian wasn't expecting it.

Alessandro swallowed a lump of food and cleared his throat, slipping into professor-mode. Rosalina had come to recognize it. He had learned to relax since he'd joined them in their treasure hunting but give Alessandro the opportunity to detail anything and he was guaranteed to deliver it as if it were a university lecture.

"While we couldn't work out much from his notes, we did notice there were nearly as many references to Singapore as there were to Saigon."

Alessandro would've been in his element if he'd had a whiteboard to scribble on as he spoke. "I obtained the Awa Maru's tabular record of movement since the day she was built. During the course of her four short years, she only visited Saigon once." He held up his forefinger. "On 24th February, 1945." He paused to drink his wine.

"How'd ya get your hands on that?" Jimmy huffed.

Alessandro shrugged his shoulders. "During the Second World War, the Japanese Imperial Navy were arguably the most powerful navy in the world. Once they were crushed under the US navy, who at the time were considered underdogs, their impeccable tabular records became the subject of comprehensive scrutiny. Everyone wanted to establish what the Japanese did wrong. Fortunately for us, the records are readily available."

"So, what's the significance of the Saigon visit?" Rosalina asked.

Alessandro picked up his fork and used it as a pointer. "By those early months of 1945, the war was drawing to a close, but the United States was growing concerned about the number of prisoners of war held by the Japanese. You have to remember that the Japanese merchant fleet had been nearly entirely decimated. That meant the Japanese were having trouble getting supplies to their own troops, let alone the prisoners."

"Come on, professor, stop with the history lesson and get to the good part." Jimmy huffed.

"Rosalina and Ginger need to know all the facts." Alessandro thrust his chin out and waited until Jimmy spooned a mouthful of risotto into his mouth before he carried on. "So, by utilizing neutral Switzerland, the US arranged for the Awa Maru to carry Red Cross relief supplies. The Japanese agreed, of course, because they saw it as an opportunity to load up the ship, which could carry much more than just the supplies, with other cargo. In particular, their precious gold bullion."

"Not just gold bullion," Jimmy added. "Diamonds, ivory, jewels, antiques. . . all sorts of precious babies."

"Sounds like a lot." Ginger grinned.

Alessandro swallowed another mouthful of food. "It was substantial. And not only would it have weighed a great deal, it would have required significant space." Alessandro waggled his fork as he spoke. "It would've been difficult to load it onto the ship without many people knowing about it."

Rosalina noticed the twinkle in his eye. "I assume you know who else knew about the treasure?"

"*Corretto.*" Alessandro's eyebrows bounced together. "I believe Kimoda Yukimura's brother knew."

Jimmy nodded, as if this was earth-shattering proof of where the treasure was.

"How did you work that out?" Rosalina cocked her head.

"Kimoda joined the Japanese navy, but his brother, Hiro, became a pilot. In 1941, he started flying the Nakajima A6M2 fighter bombers. By 1944, he was the squad leader. However, in 1944 he lost a few toes in an air battle--"

"Eeew, ouch." Ginger scrunched up her face.

". . . and Hiro was switched over to flying the Kawasaki Ki-56."

Rosalina cocked her head at Alessandro. "How did you get this information?"

Alessandro's dark eyebrows wiggled. "The Ministry of the Navy of Japan was responsible for the development and training of the Imperial Japanese Navy Air Service. Their pilot training was rigorous, selective, and meticulously documented. Much of these records were seized by the end of the war. Fortunately, many of the details are on public record. It's taken weeks to process. Ginger helped."

Ginger and Alessandro shared a look. Rosalina had forgotten that Ginger could read and speak Japanese. Although the blonde seemed so ditzy at times, she was far from it.

"So why is the plane-type significant?" Rosalina asked.

"Because the Kawasaki Ki-56 planes were freight transport planes. They could carry up to fourteen passengers and eight tons in weight."

"Ahhh." Rosalina had a sinking feeling she knew where this conversation was going. She glanced across the table and noted that everyone had finished their meal. "Should we move to the lounges?"

"Sure." Archer slipped out of the booth seat, and as he helped Rosalina with her crutches, she noticed Jimmy swipe the last slice of sourdough before he left the table.

Rosalina settled into one of the new lounge chairs, and everyone but Alessandro sat too. Alessandro stood at the front of the group with a pen gripped within his fingers.

"Are you right there, professor? Want to take a seat?" Jimmy waggled his half-eaten sourdough at him.

"*Bene, grazie.*" Alessandro took Jimmy's ribbing all in his stride. He cleared his throat, ensuring he had all their attention.

"With the help of my colleagues at the war museum, we traced the movements of the Kawasaki Ki-56 planes. There were only 121 of these planes built during 1940 and 1943. But by 1945, only thirty-four were still operational."

"Come on, Alessandro, you're really dragging this out." Jimmy was like a bear in shackles.

Alessandro pursed his lips and glared at Jimmy. "Do you have somewhere you need to be?"

"No. But we don't need to know all the boring details." Jimmy huffed.

"They're not boring to me," Ginger said.

"Nor me," Rosalina agreed.

"*Precisamente.* Shall I continue?" He waited, and Rosalina had the feeling he could do this all-night long.

Jimmy rolled his eyes, and his shoulders sagged. "Whenever you're ready."

"Okay, so the Awa Maru, with Kimoda Yukimura as the captain's steward, was in Saigon for three days from 25th February to the 28th February 1945. Nine Kawasaki Ki-56 freight planes were also there on 27th of February. I have no indisputable proof that Hiro Yukimura was flying one of those planes." He paused for effect.

"But?" Rosalina proffered.

"But only one of those planes was also in Singapore on the 28th March, 1945. That's the day the Awa Maru left on its final fateful voyage."

"That's brilliant, Alessandro," Archer said. "So, what happened?"

"The plane was next documented in Munda in the Solomon Islands."

Rosalina snapped her fingers. "Oh Jimmy, do you remember we found that gold star on Wade's globe, right over the Solomon Islands?"

Jimmy beamed. "Sure do, and that's why we're heading there."

Archer huffed and shot a glance at Jimmy. His clenched jaw showed his annoyance.

Rosalina folded her arms across her chest and turned her attention to Archer. "Oh, we are, are we?"

Archer placed his hand over hers and sighed. "I was going to talk to you about it in private later." He glanced sideways at Jimmy.

"Whoops." Jimmy got busy drinking his wine.

"We think this is worth looking into." Archer's brow furrowed as he gazed at Rosalina with pleading eyes.

"What? We're just going to sail into the Solomon Islands and find forty tons of gold sitting right there on the beach?" Rosalina ran her clenched fists over her thighs. "So far, our treasure hunting has scored us nothing but bullet wounds, knife injuries, broken ribs, broken legs, and a ruined yacht. We have nothing else to show for it." She hoped they heard the fury quivering in her own voice.

"Not nothing. We have the monkey statue. And the cannon." Archer cocked his head, and the lights highlighted the gold flecks around his irises. His signature move annoyed her this time.

She'd forgotten all about the monkey statue. It was the only piece of treasure other than the cannon that hadn't been stolen from them. It was a miracle it wasn't stolen.

Although it was heavy, Ignatius had enough men to help him lift it, so the only reason they could work out as to why the precious piece had been left behind was because Ignatius simply didn't notice it. He must've walked right past it several times when he stole all the other treasure. The cannon, on the other hand, was definitely too heavy to move.

"What's happened to the monkey statue and the cannon anyway?" she said.

Alessandro sat down beside Ginger and their fingers intertwined on her lap. "The cannon is in storage at the Accademia di Belle Arti, and the monkey statue is sealed up in a crate," Alessandro said. "We were waiting to see if all the other pieces of the Calimala treasure resurfaced, so we could document them together. But it looks like they're *finito*."

"It's hard to believe over fifty ancient relics have simply vanished." Archer's words were laced with the tone of defeat. When he curled his arm over Rosalina's shoulder, his chest rose and fell with a long sigh. She softened her resolve and snuggled in.

Rosalina hadn't had much time to think about the missing treasure. But she couldn't deny that she too was disheartened that they had nothing to show for all their hard work. Ignatius had paid for the theft with his life, but whoever he was working with had so far gotten away with a priceless fortune.

Chapter Eight

Nox's luck was finally changing for the better. After he'd walked out of the church of St Apostoli unnoticed, it had only taken him an hour to find Nurse Isabella's car.

Thanks to the little central-locking opener on the set of keys he'd found in her pocket, all he had to do was walk the streets around the church, pressing the button, until the lights on the silver Fiat Linear lit up. In addition to that lucky find, the car had a full tank of gas. The ruby red stones in the antique ring offered a warm inner glow when the dashboard lit up.

It was a sign. A very good sign.

The Linear made his mission a whole lot easier. Until he'd found the car, he hadn't really processed how he was physically going to kidnap Rosalina.

Next on his agenda was locating that old orphanage. He'd remembered it was on a cliff overlooking the ocean, and he remembered the day he, along with all the boys, had been loaded up into one of two buses and moved from that imposing building to the new orphanage next to the church of St Apostoli in the middle of Florence. If his recall was accurate, the bus trip had taken just over two hours.

Armed with that information, he headed towards Livorno. It was very convenient that Livorno was also the place where the helicopter had crashed into Archer's yacht. He just hoped that *Evangeline*, and in particular, Rosalina hadn't moved away since he'd seen news footage of the helicopter crash weeks ago.

Nox arrived at Livorno early on a Friday morning and, out of curiosity, went straight to the marina.

He parked the car, but on account of the serious security he could do little else other than glance from a distance at the rows and rows of boats lined up in the marina. There were so many boats. A ridiculous amount of money floated out there. He had viewed *Evangeline* through high-powered binoculars so often while following Rosalina and her friends in the Greek Islands that he would easily recognize the enormous yacht.

Not today, though.

Even so, buoyed by the reasoning that he couldn't possibly see all the boats in the marina from his position at the fence, he clung to the hope that Archer's yacht might still be out there.

Striding back, he spied an information booth alongside the fancy marina shops and headed towards it. As he glanced around, wishing for a chance sighting of Archer or Rosalina, he ran his hands through his hair in an attempt to smooth it down. Despite actually being a homeless person, he didn't want to look like one.

Nox walked past two restaurants. One looked very fancy, with double white table cloths, highly polished silver, and an abundance of waiters, eager to please. The other restaurant, with its wooden bench tables and glass canisters loaded with cutlery, was much more casual. The smells of bacon and tomato had his stomach snarling, and the urge to reach over one of the tables and snatch the food right off someone's plate was powerful. He resisted though and made it to the information booth without incident.

He stepped through the door and walked up to the young brunette woman at the counter. Nox refrained from smiling. His teeth were already yellow when he'd left Florence months ago; he'd hate to think what they looked like now. He had no idea when he'd last brushed them.

"*Buongiorno.*" She smiled as he approached.

"*Buongiorno. Ho una strana richiesta, sai di un vecchio orfanotrofio abbandonato qui da qualche parte?*" Nox didn't need to enter into small talk; he just hoped the woman wasn't too young to remember the old orphanage that he prayed was near here.

She frowned at him and shook her head. "*Non mi dispiace.*"

"It was a big old building that was built right on the edge of the cliff. Around here somewhere."

"On a cliff? Well from here towards the direction of Pisa there are mainly sandy beaches, so maybe heading south is the best thing to do. If you drive along the Stada Statale One you may find it." She smiled.

Nox smiled too, and when the woman eased back from the counter, he clamped his lips over his teeth again.

He left the information booth and as he walked towards the casual restaurant, a party of four people started rising from the table. Nox did a quick assessment of the restaurant and decided no staff were watching.

The foursome was no sooner off their seats than Nox was at their table, forcing as much of the leftover food as he could into his mouth. As he chomped down on the crispy bacon, he shoved a half-eaten bread roll into his pocket, along with two foil packets of butter. He was nearly through a leftover egg when one of the waiters came storming towards him.

Nox put his hands up in a 'calm down' gesture and backed away from the table. He snatched a half-empty water bottle off another table as he raced out the restaurant. They wouldn't follow him. . . of that he was certain. He'd stolen food in this fashion from restaurants on many occasions, and not once had the staff ever chased him. They probably felt sorry for him. Or disgusted. Either way, it was an ideal way to get a quick, free feed.

By the time he reached the car, he'd finished the bread roll and two small slabs of butter. Nox slipped in behind the wheel and started the engine. He didn't bother to look over the boats again. He would try again once he'd located the old orphanage.

Nox navigated his way out of Livorno, and his plan was to keep the ocean on his right. That way he could navigate his way to the road the closest to the ocean.

Within half an hour, he was on the Stada Statale One. It was a picturesque drive, with vast blue ocean stretching as far as he could see and meeting with the equally blue sky. It seemed every stretch of road had been developed with hotel after hotel, all built to maximize their exposure to the view. Occasionally the road took him inland, but before long it would swing back towards the sea again.

Twenty minutes later, the buildings became less frequent. Nox saw train tracks that ran parallel to the road. He was heading in the right direction. He had a vivid memory of seeing a train from the overcrowded bus all those years ago. It had been the first time he'd ever seen a train, despite hearing them on many occasions as he'd laid in bed at night.

It was a strange thing to be going back to the building where he'd first learned fear. The hairs on his neck bristled at the reflection.

A train suddenly appeared out of nowhere and shot past him with a fierce clickety-clack. Nox slowed down and counted the carriages as they whizzed by. Twelve. The train he'd seen last time he'd been on this strip of road had just six carriages.

Since he'd hit this road, it seemed his was the only car that skirted along the edge of the cliff. There was no barrier that would save a wayward driver from plummeting straight into the ocean some thirty or so yards below. Nox wound down his window and smelled the crisp ocean air. He wasn't too fond of that smell after spending months trapped on a deserted island with a couple of crazy twin brothers, although that time of his life already seemed like a lifetime ago.

Once again, the road veered inland, and scraggy bush that had battled the brutal ocean breezes lined the asphalt at drastic angles. A road appeared on his right, and his breath caught. It was the one. He didn't know how he knew; he just did.

After locating a place to turn, he headed back to the road and veered left into it. Disfigured trees lined the first part of the road, but that soon changed to spindly grass and ragged weeds. Within seconds, Nox spied a large terracotta rooftop. He'd arrived.

The building was impressive. A large stone castle, dominating the ocean point had it situated like a fortress. A vine that had threatened to take over the lower half of the building had long ago died. Now it resembled jagged black veins creeping all over the stone walls.

Holes puncturing the brick walls had once been windows, though their black bars remained. The dilapidated condition of the old building was a welcome sight, because it meant nobody had moved in since the children and pedophiles had been shipped out. However, it didn't stop the deep and bitter loneliness Nox had suffered as a child threatening to well up in him.

Nox shoved the untimely feelings aside as he curved around the crumbling four-tiered concrete fountain and pulled the car right up to the front steps. It was impossible to hide the car anywhere else. His only hope was that nobody would come wandering his way.

The wind caught his hair and whipped it around his face as he stepped out of the car. He pulled it back from his eyes and held it there as he shut the car door and stepped on the moldy concrete steps that curved up to the front door. He was halfway up the stairs before the wind settled enough to let his hair go.

Nox took a moment to take in the building. Three large arched windows had once been an impressive architectural feature of the grand design, but the only glass that remained was at the very top of the arch. The vine he'd noticed from afar was covered in sharp thorns that stuck out like little razor blades all over the twigs.

Some of the upper-floor windows had the remains of shutters. Two of them dangled precariously and threatened to drop off at any moment.

Nox stepped up to the front door. Someone had put a padlock on it but the metal bolt it was attached to had long ago fallen off and dangled below the lock. Nox pushed on the double doors, and the left one creaked open.

He stepped into the vast foyer. Bricks of foreboding stacked in his stomach as long-forgotten memories flooded back.

He had been a small child when one of the sisters had dragged him by the ear to this once-grand foyer and made him stand with his hands at his sides as she explained that this very spot was where his parents had abandoned him.

He couldn't remember the sister's name, but he could remember the blue veins popping out all over her hands after she'd slapped him across the face. Apparently, his parents hadn't so much as wrapped him in a blanket before they'd placed him in the cardboard box. They'd probably thought he'd have a wonderful life in the beautiful stone building overlooking the picturesque ocean setting.

He hadn't.

The entrance floor was covered in so many dried leaves, splinters of wood, and peeling paint and plaster that it was impossible to make out the black, white and red mosaic tile pattern he knew was there. As he stepped over the debris, he had the strange feeling he was coming home.

He was surprised the place wasn't covered in graffiti. Maybe it was haunted? The thought made Nox chuckle. He didn't believe in ghosts. If he did, he'd have a hell of a time sleeping at night given the number of lives he'd extinguished with his own hands.

A set of stairs to his left, also covered in peeled paint and plaster, curled up the wall to an upper landing. The steps creaked under his weight, yet they felt every bit as solid as they had thirty years ago. Decades of dust caked his hand as he glided it along the once highly polished balustrade.

At the top of the stairs was a long corridor. The sun's rays streamed in the windows at a sharp angle, creating alternate light and dark shadows along the walkway. He smelled the salty ocean air but, on his tongue, he tasted old concrete, dust and mold.

Nox knew exactly where he was going. It was like he'd walked these halls yesterday. Plaster that had crumbled off the walls lay in neat piles along the skirting boards. The door to an electrical box hung open and dozens of wires scrambled in all directions.

Nox wondered if there was electricity. He doubted it. A bare bulb that hung from the ceiling near his head consisted of jagged pieces of white glass. Just like the next three he saw along the corridor.

Nox turned at the fourth open doorway. Before him was a curved balcony. In the distance were grand high-arched windows that looked out across the ocean. Most of the glass was gone. Nox stepped up to the balustrade and looked down.

The beds were still there, dozens of them. All lined up like soldiers. Some had pillows and sheets, some were just a frame and a bare striped mattress, some were nothing more than a metal frame.

He closed his eyes and saw himself, lying in the bed sixteen along from the fireplace, his sheet pulled up to his chin, and staring up into the eyes of the monster.

Zanobi.

Chapter Nine

A lessandro hadn't been able to sleep. The excitement of what today held had kept his mind working overdrive into the small hours of the morning. Ginger, on the other hand, had slept peacefully at his side. She turned with the elegance of a ballerina, and at one point when she'd rolled towards him, he'd studied her beautiful face bathed in the glow from the moonlight filtering through a small crack in the blinds. He watched that slither of light move from her left cheek to her right, and it wasn't until it slipped into her golden hair that he finally drifted off to sleep.

The morning brought unusual chaos aboard *Evangeline*. Their typical morning routine involved a delicious breakfast prepared by Rosalina or Ginger, or both. That would be followed by plenty of discussion, usually revolving around treasure. But not today. Not after Alessandro had received the call last night he'd been waiting for ever since they'd arrived back in Italy.

Professor Sezoine from the Dipartimento di Scienze Archeologiche in Pisa had agreed to decipher the Egyptian hieroglyphics engraved into the gold monkey statue. But he was only free for six hours today before he headed to Rome for a flight to New York, so this morning it was. Jimmy and Archer would be tied up most of the morning with some of the finer details of *Evangeline*'s renovations, and Rosalina had to visit both her doctor and Nonna.

Archer had performed his usual magic, and, as he'd arranged, an armored truck arrived at 6.30a.m. at the marina gates, and the two burley security guards who were as efficient as they were unfriendly transported the sealed crate from *Evangeline*'s lounge area to the waiting truck. Under Archer's orders, Alessandro and Ginger were to remain with the crate at all times.

Alessandro was happy with that, and judging by the grin on her face, Ginger was too.

Ginger climbed into the back of the truck, skirted the wooden crate, and chose a seat at the front, up against the wall of steel that separated them from the driver's cabin. Only a rectangular glass window gave them visibility to the outside world when the doors locked them in. She patted the seat beside her as Alessandro sidled around the crate. He slipped onto the seat at her side, her arm curled over his leg and she pushed her hand beneath his thigh. She did this often, and he liked the familiarity of it.

"Do you think they can hear us?" she whispered. Her face was a delicate blend of milk and cream with the touch of makeup she'd applied today. The discrete lighting added to her ethereal complexion.

He shrugged. "I have no idea."

She looked through the glass, and when he followed her gaze all he could see was the very top of their heads.

"We could have sex in here."

Alessandro gasped at how loud she'd spoken, and she giggled at him. "I don't think they can hear us."

"Really? That was your test?"

"It worked, didn't it? They would've done something if they'd heard. Don't you think?"

Ginger's spontaneity was just one of the things he loved about her. They'd been a couple for only a few months, but he'd already decided she was the woman he wanted to marry. He hadn't asked her yet, though; he was waiting for the perfect moment.

"Oh look." She pointed up over his shoulder. "There's a button. Press it."

"I'm not going to press it." Alessandro still whispered, despite her 'test'.

Ginger jumped to her feet and jabbed at the red button. "Ciao, fellas. We're all good to go back here."

"*Grazie, signora*," a deep voice replied.

Ginger giggled as she sat back down and squeezed her hand back beneath Alessandro's thigh. "Told you they couldn't hear us."

Alessandro grinned at her.

"What?" She beamed up at him.

"Nothing." He wrapped his arm over her shoulder and tugged her to his chest.

"You think I'm crazy, don't you?"

He kissed her forehead. "I think you're *meraviglioso*."

She giggled and scrunched up her nose. "Sounds wonderful."

He laughed. "That's exactly what it means."

"That's all right then." She reached up to kiss him on the lips.

The truck kicked into motion, lunging both of them onto the floor in a fit of laughter. Alessandro crawled onto his knees and helped the giggling Ginger onto her chair before he re-seated himself. As the truck swerved, they both clutched onto their seats rather than each other.

"We couldn't make love in here even if we tried." Ginger laughed.

"I agree."

The drive to the Accademia di Belle Arti was an unpredictable trek of bumps and turns, and it wasn't until they hit the freeway that Alessandro felt like he could breathe again.

An hour and a half after taking their seats in the back of the truck, the vehicle pulled to a stop, and moments later the back doors flung open.

"*Siamo arrivati.*" The taller of the two guards announced their arrival.

Alessandro helped Ginger down from the truck, and in a matter of minutes the crate and its valuable contents were loaded onto a cart. Two of Alessandro's colleagues greeted them at the back entrance to the museum and Alessandro quickly dismissed the guards before they were whisked inside.

"*Ciao*, Leonardo and Lorenzo, this is my girlfriend, Ginger."

Ginger reached out and shook hands with each of the men.

Alessandro could just imagine what was going through his friends' minds. He'd been away for seven months and has returned with not only valuable cargo, but also a stunning Australian woman on his arm. He liked the looks the two men gave him as their glances shifted from Ginger to him to the crate. Even Alessandro had to admit he was no longer the unadventurous professor they knew him as.

He pushed the cart up to a glass door and Lorenzo swiped the key card around his neck down the security pad. The door popped open, and he pushed the cart to the waiting stainless-steel table. Alessandro used a crowbar to ease the lid from the crate and the men helped him lift it off and place it on the floor.

Nestled within the custom-built crate, the monkey statue was resting in a bath of cotton wool. Under the harsh lights it shone with a magnificent glow. Although Alessandro had been looking at it for weeks, he was still astonished at how perfectly crafted the piece of treasure was.

"Wow, Alessandro, *è magnifico*." Leonardo didn't drag his eyes from the gold as he spoke.

"Where'd you find it?"

"Sorry, but that's classified *informazioni*."

Lorenzo cocked his head. "Come on, you can tell us."

"No. We can't," Ginger said with an assertive tone he hadn't heard from her before.

That was another thing he adored about Ginger. She could switch from carefree and joyous to forthright in the blink of an eye.

Lorenzo shrugged as if he didn't care, but Alessandro knew that the secrecy ate at him. Whenever Alessandro had come to work with his lunch in a paper bag, Lorenzo always had to know what was inside. Alessandro liked the lunch guessing game, but this was a thousand times more impressive.

Alessandro glanced at his watch. Professor Sezoine should be here in about twenty minutes. Their timing was perfect. "We'll have to work together to lift it out."

Alessandro pressed a button at the side of the table to lower it to the bottom position.

Between the four of them, they managed to wriggle their gloved hands beneath the statue and stand it onto its base. From there, it was relatively easy to lift it onto the counter.

Professor Sezoine arrived and went straight to the statue that now stood proudly in the center of the room. He had a wooly head of gray hair that scrambled in all directions, and a beard to match. His eyebrows were enormous tufts of gray fluff that nearly consumed his eyes when he frowned, which he was doing now as he pointed at the decorations over the statue.

"This work is exquisite." The awe in his throaty voice was unmistakable. "Where did you find this?"

Ginger shot Alessandro a glance.

"We are not at liberty to say at this point." Alessandro shifted from foot to foot.

"Right. You said that on the phone."

Alessandro caught Ginger's eyes, and she bulged them at him. It was exciting to be sharing this moment with her. As he was the only one who didn't scuba dive, he hadn't had the pleasure of unearthing a treasure yet. Today, he and Ginger were receiving front-row seats for the removal of the monkey's head.

"This is Thoth, the god of knowledge." The professor's mouth was barely inches from the gold. "He is usually depicted in one of two ways. The Ibis head or the baboon head. The baboon is a form of A'an, which is the god of equilibrium. You have the ibis-headed Thoth here." He pointed at the three men with ibises for heads that were carved into the body of the statue. "The fact that a baboon head is on this statue means he is the guardian. But of what?" He waggled his eyebrows in a fluffy gray two-step.

"You can't tell from the pictures?" Ginger's voice elevated a notch.

Professor Sezoine glanced at her momentarily before he blinked a few times. "Patience," he said, before he returned to the statue. "I have never seen a statue of Thoth with both the baboon and the ibis. It is always one or the other. Never both." He finished his sentence with a low hum in his throat. Alessandro caught Ginger's twinkling eyes, and she winked at him. It helped to alleviate the tension in the room that was as crisp as static electricity.

Sezoine made one indecipherable noise after another as he scrutinized the statue. He paused on a symbol, and Alessandro's heart pounded in the silence as he waited for the professor to reveal the significance of the engraving.

"Can you tell how old it is?" Ginger made her impatience obvious.

"Mmmm," Sezoine mumbled. "It's fascinating. We have indications here that it's from the late period, however as it has inscriptions from Ptolemaic Egypt that would place it at a later date."

"I've never heard of Ptolemaic Egypt." Ginger voice was higher pitched than normal.

"It was a dynasty that started with Ptolemy I Soter who rose to accession after the death of Alexander the Great. Which means this magnificent artifact could date to as far back as 323BC."

Ginger whistled. "That makes it--"

"About 2,338 years old." Alessandro did the math for her; she'd pointed out many times that math was not one of her strongest talents.

"Holy shit," Ginger squealed.

Sezoine leaned in and glided his gloved finger across the symbols that ran parallel to each other at the top and the bottom of the statue. "These symbols I can translate." He pointed at what Alessandro thought looked like a large kitchen knife. "See this feather, this is I." He pointed at the next symbol, a bird. "This is watched." As he went from symbol to symbol, he translated. He stalled, looked up, and eyeballed Alessandro. He then raised one of the bushy eyebrows in a silent question.

Alessandro put the sentence together. "I watched over the building of a splendid boat of 140 cubits in length 60 cubits in breadth to transport. . ."

After a momentary pause, Ginger opened her palms. "Transport what?"

The professor lifted his other brow this time, and his eyes gleamed. "Gold."

Alessandro shared a glance with Ginger and her eyes bulged.

"The Ptolemy dynasty was noted for its extensive collection of coinage in three metals. Gold, silver and bronze. In particular, they produced large coins of substantial size." The professor's eyebrows thumped together. "Aha. . . here we have a warning."

"What kind of warning?" Alessandro asked.

"Warning us away from the urn."

Ginger put her hands on her hips. "But we are going to open it, right?"

Sezoine flicked his hand. "We must proceed with caution."

Alessandro tilted his head at the professor. "Surely nothing could have survived all these centuries in the ocean."

"Quite the contrary. If this has been sealed well enough to prevent water penetrating, then it's possible some of the mechanisms they used could have survived."

"Like what?" Alessandro asked.

Sezoine drew his lips into a thin smile. "Like mercury."

"What would that do?"

"Mercury is particularly dangerous because at room temperature it vaporizes. When that happens, tiny, invisible atoms fill the air." He wriggled his fingers in the air as if sprinkling fairy-dust. "It is both scentless and soluble in oil, so if it's inhaled it's easily absorbed into the body." He paused for effect. "That would be very bad."

Ginger twisted her hands together. "How bad?"

"It would absorb into your lungs first. From there it would enter the bloodstream, and then up to the brain."

"Then what?"

"It can take hours." He shrugged. "Or possibly weeks for the poison to work its way, but exposure will cause nerve poisoning. Sleep disorders. Paralysis. Death." Sezoine actually grinned.

"Sheez," Ginger said. "How do we make sure there's none of that stuff in there?"

"We open it up and take a peek." Sezoine's grin bordered on crazy.

"Yeah, right."

He nodded. "Seriously. But you need to leave the room. I'll put on the Hazmat gear."

"Professor Sezoine," Alessandro said, "how will you remove the baboon head by yourself? We tried and didn't get anywhere."

His jaw dropped. "Thank heavens you didn't. You could be dying of mercury poisoning right now."

Alessandro had no idea if he was serious or not. "Professor, whilst I respect your professional opinion, Ginger and I will remain in the room when you open the urn. We shall dress in the necessary Hazmat gear too." Alessandro clenched his jaw. Standing up to a man of Sezoine's credentials was not something Alessandro had done before. But this was a unique situation and he had no intention of leaving the room until he'd seen what was inside the statue.

As Alessandro waited for Sezoine to answer, he swallowed back a lump that'd formed in his throat. Everyone probably heard it in the silence.

Finally, the professor's grim look changed to a grin. "Tell me you have the necessary Hazmat gear to handle this."

Alessandro turned to Leonardo and Lorenzo, and they each shook their heads. "Ginger, can you stay here with the professor while I make a call?"

"Sure." She tugged at her plait folded over her shoulder.

Alessandro stepped from the room and slipped into the hallway. He rang Archer and explained the situation. "Make the arrangements," Archer said. "Then tell me who to pay."

"Thank you, Archer."

Alessandro hung up from Archer and it required a further four phone calls before the arrangements were made. Forty-five minutes later, the Hazmat suits arrived, and the three of them climbed into them.

"I don't get it." Ginger's voice was muffled through the clear plastic covering her face. "If we're only worried about ingesting mercury, why don't we just cover our mouths rather than our whole bodies?"

Alessandro looked to Sezoine for the answer. "Because the ancient Egyptians were also brilliant alchemists. Some of the poisons they used were effective just by touching your skin."

"Oh. Okay then." Through the clear plastic, Ginger's wide eyes. He contemplated telling her to stay outside, yet at the same time knew it was pointless. She would never miss this.

The threesome moved back into the room and Alessandro looked up, past the dangling lights. Leonardo and Lorenzo stared down at him from the balcony.

The monkey statue faced them side-on, and Alessandro admired its brilliant craftsmanship. It was impossible to believe this piece could be thousands of years old.

He marveled at the gold and contemplated its worth. A piece like this would bring out the who's who of antiquities buyers. The bidding would be fierce. But Alessandro had no intention of selling it. This piece was destined for pride of place in a museum.

He glanced at the camera set up in the corner; the red light indicated it was still recording. The video replaying the opening of the statue would make an excellent addition to the museum display.

"There's a trick to opening the urn. I've seen it before." Professor Sezoine placed his blue plastic gloves on the neck of the statue. He leaned in close and Alessandro and Ginger eased in with him. As his fingers applied pressure to the symbols on the statue, Alessandro realized he was searching for a trigger mechanism. His breath caught in his throat as Sezoine went from one symbol to the next. He gasped when a small triangle attached to a straight line, like a very simple flag, moved inwards at the professor's touch.

Sezoine moved his hands up to the monkey's head so that he could also reach the triangle with his thumb. Then as he applied pressure to the triangle, he twisted the head anticlockwise. It moved, and the ease with which he did it made it look as if the statue had been made yesterday, not centuries ago.

"Stand back." Sezoine spoke through clenched teeth.

They did as they were told. Alessandro didn't take his eyes off the statue; he didn't even want to blink. There was a muffled click, and ever so slowly Sezoine lifted the head off.

An explosion shattered the silence.

Ginger screamed, as did someone on the top balcony. Glass shards rained down and Alessandro yanked Ginger to the floor. As he draped his body over hers, red powder blossomed around them.

His heart thundered in his ears as he stared across the floor at Sezoine's bulging eyes. The professor remained still but his eyes darted about the chaos. Alessandro shifted his vision to the shards of fine, clear glass lying everywhere. His eyes snagged on a twisted spring of wire. It took him a while to realize it was the coil from a light bulb. Something or someone had shot at the lights. His thoughts snapped to Nox, and he covered Ginger more.

"Are you guys okay?" It was one of the men from the balcony.

"What was that?" Alessandro yelled.

"Something shot out of the fucking statue."

Alessandro blinked, trying to make sense of it. Professor Sezoine pushed up from the floor and Alessandro climbed off Ginger. "Are you okay, *il mio dolce?*" He wanted to cup her cheeks, to see her eyes.

She nodded. "I'm okay. What the hell happened?"

"Pressure dart." Sezoine smiled. "Lifting the lid off the statue triggered a dart. Ancient booby trap."

"Geez, lucky we weren't looking into it," Ginger said.

Sezoine ran his finger along the red dust that caked the table. "Oh dear," he said, as he stepped back.

"What?" Even through the suit Alessandro read the fear in Sezoine's eyes.

"Hematite powder."

"What's that?" Alessandro asked.

"It's a sharp metallic dust that the Egyptians used to cover tomb floors. It would cause a slow and painful death to the grave robbers who inhaled it."

"Holy shit," Ginger said, and Alessandro agreed with her.

Alessandro had to see inside the urn. His heart still thundered in his chest as he stepped forward, stood on his toes, and glanced in. A powder the color and texture of ground coffee filled the urn three-quarters full, but it was what was centered in the middle of it that caught his attention. A circle of gold attached to a blue cylinder, about three inches in diameter, protruded from the powder.

"What's that?" He pointed inside. "It looks like a cylinder."

"Mmmm," Sezoine mumbled. "An urn within an urn."

"Pull it out, let's see," Ginger said.

"No," Sezoine snapped. "It may contain another trigger."

"How do we get it out then?" Alessandro asked.

They were all silent as they contemplated the situation.

"Have you got any kitchen tongs?" Ginger suggested.

Alessandro looked at Sezoine for confirmation, and when the professor nodded, he glanced up at his friends.

"I'll be back in a sec," Leonardo said before he disappeared from view. A minute or so later, there was a knock on the door.

"Leave it there and go back upstairs," Alessandro instructed.

Once Leonardo was back up top, Alessandro opened the door and clutched the tongs in his gloved hand.

"Think there'll be any more surprises?" Ginger asked, as Sezoine reached in with the tongs.

"We're about to find out," the professor said.

Alessandro put his arm across Ginger's waist and nudged her backwards with him. He stared wide-eyed as a cylinder the color of the Mediterranean Sea was gradually lifted from the urn. Even from this distance, Alessandro noticed the intricate drawings painted in gold upon the tube.

Ginger let out a slow whistle. "Wow."

Sezoine's fingers trembled as he lowered the cylinder to the table. He let out a huge breath and stood back. "It's made from Lapis Lazuli," Sezoine said. "A semi-precious stone that's been prized since antiquity for its intensely rich blue color. They even found it on the funeral mask of Tutankhamun." His words were loaded with awe.

The base of the cylinder was a layer of gold, carved in a way to look like rope twisted around and around, gradually becoming narrower so it formed a cone and ended in a knot at the very tip. Sezoine turned to Alessandro. "This is incredible."

"What is it?" Alessandro asked.

He shook his head. "I've never seen anything like it."

"Do you think it has something inside?" Ginger said.

"I'm not sure." Sezoine rolled the cylinder over with his fingers.

"It looks like the gold cap might come off," Alessandro said.

Sezoine let out a gush of breath. "We need to clean this up first. Then we'll look."

"But that could take hours," Ginger said.

Alessandro looked around. Everything was covered in coffee-colored dust. It would take hours.

Sezoine turned to Ginger. His face was stern. "Whoever created this went to great lengths to protect whatever is inside."

Alessandro stepped forward, saving Ginger from Sezoine's warning. "Okay, what shall we do?"

Sezoine glanced at the clock on the wall and huffed. "I need to go."

"Go! What do you mean, go?"

"I have a flight to catch. I'm guest speaker at the New York Metropolitan Museum of Art tomorrow night. Sorry, but this'll have to wait until I get back."

"Wait?" Ginger thumped her sides with her fists.

He turned to her. "Yes. Wait. We can't progress without cleaning this up and. . ." he ran his hand over the blue cylinder, "I want to take my time examining this exquisite piece."

Alessandro sighed. "When do you return?"

Sezoine shook his head. "Ten days."

Chapter Ten

Rosalina had had an emotional day. It started at the doctors, where she'd held firm hope that the plaster cast would finally come off. She didn't get the news she wanted. "Three more days," the doctor had said in a chirpy voice that'd made her want to strangle him.

After leaving the Santa Maria Nuova Hospital, she'd caught the train back to Signa and hailed a taxi to take her the two miles to Villa Pandolfini. Rosalina was exhausted, sore and angry by the time she'd trudged up the gravel driveway.

Nonna's first words were. "Eat, then we talk." It was her standard approach when she noticed someone was troubled. Rosalina knew there was no point putting up a fight. Nonna was impossible to manipulate. She slumped into the kitchen chair, and within seconds Nonna placed a plate of still steaming sfogliatelle pastries before her. The tension magically disappeared as Rosalina inhaled the delicious aroma. Her shoulders sagged with relief as she bit into the buttery pastry and tasted the heavenly semi-sweet ricotta mix ingeniously pillowed inside.

This was by far one of Rosalina's favorite traditional Italian sweets, and Nonna was brilliant at knowing when she needed it. But she'd need to eat at least one full pastry before Nonna would allow her to talk. She was grateful, though because she felt much better after she'd finished.

"How are you, Nonna?" Rosalina didn't need to elaborate that she was referring to their last conversation.

"I'm okay." Nonna wrapped her soft, pale hands around Rosalina's and drew her eyes in. Nonna's eyes were clear today, thankfully free of tears and tension. "You don't need to worry about me."

"I know. Have you seen Filippo?"

Nonna shook her head and released Rosalina's hand. "Not since we last spoke."

At first, Rosalina feared that Nonna wouldn't reveal her stress even when asked, however as the hours rolled on, and Nonna showed no signs of tension, Rosalina wondered if Nonna was actually pleased to have unburdened that family secret.

When she kissed her goodbye, Nonna loaded Rosalina up with the remaining sfogliatelle pastries. By the time the taxi returned her to the marina, Rosalina was ready for a quiet night. But as soon as she heard laughter coming from the top deck of *Evangeline*, she knew that was not to be the case. As the laughter continued, she conceded that it may be exactly what she needed.

She planted a smile on her face as she hauled herself up the last set of stairs to the sundeck. Her smile broadened when she saw what was going on. Archer, Jimmy, and Archer's mother, Helen, were all in the jacuzzi. This proved that Helen was making significant progress with her recovery.

"Hey babe." Archer stood quickly, and Helen slapped his leg as she wiped away the water Archer had accidentally splashed onto her. It was exactly the silliness Rosalina needed to tip her into a better mood. She arrived at the jacuzzi and Archer wrapped his wet arms around her and drew her in for a hug.

"The Jacuzzi's finished." He pointed out the obvious.

"I can see that. Hello Jimmy. Helen." She leaned in and kissed Archer's mother on the cheek.

"Still got your cast on, hey?" Jimmy screwed up his face.

"Three more days. I should get it off Monday."

"Bugger. We were hoping we could get all six of us in here tonight. Christen it, so to speak."

The idea of sitting in that warm bubbling water was very enticing. "You're not helping, Jimmy."

Rosalina slumped into the curved bench seat that met with the edge of the bar and took the pastries out of her handbag.

"What's that?" Helen pointed at the white paper bag.

"Nonna made pastries."

Jimmy sat forward. "What sort?"

"*Sfogliatelle.*"

"Oh my God, Mom, you have to try these," Archer said. "They're magnificent."

"Okay." Helen didn't display the same amount of enthusiasm Archer did, however Rosalina was delighted that Helen had accepted the offer. It was normally impossible to get her to eat anything. Rosalina stood and reached for her crutches.

She hopped over to the jacuzzi, and with one of her butt cheeks on the edge, she held the open paper bag towards Helen. Helen reached in, and with knitted brows she withdrew a pastry. Rosalina wished the pastries were still warm so Helen could experience them the way they should be.

"I'll have one." Jimmy lunged at the bag with his wet fingers.

Archer had one too, and as the men devoured them in two or three giant bites, Helen nibbled on the pastry as if it were filled with chili peppers.

"So, is this all you boys have been up to all day?"

"No." Archer palmed his chest in mock hurt. "We stocked the bar." Archer's carefree smile flashed at her.

Rosalina chuckled. "Of course you did. So, what's a lady got to do to get a wine around here?"

Archer launched out of the tub, and Rosalina tried not to laugh as Helen held the pastry up high and once again brushed water from her face.

"Wade!" Helen fumed.

Some of the gleam in Archer's eyes faded. His mother still called Archer by her long-lost husband's name from time to time, and it was always confronting. Knowing that Archer looked like his father added to his mother's confusion.

Rosalina chose to ignore Helen's slip-up. "I see we're going to need to implement some strict jacuzzi rules."

"Sorry, Mom." Archer wiped the wet hair from his mother's eyes, then he leaned in to kiss her forehead. He plucked a towel that'd been placed on the nearest deck chair, wrapped it low around his hips and walked to the bar.

Rosalina had her wine in her hand and her feet propped up on the coffee table when Alessandro and Ginger joined them.

"What's going on here?" Ginger bounded to the hot tub and dipped her hands in. "Oooh, it's warm."

"It's great," said Jimmy. "What took you so long?"

"We've had the best day." She grabbed Alessandro's hand and swung it between them.

"Hang on. Wait till I get another beer." Jimmy reached over and plucked a beer from the ice container he'd put beside the jacuzzi.

"Maybe we should all get out so we can go over the details together." Archer returned to the jacuzzi and reached for his mother's hand. "Come on, Mom, let's get you dry."

"I was wondering when you were going to help me out. I'm beginning to look like an Egyptian mummy."

Archer laughed. It wasn't very often his mother had something to say. "It's only been about half an hour." Archer helped her down the steps and Rosalina handed over one of the white towels stacked up on a deck chair.

"How was your spa?" Rosalina asked.

Helen's smile was both incredibly rare and delightful to see. "It was lovely. Very relaxing."

Rosalina caught Archer's eye. He looked so proud.

Archer helped Helen wrap the towel around her body, and then he pulled out one of the day chairs for her to sit on. Helen sat, folded her hands in her lap and looked up at Alessandro and nodded, as if giving him the go-ahead to continue.

"This better be good, Einstein. I was enjoying that jacuzzi." Jimmy put his wet hands on Alessandro's shoulders as he spoke.

Alessandro scowled and peeled Jimmy's hands off in disgust. "You don't have to listen." He cocked his head, and by the smug look on his face, Rosalina knew he was holding the trump card. Jimmy would never miss a discussion about treasure.

"Yeah, right. You're a funny guy." Jimmy snatched a towel off the lounge and flung it over his shoulders.

Archer eased in beside Rosalina. She shuffled over, and Jimmy slotted in on her other side. Wedged in between their two warm bodies, she was consumed by the combined smell of chlorine and beer.

Alessandro remained standing as he told what had happened with the monkey statue. He described what they'd learned from Professor Sezoine in great detail, and by the time he arrived at the incident with the shooting dart and showering glass he was bursting with energy. His hands flung out and back as he recounted the blow-by-blow action. He finished with a flick of his thick black hair and presented the blue cylinder with a beaming smile.

The cylinder was passed to Rosalina, and as she studied its intricate design she was struck with a question. "I still don't understand how a two-thousand-year-old statue came to be on a thirteenth-century ship?"

She watched Alessandro think it through. "It's a mystery, I agree. Maybe we'll find something in the cylinder that will explain it," he said.

"Anyway, it's our turn in the jacuzzi." Ginger grabbed Alessandro's hand. "We're getting our swimmers on, and we'll be back up in a sec." They dashed off, and Rosalina wished she could move that quickly. *Three more days.*

Helen pushed off the lounge to stand up. "I'm going to bed. Good night."

Archer hopped up and helped his mother. They disappeared together down the stairs, and within minutes Ginger and Alessandro climbed into the jacuzzi. Rosalina would've been in there with them in a heartbeat if she could. Instead she watched from the sidelines, and it wasn't long before Jimmy climbed in too.

Archer returned and walked straight towards Rosalina to lean into her ear. "Want some quiet time?"

His words were music to her ears. She turned to him, and his eyes softened. "I'd love that."

He reached for her hand. "Rosa and I are heading to bed. See you crazy cats in the morning."

"Night guys," Ginger and Alessandro said in unison, and then laughed as they raised their glasses high above the bubbles to clink together.

"See you in the morning," Jimmy said.

Archer scooped Rosalina into his arms.

65

"What are you doing?" She playfully slapped him on the chest.

"Watching you go down the stairs with the crutches is torture. Now grab your sticks."

As directed, she picked up her crutches when he tilted her in their direction. She held them in one hand as she waved good night to the others.

"Thank you, babe. I was starting to nod off."

"I noticed. But the night's still early." He wriggled his eyebrows as he turned sideways and navigated the stairs with ease. At the bottom of the stairs, she wrapped her arms around his neck and pulled him in for a kiss. He smelled of chlorine and beer, yet his favorite cologne, offering hints of spices from the orient, still lingered.

At the kitchen, he diverted to the counter and lowered her onto it.

"Stay there." Archer kissed the end of her nose then reached up to the overhead cupboard, selected two champagne glasses and placed them on the counter beside her. He turned to the fridge and removed a bottle of Villa Pandolfini's red Chianti and a wooden box.

She cocked her head at him. "What have you got there?"

"A little surprise. Now stay there; I'll be back in a sec."

He grabbed her crutches and the other bits and pieces and dashed off down the hall. Back in a flash, he picked her up off the counter, and with her arms wrapped around his neck again, he carried her to the Hamilton suite. Archer had closed the blinds, put on some music, and lit the vanilla-scented candles on the nightstands that they'd bought from her favorite little gift shop in Livorno.

Archer carried her to the bed and lowered her to the covers. He eased her backwards, climbed up on the mattress and straddled her so he could hover above her. His pendant dangled from his neck, and she wrapped her hand around the curved finger of gold. This little piece of ancient treasure had a lot to answer for.

Archer cupped her cheeks, drawing her eyes to his. "I've missed you, babe."

She frowned, unsure what he meant.

"Tonight was the first time you've smiled in weeks. I've been worried about you."

Rosalina sighed. He was right. She hadn't been herself. "I'm sorry. I think it's this stupid leg cast; it's driving me crazy."

The candlelight danced in his dark eyes. "Is that all?"

Was that all? She'd been asking herself the same question. No. No, it wasn't all. "You mean besides nearly dying, nearly losing the man I love, and finding out my brother and I have different fathers?"

He cocked his head. "Okay, I admit they're all big things, but--"

"Huge things," she corrected.

"Okay, huge things. But I didn't die, you didn't die, and your brother is still the same man you knew a month ago." He shrugged. "Nothing has changed."

Archer had a gift at simplifying things. A smile curled at his lips and faint creases lined the corners of his eyes.

"I guess you're right."

"I am right, babe. All that matters, is that you and I are together. I lost you once. . . I'm never going to lose you again. What can I do to make you happy?"

"Take my cast off."

He scrunched up his nose. "Other than that."

She laughed and let out a huge sigh. They were good together. There was no other man in the world who could make her feel like Archer did. "You can kiss me."

He glided his thumb over her lips. "My pleasure." He lowered and as their lips met, she traced her fingers over his rock-hard pectoral muscles and placed her hands so his nipples rested between her thumb and forefinger. They hadn't made love since before the helicopter crash, and as he pushed his tongue into her mouth, she realized just how much she'd missed it.

She rolled her hands down his body, absorbing the heat of his skin with her fingers. The towel was still wrapped around his hips. She tugged it from his body and gasped. "You're naked."

He rolled his eyes. "Well I wasn't until you took the towel off."

"Where are your boardies?"

"I took them off when I brought the wine in. They're still a bit wet." His dimples punctuated his cheeks.

She suddenly remembered the wooden box he'd removed from the fridge. "Are you going to show me what that little surprise is?"

"Hmmm, you'll have to ask me nicely." The golden flecks in his eyes dazzled.

His full, kissable lips always fascinated her, and as if knowing exactly what she was thinking, Archer flicked his tongue over them. She used his gold pendant to pull him towards her for a kiss. This time she forced her tongue into his mouth, and the weeks of tension that had gripped her glided away as she tasted him. Kissing Archer captivated all her senses. . . sight, smell, taste, touch, and even sound, as little whimpers of pleasure tumbled from his throat. She cupped his buttocks, massaging the firm flesh in her fingers, and at the right moment she smacked him on the bottom.

He pulled back; eyebrows raised.

"Stop teasing me. What's the surprise?"

"I do believe, Miss Calucci, it is you that's teasing me." He gave her a quick kiss before he pushed off the bed. Just the sight of him naked was enough to set her heart racing and draw delicious heat to her loins. The muscles in his well-toned bottom bulged and flexed with each step he took to the coffee table centered between the two red leather day-chairs.

He turned with the wooden box in his hands, and a full-blown erection between his legs. The heat between her thighs hit overdrive as he stepped towards her with burning desire in his eyes.

"I thought it might cheer you up." He placed the wooden box at her side.

She propped up on her elbow to study the gift and recognized the insignia burned into the lid. "Oh, Archer. When did you go to Arte Del Cioccolato?" Roberto Cattinari was one of the finest chocolatiers in Florence, possibly in all of Italy. Rosalina had been fortunate to spend a few months working with him during her chef apprenticeship.

"I didn't. I rang Roberto and he selected out a few of your favorites."

"You rang him? How do you even know him?"

"I don't, but when I told him who the chocolates were for, he was more than willing to help. It seems you were one of his favorite students."

She frowned, completely confused. "But Archer, how did you even know that I'd worked with Roberto?"

"You told me once."

"I did?" Rosalina had no recollection of it.

Archer slid the lid back on the wooden box to reveal five rows of individual chocolates. Each one would be unique and exquisite. "We were in Melbourne, in one of those fancy mosaic-tile-lined arcades, and we stopped for a coffee and chocolate. You took a bite of your treat, screwed up your nose, and then told me about Roberto Cattinari and how amazing his chocolates were. You did that little eye-roll thing you do when you're eating something that pleases you."

"Oh babe, this is one of the most thoughtful gifts you've ever bought me."

"I wanted to make sure your taste buds were still working okay."

She chuckled. "I'm sure they're fine."

"Let's see then, shall we?"

Archer studied the pictorial chart and then, after apparently making his choice, he selected a square chocolate decorated in gold flecks. "Open your mouth." She obeyed, and he popped the chocolate onto her tongue.

"So, Miss Calucci, what flavor is that?"

She rolled the smooth chocolate around her mouth and welcomed the burst of flavor. With her eyes closed, she described what she was tasting. "It's dark chocolate with praline and orange. No, wait. . . I think it's caramelized orange."

She opened her eyes and Archer grinned. "You are correct, madam."

He moved to the base of the bed and began to roll her maxi dress up her legs. "Your prize is that I," he palmed his chest, "your humble servant, shall undress you."

Rosalina giggled as she lifted her hips so he could draw the dress up from beneath her bottom. She closed her eyes as he lifted it up over her head and his mouth found hers. Their kiss was deeper, their breathing deeper, and her want for him as deep as it could be. Archer's hand reached around behind her back, and in a flash her bra was off and his warm hand cupped her breast.

All her worries evaporated as she trailed her fingernails up his back. She wanted him. Now. She pushed at his shoulder and had every intention of rolling him onto his back and straddling him, but instead it became an awkward clumsy move that had them in a tangle of legs.

Archer blinked at her with a huge smirk on his face.

She playfully punched the mattress. "Bloody broken leg."

Archer chuckled. "What were you trying to do?

"Get on top."

"Sounds great to me." He trailed his finger from her hipbone to her breast. "But tonight, you'll have to lie back and let me do all the work."

Despite herself, she liked the sound of that. "Okay."

Archer rolled up onto one elbow and cupped her breast in his hand. "Now, where were we?" He ran his tongue around her nipple, and a thrilling tingle started at the very tip of her breast and ran all the way to the throbbing pulse between her legs. She glided her hands through his unruly curls, scratching her nails across his scalp. He sucked on her nipple, drawing it out until it snapped from his lips and a groan tumbled from her throat.

His hand roamed down her belly, over her mound and between her legs. She curled beneath him when his finger entered her hot zone. Her body clenched and released in time with his movements, taking her to the exquisite edge of release. The days, weeks, months of uncertainty evaporated in one explosive orgasm that had her clawing at the silk sheets.

"Oh, Archer. That was incredible."

"Mmmm." The fire in his eyes glazed, proving he'd enjoyed her climax as much as she had.

He moved around to between her legs and helped her bend her plastered leg at the knee. Archer reached for her hips. "Is this okay, babe?"

"It's perfect."

At first, their lovemaking was slow, and with measured control. Archer's eyes danced behind his eyelids, lost in their own blissful world. She lifted her hips, and his thrusts grew deeper. Faster. As did his breathing.

She in turn felt herself go, riding another climax that had both her and Archer catching their breath.

Archer's eyes shot open. Their eyes met and then he shut them again, gripped her hips and thrust until he collapsed onto her chest with satisfied panting.

"You're a cheap date, sweetheart." His breath was hot on her ear.

"Why?"

"Just one chocolate. And we didn't even get to the wine." He rolled to her side and circled her nipples, one then the other.

"Mmmm, I guess you're right." She leaned in for a quick kiss. "But the night is still young."

Chapter Eleven

Nox found Zanobi's bedroom. He knew it was his room because on the wooden cupboard doors hung a light gray suit coat, buttoned up the middle, as if it had been just plucked from the cupboard. Nox could vividly recall Zanobi wearing it, as he had done at every Sunday night dinner that everyone had to attend. He'd despised the smugness plastered on Zanobi's face as he'd pored his discriminating gaze over the hundred or so boys sharing the meal with him.

The fact that the jacket was still there was a testament to the speed with which the building had been vacated. So much was left behind. Again, Nox pondered the fact that the building hadn't been vandalized and the remaining pieces of furniture and clothing taken. With the amount of horrors that went on here, maybe nobody had wanted to come back.

The double bed was still made up with a blue and white checked duvet curved over the sides and up over the pillow. The powerful urge to lie flat on a real bed gripped him. He sat on the mattress and was surprised when it didn't creak. Without any regard for the decades of neglect disgracing the covers he flopped back, and a cloud of debris bounced into the air. Closing his eyes to ignore the dust cloud, he allowed the tension strangling the muscles up his back to gradually unravel.

Nox hadn't slept on anything comfortable since he'd raced out of Ophelia's place after nearly strangling her. Ophelia's chubby, rose-colored cheeks came back to him now. He missed her smile. He missed her motherly concern. He missed her cooking. He missed everything about his beautiful Ophelia. She was the only woman who'd ever shown him compassion. Maybe, when all this was over, and he'd used his wealth to fix his teeth, buy some fancy clothes, and shown the world who he really was, he could return to her. Would she accept him back after what he did?

He cast the futile thinking aside, sat up and scanned the rest of the room. A stack of wood was piled in the fireplace, as if someone was about to light it. On the mantel stood a statue of Jesus. Nox strode to it, yanked it off the marble shelf and pegged it out the broken window. He watched it bounce off the jagged rocks below and disappear over the cliff.

"Arghh!" His scream teetered between outrage and insanity.

He gripped onto the windowsill until his momentary lapse of self-control faded. After inhaling a couple of deep salt-laced breaths, he turned back to the room with fresh eyes. Nox walked calmly towards the gray jacket, plucked it off the hanger and tossed that out the window, too. It fluttered gracefully, caught in the breeze, and landed on a small patch of luscious green grass at the top of the cliff.

Nox huffed, turned back to the room and strode to the cupboard once again. The doors resisted opening before something gave, and they creaked towards him. The clothes inside had been sealed for thirty years and looked clean and ready to be worn. Nox slipped a shirt off a hanger and sniffed the fabric. It smelled stale and dusty, but other than that, it was a hundred times better than what he was wearing. He stripped off the clothes Ophelia had given him and paused open-mouthed when he caught sight of himself in the grime-covered mirror inside the cupboard door.

He turned slowly, barely recognizing the man in the reflection. His hair was long and his body was thin. He ran his fingers over protruding collarbones that he'd never seen before. His skin was sickly pale, and the spear wound to the left of his navel was a prominent bull's-eye. As he studied the raised scar, his thoughts hinged on the woman who'd shot him with the spear gun.

"Rosalina." Her name hissed off his lips. He would never forget what she'd done to him. Nox licked his lips at the prospect of squeezing the fiery cockiness from her eyes.

Pushing the door open farther so he couldn't see his reflection anymore, Nox selected a shirt and pair of slacks from the cupboard and put them on. Their fit was just about perfect.

He turned his attention to the fireplace next. The plan to live here would be impossible if he didn't activate one of the fireplaces. In his search for something to ignite the fire, he rummaged through a nightstand and found an old leather-bound bible. He hissed as he pegged it at the fireplace. It would come in handy once he found matches.

He turned his attention to the bed and made the decision to sleep in it tonight. It pleased him that he could make that rational declaration without clouding his thoughts with who had slept in the bed before, or what slept in it now. Nox yanked the duvet from the bed, and in a swirl of dust and debris, tossed it onto the floor. He did the same with the sheets and pillows.

Without finding anything else of interest, he gathered all the bedding in his arms and made his way back downstairs and out the side exit. Brisk ocean breezes licked at his face, and he welcomed the freshness.

The veranda was exactly as he'd remembered it. The white floor tiles stretched its length along the side of the building in a repeating diamond pattern. It had fared quite well, despite taking the full brunt of whatever the wild ocean weather could blast at it.

Nox gathered the linen into his arms and ignored the stale dust that powdered his tongue as he walked along the side of the building. He stepped down the four concrete steps and onto a small patch of grass. The grass met with the cliff face; a brutal contrast of soft meets hard. If he didn't know any better, he'd say someone had mowed the grass just yesterday.

Looking over the top of the bedding, he stepped onto the rocks and sought out the path he hoped was still there. It was, but the trek was steeper than he remembered. The rocks were rough and sharp. One slip here and he could lose a kneecap. He took his time, because that was the one thing he had loads of. Time.

He made it to the rock pools without incident and tossed the bedding at the water's edge. A vivid flashback of bathing here came flooding back. Nox had very few memories of his childhood, most were unpleasant. This one, though, had him in the rock pool with five other boys. It was a warm summer day, and they were jumping into the water and splashing around without a care in the world. He could remember laughing, really, truly laughing. Nox searched his brain for another occasion in his life where he'd laughed that hard. Could it truly be that the last time he'd laughed was three decades ago in this very spot?

Nox shook his head at the question and promised himself that in the future, once he had his hands on his treasure and his teeth were fixed, that he'd laugh. He'd laugh so hard the whole world would hear.

Nox stripped naked, laid the professor's clothes out in the sun, separated the first sheet from the pile, stepped into the rock pool and pushed the fabric into the water. Mesmerized by how the sheet resisted the pressure, he dunked and lifted. Dunked and lifted. It was therapeutic.

He repeated the process with the remaining bedding, and then took a few moments to wash himself. With the sun on his skin and the cool, refreshing water cleansing his body, it was as if years of persecution were being unloaded.

Once he was finished, he wrung out the bedding, redressed, and made two trips back up the cliff with the soggy linen.

In this weather, laid out in the sun and secured with a few large rocks so they wouldn't blow away, they'd be dry before nightfall. He wasn't so confident about the pillows, but it didn't matter. He'd had worse. Much worse.

His next stop down memory lane was situated at the far end of the building. The kitchen had timber paneling on the walls, white laminated counter tops and blue spotted tiles. Many of the tiles had fallen off and cracked in half as they'd hit the counter. Pots and pans hung from a wire rack over the island in the middle. Nox methodically checked the drawers, some of which broke apart as he tugged them out. He found matches in the third drawer down but after several attempts, in which every match crumbled to nothing, he threw the box into the cold fireplace.

He checked for power and gas, and as suspected, neither were working. It didn't matter; once he ignited the fireplace, he'd be living in luxury. Before the sun set, he went downstairs to fetch his bedding. Just the thought of sleeping in a real bed made him drowsy. He went out the front doors, and the wind blasted him as he stepped from the shelter of the bricks.

He gathered the dry linen into his arms and made his way to his new bedroom. As he flung the sheet so it billowed over the bed, he snapped his hand back. A rotten memory instigated that reflex. Sister Teresa, stiff, matronly, grinning Sister Teresa, loved rapping him over the knuckles for not making his bed properly. He'd forgotten about her, but now, clenching his teeth as he tucked his sheets in, he repeated her name over and over.

"Sister Teresa. Sister Teresa." He permanently wrote her name onto his revenge list.

It was almost pitch black when he crawled beneath the covers. The wind howled angry whispers through the shattered glass, and cool, salt-scented air drifted across his face. The grumbling in his stomach joined the howling wind, and he tried to ignore the emptiness screaming in his belly. In the morning, he'd stock up on food with the money Nurse Isabella provided, and with his newfound lucky streak he decided he'd swing by the marina afterwards and maybe, just maybe he'd spy Rosalina or Archer.

It wasn't long before his heavy eyelids closed, and as he pictured the abundance of delicious food he would buy tomorrow, he drifted off to sleep.

Chapter Twelve

Rosalina woke to Archer's face just inches from hers. He looked comfortable, like he'd been looking at her for a while, waiting for her to wake up. "How long have you been awake?"

He curled a slip of hair off her cheek. "A while."

She squeezed the sleep from her eyes. "You okay?"

"I couldn't be better. I was just enjoying watching you sleep."

"No nightmare then?"

"No. All good."

She studied his eyes, searching his chocolate brown irises for the truth. She saw it there; he had indeed enjoyed a night free of bad dreams. Maybe he sensed she'd arrived at that conclusion, because he bent forward to kiss her, a lingering good-morning kiss.

He pulled back and finger-combed her hair. "Are you sure you don't want me to take you to the hospital today?"

She cleared her throat. "No, I'll be fine; it's just as easy to take a train from Signa. I'll spend a few hours with Nonna this morning before I go anyway."

"Mmmm."

"Mmmm what?"

He shrugged and looked away.

She pushed up onto her elbow. "What, Archer?"

His tongue skipped over his lips. "Maybe you could talk to Nonna. You know, about us leaving again."

"I still think it's too soon."

"It's been nearly two months." He sat up and swung his legs off the bed. "I can't sit around here doing nothing anymore."

"You haven't been doing nothing, Archer, you've been repairing *Evangeline*."

"Only for three weeks. Before that, I did nothing all day."

"You were recovering from broken ribs."

"You don't get it. I can't stay here with a blank agenda day after day."

"But this is where I live."

"*Evangeline* is where you live. Your home can go anywhere."

"What's wrong with staying in Livorno? You can start your business here." Archer's treasure-hunting business, in which he created fake treasure hunts for thrill seekers with bundles of money, was a huge success. People came from all over the world to cruise around on Archer's multi-million-dollar yacht, looking for fake treasure Archer had planted. Rosalina couldn't see any reason why it wouldn't be a success here in Italy, as it was in Australia.

"I don't want strangers aboard *Evangeline* anymore." He turned to her, drilling his dark eyes into hers. "I just want you."

She cocked her head. "And Helen, Jimmy, Alessandro and Ginger. Right?"

He grinned. "I kinda like having them around."

"So, they can help you look for the Awa Maru? Or the Calimala Treasure?"

He crawled on his hands and knees to her, then straddled her and lifted her palm to his lips. "Treasure hunting is what I do, babe. You know that."

It was true. It was in his veins. She didn't know that when she'd first fallen in love with him, but she knew it now.

"I know." She lowered her eyes. "But it's dangerous."

He kissed her other palm. "But now that Nox and Ignatius are both dead, there will be no danger. Only fun."

She looked up to the gleam in his eyes, and when he tilted his head and the gold flecks in his eyes dazzled, the argument was pointless. The man she loved was a treasure hunter; he was born into it, and he was good at what he did. She was the one holding him back from living his dream. Rosalina reached up to his pendant. The ancient slice of solid gold was heavy in her palm. This very piece had changed their lives forever. She couldn't decide if the change was good or bad. "Which treasure will you go after?"

He pushed up on his hands and hovered above her so his pendant rested between her breasts. "Not me! We. I'm not leaving you, babe. We stick together. Remember?"

She cupped his cheek. The rough stubble brushed beneath her palm. "I don't know, Archer. There's no way to know how long we'll be gone, and Nonna needs me."

"Why does Nonna need you? She's as strong as an ox."

"Because of Filippo. You know he gives her trouble."

Archer rolled off her and sat at the edge of the bed again. "But why is that your problem? He's twenty-one. He needs to sort his own stuff out."

It was Rosalina's turn to crawl to him, dragging her cast behind her. "I know that. It's just. . ."

"You can't undo the past, Rosa. What your mother did was shameful, but not your fault or Filippo's. Nothing you do now can undo it. In fact, it would be better to pretend you didn't know. Then everything could carry on as it did before."

She flopped back onto the pillow, and he turned to her. "Why don't you talk to Nonna? Tell her that we're going to look for another treasure and see what she says. Good relationships are about good communication."

"Oh, really?" That was a bold statement, coming from the man whose secrets once tore them apart.

"Yes." He nodded sincerely. "I've learned my lesson."

She huffed because he was right. Being torn between her fiancé's wishes and what she believed to be her grandmother's wishes was not an ideal situation.

Rosalina had always believed in fate. Leaving Italy to discover the world when she was twenty-three had been one of her greatest leaps of it. That decision had turned out to be one of the best she'd ever made.

Maybe she'd let Nonna chose her fate this time. "Okay." She accepted Archer's challenge. "I'll talk to Nonna."

He crawled on top of her again. "Thank you, babe. I think she'll want you to go on this most magical adventure."

"Magical adventure?" She burst out laughing at the ridiculousness of his comment.

AFTER A QUICK BREAKFAST OF HAM AND CHEESE CROISSANTS AND freshly brewed coffee, Archer walked Rosalina to the front of the marina. "You're actually getting the hang of those crutches." He opened the security gate for her.

"Yeah, right. Today had better be the last day."

"I'm sure it will be." Giovanni, the driver they'd had since they'd arrived back, met them at the gate. He strode to the car opened the back door for Rosalina.

"Mr. Archer, Miss. Rosalina. Sorry, sorry, the traffic, it's bad today."

"It's okay, Giovanni." Archer assured the panicking driver by resting his palm on the man's shoulder. "We're not running late."

Archer helped Rosalina into the car and then passed the crutches into her. "Ring me with how you go with Nonna. And the doctor. Okay?"

"I will. Love you."

"Love you, too."

Archer paid Giovanni one hundred euro and told him to keep the change.

"To Villa Pandolfini?" Giovanni asked, once he eased into the driver's seat.

"Yes . please." Rosalina settled into the seat and pulled her book from her handbag. Before long, she was lost in the pages of The Rosie Project. The feel-good comedy made the ninety-minute drive disappear in a flash, and it only seemed like ten minutes before they pulled into Villa Pandolfini's driveway.

She was surprised to see the boom gate up. That meant either one of her family members had just arrived, or Nonna had gone for a quick drive to the shops. Rosalina instructed Giovanni to pull up around the back of the villa, grateful that she wouldn't have to walk too far.

She thanked him, told him she'd call later for a pickup, said goodbye and watched the car drive away.

That was when she heard yelling.

It came from the villa. A man's voice. It took a couple of seconds to recognize Filippo, but the rage in his tone drew a vice across her chest. And then she heard Nonna. Her grandmother's obvious panic had Rosalina gripping the crutches and charging at the back door as quickly as the darn aluminum sticks allowed. She burst through the door and aimed for the yelling.

"I don't care what you think, you had no right--"

"What's going on?" Rosalina cut in on Filippo as she lunged into the kitchen. He towered over Nonna, who was at the table with her hands over her eyes.

Nonna spun to her. Her bulging eyes were a mixture of relief and horror.

"That's just great. How typical that you'd turn up right now." Filippo's cheeks blazed with anger.

Rosalina hobbled to Nonna's side and draped her arm over her grandmother's shoulder. "What's going on?

Nonna wiped a tear from her cheek. "It is my fault."

"Damn right it is."

"Shush, Filippo. That's enough." Rosalina spoke through clenched teeth.

"It's not nearly enough. Right from the moment I could talk she's been demanding I keep our sordid family secret hidden. And then what do I find out? She's told you."

Rosalina's stomach lurched. "Talk to me, Nonna."

Filippo slapped his hand on the table. "Yes, Nonna." Her name snapped off his tongue. "Tell her how for years, you've threatened to cut me off if I told anyone. And yet the second *you* come home, she's telling you all about our slutty mother."

"Filippo! That's enough." Rosalina clenched her jaw and glared at him.

"Is it?" He edged up to her, jutting his chin in her face. "Did she tell you about your father calling me a bastard? Or how he slapped me for calling him Daddy?"

Rosalina cupped her mouth. Tears stung at her eyes. Her father had always treated Filippo differently to his other children. After her mother died, Rosalina had reasoned he was sad and upset. She'd never imagined this.

Filippo leaned on the table, and with a clenched jaw, he lowered his eyes to Nonna. "You allowed this to happen."

"I didn't!" Nonna stood, knocking her chair over. "I loved you; I only did the best for you." Tears streamed down her face. "I'm sorry, Filippo. I'm so sorry." She turned and fled the room. Rosalina would've run after her but couldn't. Instead, she turned to her brother. He was so dissimilar to her other brothers in both looks and temperament, yet never in her wildest imagination would she have thought he had a different father.

"Filippo, you're still the same brother to me. No matter what I know."

"Really? You can just forget that our mother fucked around and I was the result?"

She pursed her lips. "Yes! Yes, I can."

"Your father blamed me for killing Mom. Me." He jabbed his thumb to his chest. "I was a baby."

"Dad was wrong. He should never have said that."

Movement at the corner of the room caught her eye, and Rosalina gasped when the madman who lived in her nightmares stepped into the kitchen. Although he looked different, she'd never forget the pure evil in his eyes.

She backed up and screamed, a pure gut-wrenching scream of terror. The sight of the gun made her stop.

"You're. . . d-d-dead."

His eyes zeroed in on her. "So I've been told." Nox pointed the gun at Filippo.

The fear that had her rooted to the spot shot up her spine. "Get away from him."

"Who are you?" Filippo stepped towards Rosalina, and she clutched his arm.

"I am the divine Nox." Nox aimed the gun at Rosalina. "She tried to kill me. She failed."

Rosalina stepped in front of Filippo, putting herself between her brother and the madman. "I shot you with the spear gun."

"You did. I lived." Nox tossed a rope at her, and it fell at her feet. "Tie his hands behind his back."

Rosalina didn't move. She could hardly breathe.

"He either comes with us, or I kill him now. Which do you prefer?"

A vein throbbed in Nox's temple; his left eye twitched. He wasn't bluffing.

Her mind slammed to Nonna. If she came downstairs now. . .

Holding back the scream burning in her throat, Rosalina reached for the rope with trembling hands. "Where are you taking us?"

"Shut up and do it."

Her heart set to explode.

As she looped the rope around Filippo's wrists, Nox's putrid stench poisoned the air and filled her beloved kitchen with hate.

A grim smile crept across Nox's lips.

I shot him. The spear pierced his belly.

He tumbled overboard, never to be seen again. Everyone had said he was dead. Everyone. . . including the police.

She finished tying the knot. "Are you okay?" She touched Filippo's arm.

"No!" Filippo snapped. "What's going on?"

Without warning Nox lunged. In a flash of movement, he stabbed a syringe into Filippo's neck. Filippo screamed and tumbled to the floor, clutching the stab wound with his bound hands.

Rosalina lowered herself to Filippo's side. "What did you do? Filippo? Filippo!"

Nox shoved the gun at her nose. "Get up."

"No!" She glared over the barrel at him.

He aimed the weapon at Filippo's head. "Get up now or I'll shoot him." His calm voice shot fear through her.

Filippo whimpered as Rosalina clawed herself upright.

"Walk around the table."

Filippo's silence was terrifying. As was the red spider veins bleeding into the whites of his eyes.

"I'm not going anywhere." She clamped her jaw.

"You'll do exactly as you're told." Nox pressed the gun to her brother's knee.

Her stomach lurched. "No!"

"Then get moving." Nox indicated with the weapon towards the door.

She hooked the crutches up under her armpits, and with a glance at Filippo, her heart exploded in her chest as she hobbled away. Her knees nearly buckled when the press of steel nudged into her back.

"Keep moving." Nox hissed in her ear.

"I am!" She spoke through gritted teeth and took another awkward stride with the crutches. She went out the back door and saw the silver car in the driveway. Her breath shot in and out as she realized if she got in that car, it could be the end of her. She could vanish forever.

The small gravel stones made the walk difficult, but she slowed even more, praying for a miracle. She pictured smashing her crutch over his head, crushing his skull with the blow. But it would never be. She'd have no chance; her plastered leg made her movements stiff and unco-ordinated. And she needed to keep moving before Nonna came downstairs.

She'd do whatever Nox said, if it meant saving her grandmother.

But when Nox opened the car's trunk, her resolve shattered to a million pieces. Fear coursed through her veins.

"Get in." Nox trained the gun at her chest.

Bile shot up her throat. "No!"

"Get in the fucking car or your brother is dead."

If he yelled at her, even raised his voice, she would've accepted his lunacy. But it was the calmness with which he spoke that drove a gut-wrenching realization through her. He'd planned this for a long time.

She swallowed bile and revulsion as she took a step forward and leaned on the edge of the trunk.

Nox snatched her crutches out from under her and whipped the gun across her temple.

She tumbled forward. The coarse carpet sandpapered her cheek.

Her world swam.

Then everything went black.

Chapter Thirteen

Nox believed it was divine intervention that placed Rosalina and Archer at the gate of the marina when he drove that way in the morning. For three days, he'd stocked up on food and supplies and searched the marina for even a glimpse of Archer and his oversized yacht without any success. Today though, it was like finding them was meant to be.

It was a further miracle when Rosalina climbed into the black car without Archer at her side. Last time he'd kidnapped Rosalina it had been spontaneous. This time, everything was planning out to perfection.

He had intended to kidnap only Rosalina. But now, with her brother tied up in the back seat, he realized his good fortune. Torturing him to make her talk was the prefect scenario.

As he munched away on the pastries he'd stolen off the kitchen counter before he'd dragged Filippo to the car, Rosalina began screaming in the boot. But traveling at the speed they were along the autobahn gave little chance that her cries would be heard. Nox raised the music volume and attempted to sing along as he headed towards Livorno.

His luck had definitely changed, because not only was there no queues at the two toll booths, but every traffic light they approached was green. The trip through Livorno was quick and uneventful, and soon they were on the Stada Statale One, heading towards his new home.

Nox wound down the window, and as he enjoyed the ocean breezes and processed a plan to get Rosalina and the still unconscious Filippo out of the back seat, Rosalina resumed her kicking and screaming in the boot. Her screams were music to his ears. It also meant she'd be physically exhausted by the time they arrived. Perfect.

He turned into the tree-lined road, drove right up alongside the front steps, pulled to a stop and jumped out. Choosing to work with Filippo before he woke up from the sedative, Nox tugged the man from the back seat. With his hands under Filippo's armpits, he dragged him from the car and allowed his feet to fall to the ground. The man was heavy, and Nox hadn't realized how weak he'd become. He had to stop a few times up the front stairs and he was gasping for breath by the time he dropped Filippo to open the front doors.

He shoved his hands under the man's armpits again and pulled him over the threshold. One of Filippo's shoes fell off at the door, revealing a brown sock with a hole large enough for his big toe to poke through. As Nox continued all the way down the corridor and into the dormitory, Filippo's heels dragged two jagged lines through the rubble. Once in the room, Nox dropped Filippo to the floor, checked his captive's pockets, and removed a phone and a billfold.

Rosalina's turn.

Nox had the gun drawn and the crutches ready as he raised up the trunk. She lunged at him but Nox simply stepped back and watched as she grappled to avoid sprawling to the ground.

"You bastard. What'd you do to Filippo?"

"Get out and I'll show you."

She glared at him with steely blue eyes, and her chest heaved with one angry breath after another. It seemed that the plastered leg wasn't a deterrent at all. The gun in his hand was the only barrier to an all-out attack. It was a long, anxious moment before her shoulders sagged. She raised her skirt and curled one long, tanned leg over the edge of the car and found her footing on the ground. Then she leaned forward and lifted her broken leg out of the trunk.

"Give me the crutches."

He handed them forward and eased in behind her. "Up the stairs."

Rosalina walked slowly. Too slowly, and she was looking around too much. "Hurry up, bitch." He thumped the gun into the back of her head.

She flinched. "Shit! I'm going as fast as I can."

Once they were through the doors, Nox didn't care how slow she went. Now that he had her, he was planning on taking his time with her anyway.

"Open that door on your left," Nox said at the end of the hallway.

She obeyed and turned the handle. "Filippo!" She threw the crutches aside and launched at her brother. Nox shut the door, slid the new latch he'd bought into place, and returned the gun to his pocket as he strode back along the hallway. He climbed the stairs, traversed the hallway and aimed for the fourth door.

He eased up to the balcony and tingles curled up his spine as he looked down. Rosalina had Filippo's head in her lap. She wiped his cheek and her shuddering shoulders suggested she was crying.

Nox hadn't made a sound and yet Rosalina suddenly looked up at him as if she knew he'd be there. The look on her face took him back thirty years. This moment was decades in the making. He was the new Zanobi. Now he realized what the pedophile had gained from his nightly ritual of staring down at the boys. Power.

Nox gripped the railing and indulged in the thrill of domination coursing through his veins.

Chapter Fourteen

A prickle along Rosalina's spine made her look up. Above her, staring down from a curved concrete balcony, was Nox. He inclined his head, as if acknowledging an adversary. She forced herself to ignore the pounding in her chest as she took in his squared-out jaw, his pockmarked cheeks, his gray-speckled chin stubble, and his beady eyes that were the color of arctic ice. He looked triumphant. He looked calm.

His composure scared the breath out of her.

Nox slinked away from the edge and disappeared from view. She turned her attention back to Filippo. Her brother's breathing was steady, but his eyes flittered beneath his eyelids, riding out whatever torment trapped him there. A fine layer of sweat beaded his forehead, and she wiped it away with the fabric of her dress. Trying to alleviate her aching back she nudged forward and bent her leg so Filippo's neck was on her thigh.

She turned her attention to her surrounds. Three rows of beds stretched out before her. The ones closer to her were just skeletal frames, but some had mattresses and others were fully made with blankets and pillows. The beds were small, too small to be adult beds, and she wondered if this was once a boarding school, or a children's hospital. Three large windows were along one wall. She doubted they were a way out, yet she had to see. Lowering Filippo's head to the concrete floor, she used the crutches to climb to her feet.

She navigated her way through toward the windows. Glass shards struck out from the frames like shark's teeth. Black metal bars, an inch thick, ran from top to bottom. Whoever had slept in these beds hadn't stayed voluntarily.

Beyond the window, as far as she could see was nothing but ocean. In the very distance, container ships followed each other along the horizon in a conga line. The nearest port from Signa was Livorno, and if she had to guess she'd say they were about half an hour's drive from the seaside port.

Directly below the window was jagged cliff face in several shades of red. Waves crashed into rocks a long way below. The building teetered right on the edge of the cliff.

A groan alerted her to Filippo waking. She hobbled to his side, eased to the floor, and once again lifted his head onto her lap. "Hey Filippo, I'm here. Rosa."

He groaned again and raised his hand. She reached for it and cupped his palm in hers. His grip was a vice, his palm a fiery furnace. "It's okay. I'm with you."

Little by little, Filippo regained consciousness, and finally he blinked up at her.

"Hey there. Are you okay?"

He frowned and squeezed his eyes shut as if trying to change the vision.

"Do you know what happened?"

He snapped his eyes open, then shook his head. "No."

"We've been kidnapped."

"What? By who?" He continued to blink, maybe trying to shake the fog from his brain.

"Did you see or hear anything about that crazy priest I shot with the spear gun in the Greek islands?"

His eyebrows drilled together. "The one you killed?"

"I thought I'd killed him. He's kidnapped us."

He reached up to his neck and winced. "What did he inject me with?"

"I don't know. I'm just glad you're okay."

Filippo tried to push up and Rosalina helped him to sit. "Where are we?"

"I think we're in an old mental hospital or something, near Livorno."

"Where is he?"

"I don't know. He stared down at us from up there for a while." She pointed at the curved balcony that hovered above the room like a judge's bench. "But I haven't seen him since."

"How long was I unconscious?"

"A few hours, I guess. I don't know"

"What do you know?" He spat the words out.

Now that Nox was alive, she wasn't sure what she knew anymore. "I'm sorry, Filippo. This is all my fault."

Filippo used the bedframe at his side to pull himself up. Rosalina did the same with her crutches.

"What does he want?"

"I don't—" She stopped herself. "Last time he kidnapped me, he was after the Calimala treasure."

"He's kidnapped you before? Jesus, Rosalina, what're you messed up in?"

It was a good question. Treasure hunting was supposed to be exciting, not dangerous. "I don't know anymore." She shrugged. "We found a clue to a seven-hundred-year-old missing treasure in a church and ever since then people have been trying to kill us."

Filippo squinted at her. "Did you find the treasure?"

"Yes, but--"

"Well where is it?"

"It was stolen from us."

"So, if he's already stolen it, what does he want now?"

"No, Nox didn't steal it from us. Ignatius Montpellier did."

Filippo's face scrunched up. "Who?"

If Filippo hadn't been following the stories in the news, then he must be the only person who hadn't. Even her friends in Australia seemed to know everything about it. "Did you see the footage of the helicopter crashing into *Evangeline*?" Rosalina had seen the segment a dozen times over, and each time Archer fell from the helicopter and plunged into the black water, her breath trapped in her throat.

"Yes, I saw that."

"Ignatius was the helicopter pilot."

Filippo frowned. "So, the treasure was in the helicopter when it crashed."

"No. It'd been loaded onto a boat. It's vanished and we don't know who took it."

"Nox must know the treasure was stolen from you."

She shrugged. "I have no idea what he knows."

"I know your boyfriend will exchange you for the treasure." Nox's voice boomed down onto them.

"There is no treasure. It was stolen from us." She punched her clenched fist into her thigh.

"Not all of it."

She frowned at that comment. The monkey statue was the only piece not stolen. How could he know about that? Ginger? Not for the first time, her suspicions over the young Australian woman were aroused. But even as the thought flittered across her brain, she dismissed it as unfounded. It was so unlike Rosalina to be suspicious. This crazy treasure-hunting business had marred her trust, and it infu-riated her that she doubted so easily. "Ignatius stole it all. It was on the news."

"Yes, but the Calimala treasure was divided into thirds. You only found one third."

She blinked up at him. They'd already made this discovery, but how did Nox know? She decided to play ignorant. "What're you talking about?"

"I'm talking about Archer looking for the other two thirds of the Calimala treasure. When he gives it to me, he can have you."

She gasped at his statement. "But that could take months. Years."

"Exactly. That's why you're here."

That was never going to happen. Archer wouldn't do anything before he rescued her. It also meant it was up to her and Filippo to escape. But as she glanced around the room, it looked impossible. "Have you called Archer?"

"No." His eyes sharpened. "I need his number."

"I'm not giving you anything."

"What you don't realize is that I have all the time in the world. You see, as far as everyone is concerned, I died somewhere out in that ocean months ago." He pointed out the giant arched windows. "Nobody is looking for me." He turned on his heel and left.

"Jesus," Filippo snapped at her. "Why didn't you just give him the number?"

She had no idea. "I don't know."

"Of course you bloody well don't." Filippo strode to the middle of the room. "Come back. We need food and water."

Rosalina had a sudden brainwave. "Once he gives us food and water, I'll give him Archer's phone number."

Filippo turned to her. "You could have said that to him before he took off. We'll starve."

She put her hands on her hips, and it took all her restraint not to roll her eyes. "He's not going to let us starve. He needs us."

"So, what. . . we just sit here and wait?"

"No." She lowered her voice and looked squarely in his eyes. "First, we see if we can find a way out, and then if that fails, we try to make things as comfortable as possible."

"I'm not spending one night in here."

She cocked her head. "Then help me find a way out."

Chapter Fifteen

Archer wriggled the panel into place, then hammered a nail into the wood to hold it there. It'd taken all morning to measure and cut the paneling into shape, but finally he and Jimmy were at the stage of installing it. They could've organized a builder to do it. But this way, only two people in the world knew it existed. And he trusted Jimmy with his life.

"It's good. By the time we're finished, you won't even know it's here." Jimmy slapped his oversized palm onto the paneling. It didn't even sound hollow.

Archer squeezed his mate's shoulder. "That's the plan." Having the treasure stolen twice was embarrassing. It will never happen again. The new hidden compartment was in the Moreton suite, the second-largest bedroom on *Evangeline*. It had a little room to spare, and with the panel hidden behind the bedhead, nobody would find it.

"All it needs is a lick of paint," Jimmy said.

"I think we'll get Rosalina and Ginger to do that."

"Good idea. I'm shithouse at painting."

Archer hammered the last of the nails into place and stood back to admire his handiwork. It really was good. Once finished the compartment would be impossible to see.

Archer checked his watch. One p.m. He was surprised Rosalina hadn't rung him after visiting Nonna. He'd tried to call her about an hour ago but got no answer. She should be at the hospital now, hopefully getting her cast removed.

Right on cue, his phone rang and he fished it from his pocket. He smiled as he noted Villa Pandolfini's number on the screen. "Is that you, Rosa?"

A torrent of fiery Italian words was thrust at him.

"Nonna?"

"*Sì*, Nonna." Nonna slipped into hysterical speech again.

Archer's heart leapt to his throat. "Nonna, calm down. What's happened?"

"*Rosalina e Filippo abbiamo litigato e ora se n'è andata.*"

"Goddamn it." Though he couldn't understand what she was saying, he didn't miss the fear in her voice. "Hang on a minute, Nonna." Archer dashed from the room. "Alessandro! Alex, where are you?" He ran towards the upper deck. "Alex!"

"We're up here."

Archer took the stairs two at a time. Alessandro was stepping out of the jacuzzi when Archer reached the sundeck.

"What's wrong?" Alessandro's question was loaded with urgency.

Archer thrust the phone at Alessandro. "Nonna's upset. I can't understand what she's saying."

"*Nonna, è Alessandro, che cosa c'è che non va?*"

Alessandro's face twisted from curiosity to fear.

"*Hai notizie di lei?*"

Jimmy strode across the sun deck to Archer's side. "What's wrong?"

Archer clutched Alessandro's forearm. "Is it Rosa?"

Alessandro nodded, but didn't elaborate. "*Hai provato a contattare Filippo?*"

Archer recognized Rosalina's brother's name. "Filippo. What's he done?" He recalled the conversation he'd had with Rosalina that morning regarding Nonna. Whatever had happened had something to do with Rosa's brother.

Archer clutched Alessandro's arm. "Alex, tell her we're coming. Jimmy, you stay here, and let me know the moment Rosalina calls or shows up."

"Got it." Jimmy's muscles bulged as he folded his arms across his chest.

Alessandro nodded. *"Archer e io sono venuta Nonna? Fateci sapere se senti qualcosa."*

Alessandro ended the call. "She said Rosalina had gone and that she'd had a fight with Filippo." He passed the phone to Archer. "I told her to call us if she hears anything. Have you tried ringing Rosalina?"

"Yes, I'll try again though." Archer punched the speed dial number on his phone. It rang, once, twice, three times, and then it clicked.

"Rosa!"

"No, it Nonna."

It took Archer a moment to compute. Rosalina would never leave her phone behind.

"Shit, Alex. Rosalina's phone is at Nonna's. Let's go."

Ginger slung a towel around her hips as she walked up to them. Her eyes were fearful when she looked at Archer. "What's wrong?"

"We don't know."

Alessandro placed his hand on Ginger's shoulder. "Archer and I need to see Nonna. You stay with Jimmy. Okay?"

"Okay."

Archer's searing gut gave him a bad feeling, and he'd learned a long time ago to trust his feelings. The burning in his gut moved to his chest as he raced down the stairs. "Come on, Alex," he yelled, as he raced for the door.

"I'm here." It sounded like Alessandro was right behind him, and not for the first time, Archer was surprised at the Italian's speed.

Archer ignored stares from people as they raced along the marina and out the security gate. There was a line of waiting taxis, and Archer jumped into the front seat of the first one and tossed the driver two hundred euro. "Tell him where to go, Alessandro," Archer said, as soon as the Italian was in the back seat.

Alessandro relayed the address to the driver and the man nodded like he knew exactly where the villa was.

Archer clipped his seatbelt into place. "Go, go." He hurried the driver along with his hand. "Tell him to hurry."

"Rapidamente. Affrettatevi."

"What did Nonna say, Alex?"

"She said she was fighting with Filippo when Rosa walked in. Filippo kept yelling at her and she was so upset she went upstairs. She heard Rosalina and Filippo arguing and then she heard Rosalina scream."

"Scream?"

"That's what she said."

"Then what?"

"Nonna said that by the time she came downstairs they were both gone."

"Do you have Filippo's phone number?"

"I don't think so." Alessandro scrolled through the numbers on his phone. "No. No I don't."

During the drive to Signa, Archer continually checked his phone, hoping for an update, but nothing came. It was suddenly important to recall everything he'd said during this morning's conversation and with each rehash he grew more certain the issue with Filippo was his fault. But then he frowned. "Alex, did you say Nonna and Filippo were fighting?"

"That's what Nonna said. Rosalina walked in on them fighting."

Rosalina would've got involved. She had an ingrained necessity to resolve everyone's issues. "Where do you think they went, Alex?"

"Ummm."

He could almost feel Alessandro's mind ticking over, but he didn't want a summary. . . he just wanted an answer. "Come on, man, you've known their family forever."

"Wait! I'm thinking."

"I don't understand where she'd go without telling me or Nonna."

"Maybe they wanted to get away from Nonna. They could be up in the wine-making shed."

"But doesn't Rosalina's dad live up there?"

"Yes."

That didn't make sense. In light of Rosalina's new information about her brother, there was little chance she'd go near her father. Unless. . . she wanted to bring the two of them together. No. She wouldn't do that. Would she?

"Maybe they went for a coffee or something."

"Maybe. Where would she go?"

"Rosalina's favorite coffee shop is Aresi café, in the main street of Signa."

Archer hated that he didn't know that. Not for the first time, he felt crushed with inadequacy for not knowing everything about Rosalina's home town.

They drove up the cobbled main street of Signa and stopped at the lights. The road was so narrow, only a single lane of traffic could pass through at a time. As they waited their turn, Archer looked for Rosalina through the shop windows. The lights were on inside, allowing him easy viewing through the windows of the fruit shop, the bakery, the pizzeria, and the little grocer. The taxi began to move again, and Archer quickly glanced in the rest of the shops as they whizzed by.

At Villa Pandolfini the boom gate was up, and Alessandro instructed the driver to go right up to the back door. No one entered the villa through the grand front entrance.

"That's Filippo's car, Archer."

"Then they must be still here on the property somewhere."

Archer opened the door before the driver pulled up. The second the car stopped, Archer jumped out, raced to the back door, burst in and dashed to the kitchen.

Nonna was there, standing, her hands cupping her cheeks, a patch-work of fear riddling her features.

"Have you heard from her, Nonna?"

She shook her head and reached out to Archer. He gripped her frail hands in his. "She'll be okay."

Alessandro placed his hand on Nonna's shoulder. "*Non ti preoccupare, Nonna, la troveremo.*"

Archer squeezed the old lady's hands. "Filippo's car is out the back, so they must still be here. Have you looked around, Nonna?"

"Yes. I've checked all of the rooms in the villa, the downstairs cellar and the guest houses."

"Okay. Let's check all the other buildings, Alex."

Archer allowed Alessandro to lead the way, because although Archer had been here on several occasions, he'd only been into a couple of the buildings. Together, they dashed from one building to the next. They started at the laundry, then went to the pool house, the gym room, then moved onto the guesthouses. The last stop was the wine-making shed. It was one of the biggest buildings on the property, other than the villa itself.

Archer dreaded meeting Rosalina's father and yet, considering he was Rosalina's fiancé, it was well and truly time. The man had failed to show up at their engagement party, and every meal Archer had had with the family so far. It was bizarre that Mr. Calucci was a recluse on his own property.

The two giant doors were wide open, and Archer and Alex raced in and stopped in the central space surrounded by a dozen or so very tall stainless-steel silos.

"Rosa!" Archer's heart was in his throat as he screamed out for her. "Rosalina!"

Their voices echoed back to them. Alessandro picked up the pace again and raced past the silos towards the back of the shed. A man appeared from nowhere and Archer didn't need an introduction to know it was Rosalina's father.

The man had ink black hair, peppered with streaks of silver that swept back from his chiseled face. His neatly trimmed beard was also speckled with gray. He was tall and solid, and barely showed any signs of his age or the grueling manual labor he must do day to day.

Archer thrust his hand forward. "Hello, Mr. Calucci, my name's Archer. I'm Rosalina's fiancé. Have you seen her?"

The older man shook his head, frowning, and glanced at Alessandro. "*Cosa è successo?*"

From that point on, Archer let Alessandro do the talking, and it took forever. When the old man shook his head, Archer knew their last hope had been dashed. She wasn't here.

Mr. Calucci turned his gaze to Archer. "Welcome to the family." His broken English was decipherable.

"Thank you. Nice to meet you at last." Archer tried to keep the sarcasm from his voice; it wasn't his place to judge his future father-in-law. Nor was it the right time.

"She's not here," Alessandro said. "What do we do now?"

"I don't understand why Filippo's car is still here."

Alessandro's eyebrows drilled together. "Mmmm."

"He wouldn't take her into the vineyard, would he?" The acid in Archer's stomach burned. *What if Filippo had done something to her?*

"Archer?"

Alessandro had been talking to him. "What?"

"Mr. Calucci will check the vineyards. Shall we check the villa again?"

"Okay." Archer shook Rosalina's father's hand again, then he dashed out the door and down the path lined with miniature hedges. It only seemed like yesterday, and not six months ago, that he and Rosalina had walked along here hand in hand. So much had happened since then. Neither of them was the same person they were six months ago.

Maybe she'd left on purpose.

That thought was a freight train smashing through his heart.

Chapter Sixteen

Nox tore pages from the bible, scrunched them into balls and tossed them into the kitchen fireplace with a flaming match from the box he'd bought at the shops. The fire engulfed the paper quickly and soon the stack of wood he'd tossed in from beside the fireplace began to smoke. His only hope was the chimney wasn't blocked after years of neglect. The fireplace in his bedroom had worked just fine.

Mesmerized, he watched as the smoke curled out from beneath the kindling and drifted aimlessly, then, ever so slowly it trailed upwards and vanished behind the mantle. He'd know soon enough if this was going to work.

Nox stepped back as the flames took hold and within minutes he had a cozy little fire going. Holding his palms towards the heat, he sighed deeply. He could easily put his feet up by the fire and stay there for the rest of the day. If his stomach weren't gnashing at him, that was.

Earlier, once he'd confirmed Rosalina and Filippo were secure, he'd raced to the shops and bought enough food and supplies for a couple of weeks. He had no intention of going anywhere for a while. His mouth salivated as he steadied a saucepan of water onto the flames. Today's meal would be a big bowl of pasta mixed with salami, crushed tomatoes, Kalamata olives and grated parmesan cheese. Prior to these last three days, it had been a very long time since he'd had a home-cooked meal.

His thoughts drifted to Ophelia; he often dreamt about her. She was his angel. Maybe one day he could find her again. Maybe she would forgive him. She must know that he could have killed her, but he didn't. Instead, he'd chosen to set her free.

Nox tossed two handfuls of spirally pasta into the boiling water and stirred with a wooden spoon he'd found in a drawer and wiped on his shirt. Leaving the pasta to cook, he rummaged through the kitchen drawers to locate the other utensils he needed. He gave them a quick wash in the bottled water he'd bought.

When the pasta was ready, he ate straight from the pot, and paused only when it scalded his tongue. Every bite was delicious.

Soon, he couldn't eat even one more mouthful. He set the pot aside, sat back, belched and then laughed, a good hearty laugh.

When the cramping subsided, Nox grabbed a small bottle of water, a loaf of bread, a pail and a rope. Then he crept up the stairs and along the corridor. He had hoped to overhear Rosalina and Filippo talking, but other than the whistling wind, it was silent. Too silent. Panic gripped him, and he raced the final steps to the balcony and peered over. He let out his trapped breath when he saw them.

Rosalina and Filippo were seated on beds facing each other. They looked up at him simultaneously. There was something in their faces that made him pause. The anger was gone. So was the fear. It was resignation that looked up at him now. They finally knew they had no choice but to do what he wanted.

"Are you ready to give me Archer's number?"

"We want food and water first."

Rosalina was a demanding bitch.

But Nox accepted that as a fair exchange. In fact, he'd predicted it. Everything was going to plan. He put the water and loaf of bread into the pail, then tied the rope to the handle and the other end to the balustrade and lowered it over the side of the balcony. Rosalina and Filippo positioned themselves beneath it, ready to catch. Nox stopped the pail three feet from their reach and their eyes turned up to him.

"What's the pin code on your phone, Filippo?"

"One-two-four-three," he said without hesitation.

Nox removed the iPhone from his pocket and punched in the code. The screen flashed to a picture of Filippo holding a glass of red wine in his hand. Although he was smiling in the photo, Filippo had a touch of sadness about him. Nox pressed on the green phone tab. "What's Archer's number?"

"We want the food and water first," Rosalina said.

"Give me the number."

"No."

Nox shrugged and began to pull the rope back up.

"Stop! Wait," Rosalina said.

He paused to look down at her and she folded her arms across her chest. "The number. Now!"

A series of numbers snapped off her tongue and Nox keyed them into the phone. He pressed the speaker button so everyone could listen.

It was answered on the second ring. "Rosa, Is that you?" It was Archer. Nox would never forget his vulgar Australian accent.

"ARCHER," Rosalina screamed from below.

"Rosa! Where are you?"

Nox lifted the phone to his lips. "She's with me." He spoke with measured assertion. Archer would remember him; he had no doubt about that.

"Nox!" Archer said it with the right amount of shock.

"You got it in one guess."

"If you so much as lay a hand on her, I'll kill you."

"You can't kill me. Nobody can kill me. But I'll kill both Rosa and her brother if you call the police, do you hear--"

"Nox is holding us in an old build--"

Nox pressed the red button, cutting off Rosalina's rant. "Here's your food." He dropped the rope and the pail clattered to the tiled floor. "Don't eat it all at once."

Filippo scurried over to it. "That's not enough, you bastard."

"Yes, it is." It was more than enough. They could live for a week on what he'd just supplied.

"I need to go to the restroom," Rosalina yelled up at him.

"That's what the pail is for." Nox cackled. His plan was playing out like a perfectly crafted script.

As Rosalina yelled profanities at him, the phone rang.

It was Archer.

Nox let it ring as he turned and left.

Rosalina was still yelling even once he'd returned to his meal. As the phone rang over and over, the salami pasta became more and more enjoyable.

Chapter Seventeen

Rosalina accepted half the bread loaf from Filippo and tugged off small chunks to eat. Filippo, on the other hand, took huge bites, devouring it as if it were his first meal in a week. "We better save some," she said. "We have no idea when he'll give us more."

Filippo's mouth gaped, displaying bits of chewed up bread on his tongue. "You better not be serious."

"You don't know Nox. He's evil."

Filippo took another bite and washed it down with water. "How do you know him?"

"It's a very long story."

Filippo spread his arms wide, bread in one hand, water in the other. "Looks like we have all the time in the world."

Rosalina rose up, put her bread back in the pail and used her crutches to return to the window. The sun was setting and the sky had morphed into dusty pinks and purples. The ocean resembled a grand velvet blanket. It was apparent they'd be spending the night here after all.

She curled and uncurled her fists.

It would get cold. The wind had already whipped up since they'd been first thrown into this room and the sound had changed from a high-pitched whistle to a low howl.

She turned from the window and surveyed the room. There were beds. . . dozens of them, all lined up side by side in three rows with almost equal distance between them. There was a series of cupboards at the far end. She hobbled towards them and opened the doors, one by one. They were crammed with clothes, all very small and all very bland in color, mostly gray, black, and what used to be white. There were shoes, too, all black and all small. She tried to imagine why these would've been left behind but couldn't. A small pair of shoes teetered on the front shelf. She lifted them out and placed them in her hand. They barely covered her palm. The child that had owned these was very young.

Rosalina hadn't had much involvement with children. All her nieces and nephews had been born while she was overseas, and the thought of having her own terrified her. Right from the moment her mother had died during childbirth, she'd decided she'd never have children. Thankfully, she'd never needed to admit this fear to Archer. He was too caught up in his treasure hunting to think about having a family.

She put the shoe back. What happened here to make them abandon all this clothing?

She shoved the thought aside. She didn't want to know. Especially as they were sleeping here tonight.

"Filippo."

"What?" he said, with a mouthful of bread.

"It'll be cold in here soon. And dark. I think we should get some things ready now."

"Like what?"

"For starters, we'll need a bed each. We could push the sheets and blankets through the bars in the window and shake them out a bit."

"You're crazy if you think I'm sleeping in one of them."

Rosalina nodded. She'd half expected this response. With the crutches up under her armpits, she hobbled to the very far beds, the ones farthest away from the doorway. If Nox planned on coming in while they were sleeping, then he'd have to navigate all the beds to get to her.

The lump in her throat was as big as an orange. She couldn't breathe; she couldn't swallow. Soon, her chin dimpled and tears streamed down her cheeks. She flicked them away, angry with herself, furious for letting this happen again. The last time Nox had kidnapped her had been opportunistic. She'd literally walked into him beneath the Church of St Apostoli. This time, however, Nox had planned it.

That made this a whole lot scarier.

She wanted Archer. Needed him. Her heart burned. Emotion trickled through her. The sense of loss lurked like a predator. Preying on her weakness. Making her nothing but a hollow shell.

It was a long while before she was able to slap herself into action. Soon they'd be sitting in the dark, and that image got her moving again.

She chose the fully made-up bed against the wall, tugged off the blanket and linen, and began sneezing from the dust. With the sheets over her arm, she abandoned her crutches and hopped to the window. The glass had long ago fallen out, and fragments of it, big and small, littered the floor. One of the pieces was a pointy triangle. Remnants of an intricate stained-glass pattern in blue and green hues covered half of it. She lowered her sheets to the floor and picked up the glass shard. It would make the perfect weapon. And when the time came, she'd have no hesitation in using it.

She'd killed Nox before. . . she'd do it again. This time, she'd do it properly.

Rosalina placed the potential weapon on the bed nearest her and turned her attention back to the sheets. She unravelled one, threaded it between the bars in the window, then she passed it along the outside of the bars so she could spread it as much as possible and shook it out. It billowed like a sail in the wind, and just as another idea came to her, Filippo arrived at her side.

"Here, let me help you." He reached for one of the ends, and together they shook all the forgotten years off the sheet. They repeated the process with the rest of the bedding. Filippo then stripped the bed beside the one Rosalina had chosen, and they did the same with his linen.

They moved back to the beds and worked together to flip the mattresses over. Rosalina didn't even want to think of what had happened to the children who'd slept in her bed.

"Are you going to tell me about Nox?" Filippo asked as Rosalina flicked her sheet out over her mattress.

She didn't want to, but now that Filippo was involved it was only fair that he knew just how dangerous Nox was.

It was hard to know where to start. She decided Archer's necklace, the place where the whole treasure hunt journey started, was the obvious place.

"Have you noticed the pendant Archer wears around his neck?"

"The ugly gold thing?"

She chuckled. "Yes, that's the one. Archer found it when he was eleven years old. He was scuba diving with his dad when they discovered it off the Greek Islands. But then his dad was killed by a shark."

"Oh shit. You never told me that."

She shrugged one shoulder. "You and I rarely talk, so why would I?"

"That's not my fault. You always hated me." Filippo tossed his mattress over with unnecessary aggression.

"I never hated you." Rosalina palmed her chest. "What're you talking about?"

"You never involved me in anything. I was always the last to hear about whatever was going on. You knew what went on. And now that you know I'm the family bastard, you know why Dad treated me like shit too."

"Filippo." She hopped around the bed, trapping him between her and the wall. "Look at me. Filippo, please." He turned, with anger burning in his eyes. "You're still the same brother today as you've always been. Nothing has changed."

"Yeah, right. Every time you look at me, you'll know why I'm not like your brothers and sisters."

"Our brothers and sisters," she corrected him.

"Not according to your father. He tells me I'm not a Calucci."

Her pulse rocketed. "He's wrong. He has no right to say that. You were Mom's child, and that makes you a Calucci."

The tendons in Filippo's neck bulged. "She died because of me!" He shoved Rosa aside to stride to the window.

There were no words that could ever make up for what had happened. "Filippo, I can't imagine what you've been through, but--"

"Nonna had no right to tell you. Now every time you look at me, it'll be different."

Rosalina hopped towards him. "No. It won't." She reached for his arm, but he snapped it away.

"I don't want to talk about it." He strode off again and this time she let him go.

As she watched him walk away, she slumped to the nearest bed. There was no point talking about it while he was churning with fury. It seemed like almost every time she saw him, anger itched at the surface.

Her hand fell on the long, pointy shard of glass she'd placed on the bed earlier. She picked it up and turned it over in her hands. With her fingers wrapped around the broader part, she held it like a knife and pretended to stab. She pictured Nox and stabbed again. The edges were sharp; for this to work, she needed to cushion the handle.

Using the glass as a knife, she cut a long, narrow strip from a bed sheet. Once she had enough, she sliced one end of the strip up the middle like a forked tongue. She tied it into a tight knot halfway along the glass, and then wound the strip around and around the shard. At the other end of the strip, she sliced it into a fork, too and tied it around the padding to finish off. She gripped the new weapon, pleased with how well her fingers were protected. All she needed now was an opportunity. But if Nox only spoke to them from twelve feet above, then there was little chance she would get one.

"Where'd you get that?" Filippo said.

"I made it."

If Filippo was impressed, he didn't say so. But he did bend over and forage for another suitable piece of glass.

While he was searching, Rosalina cut a strip of sheet for his weapon.

"I thought you'd killed this Nox guy."

"Me too."

"You must've missed then."

The image of the fishing spear shooting at Nox's belly darted through her brain. She'd seen the five-foot rod hit him. When Nox went overboard, he had a spear still pierced through his torso. "No. I didn't miss," she finally said. "Somehow, he survived."

"How come he knows so much about the treasure?"

"We found the first clue to the treasure in the Church of St Apostoli in Florence. That's where we found Nox, too."

"So why doesn't he just go after it?"

Filippo finished wrapping the strip of bed sheet around his shard of glass and Rosalina helped him tie it off. "Treasure hunting isn't that easy, Filippo. Archer has been doing it for decades, and before that, his father had been doing it his whole life, too."

"Does Archer know where the other two thirds of the treasure are?"

"No. We were going to leave it for a while and look for a different treasure."

Filippo's tilted his head. "There's another treasure?"

Rosalina hesitated. She wasn't accustomed to discussing their treasure-hunting secrets with anyone besides Archer and the other people who lived on *Evangeline*. But not answering Filippo's questions would imply she didn't trust him. And now would be the worst time to show that. The squeeze of indecision tormented her. She decided to be vague with her answer.

"There are hundreds of treasures lost at sea. The hard part is finding them." She shifted her weight on her crutches. "It's getting dark," she said, diverting the conversation. "We need to get something over these windows to stop the breeze; it will be really cold in here very soon."

She moved towards the beds nearest the windows. "We can move one of the beds to below here and then stand a mattress up on its end to cover at least half the window."

Filippo helped her drag the small bed over. She was surprised at how heavy they were. They battled the breeze to stand a mattress up against the open window, but every time they propped it up, it fell down again. "I know." She clicked her fingers. "I'll cut some more strips of sheet, and we'll tie the mattress to the bars."

Her plan worked, and soon they had three mattresses up against the windows and the sound of the wind changed with the blockage; now it was a howling dog. It wasn't perfect, because there was still one third of the shattered window above the mattress that remained uncovered.

Rosalina couldn't ignore the pain in her belly any longer. She needed to use the pail. "Filippo, I want to put two beds up on their ends here and here." She indicated to two spots either side of the corner.

"What for now?"

"So I can hang a sheet across for a bit of privacy while I go to the toilet."

"Oh." He dragged a bed over and popped it up on its end, just like she'd instructed. While he did that, she stripped another bed of its linen and tied one corner of the sheet to the upended bed. When he finishing maneuvering the second bed into position, she tied the other end of sheet to it, creating a small cubical for a bit of privacy.

Without instruction, Filippo fetched the pail. Rosalina snatched another sheet off a bed, and using her knife, she tore it into pieces that they could use for toilet paper. Filippo removed the remains of her bread from the pail and scrunched up his face as he handed the pail to her. As she ducked in behind the drape, Filippo walked away.

It was nearly completely dark. The mattresses over the window hastened the darkness. She finished in the makeshift toilet and decided to have another look in the cupboards. The clothes were all hanging on wire hangers and she tugged one of them off the hook and allowed the shirt to fall to the floor. As she pulled and twisted at the hanger, she noted it was easily manipulated, making it potentially useful as a weapon. Although she wasn't sure how. Yet.

She put the hanger on the floor, picked up the shirt that had fallen and tossed it towards her bed. It landed on her pillow.

As a shiver ran up her spine at the thought of sleeping on that pillow, she formed another idea. She tugged another shirt from the cupboard and smelled it. Other than being dusty and a little bit stale, it wasn't too bad. She grabbed a few other shirts and stuffed them into the first. When no more could fit, she assessed her creation. This was a much better idea for a pillow. She tossed it towards her bed and did another one for Filippo.

She could just make out Filippo's shape in the darkness; he was sitting on his bed. "Here, catch." She tossed him the makeshift pillow. She picked up the coat hanger from the floor.

"You're really clever."

"Thanks." She'd take that compliment. Coming from Filippo made it extra special.

She hopped over to her bed and the springs creaked as she sat upon it.

"What's the coat hanger for?"

"I don't know yet."

"Are you going to tell me the name of the other treasure you're looking for?"

Rosalina had hoped he'd forget about that, but at the same time, she felt heaviness in her heart for being unwilling to share it with him. Her own brother. "It's called the Awa Maru."

"Funny name. What is it?"

She kept it brief at first, skimming over the details. But once she started, she found she didn't want to stop. Rosalina told him the ship's history, from when it was built to when it sank. Filippo prompted her with a myriad of questions, and she told him all about the fortune that went down with the ship and the priceless skulls that vanished, too. Just talking about something else allowed her a brief reprieve from their current nightmare. The joy of piecing together an ancient treasure mystery took over.

"If you know where the Awa Maru sank, then why can't you just go down there and get the treasure?"

"The Chinese searched for it in 1980, but they found nothing."

"Huh. So, what happened to it?"

"We believe it was put on a plane and taken to the Solomon Islands."

"Really? How do you know that?"

"This is what we do, Filippo. Treasure hunting is all about putting together pieces of a puzzle. It takes time. And luck. It can be fun. It can be very dangerous, too."

The cold was too much to handle and she cringed as she crawled beneath the sheets and pulled the blanket up over her shoulders. The bedsprings twanged beside her confirming Filippo was doing the same.

"I'd like to go treasure hunting with you sometime."

It was ironic to hear those words from him.

Because Rosalina didn't want to go treasure hunting ever again.

Chapter Eighteen

Archer's mind exploded when he'd heard Nox on the phone. But when Rosalina screamed in the background, he was stung with the horrifying premonition of loss. His knees threatened to buckle beneath him at Nox's words. . . 'She's with me.' He'd said it with the brutal calmness of a madman in control.

Archer bit back the chill of desperation to hash out his options. There were so few. He clutched Alessandro's forearm as they neared the back door to the villa. "Tell Nonna we're taking her car. But whatever you do, don't mention Nox."

"Where are we going?"

"That church where Nox kidnapped Rosa last time." It was the only place Archer could think of.

"You're telling the polizi. Right?" Alessandro's voice was strained.

"No, he said he'd kill them if we go to the police, and we know what he's capable of."

"Did he say he'd kill her?"

Archer drove his fingers through his hair. "Yes, and Filippo."

"But how will he know?"

"I'm not telling the police to find out, so calm down and think."

"Calm down! Look at you. . . you're nearly frothing at the mouth."

"Look. . . he'll kill her if we involve the police. We didn't call the police in Florence and we found her. Don't argue with me, Alex. I'm not in the mood."

Last time they'd rescued Rosalina they were both fighting for her love. It was different now, yet Alessandro would still do anything for Rosalina.

Alessandro held his glare. "Okay, but if we don't find her at the church, I'm going to the polizi."

"Come on." Archer dashed through the door.

Nonna stood as they lunged into the kitchen. "Did you find them?"

"No, but we think we know where they are."

Alessandro spoke to her in Italian, and Nonna turned and lifted a set of keys from a hook over the fireplace. Before Archer grabbed them, she gripped his hands in hers. She captured him with her large stricken eyes. "Don't hurt him?"

Archer blinked at her, confused. He had every intention of killing Nox when the time was right. It was a few beats before he realized she was talking about Filippo. "I won't, Nonna."

Archer and Alessandro ran together towards Nonna's car. Archer aimed for the right-hand side and then, realizing the driver's side was on the left, he switched at the last second and collided with Alessandro.

"What're you doing?" Alessandro shoved him.

"I'm driving."

"No, you're not. You've had little experience driving in Italy, and you have no idea where you're going. Give me the keys."

"Don't argue with me. I'm driving." Archer's despair goaded his anger.

"Then I'm not coming with you. Good luck finding it."

"Fucking hell. Can't you just work with me?"

Alessandro folded his arms. "I am working with you, and don't swear at me."

"I'll swear at you if I fucking well like."

"Fine then. But if you want to get there quickly, then I should drive."

Archer hissed out a breath. Alessandro was right, but it really pissed him off. "You better drive fast."

"And get pulled over for speeding. That will take more time."

"Arghh!" Archer tossed him the keys and clenched and unfurled his fists as he climbed into the passenger seat. "Hurry up."

"Shut up." Alessandro punched the Fiat into gear, launched out of the garage, and kicked up a barrage of stones as he careened down the driveway.

Archer gripped the door handle, but the moment they hit the road it all changed. Alex stuck to the speed limits, driving as if they were heading to a Sunday picnic. Archer's heart was a pounding earthquake at the uselessness he felt.

"How on earth would Nox kidnap two people and take them both into the tunnels of that church in Florence?" Alessandro had waited until they were on the autobahn heading into Florence before he spoke.

"That's what's pissing me off. I only heard Rosalina's voice on the phone. We may be too late for Filippo."

"Oh my God. Are you serious?"

"I don't know. But I agree with you. How does someone kidnap two people at once?"

Alessandro shrugged. "With a gun."

"Okay. . . so he has a gun." Archer attempted to lay it out. "He must've moved them one by one from the car. You saw those tunnels in that church. He would have to be damn lucky not to run into anyone. Twice."

"And Rosalina has a broken leg."

Archer hadn't thought of that. It made the whole scenario even more implausible.

Alessandro shook his head. "It's not looking good, is it?"

"For Filippo?"

"For either of them. I don't think they're going to be at the church."

Archer's shoulders slumped. "I doubt it. But we have to start somewhere."

Alessandro turned off the freeway and headed towards the ancient city of Florence. As Alessandro drove the car with unerring direction, Archer realized the Italian was right to have driven. "I'm sorry I argued with you. I'm glad you drove."

"Why, thank you, Archie."

"Do you want a smack in the nose?" He glared at the Italian.

Alessandro offered a lopsided grin and ramped up his speed.

Once they hit the busy Florence streets, they had to slow further. That only made Archer's heart race faster. Time was ticking and every second counted. Nox's ugly head appeared in his mind. The last time Archer had seen him, the crazy priest had a gun in his hand and madman blazing through his eyes.

He'd looked comfortable with the gun, too.

That admission bristled the hair along Archer's neck. Rosalina was a fighter, but she was already feeling down, both with her broken leg and, after the discussion they'd had this morning, it seemed like she was over the treasure hunting, too.

Alessandro turned the Fiat into yet another one-way street, and a wall of flashing lights hit them. "Oh Jesus, this is not good," Alessandro said.

Archer's fear hit overdrive at the sight of the police cars. "Pull over." He opened his door.

"Shut your bloody door."

Alessandro never swore, and Archer gawked at him.

"Wait until I find a place to pull over. You don't want to draw attention to yourself."

Once again, he was right. Archer clenched his jaw and with each flash of the lights in the distance, the vice around his chest tightened further. Alessandro pulled to the curb and both of them jumped out.

"Don't run." Alessandro was forceful, and it took Archer's full restraint not to sprint full-tilt to the church. Although there were probably fifty buildings in the vicinity of this street, Archer had no doubt the abundance of police and emergency vehicles were here for the Church of St Apostoli.

Archer couldn't breathe as he rounded the corner. When he saw the line of police and ambulances right outside the church his throat constricted altogether.

Dread ate a hole in his stomach. A crowd had formed around a police barrier and Archer and Alessandro moved in with them. "What's happened?" Archer asked the curly-haired man near him.

The young man glanced at him with mild curiosity. "Don't know, but it must be huge."

The mumbling crowd grew louder and a stretcher with a white

sheet draped over a body was wheeled to a waiting ambulance. The body was too big for Rosalina, but it could be Filippo. Or Nox. "Jesus, Alessandro." Archer prodded him with his finger. "Find out who that is."

Alessandro's dark eyes drilled into him. "What? How?"

The crowd gasped again, and another sheet-covered body was wheeled out. It was much smaller this time. "Oh Jesus." Archer plowed through the crowd, ducked under the tape, jumped the barrier and raced towards the stretcher. He was there before anyone could stop him.

A scream trapped in his throat as he ripped off the shroud.

It was a woman. Half her head had been smashed in. Her hair had a red tinge, her complexion was pale. Her body was bloated and her swollen tongue poked out. He was no expert, but this woman had probably been dead for days.

Archer nearly collapsed with relief.

Rough hands clutched his arms, dragging him away.

His legs threatened to crumble. As he doubled over, gasping for air, his mind was a landslide of rotten thoughts as he grappled over where Rosalina could be.

Chapter Nineteen

Nox woke with the early dawn and the thick duvet still tucked up under his chin. He lay awake, listening to the therapeutic sound of the waves crashing into the rocks below. When his stomach began to grumble, he flicked back the covers, sat up, and stretched his back. He felt marvelous, something he hadn't experienced in a very long time.

He made his way to the balcony to see what his guests were doing. Rosalina and Filippo were seated opposite each other on the two beds at the far end of the dormitory. Nox frowned at the upended mattresses at the windows, but when he realized it was to block the breeze, he grinned. He had no objections to them making themselves at home; they were likely to be here a long time.

"We need food and water." The defiance in Rosalina's voice was unmistakable.

Once again, he had no idea how she knew he was there. "I already gave you some."

"It's not enough."

Nox laughed. "It was more than enough."

"What do you want?" Rosalina said.

"I told you. The rest of the Calimala treasure."

"But we don't know where it is. Searching for it could take years."

Rosalina stood and moved with her crutches towards the balcony. Filippo sidled up beside her.

"I don't care how long it takes. I've waited decades. I can wait so much more."

"What about if we give you the Awa Maru treasure instead?" Filippo said.

As soon as Filippo spoke, Rosalina turned to him and he stepped back. Nox watched with interest. Clearly this was not something she'd planned to mention.

"I'm listening," Nox said.

"It's nothing," Rosalina said. But her reaction confirmed it was something.

"If you tell me about it, I will deliver more food and water."

"It's a Japanese warship."

Rosalina shoved her brother and he stumbled backwards. "Shut up, Filippo. It's not helping."

Filippo got up from the floor and stood, legs apart, hands on hips, glaring at Rosalina. Nox enjoyed the floor show. A dispute between these two could only work in his favor. Nox turned on his heel, deciding to leave them to battle it out.

He went downstairs and fed the fire more pages from a bible and slabs of wood. When the flames blazed, he filled up a pot with water and placed it on the heat. He could almost taste the coffee before he'd poured it. He heated up last night's pasta and turned on Filippo's phone to search Safari for a Japanese warship named Awa Maru.

By the time he'd finished his meal and enjoyed two more cups of coffee, he had enough notes and sufficient ammunition to ring Archer again.

Archer's phone was answered on the first ring. "Filippo!"

"Guess again."

"I'm going to kill you."

"You already tried that."

"I'll make sure of it this time, you bastard," Archer yelled.

Nox picked at something wedged between his front teeth. "You'll have to find me first."

"Finding things is what I do."

"Exactly. That's why I'm calling." Nox sipped at his coffee, making

Archer wait a moment or two before he continued. "I have a proposition."

"Yeah! What?" Archer snapped.

"You shall see your precious Rosalina again when you bring me the Awa Maru treasure." He heard breathing on the other end of the line but it was a long moment before Archer spoke again.

"I want to speak to her."

"Do we have a deal?"

"Not until I speak to her."

Nox ended the call; he couldn't risk Archer tracing the phone. As he walked up the stairs, the phone rang again. He waited until he was halfway along the corridor before he pressed the answer button. At the edge of the balcony, he looked down. One of the mattresses had been pulled down from the window, letting in more light. He found Rosalina and Filippo on the same two beds they were on earlier.

"Archer wants to talk to you." Nox pressed the speakerphone button.

"Archer!" Rosalina yelled.

"Rosa!"

"I'm here, babe." Rosalina stumbled to the center of the room.

"Has he hurt you?" Archer's voice cracked with concern.

"No. Filippo is here with me."

"Make sure you protect her, Filippo. I'm coming to get you."

"No, you're not," Nox said. "Filippo, tell Archer what the deal is."

Filippo looked at Rosalina before he spoke. "He wants to exchange us for the treasure."

"Tell him which treasure," Nox said. Nox was certain the Awa Maru treasure would be easier to find than the seven-hundred-year-old one. He could pursue the Calimala treasure next.

"He wants the Awa Ma--"

"We're in a big old building near Livorno." Rosalina cut Filippo off.

Nox jabbed the end button, certain he'd done it before she'd said Livorno.

How the fuck did she work that out?

He glared down at her with all the loathing he could muster.

Chapter Twenty

As the morning glow peeked over the top of the stood-up mattresses and crept up the wall behind her, questions spun through Rosalina's brain like a roulette wheel.

Had Archer heard me call out Livorno?

If he did, was I correct?

Would Archer ever find us?

Her questions morphed into anger over Filippo revealing the Awa Maru treasure to Nox.

How the hell did I get captured again?

Her hunger pains groaned like rabid dogs. Her leg throbbed like crazy. And she was beyond exhausted. In the last twenty-four hours, all she'd had to eat were a couple of chunks of bread.

"Jesus, I'm hungry." Filippo's first comment of the day was, as expected, a complaint.

"Hopefully we'll get something to eat this morning."

"We better."

Or what? Nox had complete control. Nothing they could do would influence him. They'd already lost their one bargaining chip, thanks to Filippo.

"Did you sleep okay?" she asked.

"What do you think?" He glared at her with anger-filled eyes.

She refrained from pointing out that she'd lain awake most of the night listening to a combination of the howling wind, crashing waves, and Filippo's constant snoring. In her opinion, he'd had a decent night's sleep. . . compared to her.

Rosalina flipped back her covers, and without her crutches, made her way to the makeshift restroom to relieve herself. Trying to squat was difficult with her plaster cast.

Damn it. I missed my appointment at the hospital.

The cast would've been removed yesterday. It took all her might, not to scream at the top of her lungs.

She came out from behind the drape and shuffled to the first window and willed the beautiful scene of the golden sun glistening across the ocean to relax her simmering fury.

"How much do you think the Awa Maru treasure is worth?"

She spun to him. "Shut up, Filippo."

His eyes bulged. "What? Why?"

"You're a fool. That was our only bargaining chip. We could've traded information on the treasure for food and water. And other things. But now. . ." she clenched her fists at her side, ". . . because of you, we have nothing."

"How was I to know?"

"You don't think. Everything is always about you. You never stop to think about anyone else."

"Piss off. You don't even know me. You take off overseas for years then come back and try to take over."

"How did I try to take over? I was protecting Nonna."

"She doesn't need protecting. She started all this by trying to protect the fucking Calucci name."

If he was within reach, Rosalina would've slapped him across the face. "Shut up. I don't want to hear another selfish word from you." She moved to the window farther away from him and inhaled deeply, smelling the fresh sea air. With each breath she yearned to be back on *Evangeline*. To be folded up in Archer's arms. Without Archer at her side, the breeze seemed to blow straight through her, chilling her to the bone. There was no doubt he'd come for her. But if he didn't come soon, she feared her resolve would crumble to dust like the building surrounding her.

She didn't speak to her brother for the rest of the day, and he didn't seem to miss it either.

It wasn't until late in the afternoon that Rosalina remembered an idea she'd thought of yesterday. She got up and stripped yet another bed of its linen. Then she tugged a couple of beds apart so she could lay a sheet out flat.

Filippo watched with disinterested eyes.

Now she just had to find something to write with. The sheets were a dirty shade of white so all she needed was something dark. Even dirt would do. She ran her finger over the floor and thick black dirt caked her fingertip.

She went to the makeshift toilet cubical and carried the pail back to the laid-out sheet. Filippo watched her but didn't move. Then she went to the cupboard and snatched one of the shirts off its hanger. Rosalina knelt on the floor beside the sheet, and with the kid's shirt wrapped around two of her fingers, she dipped it in the urine in the pail and then dragged it along the floor. Using it like a paintbrush, she began to write enormous letters across the sheet.

"What're you doing?"

"You'll see." By the time she'd finished, the word HELP dominated the sheet.

"Where are you putting that?"

"Outside the window."

He looked out the window, then glanced down at the sheet. "I don't think the ships out there on the horizon will see it."

"Thank you for that observation, Mr. Pessimist." Afraid of what she might see, she refrained from looking at him. She picked the sheet up by the corners, led it to the window, threaded it through the bars and tied each end to the cold metal. Rosalina was happy with the result; she just hoped that if somebody did see it, they were curious enough to investigate.

"You're wasting your time."

"When did you get so bloody negative?" She rolled her eyes at him.

He cocked his head. "When my father called me a murderous bastard."

Rosalina clenched her jaw and slammed her fists on the window bars. The bars moved. It was only slight, but they did move. She banged on them again, and sure enough, the base of the bars, where they penetrated the concrete, moved a fraction. The one-inch bars may be rock solid, but the bricks and mortar holding them in place were not. She turned, hopped to the floor near her bed and snatched up the wire coat hanger she'd played with yesterday and returned to the window.

"What're you doing now?"

"Getting out of here."

She manipulated the wire so the hook became as straight as she could get it. Then she folded back the hanging parts of the wire, giving her something to hold onto. Climbing up onto the wire bedframe so she had a bit of weight behind her, she then poked the point of the hanger into the small divot she'd created around the base of the metal bar and flicked it. A small piece of gray concrete bounced out and plummeted towards the rocks below.

She did it again. And again. Focusing her attention on the outside of the bar. Over and over the concrete crumbled under her attack and tumbled down to the cliff face. When a decent chunk of concrete released, she put the wire down and banged on the bar again. It moved about an inch this time. Getting excited now, she moved onto the next bar and Filippo sidled up beside her with his own coat hanger tool. They worked silently together, piece by piece, fashioning their escape. The sky outside began to morph into reds and oranges as the sun began to set. Soon they'd be in complete darkness.

"Filippo, let's give it a good bang and see what happens." They dropped their hangers to the floor. "Ready. One, two, three."

Together they slammed their fists onto the bars, and it moved a good four inches. The bar Rosalina was concentrating on released from its foundation, along with a large chunk of concrete. It now stuck out beyond the windowsill.

"It's working." Filippo sounded surprised.

"Keep going." They worked furiously and it seemed the more they dug, the larger the chunks became. "Let's bang on them again." It was Filippo's turn to make a decision.

They banged again, and two of the bars released. "Again!" he said.

One more popped out. Rosalina grabbed one of the released bars and pushed with the hope of making it extend farther than the windowsill. "We need to push them farther."

Filippo helped her and soon a significant gap opened up.

"I think I can fit through that," she said.

His eyes shot to her. "What about me?"

"We're going together, Filippo, so keep digging."

"No!" Nox's voice boomed from above.

Rosalina's heart leapt to her throat.

Nox turned and ran.

"Shit. He's coming. Push!" She grabbed the bars and pushed with all the strength she had. But it was too late; the gap wasn't big enough for her brother. She turned to him and by the look in his eyes, they both came to the realization at the exact same second.

"Quick, you have to go." Filippo grabbed her shoulders and twisted her towards the window.

"I'm not leaving without you."

"Yes, you are. Find Archer and come back for me." He grabbed her cheeks and kissed her forehead. "Go."

She launched her good leg over the windowsill. Halfway across, she stopped. "Grab our knives." He raced to their beds and ran back with a knife in each hand. She reached for her weapon. "If you get a chance, kill him. Understand?"

He nodded, but by the look of fear contorting his face, she wasn't sure he could do it. She hoped for his sake she misread him.

She shoved her knife down her dress, securing it just above the elastic waistband, then swung her broken leg over the windowsill. With a grip on the bars she stretched out, hoping for footing, but there was nothing. She dangled there for what seemed like minutes, stretching out as much as she could.

"No!" Nox's voice boomed loud and clear.

She had no choice. With her heart in her throat, she clutched the billowing sheet tied to the window bars and let go.

The cotton whipped through her fingers. She had no time to think. Jagged rocks sliced her cheek. Her feet hit a ledge. Pain shot up her legs. A desperate shriek tore from her throat. She clawed at the sheet desperate to stop her fall backwards.

Above her, rising straight up from the cliff was the solid block wall of the building. She tried to ignore the yelling from the window as she searched with her feet along the very narrow ledge she'd fallen onto. Below her was nothing but steep cliff face that met with the churning ocean. The ledge was barely a foot wide; she was lucky to be alive.

The realization was a punch to her stomach.

Night was encroaching. Fast. And she needed to get off this precipice while she could still see. Pulling herself back up the cliff was not an option; her upper body strength had never been great. She glanced left and then right, trying to establish the best way. Neither looked better than the other. In the end, it was her broken leg that dictated her decision. She needed her good leg to take her weight before she could find a spot for her cast.

"Go Rosalina, run." Filippo's shrill voice pushed her to action. With her breath trapped in her throat and her heart pounding in her ears she let go of the sheet, and searching for rocks to grip onto, she took a hesitant step. The measured precision made her progress painfully slow and with horror she noticed she wasn't going up at all. Nor was she going down. She was traversing along the cliff face parallel, and about seven feet below where she wanted to be.

Her foot kicked at something. Thinking it was a rock, she looked down and saw a statue of Jesus. She blinked, certain her mind and the fading light were playing tricks on her. Jesus held his arms out to her, like he was willing her to embrace him. Not believing her eyes, she tapped it with her foot, and the statue didn't move. The irony wasn't lost on her. Somewhere above her was an evil priest who wouldn't hesitate to kill her. This statue was telling her to have faith. She'd always been a believer in fate. . . landing on this ledge was a sign of that. Assuming the statue was offering something in the grand plan, she eased down and picked it up.

It was heavy and awkward, but upon slotting it down her top so it nestled above the waistband of her dress with the glass knife, she was heartened by the curious find.

Darkness came swiftly, and soon she was operating in a complete blackout. Her fingers and arms ached, as did her good leg. Her cast was a dead weight that grew heavier with each step. She couldn't go much farther, yet she had to.

Despair gripped her. Tears tumbled down her cheeks. Unable to wipe them away, she let them fall onto her chest.

Salty air and dirt lined her tongue. She swallowed back the dryness and reached for her next foothold. A faint voice in the distance carried to her and she paused to listen. Her heart was in her throat as she begged for it to be Filippo; she grew frantic with the knowledge that it was Nox yelling somewhere above her, not her brother.

Her chest squeezed as she thought of Filippo still trapped with Nox. She felt no elation or satisfaction over her escape; her thoughts were shackled by what Nox was capable of. Squeezing her eyes shut, she prayed for her brother, something she hadn't done in a very long time. But then she realized that Nox needed Filippo. Her brother was Nox's only leverage against the treasure. She forced herself to believe this concept would keep her brother alive.

She reached out with her hand for the next rock to grip onto, but there was nothing. Her fingers grasped at the void. Her knees wobbled as she stretched farther, hoping to reach something. Still, there was nothing. She snapped back, and her arm slapped on the rock at a ninety-degree angle. She'd come to a corner of sorts. Putting all her weight on her broken leg, she reached out with her good leg and her toes found flat ground.

It was an excruciating amount of time before she crawled onto the relatively flat surface. In the pitch black, she felt out the space. She'd found a small cave, about the size of an arm chair, large enough for her to sit cross-legged, but not big enough for her to lie down and stretch out her aching back muscles.

She removed the knife and the statue from down her dress and stood the figurine at the edge of her cave, watching out for her. Cuts on her cheek and hands stung, and her fingers almost screamed with a crippling ache. She massaged her toes and calf muscle until some feeling returned.

Rosalina closed her eyes and the sound of the crashing waves helped steady her erratic breathing. When she eventually looked out over the ocean, a sliver of moon hung high over the ocean. As it gradually lowered into the horizon, gracefully concealing its thin curve, she made the decision that this little cave would be her bedroom until sunrise.

With that choice made, she explored the cave for ways to make it warm and comfortable. Scraggy weeds popped out of many crevices and she tugged as many of them as she could free from the rocks and shoved them down her dress. It wouldn't be enough insulation, but it was all she had. A couple of the weeds wouldn't budge, and she reached for the cloth-wrapped shard. The light of the moon caught in the edge of the glass, casting a rainbow pattern on the cave wall. Her Nonna came to mind, as did one of her grandmother's favorite sayings. "To get a rainbow, you must have a little storm."

"That's what my Nonna's fond of telling me," she told the statue. "I think I've had enough storms."

Rosalina twisted the glass side to side a couple of times, admiring the colorful spectacle before she hacked off the last of the branches, cut them into smaller pieces and shoved them down her dress. The branches were prickly and uncomfortable, but with the dropping temperature they were necessary.

With the moon nearly gone, the breeze picked up, blowing cool air into the cave. Dirt swirled up into her face and she closed her eyes as she shivered. She curled into a ball, tucked her leg and plaster cast up under her dress, and hooked the thin fabric over the top. When her teeth began to chatter and her back ached with the cold, she made a drastic decision.

She dragged her plastered leg out from beneath her dress, and with the knife, began to cut the cast off. The cotton wool inside the cast may be enough insulation to help her get through the cold night. She started at the top, near her knee, and sawed back and forth, applying as much pressure as she could with her fingers. Pausing constantly to gage her progress, the split deepened. Concerned that she'd cut herself, she alternated between sawing back and forth and prizing the cast apart with her fingers.

Finally, she had a breakthrough and peeled the plaster off and placed the shell to the side. She rolled her ankle around and breathed a sigh of relief at the minimal pain. She flexed her foot back and forward. Again, not much pain. She put the knife aside, and using her fingers, tugged the layers of cotton wool from her leg. Cool breeze licked skin that hadn't felt fresh air for seven weeks.

The sense of freedom was fantastic. When all the wool was

removed, she rubbed her leg with a bunch of it, scratching at her scaly skin. After separating the condensed cotton wool and fluffing it up as much as possible, she lay on her side, curled her legs and packed the wool around them. Then she draped her skirt over her legs and tucked the fabric around her feet.

She felt for the knife and placed it within easy reach, then she grabbed the plaster cast and nestled it into the crook of her neck as a pillow. It was hard and uncomfortable, but at least her head wasn't on the rough ground. Her arms were freezing and when she ran out of energy to rub warmth into them, she tucked her arms inside her dress and hugged herself.

There was nothing left to do now but wait until sunrise. She closed her eyes, imagined Archer's arms wrapped around her, and told herself to go to sleep.

Chapter Twenty-One

Nox wiped dried blood off his arms with a T-shirt he'd grabbed from the upstairs cupboard. The jagged cuts from Filippo's knife attack may have been shallow, but they still stung. Five in total, ranging from a small nick on his cheek to the three-inch one on his forearm. He couldn't believe he had yet more wounds to tend to. Fortunately, these were nothing compared to the injuries he'd suffered in the past few months.

He tossed the bloody T-shirt into the fire and watched as it became an explosion of flames and black smoke. Soon, all evidence of the fight would be gone. Just like Rosalina. Stupid woman had fallen to her death. He had no doubt about that. Nox knew what was outside the dormitory windows; he'd tossed many things out there as a child. None of them ever turned up again.

With luck, Rosalina's battered body would be dragged out to sea, never to be seen again. It was fortunate he'd caught them in the middle of escaping or else both of them would've plunged to their deaths, ruining his entire plans.

Filippo was unconscious when Nox had tied him to one of the beds. By the time Nox had run upstairs to unhook the rope from the balustrade and returned to the dormitory, the lump on Filippo's head had grown to the size of a walnut. Nox had checked the man's bullet wound while Filippo laid passed out. It was just a graze, barely skimming his bicep. He was lucky Nox hadn't killed him. As was Nox. He needed the stupid shit.

Shooting him had given him the edge, though. Until then, Rosalina's crazy brother had slashed wildly with a piece of glass. He'd fired the gun as a warning and when Filippo screamed and gasped at his bullet wound, Nox had smashed the gun across his temple. Filippo had hit the floor like a dead man.

Once Rosalina's brother was tied up, Nox had gone outside to find her. He'd called out a few times and looked over the edge. But without a flashlight it was pointless and dangerous; he was just as likely to tumble over the cliff himself.

He'd seen a boy do that once. Santo was his name. There was some debate at the time over whether or not he'd jumped, fallen or been pushed. Nox had been only a few feet from him when he'd plunged, but he'd seen the look in Santo's eyes. Sadness had emanated from his tiny body, from his vacant eyes, his sagging shoulders to his wobbling knees. The boy had definitely jumped. It was many years before Nox knew why.

Santo had been chosen by Zanobi the night before, and Nox could remember thinking how lucky Santo was. To be chosen by Zanobi meant you were given special treats like ice cream and candy, new clothes and new shoes. Those chosen by Zanobi were also saved from the chores. Not Nox, though; he'd cleaned the toilets hundreds of times. The stench of it was still right there in his nostrils. Not once did he see any of Zanobi's boys clean the toilets.

If he could've begged Zanobi to choose him, he would have. Other than Sunday dinner, the only time Zanobi showed his face was above the beds at night. He'd hover over them in that balcony like God. Nox had stared into his dark eyes, willing the man to look at him, to point his bony finger at him, and say 'you. I pick you. But Zanobi would always glance right over bed number sixteen as if there wasn't a soul in it.

Maybe Nox had already lost his soul by then.

Santo was the first person Nox saw commit suicide. Three more boys jumped off that cliff before the facility was shut down. The authorities were told it was too dangerous. That was what they told the concerned public, too. It was many years before the real truth came out. By then, though, Zanobi was a long way up the food chain.

Santo's body was the only one they'd ever recovered; he'd hit the rocks so hard he wasn't going anywhere. The other three boys vanished. Each of them were washed out to sea and never seen again. And now Rosalina had suffered the same fate.

It suddenly occurred to him that Archer didn't need to know what had happened. If good fortune was on his side, Rosalina would never be seen again, and that suited him just fine.

When the pot of water in the fireplace boiled, Nox tossed in the pasta. His hunger pains were back. It was a familiar sensation, but he was sick of it. He missed Ophelia's incredible cooking. He came to her as a battered, starving man. When he'd scrambled away, he was strong, healed and cured.

Nox sucked in a deep breath, closed his eyes, and Ophelia filled his vision. Her arms were wrapped around her two sons, and she smothered them with kisses. Nox wanted that. He wanted Ophelia.

He snapped his eyes open, furious that he'd gone back there. It could never be. He could still picture his hands around her neck, her bulging blood-shot eyes, her swollen tongue. It was a miracle that he'd stopped squeezing when he did. She would never forgive him after that, and he didn't blame her.

He needed to move on from her. Once he had his treasure, he could fix his yellowed teeth and become handsome. With good looks and bucket-loads of money, he'd be able to choose a lover. But even as he thought it, he knew in his heart that Ophelia was the only woman he wanted.

Nox mixed his cooked pasta with tinned tomato, salami and cheese and gulped it down, eating until he was beyond full. He felt sick when he finally stood up from the table.

It was time to check on his prisoner. With Rosalina's brother tied up, it was not necessary to view him from the balcony. Nox strode to the dormitory door, put his ear to the wood and heard nothing, and so he entered.

The door creaked loud enough that his entrance couldn't go unnoticed. Filippo turned his head in Nox's direction.

"Good. You're awake."

"Let me go!" Filippo pulled against the restraints that held his arms above his head.

"You've been a very bad boy, Filippo. Do you know what they did to naughty boys here?"

"You're a sick bastard."

Nox huffed. "They tied them to the beds. Just like you are now. For days and days."

"Let me go, or else."

"We had to lie in our own piss and shit until the entire room reeked."

"Jesus. What the fuck did I ever do to you?"

The question caught Nox off guard. Filippo was an innocent bystander. Much like Nox had been for the early part of his life. He was eleven when he stopped being a bystander. And innocent, for that matter. "It's not what you've done. It's what you're going to do."

"I'm not doing a damn thing."

Nox let out a long, slow sigh. "Then I guess you'll starve to death."

"Arghh!" Filippo rattled the bedframe and screamed until spittle frothed at his mouth. "Where's Rosalina?"

"She's dead." Nox shrugged nonchalantly. "From that window." He pointed at the window Rosalina had jumped out. "There's nothing but sheer rock wall all the way down. Every bone in her body would've shattered when she hit the bottom."

Filippo's jaw dropped then he squinted at Nox. "You don't know that. It's dark outside. She could've escaped."

"Not likely. I've seen four boys jump off that cliff. Three of them were never found again. The fourth, well. . . let's just say they let nature take care of what was left of him, too." Nox let that comment sink in. "I'm afraid your stupid sister jumped to her death."

Filippo squeezed his eyes shut and shook his head. "I don't believe it."

"That's up to you." Nox shrugged. "In the meantime, we need to talk."

Filippo snapped his eyes to Nox. "I'm not talking until you untie me and give me food."

"Fine then." Nox moseyed towards the door.

"You need me, Nox." The way Filippo said it, bristling with authority, had Nox turn to the prisoner. "That's right." Filippo squared out his chin. "Without Rosalina, you need someone to trade." Despite being tied to the bed, Filippo looked cocky.

"Does this mean you're willing to talk?"

"I'll do better than that." Filippo paused and Nox watched his Adam's apple bob up and down. The man seemed uncomfortable with what he was about to say. Then his already dark eyes darkened further. "Between what you know and what I know, we can work together."

Nox laughed, a hearty belly laugh. "That smack to your head has rattled your brain."

Filippo met his eyes. "I know a hell of a lot about Archer and the treasure. I assume you know things about the treasure that they don't. Working together makes sense."

Nox prowled the room. He didn't work with people. He used people. Or, to be more precise, blackmailed people into helping him. What Filippo was proposing was ludicrous and yet, he found himself curious. "Why would I trust you?"

"Because Rosalina has always been a bitch to me. As have the rest of my family. I owe them nothing. Working with you to get the treasure and watching that cocky bastard Archer suffer would be the best start to my revenge."

Filippo hit the golden words with the idea of making Archer suffer. That bastard had been a thorn in Nox's plans for way too long. The proposition became interesting. "You need to prove it."

"How?"

"Convince Archer to get the treasure."

"Untie me. Get me food. And I'll do exactly that."

Chapter Twenty-Two

Archer couldn't stand sitting around doing nothing. For hours they'd been in Nonna's kitchen, listening to Nonna rehash the argument she'd had with Filippo. He'd thought she was going to have a heart attack when they'd told him that Nox had kidnapped them.

She'd heard about Nox before, but only after Rosalina had supposedly killed him. Now that he was back from the dead, he was not only real, he was terrifying. Archer knew what he was capable of. . . he'd seen it in the Greek Islands, and he'd seen it today in Florence. Nox must've been crazed when he'd smashed that woman's head in. Archer was destined to see that image for the rest of his life. He dug his thumbs into his temples as he pictured Rosalina trapped again with that madman.

He paced the room, striding the five paces back and forward.

Alessandro stood up from the table and drove his fingers through his hair. "I'm calling the polizi."

Archer didn't stop him. He watched on helpless at Alessandro's foreign exchange on the phone. He had no hope of following the conversation, but he heard the names Rosalina, Filippo and Nox, and he watched Alessandro's expression plummet into deep distress.

Archer turned his attention to Nonna. She'd stopped crying for the moment, but her eyes looked to be bleeding. The puffiness below them were dark pillows threatening to render her blind at any moment. Archer placed his hand over Nonna's trembling fingers.

"Did Nox kill those people in Florence?" she said.

Archer nodded. "We think so." The news footage said the people in the church had been murdered days ago but hadn't been discovered until today. Archer couldn't shake an eerie feeling Nox had been watching them for days, waiting for the perfect moment to attack.

"All this stupid treasure hunting. It brings the bad men." Her eyes glossed over again, and Archer turned away. Her statement cut very deep.

Alessandro put his phone down and drove his finger through his hair. "They have no evidence that Nox killed those people in Florence. They still have him listed as dead. We have to wait at least twenty-four hours before they will commence searching for Rosa and Filippo." He drove his hand across the back of his neck then slammed his fist on the table. "*Stupido*."

Archer's phone rang. He snatched it from his pocket and jabbed the answer button. "Archer."

"Archer, it's me, Filippo."

"Filippo! Where's Rosa?"

"I. . . I don't know."

"What do you mean you don't know?" Archer tried to ignore the fear in Filippo's voice and Nonna's eyes.

"She tried to escape. I don't know where she is. He shot me, Archer."

"Shot you? Are you okay?"

"I think so. You need to help us."

"Where are you?"

"We're in a building. . ." There was a loud thump and then a scream. "Don't hurt me!" Filippo wasn't talking into the phone. Archer's heart exploded as he heard the beating and Filippo's cries in pain.

"Stop it!" he yelled into the phone.

Soon there was silence. "Filippo!"

"Filippo's asleep now." Nox had a confident purr to his voice.

"You bastard. Where's Rosa?"

"She's sleeping, too."

"I'll kill you." Archer spoke the words with measured control.

"You already said that."

"What do you want?"

"I want the Awa Maru treasure."

"We don't have the fucking treasure."

"Find it. I'm a patient man. Take as long as you like. But. . ." Nox paused. "Rosa and Filippo may not have so long."

Archer strangled the phone. "I swear if you hurt her--"

"The sooner you get the treasure, the healthier they will be."

"Let me talk to her."

"No. Oh, and one more thing. Remember, do not tell the police or I will kill one of them." The phone clicked dead.

"Christ!" It took all Archer's restraint not to hurl the phone across the room.

"What did he say?" Nonna clutched his wrist. "Are they okay?"

"Filippo is alive, but. . ."

Nonna's chin quivered. "But what?"

"Nox shot him, and I just heard him beating him, too."

Nonna covered her mouth, tears spilling over her cheeks. "And Rosa?"

"I didn't speak to her." It wasn't possible she was gone. He'd feel it. He'd know deep down if she died. Of that he was certain. He had to believe that his fiancée was okay. "I know she's alive."

"How do you know?" Alessandro placed both hands on the table and leaned forward.

"Because he said he'd kill one of them if we contacted the police." He hung onto Nox's words like they were his last breath before he sunk into an ocean of dread.

Nonna covered her eyes. Her shoulders heaved and it was a long moment before a tortured sob released from her throat.

Alessandro balled his fists on the table. "What does Nox want?"

"He said he'd exchange Rosa and Filippo for the Awa Maru treasure."

"But that could take forever. What do we do?" Alessandro said.

Nonna reached for Archer's hand and clutched it in hers. "Get that *stupido* treasure and bring me back my granddaughter." She clenched her teeth so hard her chin quivered. "Then you kill that *bastardo*."

Archer's blood was ready to boil as he stood to kiss Nonna's furrowed forehead. "I will, Nonna. I promise."

He strode to the car with Alessandro hot on his heels. "What do you want me to do?"

"Help me figure out the clues to that treasure."

"That could take weeks."

Archer jumped into Filippo's car; his keys were still in the ignition. "We don't have weeks."

Alessandro climbed into the passenger seat, and Archer punched the car into drive and careened over the gravel. He launched out of the driveway and onto the main street of Signa.

It was Alessandro's turn to grip the door handle. "If you don't slow down, you'll either kill us or have us arrested, and neither will help Rosalina."

Archer hated how practical Alessandro was, but he slowed down all the same. He fished his phone from his pocket and dialed Jimmy. After a heated summary of what was going on, and Jimmy's just as heated response, they got down to business.

"We're flying to the Solomon Islands."

"Flying? What about *Evangeline*?" Jimmy asked.

"It'll take too long. I'll look after the flights. We need all Dad's books and things packed up and ready to go. We're on our way; see you in an hour or so." He clicked off the call.

"I'll text Ginger to start packing her stuff."

"No. Ginger can stay here."

"Like hell she is. We're a team, and she's coming with us."

"But I need someone here looking for Rosalina."

Archer felt Alessandro staring at him as he accelerated onto the freeway.

"Well, I'm not leaving without Ginger."

"You can both stay then."

"That's ridiculous. . . you need both of us to find the treasure. Besides, I have all the connections at the Accademia di Belle Arti museum, and Ginger is the only one who speaks Japanese."

Damn, Archer hadn't thought of that. "But I need someone here for Rosalina."

"Nonna will be here," Alessandro said.

Archer's mind spun like a bloody tornado. Maybe Alessandro was right. Damn it. He slammed his fist into the steering wheel.

"Calm down, Arch." Alessandro placed his hand on Archer's shoulder. "That isn't helping."

"Okay." Archer strangled the steering wheel. "Okay. Sorry. This is fucked up."

"I know. We just have to be smart about things. The four of us working together will be better than just you and Jimmy."

"All right. Find out when the first flights to the Solomon Islands are."

Alessandro grabbed his iPhone and started searching Safari.

Archer glanced at the clock and clenched his jaw. It was already nine p.m. There was little chance they'd get a flight tonight.

"This isn't looking good," Alessandro said, after much huffing.

"What?"

The quickest airline takes forty-one hours."

"What? That can't be right."

"From what I can tell we have to go from Rome to Singapore to Brisbane, and then finally to Honiara."

"Shit."

"Then from Honiara we'll need another flight to Munda."

"How far is it in nautical miles?"

Alessandro was quiet as he did the search. "8224 nautical miles."

Archer did the math in his head. "*Evangeline* will take twenty-two days, and that's without stopping."

"That's too long."

Archer agreed. Everything was taking too long. He pressed his foot on the accelerator. Then an idea hit him. "I'll charter a plane."

"Really?"

"I've never done it before, but it can't be too hard."

Alessandro rubbed his hands together. "All right. That's a great idea."

"Then we can take as much luggage as we want. Including the scuba gear. We may need it." He turned off the highway and aimed for the bright lights of Livorno.

Alessandro flicked away on his phone then sucked in through his teeth. "Jesus, the private jets in Florence charge four thousand euro per hour."

"And?"

Alessandro eyed him. "If it takes forty-one hours, then that's. . ." he rolled his eyes skyward, "that's, one hundred a sixty-four thousand euro."

"I'll make sure it doesn't take forty-one hours."

Chapter Twenty-Three

Alessandro sat forward on the lounge and slipped his fingers into Ginger's hand. Together, they watched Archer pace backward and forward. Jimmy was seated forward in an armchair with his hands clamped between his knees and a scowl drilling the lines on his face deeper.

"We can't fly till three p.m. tomorrow." Archer dug his thumbs into his temples. "It's too late; everything is taking too long."

"Why so late?" Alessandro asked. "I always assumed private planes were available any time, day or night."

"Because of the number of passengers and the amount of gear we want to take, we need the Hawker Beechcraft 800. It's not due to return until one-thirty tomorrow afternoon, and then they have to clean it and refuel."

"To be honest, it'll probably take us until then to pack up all the equipment and research notes anyway. And we'll need two or three cars to transport it all."

"I'll arrange it." Archer flicked Alessandro's points away with the back of his hand.

Alessandro heard the fear in Archer's voice and felt it in his movements. But it was imperative that they remain smart about this. Nox had deceived them once before. Not just them, either. Everyone, it seemed. The police, the church where he lived, and probably friends and family, too. If he had any. It was impossible to imagine someone vanishing for that long and then just turning up without anyone seeing him. Alessandro clicked his fingers. "He's changed his appearance!"

"Who?" Archer said.

"Nox. That's how he was capable of walking through that church without being seen."

"We did it, remember?"

That was true; they'd managed to sneak in and rescue Rosalina without bumping into anyone. Until they were on their way out, that was.

"Maybe we can work out where he's hiding." Ginger tugged her blonde plait over her shoulder.

"How?" Archer snapped.

"Calm down, Archer. You're not helping."

"I can't. That bastard has Rosalina again, and there's nothing I can do."

"We are doing something. Let me grab the whiteboard." Alessandro launched out of the lounge and strode to the study.

Ginger met him there. "Boy, is he wound up."

"*Naturalmente.* It's unbelievable this has happened again."

"Yes, but it's not like we can do anything right now."

"We can start by processing all the clues again, so when we reach the Solomon Islands we've documented as much information as we can."

They each grabbed an end of the whiteboard and wheeled it to the lounge area. Archer had flopped into a seat but he still looked like a caged animal about to break out.

Alessandro grabbed his whiteboard pen and divided the board into four columns. He cleared his throat. "By my assessment we have four options." He wrote a heading in each column as he spoke. "First, we try to find Rosa and Filippo. Second option is that we find the Awa Maru treasure. The third choice, and in my opinion the least practical, is to find the Calimala treasure that was stolen from us. Finally, we could investigate the Egyptian angle of the Calimala treasure, but given our limited knowledge there, I don't think that's a good idea either."

Archer looked up at him, but from his blank expression it seemed his mind was a long way from this discussion.

"The trouble with trying to find Rosa," Alessandro continued, "is that Nox could have taken her anywhere in Italy. It seems that since we last saw him, he's been able to blend in without anyone noticing. He could've been setting up this location for weeks. Months. We can assume he's changed his appearance. Let's start with what we know. First, he grew up in Florence so--"

"How do you know that?" Jimmy waggled his finger at Alessandro.

"It was detailed in the news when he went missing last time. He grew up in the orphanage attached to the Church of St Apostoli."

"Any family?" Archer asked.

"Not that anyone knows; he was abandoned when he was five."

"That's sad." Ginger scrunched up her nose. "No wonder he's so screwed up."

"I grew up in an orphanage." Archer glared at her. "And I don't go around killing people. Although that'll change when I get my hands on Nox."

Ginger's eye's bulged. "Sorry, Archer. I forgot."

Alessandro tapped the whiteboard, drawing Archer's hurtful glare from Ginger. "Nox was moved from the orphanage to live in the church when he was twelve. Brother Benedici became his guardian."

"Hey," Jimmy said. "Maybe this Benedici character can tell us more about Nox. Something might come up."

"Brother Benedici died last year. Apparently, he ate poisonous mushrooms."

"Yeah, right," Archer said. "My guess is Nox killed him."

Alessandro frowned. "Nox did disappear not long after that. . . the next time he resurfaced was when he started chasing us."

Archer stood up and paced the room again. "So as far as we know he's lived in two places. . . the orphanage and the church. Is that right? Seems a little odd to me."

"*Correcto*. He's never moved out."

"How old is he?" Jimmy asked.

"Nearly forty."

Everyone was quiet.

Archer sat again. "Nox could've taken them anywhere. I can't see how this is helping."

"We're trying to establish what we should do next."

Archer cocked his head. "I don't see how discussing Nox's fucking history can help."

"Okay, let's move onto the Awa Maru then." Alessandro drew a line through option one on the whiteboard and pointed at column two. "Do you all concur that the Solomon Islands is the *correcto* place to start?" He turned to them, and all three nodded in agreement.

"You do know the Solomon Islands is made up of hundreds of islands."

"We'll start at the island where the photo was taken," Archer said.

"*Si*, Munda Island." Alessandro listed it on the board.

"What do we know about that island?" Archer said.

"Hold that thought; I need my laptop." Alessandro raced to his bedroom and returned moments later to place his laptop on the table.

"The Solomons was one of the focal points of the Second World War," Jimmy said.

Alessandro glanced over at Jimmy. Jimmy wasn't usually the one revealing facts.

Jimmy shrugged. "My dad did a stint there working for some Aussie guy who had a coconut plantation. He said the place was a hell hole. Bugs galore and hot as Hades."

"Oh, I hate bugs, but they like me, for some reason," Ginger said.

"This is what we need." Alessandro found the Solomon Islands official website. "Solomon Islands is known for its scuba diving and World War Two relics. There's a place called Iron Bottom Sound, which is reported to be littered with dozens of sunken warships."

"We don't want ships, Alex. We want planes." Archer clenched his jaw again.

Alessandro ignored Archer's impatience and continued looking. "Okay, according to this scuba diving website, there are war planes everywhere, too."

"Alessandro!" Archer growled, and Alessandro shot him a look.

"This kind of research takes time, Archer. Why don't you go have a shower or something? We'll keep researching."

Archer squeezed his temples as if trying to force out whatever horror was tormenting his thoughts. Then he sighed. "Okay, I'll be back in a minute."

"Take your time."

Archer strode off.

"This is going to be a very long night." Jimmy huffed.

"Not for me. I'm already pooped," Ginger yawned.

Alessandro nodded. "Me too. We have a busy day tomorrow. . . maybe we should try to sleep."

"You kids go on; I'll keep Archer company." Jimmy tapped his fingernail on the beer can in the cup holder of his chair.

Alessandro raised an eyebrow at Ginger, seeking her thoughts, and she nodded back. She looked as exhausted as he felt. "Thanks, Jimmy. We'll finish this, and then we'll go to bed."

Within five minutes, Archer strode back into the room looking only slightly refreshed in jeans and a white T-shirt. "What'd you find?"

Alessandro cleared his throat. "There are three known wrecks of Kawasaki Ki-56 planes in the Solomon Islands. One is near Wake Island, one on Savo Island, and one just off the shores of Munda Island."

Archer clicked his fingers. "That's where the photo was taken of Kimoda and his brother, Hiro."

"*Correcto.*" Alessandro pointed his pen at Archer.

"That's it then," Archer said. "We'll check out that plane and see if it's the one Hiro flew."

"How will we know?" Jimmy said.

"Each plane has a serial number, like a car's number plate," Alessandro said. "It's usually on the tail."

Archer thrust his chin out. "This one, off Munda, how far down is it?"

Alessandro checked the dive company's website, seeking the answer. He huffed. "I can't see that information here."

There were plenty of pictures of the plane and he scanned one after the other, curious to see if any highlighted the plane's serial number, but he was unsuccessful. Alessandro paused to look at Archer. "You do realize there's a high possibility the numbers are gone, either from the crash or rusted over from decades in salty water."

"We'll take that risk. Did you work out how deep it is?"

Alessandro drove his mouse around the computer, scouring the details. Finally, he found what he was looking for. "It's forty-five feet deep, according to this."

"So, let's say we find the plane Hiro flew." Ginger flicked her plait around her hand. "If it's lying at the bottom of the ocean, you don't really expect to find treasure still in there. Do you?"

"Yeah, right!" Jimmy snorted.

"It's just the next step in tracing where the treasure went." Archer flopped onto the lounge chair and looked utterly defeated. "If our theory is right and Hiro flew the treasure to Munda, then we'll just have to pick up the trail from there and try to figure it out."

"That could take ages," Ginger said, and Archer shot her a death stare.

"Sorry Archer, I'm just trying to be practical. Nox is nuts if he thinks this'll be easy."

"Nox is nuts. And he doesn't think. But this is the only thing we can do."

Alessandro couldn't remember a time when he'd seen Archer look so deflated.

Ginger yawned, and Alessandro used it as his motivation to stand up. "We're going to bed now." He reached for Ginger's hand. Alessandro decided on a quick escape. They could be up all night searching for clues, otherwise. "See you early in the morning. Good night."

"Good night," Archer and Jimmy said in unison.

Alessandro wove his fingers between Ginger's, and he marveled at how lovely they fit with his. Being at her side felt so comfortable, so honest. He had to remind himself they had only been together for a few months. It seemed like forever. She was the most relaxed woman he'd ever met, yet she had the power to move him in ways he hadn't experienced before. . . not even when he was with Rosalina. That time in his life finally felt like a distant memory.

Ginger didn't seem to have a care in the world. But then, a twenty-one-year-old traveling the globe on a multi-million-dollar yacht looking for treasure probably didn't have a care in the world. He smiled at that; he couldn't believe he himself was doing this. His entire twenty-nine years of living had been dedicated to history. First, he lived amongst it in Florence. He'd studied it and followed that up with lecturing it. Now, with the treasure hunting, he was unearthing it.

He opened the door to the Fraser suite, flicked on the lights, turned to the music panel and chose a little opera. . . something sensual to override the stressful day they'd had.

Ginger turned to him and placed her hand on his chest. Her azure eyes caught in the light, and he believed he could connect with her soul. "Will you make love to me, please?"

His heart skipped a beat. "Is that a trick question, *la mia bella?*"

She pouted. "No, it's a very serious one. I feel so bad about what's happened to Rosa, and I know I won't be able to sleep without. . ." She rolled her eyes, as if searching for the right words, "without feeling loved." She shrugged one delicate shoulder. "I guess."

Alessandro cupped her cheeks and eased forward to kiss her. Their lips met, soft and delicate, and he flicked his tongue out to taste her. He curled his fingers around the heat of her neck and pulled her closer. His tongue probed and slowly entered her mouth, savoring the sweetness. Her hands found the inside of his shirt, and his skin prickled as her fingers roamed up his back. She melted into him, pushing her breasts to his chest, and he clutched his arms around her. They kissed until all the madness in the world evaporated. There was nothing left but the two of them.

He pulled back, bent over, and lifted her into his arms. "You never have to worry again, *la mia bella.*" She clutched her hands around him, and her hot breath made the hairs on his neck rise as he carried her to bed. He eased her onto the covers and ran his fingers down the line of buttons on her shirt, stopping at the very bottom one. His hand was unsteady as he weaved the button through the hole. After releasing two buttons, her navel appeared, a lovely shallow dip in her perfectly sculpted torso. He bent forward and ran his tongue around her belly button. Her skin was hot as if burning with desire. A low hum thrummed from her throat as her long legs wrapped sleekly around him.

He worked the rest of the buttons free and tugged her shirt open. Her baby blue lacy bra complemented her milky smooth skin. She curled her hand behind her back and sprung the clasp free, revealing perfect mounds that wobbled delightfully with her movements. Her nipples were pink buds, as pronounced as cherries on a cupcake. She watched him explore her body, allowing him to devour every inch of her flesh with his eyes.

Alessandro tore his shirt off, tossing it aside, and his trembling fingers struggled with his belt and pants. But soon he stood naked before her. It was her turn to ravish him with eyes that were warm hands caressing him with their intensity. He undid her shorts and tugged them down her long longs. Now she was wearing nothing but baby blue lace underpants. His manhood throbbed, pounding out an urgent beat.

Ginger's body was exquisite, her skin a luscious blend of peaches and cream, soft and silky beneath his fingers. She had curves in all the right places. He crawled onto his hands and knees, directly above her, and looked into her stunning blue eyes.

"I'm the luckiest man in the world."

She giggled and pulled him onto her.

Chapter Twenty-Four

Rosalina woke with a fright and it was a couple of stressful heartbeats before she remembered where she was. Her body ached all over, but she was too cold to move.

The darkness was complete. . . no variations, no shadows.

As the waves crashed into the cliff below with the regularity of a heartbeat, her mind drifted to the people she loved. She imagined Archer wouldn't have slept through the night. He most likely paced the lounge room back and forward, trying to piece the puzzle together.

She wondered if Nonna knew. The last thing Rosalina wanted to do was hurt Nonna. Since Rosalina was seven years old, Nonna had been both her grandmother and her mother. Filippo never knew their mother. Now that Rosalina knew about her mother's affair, it made so many things fit into place. Her heart ached over what her own father did to Filippo. He didn't deserve any of the hatred directed at him.

When her mother had died, her father became a different man. She'd always thought he was a mourning widower, but it was so much more. She remembered the months prior to Filippo's birth. . . it was a time of tension and unease in the home that, until that point had always been warm and welcoming. Her parents had fought often and loudly. Before that, she'd barely seen her father. Nothing much had changed. Her mother had always been so quick with a cuddle but as her belly grew her hugs became less frequent. Sadness had taken over. Rosalina now knew why.

It was hard to imagine how different her life would've been had her mother lived. Their fighting may have continued, possibly to the point of divorce. Then who would own Villa Pandolfini? That was her home. It'd been a Calucci home for nearly two hundred years. And hopefully, for many, many more. Rosalina's greatest wish was to own Villa Pandolfini one day.

It suddenly occurred to her that it should never be hers. Rosalina didn't want children, and if the villa was to be handed down to the next generation, then one of her siblings should take rightful owner-ship. Her brothers and sisters had their own homes now, all within walking distance of Villa Pandolfini. She'd never imaged spending her married years living anywhere else. But maybe she had to.

Somehow, she would ensure Nonna gave the villa to one of her sisters or brothers.

The sky in the very distance began to lighten. Ever so gradually, it changed from black to golden. She sat up, rolling her neck from side to side, trying to release the stiffness. She flicked her skirt aside and straightened her legs so her ankles and feet dangled over the edge of the cliff. Her right leg felt alien with long hairs and scaly skin and her muscle was soft and malleable. Rolling her foot around, she felt no pain. As the sun illuminated the horizon, she welcomed the light and warmth of a new day. She was beginning to feel normal. Hungry, thirsty, tired and sore. . . but at least she had the use of all her limbs again.

She tugged the leaves and twigs out of her dress, then using the knife, she cut two long, thin strips from her dress, and tied the knife to her thigh.

"Check this out," she said to the Jesus statue. "Lara Croft eat your heart out."

She laughed. The knife wouldn't be easy to get at, but she felt better knowing the weapon was there if she needed it. This also kept her hands free for scaling the cliff face.

Rosalina crawled on her hands and knees to the edge of the cave and looked down. It was about fifteen feet to where jagged red rocks met with the ocean. To her left was the ledge she'd crawled along. Her stomach flipped at the sight of it. It was a wonder she'd survived at all. To her right, the ledge continued. At some point in the last billion or so years the earth had slipped sideways, creating this fissure; she was eternally grateful for that, or she would've died upon releasing from the window last night. Now, she had to step onto the ledge again. Just the thought of it made her queasy.

She rolled her tongue around her mouth, trying to produce moisture, but it was futile. Ignoring it, she curled to her feet.

"Thanks for your company." The sun's morning glow silhouetted the statue. As much as Rosalina wanted to take it with her, she didn't need its weighty burden. "This is where you and I part ways."

With a decent hold on a rock, she ducked out from the overhang, stepped onto the ledge, and didn't look back. With the use of both her feet, it was much easier. Her leg appeared to have healed perfectly.

Time stood still. Every step was a stressful repeat of the one before. Her only judge of time was the sun's appearance over the cliff above her. She glanced at it regularly over her shoulder. It was high off the ocean, pouring heat onto her back and bouncing off the rocks, creating an intense furnace. Sweat dribbled down her lower back. Her fingers, knees, toes, hell. . . her entire body ached. Yet she continued along the never-ending ledge. It was impossible to judge how far she'd come, but it had to be at least half a mile from Nox's hideout.

She heard laughter and froze. *Am I going mad?*

Her breath captured in her throat. There it was again. Talking, too. She looked down and there, farther along at the base of the cliff was a small boat anchored near the shoreline. Two young men, shirtless and tanned, stood in the boat, glistening wet.

"Help." Her throat was too dry; barely a whisper came out.

"Help," she screamed again. It was louder, but not by much.

The men jumped off the boat and vanished beneath the water. Rosalina shuffled along, desperate to shorten the distance between her and them. With one eye on the cliff and one on the boat, she readied for them to resurface.

They popped above the surface together, laughing as they held something up out of the water. "Help." They turned around, maybe looking for the source of the voice.

"Help! Up here."

The men climbed onto the boat, shielded their eyes from the sun's glare to look up at her.

"Help me."

"What are you doing, lady?" the one with long hair said.

"Help me, please."

"How did you get up there?" The other one said.

"Can you help me get down?"

There was a brief silence. "You have to jump."

She looked down. It was at least twelve feet. "What about rocks?"

"It very deep here. . . goes straight down. Thirty-foot drop. You'll be fine. Just push off the wall."

Push off the wall? She could barely stand, let alone push off the wall.

The men dived off their boat and swam towards her. She still faced the rocks and when she lost sight of them, she assumed they were directly below her.

"Come on, we'll rescue you."

"Yes, we'll save you."

She sucked in a few calming breaths to steady her racing heart. Then, ever so slowly, she picked up her left leg and put it at a right angle to her body, facing the ocean. Then she let go of her left arm and twisted around. With a gasp, she now faced the ocean and had her back to the rock wall.

"Come on. Jump. We'll save you."

She tried to steady her breathing. "Okay. Okay. Wait."

She glanced down again. The two men were apart from each other, making a gap for her to jump into. They seemed a long way out. The sun blazed a furnace on her face. The rocks at her back were just as hot. Sweat trickled down her temples, and her throat was as dry as desert sand. She had no choice.

"Okay. I'll do it. I'll jump." She straightened her back, then sucked in a deep breath and let it out very slowly. "Ready?"

"Yes."

"Yes."

She rocked back and forward, trying to build momentum. Her breath shot in and out. She sucked in a huge breath, gritted her teeth and jumped.

Rosalina screamed as her dress billowed up around her face. She was only airborne for seconds before she hit the water. It was like plate glass, smashing the wind out of her. She swallowed mouthfuls as she tumbled in a frenzy of bubbles. Hands were suddenly on her, dragging her towards the dazzling surface.

Punching into the fresh air, she gasped for a breath.

"We've got you."

"You're okay now."

The men laid her back and as they floated her to the boat deep, wracking sobs overcame her. She could barely breathe and lying flat only made it harder.

"Don't cry, lady. You're safe now."

She reached up and wiped away her tears but still they came. In a cloud of exhaustion and relief she allowed the men to lift her into the boat and lie her down at the back. A water bottle was handed to her, and she swallowed huge mouthfuls of the cool liquid.

"Are you okay?"

"What happened?"

"How long have you been out there?"

"Where did you come from?"

They alternated questions, and it seemed they didn't need an answer because they kept going. It was suddenly important that she didn't mention Nox. At least, not until she knew what was going on with Filippo.

"Do you need a doctor?"

"Or the police?"

She wiped her mouth and her eyes. "No. I'm good now. Thank you so much. What are your names?"

"I'm Mario." The one with long dark hair that settled on his shoulders palmed his chest.

"I'm Marco."

Rosalina laughed at their boyish exuberance. "I'm Rosalina." They were delightfully happy. Exactly what she needed. She rolled the ankle of her left leg and it felt fine, no pain. . . hopefully that meant she'd done no damage when she'd jumped. Mario held a Tupperware dish towards her and peeled back the lid. It was filled to the brim with panforte and biscotti. She just about melted at the sight and reached for a piece of each.

"So. . . you going to tell us how you got out there?"

"Let me catch my breath first." She ate a bite of the panforte; it was full of nuts and fruit, and beyond delicious, and she devoured it in seconds. The biscotti too was gone in a flash. Mario opened the lid again, but this time he placed the Tupperware container at her side.

"Are you all right, Miss. Rosalina?"

His concern melted her heart. Her chin dimpled, but she fought back the tears. "I am now. Thank you so much."

"What you like to do?"

"Do you have a phone?"

Marco playfully slapped Mario on the chest. "I always says to him bring a phone. For emergencies. You know. But he says we haven't had an emergency in twelve years, we're not having one now."

"This isn't an emergency, right, Miss. Rosalina?" Mario looked at her with pleading eyes.

She wanted to say it was. A life-and-death emergency, actually. But she couldn't. "No, it's not an emergency."

"See, I told you." Mario flicked Marco on the shoulder.

She needed Archer; she just hoped he was at *Evangeline*. "Can you boys take me to Livorno marina? I'll pay you for your time."

"No need to pay us, Miss. Rosalina. It's not every day we rescue a damsel in distress. But you have to tell us what happened."

She laughed again, reached for another biscotti and sat up a bit.

Mario climbed over the seats to the motor behind her and pulled on the rope. The engine roared to life, and as the front of the boat lifted and they scooted parallel to the shoreline, Rosalina invented a story about drinking too much and falling off the cliff. To her it sounded completely implausible, but the young men lapped up the story as if it were gospel.

Mario and Marco made the journey a delight, telling her all about their lives. Marco displayed today's catch. The white octopus' tentacles nearly touched the bottom of the boat when he held it high in his arms. When Rosalina said she was a chef, they asked her opinion on how she'd cook it. Her suggestion of chargrilled octopus and haloumi salad had them both kneeling at her side as she described how she'd make that.

It seemed like hours before the masts of the enormous yachts came into view. By that time, Rosalina was sitting on one of the bench seats, and her dress and hair were dry. Her tummy was full too from more than enough delicious treats.

For the first time since they'd moored *Evangeline* at Livorno, she was grateful the yacht was in one of the outer births. She stood and started yelling before they were even near. "Archer."

"Archer!" Mario and Marco helped her.

"Archer!"

They were nearly at the dive deck when Archer appeared. The sight of him melted her to tears.

"Rosa!" Archer jumped down the stairs in one fluid motion and met them at the dive platform. Archer jumped into the boat and wrapped his arms around Rosalina and squeezed her until she could barely breathe. Tears tumbled down her cheeks.

Jimmy, Alessandro and Ginger were soon there, too.

For the second time that day, she allowed herself to be lifted up and carried. Archer took her up the stairs and rested her on the lounge. Mario and Marco accepted a beer from Jimmy and told their story by bouncing the sentences between each other as they detailed rescuing Rosalina from the cliff.

"Hey, your cast is off?" Ginger said.

Rosalina nodded, not wanting to elaborate.

"Hey, babe." She squeezed Archer's hand. "Can you please give the men a reward for rescuing me?"

"It's okay, Miss. Rosalina. We had fun."

"It's only fair that I pay you for your time, fellas." Archer clapped Marco on the shoulder as he strode past them.

"Are you Australian?" Marco asked.

"We sure are," Jimmy responded, as Archer carried on walking. "What were you boys catching out there?"

"Today we caught a beautiful octopus. Want to see? It's a good one, too. Should feed the family for a few days."

Rosalina smiled. Sometimes she wished her life was as simple.

Archer returned with five hundred euro for each of them. The men were a babble of excitement as Archer indicated that Rosalina might need a rest after the night she'd had.

"Bye Marco and Mario, thank you so much." She blew each of them a kiss.

"Thank you. We will never forget you."

"You our lucky charm, Miss. Rosalina."

Rosalina laughed as Archer directed them back towards their boat.

"Would you like something to eat, Rosa?" Ginger offered.

"No thanks. Have you heard from Filippo?"

"Archer did, last night." A dark shadow crossed Alessandro's eyes.

"Is he okay?" Her heart squeezed as she recalled the yelling she'd heard when she dropped from that window.

Alessandro grimaced and she dreaded his answer. "Nox shot him, but he seemed okay. He was able to talk."

She covered her mouth. Her chin quivered. "We have to find him."

Archer returned, helped her to stand and pulled her in for a hug. "Are you okay?"

Rosalina nuzzled into his neck, squeezing him tight. "Yes, I'm good but we need to save Filippo."

Archer eased back and put his hands on her shoulders. "Do you know where Nox took you?"

"It's a big old building on the cliff. It should be easy to find. It's time to call the police."

Archer shook his head. "No. If we do that, Nox will kill Filippo. I'm certain of it."

"What do we do then?" Rosalina's heart was being torn out piece by piece.

"We'll go get him. But we need to send him a message first, let him know we're coming so Nox keeps him in that building until we get a plan."

"How?" Rosalina frowned.

"I'll try calling. Maybe I can convince Nox to let me talk to him." Archer reached for his phone, pressed the screen, and held it to his ear. Rosalina raised onto her tiptoes, desperate to hear her brother's voice.

"Nox." Archer scowled into the phone, and his expression clouded over as he spoke to the madman on the other end of the line.

"I'm not doing anything until I talk to them." Archer blinked several times, listening.

"No! Put them on." Archer clenched his jaw, squaring out his already chiseled jawline.

"Filippo! Are you okay?"

Rosalina wanted to hear his voice but couldn't, so she watched for Archer's expressions.

"Good. Can Nox hear me?"

Archer raised his eyebrows at her.

"Okay. Listen, we know where you are. We're coming to get you."

There was a long pause and Archer frowned. "Do you know where?"

"Shit!"

Archer's dark eyes darkened even further as he shook his head. "But that will take weeks, Filippo. Months even."

Archer lowered his eyes and the despair in them made her heart squeeze.

"Okay. Okay. We'll do it. As long as you're sure. Put Nox on."

"If you hurt him again," Archer's voice changed to deadly serious, "I'll kill you."

Nox must've ended the call because Archer lowered the phone from his ear. "We're too late. Nox moved him last night."

Her chin quivered. "Where?"

"Filippo doesn't know. Last night Nox threw him in the trunk of a car and whacked him over the head with the gun. He woke up in a room without any windows."

Tears tumbled down her cheeks and Archer pulled her to his chest. "What do we do now?"

"Filippo wants us to go after the treasure. He says Nox won't hurt him because he needs him for an exchange."

"What? That could take weeks." She pulled back and studied Archer's eyes.

"I know, and there's something else." A deep frown drilled across his forehead.

"What?"

"For some reason, Filippo still thinks Nox has you."

Chapter Twenty-Five

Nox clicked off the phone, aware that Archer may be tracing the call. He stepped back from Filippo and viewed him from a short distance. He was a typical Italian man with thick dark hair and a permanent facial shadow. His heavy brows hooded eyes that shifted from fear to defiance in a split second. He was average height, slightly smaller than Nox, and his build said that the man did little or nothing in the way of physical labor. If he had to, Nox could overpower Rosalina's brother easily. Pure determination was a mighty weapon.

Nox had killed with his bare hands before. He wouldn't hesitate to do it again.

"Untie me!" Filippo tugged on the ropes that bound his hands above his head.

Nox shook his head. He had no idea what to do with the man. Since they'd messed with the window bars, the room was no longer secure, so he had no choice but to keep him tied up.

"I did what I said I'd do." Filippo squared out his chin.

He certainly had, and it surprised Nox. Maybe he was telling the truth about hating his family. Nox could relate to that; he'd hated his family for decades. "Are they going after the treasure?"

"Archer said they were." Filippo looked squarely into Nox's eyes.

Nox sneered back. "Why did you tell him I'd moved you?"

"Because they said they knew where I was, and they were coming to get me."

"What? How did they figure it out?"

Filippo shrugged. "Don't know. Now untie me!" He spoke through gritted teeth. "We're in this together."

It was an interesting partnership. For the moment, anyway. He'd do whatever was necessary to get his hands on the treasure, but he had no intention of sharing the riches with anyone. "That was clever thinking, telling him I moved you. Do you think he believed it?"

"He's got no reason not to."

Nox was impressed with what Filippo did. If he hadn't done that, Archer would have ruined his plans yet again. He was looking forward to the day when he squeezed the life out of that cocky bastard.

Filippo's quick thinking had helped him. Nox couldn't remember a time when someone had been on his side. Maybe working with Filippo was a good plan after all. It certainly wouldn't hurt to find out what he knew about the treasure.

If they did form this unlikely duo then Filippo wouldn't realize that Nox had no intention of sharing the riches. . . until it was too late, of course.

"I need to find another room to put you in. Once I've done that, I'll get you food." Nox turned on his heel and as he walked over the threshold and closed the door behind him, Filippo started yelling.

"Nox, you bastard. I helped you."

Even though Filippo couldn't go anywhere, Nox still turned the latch to lock the door. He walked along the corridor to explore other options. He hadn't had time to investigate the entire building since he'd arrived; everything had happened so quickly.

The dormitory was a large room centered along the ocean side of the building. From there, the corridor led him to the classroom. The door hung open, and the moment he stepped through the doorway he stepped back in time.

He'd learned English here and math. He'd also learned the sting of a ruler across the back of his knuckles and the humiliation of mental inadequacy. The desks and chairs were still here. Most of them were bunched up in a corner but some still faced the long blackboard, like they always had. A large potbelly stove stood off the wall, but the black pipe that fed the smoke outside had long ago corroded and fallen to the timber floor.

The blackboard still had writing on it. 16 January, 1983 was scrawled across the top. He remembered that day well. It was the day before his tenth birthday. Although he later found out that it was unlikely to be his real birth date. Because he was abandoned, there was no record of his actual birth. For all he knew, he could be years younger than he stated. Or older. The sisters had declared the 17th of January his birthday, and his tenth birthday was going to be celebrated. They'd said they'd have a little party with cupcakes and music. He would get presents like he'd seen other boys receive; stuffed toys and matchbox cars were the most common.

But the sisters had lied. The day before his birthday, they were evacuated from Provenzia as if it were about to crumble to the ground at any moment. As they were being rushed from the building to the buses with only the clothes on their backs, his questions about his party were answered with a slap across the cheek. Sister Teresa said there were much more important matters to attend to. Not for Nox though. Nothing had been more important.

He never had his party. No cupcakes. No music. No toys. What he did get was another nickname. . . Party Killer.

Sister Teresa didn't remember inventing that nickname for him. But he'd reminded her. It took him fourteen years to exact that revenge and when he did, it was perfect. He'd caught her in her bedroom, half dressed for her own seventieth birthday party. The irony wasn't lost on him. She was surprised to see him, although she'd acted like she had no idea who he was. But as Nox wrapped his fingers around her throat, he'd said, "I'm the party killer . . . remember?" And when her eyes lit up, he had no doubt she remembered the little boy he once was.

Nox picked up a stick of chalk that rested on the ledge at the bottom of the blackboard. He reached up and rubbed out the number six. At first touch the stick snapped in half, but with the remaining piece he changed the date to 17 January, 1983, and then he wrote happy birthday.

The boards creaked beneath his feet as he stepped back to admire his handiwork.

Satisfied, he left the room and headed towards the pavilion. It was a hexagonal-shaped room where the grand windows overlooked a panoramic view of the ocean. The room was a mess, with rubbish and debris covering the entire floor. All the windows were broken and shattered glass mingled with wooden pieces, leaves and peeling paint.

A long bench seat lay beneath a couple of the windows and Nox remembered sitting on them as a boy to listen to the piano. He turned to where the piano used to be and his eyes bulged. The piano was still there, tucked in behind the door.

He stepped over a rubbish pile and shoved a broken wicker chair aside to reach it. The chair to the piano was in its original position, but he daren't risk sitting on it. Nox pressed one of the white keys, and a high-pitched thrum released. He pressed another, then another. Each one radiated a different sound.

He poked at the keys, creating a random tune that echoed about the sparse room. It took him back to Ophelia and the lovely melodies she would hum as she tended to his wounds. She was an angel. His angel.

"Ophelia." Her name floated off his lips. His breath caught in his throat. He was crazy, stupid in love with her.

The phone in his pocket buzzed and he jumped. He jerked it out. It was Archer.

"You better be on your way to the Solomon Islands," Nox said.

"We're leaving soon, but we're cruising there, not flying. So it will take longer than originally planned."

Nox grew wary. "Why aren't you flying?"

"Because once we get there, we'd have to hire boats and diving gear, and we run the risk of people finding out what we're doing. Which is a huge security issue."

His reasoning was plausible. "How long then?"

"At least three weeks to get to the Solomons. After that, it's anyone's guess."

He could accept that. Nox had been waiting a lifetime, so in the scheme of things, this was barely a bump in his grand plans. And after seeing how quick they were at finding the treasure in the Greek Islands, he was confident he wouldn't have to wait long.

"Don't take too long, Archer, or--"

"Or what, Nox? You'll kill one of them?"

Nox paused. The confidence in Archer's voice was alarming.

"Rosa escaped, Nox. She's with me."

The blood drained from Nox's face. He squeezed his fist until his fingernails bit into his flesh. How could that be? She should be dead.

"What?"

"Ahhh, you didn't think she survived that jump. Did you?" Archer was all cockiness. "So, here's how we're going to do this. I'll look for that treasure, but if anything happens to Filippo, you won't see one piece of it. Do you hear me?"

Nox couldn't think, let alone speak. How the hell had she survived?

"Nox!"

Nox lurched out of his blind fury. He needed damage control. "Her brother will remain alive, but the longer you take, the less healthy he will be."

"I mean it, Nox. Whenever we call, if we don't talk to him, the deal is off." Archer hung up.

Nox slammed his fists onto the piano, producing a pained high-pitched wail.

Chapter Twenty-Six

A rcher pressed a button and *Evangeline's* anchor chain climbed up out of the water and disappeared into the hole in the hull. Once the anchor was visible, he signaled Jimmy to cast the ropes, and he eased the throttle to release *Evangeline* from her mooring. It was nearly midnight and the moon was barely a sliver above the ocean as he navigated out of Marina Di San Vencenzo and directed her nose towards the flashing beacon in the distance.

Rosalina was at his side. It was hard to believe she was still awake. Her stubbornness was probably the only thing keeping her standing upright.

It had been an afternoon of debating that resulted in them cruising to the Solomon Islands rather than chartering the plane. There were many pros and cons to each, but finally it was the ability to keep the details of what they were doing contained that dictated cruising. If they'd flown, yes, they would have saved time, but once they got there, they'd have to hire dive boats, gear and possibly storage and guards if they actually found what they were looking for. Keeping anything secret would've been impossible.

Once the decision was made, it was a grand scramble to stock up *Evangeline* with all the necessary equipment, food and fuel. Of course, Rosalina also had a heartfelt hello and goodbye with Nonna. Once she finished with Nonna, Rosalina conceded they were doing the right thing. Nonna had been surprisingly supportive of their plans and for that, Archer would be eternally grateful.

Even though Filippo was still captured by Nox, Archer was positive he'd remain unharmed. Nox needed Rosalina's brother to exchange for the treasure. If they found any treasure, that was. With a bit of luck, they'd find bucket-loads of it and Archer hoped he could show Rosalina just how exciting treasure hunting could be.

Archer had offered to take the first shift while Jimmy got some shut-eye. Jimmy would take over at four a.m., and the rotation would continue all the way to Alexandria, Egypt.

Archer tugged his beautiful Italian woman to his side. "Are you okay, sweetheart?"

She nuzzled in. "Yes and no."

He knew exactly what she meant. After the night she'd been through, she'd welcome her safety, but knowing her brother was still captive would be eating her up. "If you want to go to bed, I won't mind."

"I want to stay with you."

He kissed her forehead. "Okay."

After a while though, she couldn't hold her eyes open a moment more. Archer set the yacht on autopilot and guided her to their bed. He tucked her in, kissed her goodnight, and returned to his place on the bridge.

Their first stop at Alexandria, Egypt, was set to take three to four days. He'd make it in three.

DAY AFTER DAY THEY CRUISED THE SPARKLING BLUE MEDITERRANEAN Sea beneath the cloud-dotted sky. Bottlenose dolphins raced alongside for a while, and both Ginger and Rosalina squealed each time they launched from the water. Archer smiled along with them at Rosalina's childish glee and nature's impromptu show. Despite seeing her laugh, she was brooding over some deep stuff inside. He hoped this change of pace would help her release it soon and let his fun-loving Rosalina return.

Alessandro continued to receive fishing lessons from Ginger, and thanks to Rosalina's magnificent cooking skills, they feasted on seafood dishes with flavors from all over the world.

Late after their third night cruising, Jimmy sidled up beside Archer in the bridge. "Give me a meat pie any day."

"Had enough of the fish, buddy?"

"Haven't you? I miss my meat. I'll tell you somethin' the second we land in Darwin, I'm off to find me a good Aussie T-bone steak. When was the last time we had something like that? All this fancy food is driving me crazy."

"Do you want me to let Rosa know?"

"No. Don't. I'm sure this cooking is taking her mind off things."

Archer sighed. "Every day she's getting better. I think we should check out the diving in Alexandria. Just a fun dive. . . no treasure hunting."

Jimmy's eyes lit up. "Fuck yeah." He slapped Archer on the back. "Is it good diving?"

Archer smiled at his best mate. "Some of the most interesting in the world. Ask Alessandro to give you a history lesson."

"Ah, no thanks."

"I'm serious. You'll be intrigued."

IT WAS ELEVEN O'CLOCK THE NEXT MORNING WHEN JIMMY SPIED THE Egyptian shoreline on the horizon through the high-powered binoculars.

"I'll get the tender ready." Jimmy strode away, and Archer didn't bother to tell him to wait. They were still at least an hour before anchoring and the tender was already primed for use. Jimmy was going a little stir-crazy. Archer, on the other hand, could cruise the world, never leaving *Evangeline*, and be a happy man forever. . . as long as Rosalina remained at his side.

Once Archer let the anchor go, he called everyone to the lounge area. Rosalina looked magnificent in a powder blue maxi dress with a split that allowed her long legs to peek through as she walked. She was way overdressed for shopping in an Egyptian market, but he'd have no hope of getting her to change. Which was why he was happy he'd made some pre-arrangements.

He checked at the clock in the galley, their timing was perfect. "Okay ladies, I've organized a driver to take you to a traditional food market away from the tourist areas. Whatever you do, don't leave his side, okay, Ginger?" He was certain Rosalina would be enthralled enough by the abundance of food variety to keep her contained in the market area. Ginger, on the other hand, was likely to wander off at any random point.

Ginger's eyes widened. "Is it dangerous?"

"Some areas are known to be dangerous, but with your blonde hair you'll be hounded from the moment you step on shore. Which is why you need to hang with the driver. Understand?"

"Yeah, sure." Ginger still sounded flippant. She clearly had no idea what it was like to be heckled. Archer wondered if she could handle it. She could be ditzy sometimes, and then other times she appeared mature beyond her years. He was still trying to figure her out.

"See if you can get some meat," Jimmy said.

Rosalina placed her hand on his forearm and smiled. "I'll try, but no promises."

Archer turned to Alessandro. "I've arranged for another driver to take you to the museum in Alexandria."

The Italian's eyes just about popped out of his head. Alessandro rubbed his hands together. "*Fantastico*."

"You can have a quick look around, but your plan is to meet people, get to know them, and see if you can make friends who may be able to help us if. . . no, when we return to Egypt. Jimmy and I'll load up *Evangeline* with fresh supplies and, all going well," he glanced at the clock again, "we'll all be back on board by four."

"I thought we were going diving?" Jimmy scowled.

"We are. Don't worry, we'll have heaps of time. If not, we'll have a night dive."

"You're diving at night?" Alessandro's bulging eyes showed his horror.

"Of course. It's fun," Jimmy said.

Alessandro shuddered.

The sound of a horn had them all turn to the shore. Two black

Renault sedans were waiting. Their drivers climbed out and waved in their direction. "Good, they're on time. I'll take you all over."

They loaded into the tender, and Archer navigated the abundance of children in tiny little handmade boats that looked likely to topple over at any second. They were selling all manner of wares, from clothing to food to souvenirs and they sang *'row, row, row your boat'* at the top of their lungs. Ginger and Rosalina playfully waved to the kids and sang along with them. But their reckless attempts to intercept his course, had Archer dodging around them the entire way. He managed to avoid a catastrophe though and successfully arrived at the jetty ten minutes later.

Alessandro climbed out first and helped Ginger from the boat.

Archer cupped Rosalina's cheeks. "Be careful, babe. Stay with the driver the whole time."

"I will." She reached on her tippy-toes and kissed him. "Don't worry."

"I'll stop worrying when you're beside me again."

When she smiled her eyes lit up. This little shopping expedition was exactly the distraction she needed.

He kissed her again and watched her until she was secure within the vehicle.

Then he pushed off the jetty and dodged the water sellers back to *Evangeline*.

Chapter Twenty-Seven

Rosalina clung to the door handles as the driver zipped through the packed Egyptian streets at a reckless speed. One glance at Ginger was enough to know she was just as terrified. Horns blared, tires screeched, and drivers flung abuse out their windows. Every car she looked at had scratches and dents marring it. Some shouldn't have been on the road at all.

People were everywhere, young and old, smiling and scowling, colorful and drab. When they finally stopped, Omar, their driver, helped each of them out and instructed them to follow him.

From that point on, everything was an explosion to her senses. The smells were sweet and spicy, delicious and rank. A kaleidoscope of colors bombarded her from every angle, and the noise was the constant drone of busy Egyptian life.

Rosalina loved it all.

Omar led them to the spice market stall first where dozens of wicker baskets were filled to overflowing with a vast variety of colorful aromatic spices, some she recognized, some she didn't. It was over-whelming, and after ten minutes of trying to work out which ones to choose she decided to get one cup of each of them. When Omar explained what she wanted, the spice vendor flashed his toothless grin, and Rosalina chuckled at how happy he was.

The next stall overflowed with fresh vegetables, again, some she recognized. . . tomatoes, beans, cucumbers, courgettes, eggplant and lemons, but some she didn't. She couldn't decide again, so this time she bought the foods she didn't recognize and added some of her favorites.

The next stall offered freshly baked bread.

"Oh Rosa, let's try some." Ginger hooked her hand through Rosa's bent elbow and guided her into the stall. The owner was a woman whose smile were as big as her welcome. She was flamboyant in her sales routine and insisted they sample almost everything.

"Omar, what's this bread called?" Rosalina pointed to a flat round disc the size of a dinner plate that had a layer of what looked like finely ground corn grains on the bottom.

"That's eesh baladi, a traditional Egyptian bread."

He spoke to the woman behind the counter and with tissue-covered fingers, she picked up the bread and handed it to Rosalina. She broke off a bite-sized piece and sampled it. The bread was quite dense. It was simple, yet fresh and delicious.

"Can you ask her name please?"

"Yasmin," Omar said without asking. Omar probably knew every vendor along this strip and would be receiving a kickback for taking her and Ginger to these stalls. Rosalina didn't mind; this was how the world worked.

"Can you tell Yasmin I'm a chef, and I'd love to learn how she makes this bread?"

Omar puffed his chest out with her request and before Rosalina had a chance to think about it, she was whisked into a back room. Her concern was only brief though as she was treated to a hands-on demonstration of traditional Egyptian bread-making.

At the back of the room was an enormous brick and stone oven, and from the distance she was standing she could not only see the flames, she also felt the heat. Three men in long white robes where positioned around a high wooden table. One shaped the dough into circular discs and threw them into large pans of the pale-yellow grain. The second man loaded the round discs onto giant metal shovels that the third man fed into the oven's mouth. A young boy, also wielding a long-handled shovel, removed the baked bread and placed it onto a nearly full tray on a wheelbarrow. As one of the breads was plucked from the oven, Yasmin swiped it with a paper towel and handed it to Rosalina.

The heat was intense but she daren't complain, aware that she may offend. She divided it in half and offered a share to Ginger. Rosalina closed her eyes and inhaled. It smelled of flour and yeast and a hint of smokiness. When she bit into it, the outer layer cracked with a crispy crunch but the middle was soft and doughy. The layer of bran on the bottom gave it an interesting grainy texture.

"Yum," Ginger said.

Rosalina nodded. "Please tell Yasmin this is delicious."

When they finally left the bread vendor, they had enough bread to feed a small village. Omar waggled a finger in the air and two young men were instantly at their sides, offering to carry the bags.

The next stall offered fresh and dried meats. At first, the smell made her stomach flip. It was an unexpected reaction, and she shrugged it off as she scoured the glass cabinet searching for something to please Jimmy. She turned to Omar. "What is a local meat favorite?"

He smiled, showing off a gold-capped front tooth. "Pigeon."

"Oh no." Ginger shook her head.

Rosalina was not expecting that and wondered if she'd understood his accent correctly. "Did you say pigeon? As in, the bird?"

"Yes." He pointed towards the counter with a grin. "Pigeon."

Sure enough, dozens of plucked birds were lined up in rows at the far-left side of the display cabinet. She shouldn't have been surprised; pigeon pie had been around for centuries.

"How do you cook it?"

"We stuff it with rice and herbs and roast it."

It would probably taste similar to chicken only a bit more gamey, like pheasant or quail. She could already picture a delicious dish, but she'd have no hope of getting Jimmy to eat it.

"What else, Omar?"

"Lots of choice, Miss. Rosalina. We have goat. Rabbit. Turkey. Liver. And of course, beef."

"Yes. Beef. We should get beef for Jimmy." Ginger jiggled with eagerness.

"Thanks, Omar. Show me the beef."

By the time they walked out of the shop, Rosalina had five kilos of rib-eye steak cut nice and thick. Jimmy would be a very happy man. After a few more stops where they purchased plump dried dates, creamy buffalo mozzarella, and an assortment of fresh herbs and nuts, they stopped at a street seller offering ready-to-eat foods. Rosalina chose lamb koftas on a skewer and Ginger chose a chicken shawarma, where spicy chicken and tahini sauce was wrapped in a fresh pita bread. As they ate their meals, they meandered back to the car.

The driver rang ahead and Jimmy was waiting for them when they arrived back at the jetty.

"Where's Archer?" Rosalina asked the moment Jimmy stepped up to help with the bags.

"He's playing with the kids."

Rosalina chuckled. "What?"

"You'll see."

Jimmy thanked Omar and gave him a generous tip before helping the ladies and their multitude of bags into the boat. He untied the rope, pushed off and started the engine. "How'd you go with my steak?" Jimmy said as he steered towards *Evangeline*.

"We scored well! Lots of steak," Ginger said with a grin.

"Good."

They dodged all the little children in tiny boats that they powered by using their hands as paddles. Rosalina wished she'd purchased a little something to give to them. As they neared *Evangeline*, there was a splash off the dive deck, followed by a couple of smaller splashes. It was only when she saw Archer climb up out of the water that she realized what he was doing. Archer was jumping off the yacht with the kids.

He waved at her. His chiseled muscles glistened, and he smiled with boyish glee. Rosalina had never seen Archer with children before. Not like this, anyway. She suddenly realized how odd that was. They'd been together for five years, and although she grew up almost surrounded by children, she didn't have any interaction with kids the whole time she was in Australia. Archer tugged one of the boys to his side and motioned for all the boys to keep out of the way as the tender pulled up alongside the yacht.

"Looks like you've had fun." Archer pulled her in for a kiss, and all the kids giggled. He picked up one of the boys and the child squealed as Archer tossed him overboard. That created an avalanche of pleas to be thrown overboard by all the other boys. "These guys are insatiable."

"I can see that."

"Okay. Okay. Enough." Archer held up his palms. "Off you go now."

Rosalina picked up a couple of the shopping bags, and as she carted them up the stairs, she glanced over her shoulder to see Archer give each of the boys' money and then toss them off the yacht one last time.

She smiled on the outside, but on the inside, she was torn. They had never talked about having children, and she'd always thought his business mattered more than a family of his own, which suited her fine. After what happened to her mother, Rosalina had sworn off having children forever. But now, after seeing how happy Archer looked as he played with them, she had a horrible feeling she'd read him all wrong. Her stomach curdled at that thought.

As Rosalina instructed Ginger about where to store the food, Archer strode into the room, tightening a towel around his hips. "I hope you have something huge planned for dinner, Rosa, because Jimmy's talked about nothing but scuba diving and steak since you left. He's driving me crazy."

She laughed. "Well, I can solve the steak part."

"And I can solve the scuba diving part. Want to come with us?" He cocked his head, and the way he did it had the afternoon sun highlighting the gold flecks around his dark irises. Out the corner of her eye she saw Ginger jiggling from foot to foot.

"Okay."

"Yay. Can I come too?" Ginger said.

"Of course. We'll get the dive gear ready and we'll head out to Palais of Cleopatra."

"Sounds exciting."

"Sure is. From what I understand, the visibility is really crap, but with a bit of luck we should see the palace and temple complex of Cleopatra."

"What? Queen Cleopatra?" Rosalina raised her eyebrows.

Archer nodded. "So they say."

It was another half an hour before Alessandro returned, bursting at the seams with excitement. Rosalina felt sorry for him as they left him with all that energy and prepared for their dive.

Archer maneuvered *Evangeline* to near the dive site, and by the time he let the anchor go they were all kitted up in their scuba gear. Rosalina put her regulator in her mouth and tested it for air. Then, her and Ginger took a giant stride overboard and dropped into the murky Egyptian waters. The green haze briefly filled her vision before she popped back up to the surface to indicate she was okay to Archer and Jimmy.

As soon as the men plopped in beside them, the foursome lowered below the surface. At first Rosalina could barely see her fingers before her mask, but the deeper they went, the clearer the water became. Soon she could see all three of her dive buddies around her.

The bottom was at a depth of just thirty feet but, careful not to stir up the sediment, they hovered about six feet off and swam along in pairs. It was a different dive to what she was used to, as there was literally nothing to see. No marine life, no coral, no plants. No color. It was like swimming in a moldy bath.

A shape materialized out of nowhere and Archer played his flashlight over it. It was a large column, like the kind you'd see at a temple. It appeared to be made of red granite, and it was centered on a giant rectangular pedestal. Beyond that pillar was another and another.

In amongst the pillars was the statue of a lion. The beast was as big as Jimmy. The head of the lion was carved to show off a thick mane of hair, and the lion's mouth was open, like it was letting out an almighty roar. Rosalina was amazed that it still had teeth. Resting beneath the lion's paw was a sphere.

Jimmy had moved farther away, and his flashlight was centered on the face of an enormous statue of a man with a long rectangular beard. The statue was easily five times Jimmy's size.

Rosalina's mind raced over questions that she had no answers for. How the statues came to be there was at the top of her list. They looked like they'd been positioned on purpose. If they'd fallen off a ship, then surely some of them would be on their sides. But they were all upright. And, once they'd been discovered, why weren't they put into a museum? Their sheer size may've been the answer to that. Raising them to the surface would be a mammoth effort. The ancient cannon they'd raised in Anafi was only a fraction of these in size, and yet it took some serious planning to lift it onto *Evangeline*.

A little farther along was another group of columns, however these had tumbled over. Just one statue stood amongst them. It was a man draped in a robe, and he clutched at something. . . a jar maybe. She couldn't quite work it out.

Their evening was going to be filled with Alessandro's history lesson about this area, and after seeing this, she was looking forward to it.

It only seemed like twenty minutes and not an entire hour had passed before they headed back up the anchor line to *Evangeline*. They stopped at the fifteen-feet mark to decompress, and it was only now that marine life materialized. Small silvery fish, no bigger than her hand, appeared by the hundreds. They swam about in a massive school and seemed to be in a hurry to get where they were going. It was a great distraction as they waited to push through the green murk to surface.

The second she was topside, she popped the regulator from her mouth. "That was amazing."

"Holy shit, those things were huge." Jimmy tugged his fins off and tossed them onto the dive deck. "What the hell are they still doing down there?"

"No idea." Archer removed his tank and climbed up the ladder.

Rosalina unclipped her buoyancy vest and air tank and maneuvered them to the edge so Archer could lift them onto the dive deck with his own gear. "I think we're in for one of those nights were Alessandro gets center stage," she said.

"Shit," Jimmy said with a smirk. "I better get my good rum out then."

Ginger slapped him on the shoulder. "You love it."

"Yeah, like a hole in the head." Jimmy grinned.

He really did love it. They all did.

Rosalina left the men to sort out the dive gear and headed straight to the master suite for a quick shower. Being as hungry as she was, she knew the others would be too. The dish she planned to cook required a little preparation, so she needed to start quickly or she'd have a mutiny on her hands.

She towel-dried her hair, tossed on a maxi dress and headed to the kitchen. Ginger and Alessandro walked in moments later, holding hands.

"Want some help?" Ginger offered.

"That'd be great."

As Rosalina started placing ingredients on the kitchen counter, Helen walked into the room. Archer's mother looked tired, although that wasn't unusual; she often looked that way. It was likely that she'd only just woken up.

Rosalina walked around the counter and gave her a hug.

"Where are we?" said Helen.

"Egypt."

Helen nodded, as if waking up in Egypt was something she did every day. "Are we looking for *Occhio del Vento*?"

Eye of the Wind, Rosalina translated in her head, and frowned at Helen. "What's that?"

"One of the ships that held the Calimala treasure. It went to Egypt. Didn't you know?"

Rosalina bulged her eyes and Alessandro and Ginger both spun around. "No. We didn't know." Her heart skipped a beat. This was a significant clue to finding the Calimala treasure and Helen had probably known it all along. It was times like this, when Helen had a breakthrough, that made Rosalina realize just how exciting her life must've been prior to the shark attack. Helen and her husband, Wade, had traveled the world looking for treasure, and they didn't stop when Archer was born either.

Archer strode into the room, running his hands through his crazy mop of hair. "Archer." Rosalina couldn't mask the urgency in her voice. "Your mom was just telling us about *Occhio del Vento*, the ship that carried some of the Calimala treasure to Egypt."

It was Archer's turn to bulge his eyes. "Is that right? What were you saying, Mom?" Archer, as always, kept his tone with his mother very natural, and Rosalina was impressed at how he did it.

"Oh well." Helen placed her palm on her chest. "When Rosalina said we were in Egypt, I thought we might be looking for the Calimala treasure here."

Archer pulled out a kitchen bar stool and guided his mother onto the seat. "Why Egypt?"

Jimmy walked in, and out of the corner of her eye, Rosalina noticed Ginger hold her finger to her lips and wave him over.

"Three ships left Italy as a convoy, but after a brief stop at Malta they separated. The Flying Seahorse headed for Greece. *Occhio del Vento* headed towards Egypt and. . ." she rolled her eyes and sighed, "I can't remember the third one. It will be in Wade's notes."

"Do you think you can show us where?"

"Where what?" She blinked up at him.

"Where Dad wrote the notes about these ships in his book."

"Oh." She blinked some more and then huffed. "He was always so funny with his notes. He wrote in lots of fake information so if anyone found the books, they wouldn't be able to work out what was real and what was a decoy."

Jimmy huffed. "You're not bloody wrong."

"What's wrong with you?" Helen scowled at Jimmy like he was a naughty child, and Archer's jaw dropped. His mother hadn't done anything so forthright since he'd found her at the nunnery.

Jimmy scratched his hairy chest. "That husband of yours has had us guessing for months about what's in them notebooks."

"Well then." Helen put her hands on her hips. "That's why you need me."

Chapter Twenty-Eight

Alessandro worked quickly, laying out Wade's scrapbooks in order across the carpet. Other than typical wear and tear, each of them looked identical from the outside. Inside, they contained a crazy concoction of Wade's musings, and the cryptic notes had been driving him crazy. Drawings. Words Dates. Names. Places. Paper clippings. All of it random and in no specific order. Alessandro was more of a details man. If he'd created these books, there would be an obvious system to the notations, and they'd be cataloged and charted in various spreadsheets and then stored in several locations for safe-keeping.

The only matching information each book contained was a list of four different countries inside the front cover. In addition to that, the middle of each book, where staples held the pages together, had a number with a circle around it. They numbered from one to thirty-four.

Rosalina's cooking had the area smelling amazing, and Alessandro tried to ignore the grumbling in his stomach as he focused on extracting important details from Helen before she tumbled back into the horrible world that trapped her.

"Helen, would you mind telling us which book has information on Egypt?"

He enjoyed watching Helen's face light up. She sat forward on her seat. "Inside each book you'll find a list of countries. Show me one that has Egypt."

Alessandro flicked from book to book, opening the front cover and searching for the word Egypt written in Wade's rough scrawl. "*Va bene*, here's one." The book he'd selected had Hong Kong, Egypt, Germany and Brazil listed as the four countries.

Helen accepted the book from him, but she paused, not even turning the cover. Alessandro struggled to read the look on her face. Was it fear? Awe? Confusion? It was a long moment before she opened the flimsy cardboard cover. She turned it slowly and ran her finger down the list of countries.

"Hong Kong. Egypt. Germany. Brazil." The countries whispered off her lips.

Alessandro leaned forward, not wanting to miss a single word she said. Helen blinked few times and frowned, as if searching for a way to arrange the words she wanted to say. She turned to the middle of the book where the staples were and put her finger on the number in the middle. "Seven. Can you find me book nine please?"

Alessandro located book nine and brought it back to Helen. She grasped the book briefly, then handed it back. "This book will have information on Egypt."

Alessandro's jaw dropped. "How do you know?"

She turned to Archer. "Don't you remember your own system, Wade?" Her tone was incredulous.

Archer's shoulders sagged. "I'm Archer, Mom."

"Oh." Helen's face crumbled. In a flash, the clarity in her eyes vanished, and she was lost again.

"Come on." Archer led her to the stairs. "Let's have a look at the Egyptian sunset."

Alessandro waited until they'd left the room before he spoke. "I feel terrible."

"It's not your fault." Rosalina's lips drew into a thin line. "Helen is always confusing Archer for Wade. She told us once that he looks exactly like Wade did, and she gets muddled up sometimes. It must be awful." Rosalina shook her head and turned back to open the oven door.

Alessandro loved researching the past, but he couldn't imagine being trapped in one. Especially one with such horrific circumstances. He turned his attention back to the book in his hand and frowned. "How did she know this was the book?" Inside the cover were four countries. Ireland. Brazil. Australia. Italy. "I don't understand. Egypt isn't even listed in the front cover."

He turned over page after page, trying to work out Wade's logic. Some pages were filled with Wade's scrawl, some barely had two words. There were drawings, names, dates, and entire paragraphs of handwritten text. A drawing about a third of the way through caught his eye. It was a baboon.

"Look at this." He laid the book out on the kitchen counter. "A baboon."

"Looks like a monkey to me." Jimmy smirked.

"We've already been over. . . never mind." Alessandro dismissed Jimmy's comment. He'd previously attempted to point out the obvious differences between monkeys and baboons, but the man didn't really want to know.

"Hey, look at that." Ginger pointed at a drawing on the other side of a seahorse. The artist, presumably Wade, had drawn oversized wings with the deft strokes of a pencil. The way they were drawn made it look like the seahorse was an angel about to take flight.

"The Flying Seahorse!" Rosalina, Ginger and Jimmy all said in unison. Together they burst into laughter as another piece of the scrapbook puzzle slotted into place.

"We need to pay more attention to Wade's drawings."

Ginger squeezed his arm. "It's like playing Pictionary."

A beeping behind Rosalina had her turning away. She opened the oven door and the aromas of roasted potato and rosemary filled the room.

"Damn that smells good." Jimmy rubbed his stomach. "I'm so hungry I could eat the arse off a flying duck."

Alessandro gawked at Jimmy. "That's disgusting."

"What?" Jimmy shrugged.

Rosalina shut the oven door. "Well, lucky for you, we're having steak. Now, can one of you boys start the barbeque for me please?"

"I'm onto it." Jimmy strode off towards the stairs leading to the sun deck.

Alessandro tugged a bar stool out for Ginger and chose one for himself, too. "I still don't understand how Helen knew this book would have Egypt in it."

"I think Helen knows a lot about Wade's treasure hunting," Rosalina said. "But going back to that time hurts so much, she forces those memories away."

Alessandro couldn't imagine living with so much horror. "It would be lovely if we could involve her somehow."

"Maybe it would help," Ginger said. "I mean, if it were me, I'd like to have something to do."

"Everyone grieves differently." When Rosalina looked away, Alessandro assumed she was referring to her father's reaction after her mother died. She'd told him once that her father had never been the same after her mother had passed away.

Ginger turned the pages over one by one, and her hand fell down between his knees, dragging his thoughts from the past. She stopped on a page that had Egyptian hieroglyphics. "Looks like Helen was right about this book having Egypt in it."

"But how?" Alessandro flipped to the front. "Egypt isn't listed in the front."

"I'm going to get these on the barbeque." Rosalina loaded up a tray with enormous steaks, and Alessandro's mouth salivated just looking at them.

"We'll come up soon."

"Actually, you can bring up the salad and potato bake when it's done."

"*Va bene.*"

Rosalina left the room, and Alessandro turned his eyes back to the notebook.

"Show me the first book you gave her," Ginger said.

He reached over and handed her book seven. Ginger opened it to the inside cover and studied the four counties, then she jumped in her seat. "I know." She beamed up at him.

"What?"

"I know how Helen did it. You'll figure it out."

Alessandro reached for book seven and searched for something that indicated where to look next, like a hidden symbol or inscription.

"You're looking too hard." Ginger was wriggling on her seat now. The grin on her face was adolescent in its exuberance.

"Tell me."

"No." She slapped him on his knee. "You have to work it out. I know you can."

"Mmmm." He turned his attention back to the book. When the answer hit him, he felt like a fool and rolled his eyes at Ginger. "Egypt is the second country listed, so the information is in the second book after this one."

"You got it." She reached up to plant a kiss on his lips. "I knew you would."

"*Il mio dolce*, you're brilliant."

"So are you."

Alessandro clicked his fingers. "Let's find the Solomon Island notebooks."

They jumped off the barstools simultaneously and dropped to their knees on the plush carpet to open the front covers one by one. Once finished, they had five books that supposedly contained information on the Solomon Islands and hopefully the Awa Maru treasure.

"Let's go tell the others," Ginger squealed.

Alessandro clutched her arm before she scooted off and drew her in for a kiss. Their lips met, and it was perfect, like a puzzle piece slotting into place. Her mouth was hot and soft, yet hungry at the same time. Their kiss deepened, and their probing tongues molded together in a delicious tango. Her warm hand on the back of his neck had little fireworks blazing through his body.

She pulled back all too soon. "What was that about?"

"You. You're adorable." He wanted to kiss her all night long.

Her smile lit up her face. "You can tell me again later." She reached up on her tippy-toes and gave him a brief kiss on the lips "Come on." She grabbed his hand, and giggling, they raced up to the top deck.

The smell of steaks cooking on the barbeque set Alessandro's stomach grumbling again.

"We solved it," Ginger said, as soon as the others were in view.

"Ginger solved it," Alessandro corrected her.

"Solved what?" Rosalina said from the barbeque.

Helen sat at the bar with her fingers wrapped around the stem of a wine glass. She didn't look sad. She didn't look happy, either. It was more a look of numb indifference. Archer was at his mother's side, and Jimmy was behind the bar with a beer in his hand.

"We worked out Wade's system to determine which books contained information of each country."

"How?" Archer jerked his head in their direction.

"Go on, tell them." Ginger squeezed his hand.

"You worked it out; you should tell them."

"Bloody hell, one of you tell us." Jimmy grumbled.

Ginger looked up at Alessandro, her long blonde lashes flicking up and down, and he squeezed her hand again. "You tell them," he said.

She jiggled her head. "Okay." At the bar, she opened up one of the books and explained how it worked.

Jimmy slapped his hand on the marble top, and the sound was like a cracking whip. "Fucking genius. Sorry, Helen."

"You're forgiven. Just don't do it again." When a smile crept across Helen's face, Jimmy laughed, and soon everyone laughed along with him.

Rosalina tapped the tongs on the barbeque. "Okay you lot, dinner is served."

"Oh shit," Ginger said. "Come on, Alex, we'll get the potato bake and salads."

Before Rosalina had a chance to rouse on them, he dashed after Ginger.

Dinner was a fun affair. The steaks were perfectly cooked, juicy in the middle and just the right amount of char on the surface. The lights of Alexandria in the distance matched the abundance of stars above them. During the meal, the conversation revolved around the markets Rosalina and Ginger had gone to and the scuba diving afterwards. This was the first time Alessandro was actually jealous about them diving. To have seen those ancient treasures sitting at the bottom of the ocean would've been incredible.

"Do you know how those statues and columns got down there?" Archer asked.

"I bet Professor Alex is about to tell us." Jimmy swigged on his beer.

Alessandro played his aloof card and shrugged. "I don't have to."

181

Ginger placed her hand on her forearm. "Go on, honey, tell us. Don't worry about him."

"Yes, honey, tell us." Jimmy's grin was contagious, and Alessandro found himself grinning despite himself.

"Alexandria's Royal Quarters, including the palace and temple complex where Queen Cleopatra lived in 30BC, slipped into the sea after an enormous earthquake in the fourth century."

"That's a bloody long time ago. It's a wonder it's still there," Archer said.

"It was only discovered in 1996. Until then, centuries of sediment had protected it from the salt water."

"Even so." Archer waved his fork at Alessandro. "Why is it still there?"

"Some of the pieces weigh tons, so raising them from the water would be a logistical challenge. Interestingly, the Council of Antiquities have decided to leave the bigger pieces down there and are considering making an underwater museum," Alessandro said. "I must say, I was surprised that you could dive down there. I would've thought there'd be all sorts of red tape to dive in a significant site like that."

"Oh there was," Archer said. "But cash in the right people's pockets encouraged them to turn a blind eye."

Alessandro shook his head. That sort of thing horrified him. Priceless artifacts like that should have strict rules about who went near them, no matter how much money they had.

"Speaking of the Council of Antiquities," Rosalina said, "how did you go today, Alessandro?"

"Oh." He swallowed his mouthful of steak and placed his knife and fork on his plate. "It was amazing and horrifying at the same time. They have hundreds of incredible ancient relics scattered around everywhere. People can touch them. These pieces are priceless and should be secured behind glass facilities to protect them."

"This is Egypt," Helen said. "That's how things have always been done."

Archer grinned at his mother's comment.

"Yes, I understand. But just because it has always been done this way doesn't make it acceptable." He shrugged. It was an argument for another day. "I saw many sarcophagi of all different shapes and sizes.

Some were as small as a child, some were as big as a van, and all were detailed with hieroglyphics. Oh, I saw a five-thousand-year-old wooden statue and the remains of a queen's intestines that had been preserved in alabaster jars."

"Ewww, gross." Ginger scrunched up her nose.

"No, not at all. It's marvelous."

"Did you just swan around, or did you actually meet anyone who might be able to help us?"

"I didn't swan around, Jimmy." Alessandro huffed. "But I didn't get behind the scenes, as you say. Although, sadly, I have the impression that if I was willing to pay, like you did with the scuba diving Archer, I would've progressed much further."

"Remember that for next time," Archer said, as he pushed his plate forward and leaned on his elbows. "So, I guess we have a decision to make." He quickly glanced at all of them. "As we're already in Egypt, do we go after the Calimala treasure, or do we carry on to the Solomon Islands and look for the Awa Maru treasure? I'm sure Nox doesn't care which one, as long as he gets a treasure."

Alessandro was running through the pros and cons in his mind when Helen cleared her throat.

"You go after the easiest one," Helen said.

Archer blinked at her and then frowned. "And which one would that be, Mom?"

"The Awa Maru of course." She said it like Archer was a fool, and he laughed.

"Okay. I'll bite. Why is that one easier?"

"Because the Awa Maru mystery is only sixty or so years old. The Calimala treasure, on the other hand, is over seven hundred years old."

Archer nodded, draped his arm over his mother's shoulder, and pulled her in to kiss her forehead. "Brilliant decision. Does everyone else agree?"

"I'll drink to that." Jimmy held up his beer.

"You'll drink to anything, Jimmy," Alessandro said.

"Bloody oath. Life's too short."

"I'll drink to that," Helen said, and raised her glass with everyone else.

Chapter Twenty-Nine

Nox wandered the halls of Provenzia orphanage, searching for an ideal room to detain Filippo. In the end, there was only one room that didn't have windows. . . the medical center. It was an odd half-hexagonal-shaped room positioned beneath the stairs, as if an afterthought. The unusual stepped ceiling was the only part of the room that wasn't covered in blue three-inch square tiles, although many of those tiles had fallen off, leaving cracked glue residue after their departure from the wall.

It was in this very room that Nox had experienced his first and last legitimate dentist visit. The chair he'd sat in was still there, stuck in a disjointed three-piece position, making it impossible to lie down flat. Above it hung a giant metal cylinder pockmarked with holes that once housed seven bright lights. He was only nine years old when he'd laid upon it and the dentist, with most of his face hidden behind a yellowed mask, had looked down at him with ghoulish black eyes. It didn't matter how much Nox had screamed, or how much blood he'd swallowed, the dentist had continued drilling and scraping until Nox had passed out from the pain.

He ran his tongue around his mouth, feeling the fuzz beneath. He skipped to the gap in his teeth and his thoughts slammed to that moment when Archer had knocked that tooth flying. Yanking a couple of Archer's teeth out when they next met would be grand revenge.

When Nox moved Filippo here by gunpoint, Filippo's only complaint was the lack of bedding. Strange, really, given there were so many other things he could have complained about. Nox relented and allowed Filippo to drag a cot and a mattress from the dormitory to the medical room. Nox didn't help. Filippo wanted it; he had to do it himself.

Later that afternoon, Nox peeked in through the small pane of glass in the door, and upon seeing Filippo sitting on the cot, he entered with his gun held snugly in his hand.

Filippo looked up with insolent eyes. Most people looked at him with fear or disdain. Filippo had a flippancy about him that suggested he was confident that come the end of this situation, he would walk away a rich, happy man. Nox almost chuckled at the notion. Filippo was a long way from reality. Nox was willing to indulge him, though. . . for now.

He handed Filippo a phone. "Make the call." Nox had heeded Filippo's suggestion of using several phones and to randomly dial either Archer's or Rosalina's numbers. By alternating between using Filippo's phone and the three new phones he'd purchased with Nurse Isabella's money, Archer shouldn't be able to trace the calls. The idea was brilliant; the cost to buy the cheap phones, however, had decimated Nox's dwindling cash.

He listened in silence to Filippo's side of the conversation. It was brief, as usual, another device to lessen the chances of the call being traced.

"What did she say?" Nox asked Filippo the moment he ended the call.

"They're in Egypt."

Egypt already! That was excellent news. But then he frowned. Whilst he knew a third of the Calimala treasured was destined for Egypt, he had absolutely no idea how Rosalina could possibly know that. Filippo had more; he was sure of it.

"What else?" he demanded.

"They've figured out how to decipher Wade's notes, and they're heading to the Solomon Islands."

Now he was even more confused. Maybe they didn't know about the Egyptian angle after all. "Who's Wade?"

"I'll need some food for that answer," Filippo said, deadpan.

Nox turned on his heel, left the room and locked it. He went straight to the kitchen, put together some leftovers for Filippo, and then returned to his prisoner. He checked through the glass peephole and, confident that Filippo was where he'd left him, he re-entered the room.

He placed a bottle of water and a bowl of spaghetti bolognaise on the blue tiled counter top, and from his coat pocket, he tugged a dinner roll that he'd pinched from the marina a few days ago and placed it upon the pasta. "Who's Wade?" He repeated his earlier question before he stepped back.

Filippo slipped off the stained mattress and wandered to the bowl. "Wade is Archer's father. He was a treasure hunter."

That may explain why they had seemingly extensive knowledge in a short amount of time. "So, is he helping them, too?"

"He's dead. Died when Archer was a kid."

Nox cocked his head at Filippo. "Did he leave behind notes on where to find the treasure?"

"Yes, but it's as cryptic as hell. According to Rosa, the notebooks are full of both legitimate and fake clues. The hard part is working out which is which."

Nox needed to get his hands on that information, and Filippo was his key to getting it.

Filippo scooped mouthfuls of food with a fork and made annoying slurping noises as he sucked the spaghetti into his mouth. "What's your story, Nox?" Food rolled around Filippo's mouth as he asked the question.

"Story?"

"Yes. What makes a priest become a killer?"

Nox rolled the question around his head, trying to piece together exactly which murder Filippo was referring to. "You shouldn't believe everything you see in the news."

Filippo sucked up a string of spaghetti, then wiped his chin with the back of his hand. "You're not a murderer?"

"No. I'm not a priest." Nox's laughter echoed about the tile-lined room.

Filippo's bushy eyebrows thumped to his hairline. "You did murder your father then?"

Ahh, mystery solved. "Like I said, don't believe everything you hear."

Filippo placed his bowl at his side and wiped his fingers on his pants. "They said you poisoned your father in the church."

"No. My father abandoned me on the steps of this very building when I was five years old. But. . ." Nox shrugged, "if I ever find him, I'll have no hesitation in killing him."

Filippo sniffed. "I don't know my father either."

Nox raised one eyebrow at that.

"My mother screwed around." He shrugged. "I was the result. She never told anyone who she was fucking, and when she died giving birth to me, that secret went with her to the grave." He actually looked pained by the statement.

The revelation, though, was an interesting twist to Rosalina that he hadn't expected. She'd always seemed so wholesome. A woman who had everything and was loved by everyone.

"The entire Calucci family blamed me for killing my mother." The hatred in Filippo's eyes bubbled like sulfuric acid, yet he chuckled. "You and I are both killers."

"So it seems."

Filippo's eyes widened. "Did you kill that guy in the church, or not?"

The idea of sharing his adventures was suddenly appealing. Decades of skilled revenge would go to the grave with him if he didn't share it with someone or document it somewhere. He smiled and showed off his yellowed teeth, a rare and ironic move given the room he was in.

"Father Benedici was the man who was charged with caring for me after I was removed from the orphanage." When Nox had confronted Father Benedici about the treasure, his first stance had been to pretend that the treasure was a complete fallacy. When Nox told him things that a teenage boy simply shouldn't know about a seven-hundred-year-old missing treasure, Benedici tried to beat the basis behind the information out of Nox. When Nox had his first solid lead as to where the treasure went, Nox gave Benedici one last chance to share his knowledge with him. His failure to do so resulted in his ultimate demise.

"He was a dominating sadistic bastard who didn't agree with my plans. So, yes, I killed him." Nox had never openly discussed such a thing before. It felt strangely satisfying to admit aloud the reason why he'd killed the man who supposedly did everything for him.

"Have you killed anyone else?" Filippo was just a little too eager for the answer. Given their situation, it wasn't the reaction he would have predicted.

Nox simply nodded his head.

"Tell me."

Nox debated over how much to tell him. Had he already said too much? Then again, it didn't matter what he said. Filippo was never going to see outside these four walls again. But where to start?

"You're a fascinating man, Nox."

It was Nox's turn to be surprised. No one ever called him that. "What makes you say that?"

"You grew up in a church. And now you're a kidnapper, a killer, and a man with information about one of the greatest missing treasures."

Filippo certainly made him sound interesting.

"I thought Rosalina was exaggerating when she spoke about you."

"Really? What did she say?"

"She said you were an evil bastard who. . ." Filippo paused.

"What?"

"She said you had a. . ." Filippo cleared his throat, ". . . a horrible smell about you."

He was surprised Filippo hadn't noticed his condition. "It's true." Nox nodded. "I have Trimethylaminuria."

"What?"

Nox couldn't believe he was about to tell a complete stranger about the disease he'd been hiding from his whole life. "Trimethylaminuria. It's also called Fish Odor syndrome. It's a rare metabolic disorder that makes me smell like rotten fish sometimes."

"Huh. I hadn't noticed it."

Nox blinked at the man; he had thought everyone noticed it.

"The papers said you grew up in the church. How does someone go from that upbringing to the person you are now?"

"It's a long, long story."

"And we have lots of time." Filippo settled on his mattress and leaned his back against the tiles. "Indulge me."

It occurred to him that Filippo was stroking his ego. No one wanted to talk to Nox. Ever. He'd seen shows about serial killers who'd reveled in their fame, detailing their brutal crimes to the documentary-makers like they were describing how to bake a cake. He'd always thought of them as show ponies. But now, faced with the same scenario, he appreciated the sense of power it gave. To be able to talk about every one of those killings and give the justification behind them could be cathartic, like applying balm to his soul. Yet even with that notion, he was surprised he was considering it. Until now, he'd gone to great pains to keep every aspect of his life a secret.

"Come on. It's not like we don't have time."

That was true. It could be weeks before Archer returned. Although that still might not be enough time to go through everything.

Filippo crossed his legs and leaned forward. "Just start at the beginning."

Nox's stomach fluttered at the prospect of what he was about to do. He eyeballed Filippo. "We will exchange stories. For every piece of information you give me, I'll tell you something about my life."

"Done." Filippo smiled a stupid lopsided grin.

Chapter Thirty

Rosalina woke with a churning in her stomach that had her striding to the restroom and sucking in shaky breaths to force down the nausea. As cold sweat blanketed her body, she splashed water on her face. A glance in the mirror reflected a puffiness below her eyes that wasn't there yesterday.

Loud shouting snapped her out of the queasiness and she grabbed her robe, bolted out of the Hamilton suite and dashed towards the kitchen, but nobody was there. With her heart in her throat, she raced up the stairs to the sun deck. The blinding morning sun dazzled her eyes, and she fought the black spots to see what was going on.

"Hey babe." Archer voice was full of confusion. "You might want to put something else on; there are kids around."

Blinking away sleep, she sighed with relief that everything was okay. "What's all the yelling?"

"The kids below. Take a look." He pointed overboard. "We're a captive audience."

She clutched her silk robe around her waist, and as she peered overboard, she had to duck as a projectile suddenly launched at her. The package landed behind her, and she bent over to collect it.

"Take a look," Archer encouraged.

Rosalina frowned as she slipped her finger beneath the sticky tape to open the clear plastic sleeve. Out tumbled a long black dress with gold embroidery and colorful beading.

"It's a jalabiyas," Archer said. "A traditional Egyptian dress."

She giggled. "It's lovely. So, they just throw it up." With the dress in her hand, she looked over the railing and another cloth package was launched at her. She stepped back and several more came.

"I have your size, pretty lady," a voice called from below, and Rosalina giggled some more.

The packages kept coming.

"Quick, make a choice before we're buried under them." Archer laughed as he ducked away from a package.

She held up dress after dress, all brightly colored in blues, pinks, greens and reds, and all intricately decorated in embroidery and beading. "I can't. There are so many and I like them all."

Three more packages came in quick succession and Rosalina had to be fast to dodge them.

"Hurry," Archer said. "Pick a couple for you and Ginger and toss the rest back down."

In the fastest shopping spree she'd ever done, Rosalina chose six dresses, each of a different color. Then she leaned over the railing and with careful aim at the little boat below, threw back the ones she didn't want.

"How much are they?" she asked Archer. "Do I go down to the dive deck to pay him?"

"God no. If you go down there, you'll buy everything in his boat. Put the money back in the plastic bag and toss it to him from here. How many did you chose?"

"Six. Three each."

"So, ask him how much for six."

"Hello." Rosalina leaned over the railing. "How much for six dresses?"

"For you, pretty lady, we have a special price."

"Of course he does." Archer rolled his eyes.

"Special price, one thousand five hundred Egyptian pounds." His broken English was easy to understand.

"Pfft, I don't think so," Archer mumbled.

She turned to him. "How much is that in Euro?"

"About one hundred and eighty euro."

"That's thirty euro each."

"Yeah, like I said, too much. Offer him five hundred Egyptian pounds and one of your best smiles."

Archer waved away her frown. "Go on."

Rosalina turned back to her waterside seller and he was standing on the blue-painted platform at the front of his boat. "I have more dresses."

"Oh. No thank you. Will you accept five hundred Egyptian pounds for the six dresses?"

"Ahhh, too cheap, pretty lady. I have six children to feed."

"Ha, he's good. Ask him for a better price. Quick." Archer urged from behind her.

"Can you give me a better price please?" This time Rosalina gave an exaggerated smile.

"Pretty lady, you break my heart. I give you extra discount. One thousand pounds."

"What's going on?" Ginger arrived on the sundeck.

Rosalina showed her and when Ginger's eyes lit up, Archer threw his arms in the air. "I'm outta here. You ladies can do the negotiating."

The bombardment of plastic-wrapped packages commenced the moment blonde-haired Ginger peeked over the railing. This time not only did they contain dresses but they were also shown scarves, rugs and gaudy trinkets.

In the end, Rosalina paid two thousand Egyptian pounds for eight jalabiyas, five scarves, two rugs, and a little brass lamp that looked like a genie would pop out if she rubbed it hard enough. Rosalina could've haggled more, but seeing the smile on the diminutive Egyptian man's face was better than any bargain.

The thunder of an engine indicated the anchor chain was on its way up, which meant they were about to have their turn along the Suez Canal again. As they began to pull away, the water-bound peddler waved them off, and Ginger and Rosalina collected their merchandise from the deck and went downstairs.

"That was fun." Rosalina placed her purchases on the dining table.

"Holy cow," Archer said after a quick look. "Thank God we're moving again or I'd have to build you a bigger closet."

"Ha ha. Only five dresses, Mr. Exaggerator."

"Five! When I left, you only had three."

She reached up on her toes and gave him a quick kiss. "You're not mad, are you?"

His dimples punctuated his cheeks, and he pulled her in for a hug. "Of course not, babe. I'm glad you had fun. I'm going to help Jimmy on the bridge. Now that we're moving again, we should be on the Red Sea before you ladies have cooked breakfast." Archer wriggled his eyebrows.

Her stomach grumbled as if it knew what Archer had said.

The journey to the Maldives was expected to take seven days. On day three, they stopped briefly at the port of Aden in Yemen for refueling. While Jimmy and Archer made the necessary arrangements, Rosalina received an unexpected call. She frowned at Filippo's number on the screen. All contact so far had been with numbers she didn't recognize. She jabbed the button. "Filippo, hello. Are you okay?"

"Hello Rosalina."

Her stomach twisted at the sound of Nox's voice. "Put Filippo on."

"Hello, Rosalina. Lovely to hear your voice."

"Put Filippo on!"

"Not in the chatting mood today?"

She clenched her teeth, resisting the urge to tell him exactly the mood he lowered her to. "Put Filippo on."

There was a long, silent pause before Nox spoke again. "She wants you."

"Hello." Filippo sounded weak.

"Filippo, are you okay?"

"Yes, I'm okay."

"How about your wound? Has he given you treatment?"

Filippo moaned. "It's all right; he gave me antiseptic and bandages. It's nothing serious, I promise. I'm just. . ."

"Just what?"

"He has me tied up all the time on the cold floor. And I'm starving too; he never gives me enough food."

A sob released from her throat. Rosalina replayed her escape in her mind. The blazing panic in Filippo's eyes was a vision she'd never forget. "I'm so sorry, Filippo. I shouldn't have gone without you."

"There's nothing you could've done. I'm glad you got out. I couldn't stand it if you were trapped here with me."

"Oh Filippo--"

"How much longer do you think you'll be?"

"We're at Yemen now, just to refuel. We should be at the Maldives in four days."

"Okay." He sighed.

"This is crazy, Filippo. I should come home and try to find you."

"No." He sighed. "We need to end this. Once you find the treasure and give it to him, he'll be out of your life forever."

She could only dream of it being that easy. "But it could take weeks. Months."

"It's okay, Rosa. Really. It's the only way." An eerie crackle on the other end of the phone filled the silence.

"Are you making any further progress with Archer's father's notes?"

The eagerness in his voice caught her off guard and it was suddenly important to prove to him they were doing everything they could to save him. "Actually, yes. We had a huge breakthrough. We've worked out the system he used to assign each notebook to a country. It had us completely baffled until now."

"That's great Rosa. You'll find the treasure. I know you will. You're so smart."

For the last couple of years, whenever she spoke to Filippo, anger always brimmed in his voice, but now he seemed gentle, almost as if he cared for her. The irony about this situation was that it allowed her to speak to her brother more than she had in years. But her stomach churned as she imagined him starving away on the cold concrete floor. "Are you sure you're okay?"

"I'm good. Really. Just uncomfortable. And the rations of food he does give me are disgusting. No! Aaarrgggh! Shit!"

She strangled the phone at the agony in his voice. "What happened? What did he do?"

"He kicked me."

"Oh Jesus!" She could picture her brother tied up by the wrists, curled up on the floor while that stinking bastard kicked him. The thought of that madman being near anyone she loved drove the acid in her stomach right up her throat. But as she processed that image, she wondered how Filippo was holding the phone if his hands were tied.

"Rosa?"

"I'm here, Filippo."

"Just get that treasure as quickly as you can."

"I will. I promise. I love you." The phone clicked, and she listened to the silence for a short while before she realized he'd gone. As she placed her phone on the kitchen counter, she wondered if it was Filippo who'd ended the call or Nox.

Archer walked into the galley with a bundle of paperwork. "Hey babe, we're ready to get going again."

"Okay."

He frowned at her. "What's wrong?"

"I just spoke to Filippo."

"And?"

"He's okay. He was actually chatty. Usually he's angry with me, and right now he has every reason to be. Yet we had a conversation as if everything was. . ." she shrugged, "normal."

Archer cocked his head. "Nox must be treating him all right then."

She tugged at her gold loop earring. "He's not giving him enough to eat and has him tied up on the floor. And while we were talking, Nox kicked him."

"Asshole!"

She nodded. "Filippo still wants us to go after the treasure. He said it's the only way to end it all."

Archer reached for her hand, and his lips curved to a smile showing off his dimpled cheeks. "Let's go get it then."

THE AFTERNOON BEFORE THEY WERE EXPECTED TO ARRIVE AT THE Maldives, they hit a huge storm. While Jimmy and Archer coaxed the yacht into doing what she did best, *Evangeline* bucked and kicked over the huge waves. Rosalina and Helen were sitting on the lounges to ride out the storm when Alessandro appeared from the hallway, bounced off one of the walls and launched himself onto the La-Z-Boy recliner chair.

"This is horrible. How much longer?" His lovely olive skin had a ghastly shade of green to it.

"I have something that'll help." Rosalina strode to the kitchen and raided the first-aid kit for seasickness tablets that had come in handy with many of the Japanese tourists Archer chartered around. "Take these, then go lie down." She folded the tablets into his palm. "Trust me, it works."

Alessandro growled as he stood with unsteady legs. He bounced off a wall before he disappeared down the corridor.

"I never had any problem on the waves," Helen said. "I always thought it was fun."

Rosalina sat back on the lounge beside Helen and turned her knees towards her. "You and Wade must've been through many storms like this."

"Oh, dozens. His boat wasn't as smooth as this one though." She chuckled. "He called her the Dancing Princess, and he'd say, she's really kicking up her heels now." Helen said it in a deep voice, impersonating Wade, or so Rosalina imagined.

"It was a Conrad Cabin cruiser. . . a real gentleman's boat. He loved it. So did I, for that matter." Helen's eyes were distant, as if picturing the Dancing Princess. "The deck was this beautiful rich teak wood, like molten honey. We'd sit out there with our morning coffee, and as the sun dried the overnight dampness the decking would change from a dark cherry color to a lovely golden shade."

"Sounds wonderful. What happened to the boat?"

Helen blinked at her and then placed her palm on her chest. "I asked one of Wade's friends to look after it. David Clementine. I wonder if he still has it. Wouldn't it be fabulous if he did?"

Rosalina blinked at her. With the way Helen has resisted any mention of the past, she had thought something as memory-filled as Wade's boat would be the last thing she'd want to see. "That would be perfect. I'm sure Archer could locate David and ask him." Rosalina tried to commit David Clementine's name to memory by saying it three times in her head.

196

"Mmmm," Helen mumbled, as she played with the string of pearls around her neck.

The sun found a hole in the blackness outside and speared light onto the boiling sea. "What was your favorite country you visited?"

Helen turned to her. The older woman's eyes were as green as freshly podded peas. "Oh, there were so many." She blinked a few times. "I love the color and vibrancy of Morocco. I love the food in Italy. I love the raw beauty of Australia. Thailand has dazzling scenery. Shall I go on?"

Rosalina laughed. She'd be happy if Helen talked all night long. "Yes, please."

"Okay, let's see. I was born in England, and I've been back--"

"Were you?"

"Yes." Helen's brow's furrowed. "Where did you think I was born?"

A flash of lightning lit up the sky, and twin forks hit the ocean in the distance. "To be honest, I don't know. I guess because Archer lived in Australia, I assumed that's where you grew up too."

"Oh, I did grow up there. But I was born in England. My parents immigrated out when I was eight. They were what you'd call ten-pound Poms. Eight weeks they took to travel from England to Sydney." Helen puffed her cheeks out and shook her head. "I can't imagine how horrific it would've been to cross the ocean on those giant rust buckets."

The boat lurched and the roar of *Evangeline*'s thrusters kicked into gear. "Me neither. We certainly have luxury these days."

"You do."

Rosalina laughed. "Yes, I do. Archer's yacht is incredible. So, you lived in Australia until you met Wade?"

"Yes. Once he lured me onto his boat, and I can tell you that was no easy victory. The thought of living in that steel hull for months on end turned my stomach. At first, anyway. I grew to love it. Taking your home with you as you explore the world is the best way to live."

A wave bigger than anything Rosalina had ever seen washed over the yacht. She guessed a twenty-foot swell. It was like liquid metal driving into the side of *Evangeline*.

Helen reached for her hand. "Don't worry," she said. "Archer knows what he's doing."

It was a relief Helen didn't mix Archer up with her husband. "I'm not worried." It was true. She'd seen Archer navigate many storms where she'd felt like her stomach was being ripped out. Riding a storm was part and parcel with owning a boat.

A crack of lightning exploded outside the window. The noise was a wrecking ball smashing into solid wall. The lights dimmed and bounced back, but the digital clock on the oven remained off, which meant one of the transformers had been hit.

"Let's go to the bridge and see if Archer and Jimmy need help."

"Okay." Helen slid forward on her chair.

Rosalina helped her to stand, and together they bounced off the walls as they walked along the hall to the bridge. They stepped over the threshold just as a wall of water tumbled over the front bow, smothering it in swirling foam. The Arabian Sea was putting up a serious fight against the wind.

"Are we having fun yet?" Rosalina said.

"Hey ladies." Archer's grin proved the adrenalin pumping through his veins had him wired.

Rosalina clutched the console. "Some of the power has gone out downstairs."

"Figured it might have," Archer said. "That last crack of lightning hit us."

"Don't worry, ladies." Jimmy didn't raise his eyes from the console as he spoke.

"We're not worried. We thought you might like help."

"No need, we've got this. Right, Jimbo?"

"Sure do." Jimmy beamed.

"Take a seat and enjoy the show."

Rosalina helped Helen into a bolted down chair and then slipped into the seat beside her. She ran her eyes over the instrument panel. Archer had shown her how to use the equipment many years ago. He'd said if ever he was incapacitated for any reason, she'd have to know what to do. The thought had terrified her at the time, but the lessons had proved useful over the years.

Evangeline rocked and rolled with the waves, not in jerky movements, but more like she was taking it all in her stride. It was five hours before they punched out the other side of the storm, and soon the ocean was a smooth sheet of glass reflecting the almost luminous white clouds like a mirror. The rainbow that arched the full length of the horizon was crisp and complete. Rosalina breathed in the fresh ocean air and smiled as Nonna's saying, '*to find a rainbow you must ride out the storm*', once again flashed through her mind.

Chapter Thirty-One

Archer led his mother upstairs and found everyone else already on the sundeck. Ginger and Alessandro were in the jacuzzi, nursing their sore stomach muscles from yesterday's seasickness, and Jimmy was in his new trademark position behind the bar. It didn't matter that it was only nine a.m.; he looked like he'd be ready to crack open a beer at any moment.

Rosalina too was at her new favorite place on the yacht, behind the barbeque. Bacon sizzled and the aroma had Archer's stomach growling to attention. He led Helen to the bar and helped her onto one of the bar stools.

Archer walked towards the barbeque with his mind set on pinching a few slices of that crispy bacon. "Hey Arch," Rosalina said, "I forgot to tell you, yesterday afternoon your mom mentioned that a man by the name of David Clementine was asked to look after the Dancing Princess for her. Helen was wondering if he still had it."

He paused before the bacon and turned back to his mother. "Really, Mom? That'd be fantastic. I was only telling Rosalina about the Dancing Princess recently. So, who's David Clementine?"

"He was one of your father's boating friends. I think they were in the navy together."

Archer stopped his attack on the bacon and walked back to his mom. "Dad was in the navy?"

"Yes. For about ten years. He was very handsome in his uniform." Her cheeks flushed. "He stood out in a crowd like a flashing lighthouse."

"Ha. I never knew that about Dad." His dad had always been very carefree and unorganized. He couldn't picture him living the regimented life of a navy man.

"It was well before you came along," Helen said. "The navy was where he fell in love with a life on the sea."

Alessandro came over with a towel wrapped around his hips. "*Scusami*, Archer, how long before we *arrivare* at The Maldives?"

"Should be about two or three this afternoon."

"Would be a good time to review Wade's notes together."

Archer shrugged. "Sure. Set it up and we'll have a look after breakfast."

Alessandro cleared his throat. "Would you like to help, Helen?"

Archer watched for his mom's reaction. She wasn't always keen on dragging up the past, but yesterday had been one of her most receptive days yet and Alessandro probably wanted to capitalize on that.

Helen nodded. "I'll try. My memory isn't like it used to be."

Archer put his hand on her arm. "You're doing great, Mom."

Breakfast, as usual, was delicious. . . bacon, eggs, grilled mushrooms stuffed with buffalo mozzarella and pine nuts, his favorite ham-flavored baked beans, and toasted Turkish bread lavished with real butter. It hadn't been until he'd started eating that he'd realized how hungry he was.

Straight after breakfast, Jimmy left to go to the bridge to set them on course again, and the rest of them moved downstairs to the lounge area where Alessandro had the space set up like a military strategy room. He'd gathered some chairs around, taped a giant map to the window, and put the whiteboard at the front of the seating area. Five of Archer's father's notebooks were laid out on the table and there were several of his boxed-up things centered on the floor. Everyone sat except for Alessandro, who, as Archer had expected, stood up before them like a teacher at the head of a class.

Alessandro cleared his throat. "Okay, we'll start by reviewing the five notebooks that supposedly contain *informazioni* on the Solomon Islands. Conveniently, that means one for each of us." Alessandro handed them out. Archer grabbed his and flicked over the front cover to the four countries. Japan. Turkey. Spain. Costa Rica. He turned to the middle pages and noted he had book number nineteen.

"What I want you to do is call out anything that looks significant, and I know that's cryptic because we haven't established what we're searching for yet. But, "he pointed his whiteboard marker like a magic wand, "I'm anticipating that between these books and all the paraphernalia in Wade's boxes, we will be able to match some clues together." He wriggled his bushy eyebrows.

"This is going to be fun," Ginger said in an adolescent high-pitched voice.

"So, Alessandro," Helen said, "for example, I have a donkey on my second page. I don't see the relevance of it, but is that the sort of thing you want me to tell you?"

Alessandro shrugged. "It will be difficult to know what is important and what's not. So, I'll write 'donkey' on the board and see if it coincides with anything later."

"I wonder if it's a reference to that time Dad and I rode the donkeys in Santorini, Mom. Do you remember me telling you about that? When he bought you that pearl necklace?"

"Yes, I remember, but I don't know if it's relevant." Helen touched the pearls at her neck.

"I have a fish." Ginger turned it around for the group to see, and Alessandro wrote fish on the board.

Archer flicked over his pages. The first page had a paragraph of his father's rugged scrawl, which he read it to himself. It was a description of a poison ring, which was also referred to as a pillbox ring. The ring was designed to contain something hidden under a decorated lid. A passing glance wouldn't reveal the little hinges that lifted the lid to expose whatever was hidden beneath. Throughout history, they'd been used to carry perfume, locks of hair, messages, keepsakes and poison.

"I have a paragraph on a poison ring." Archer went on to summarize what it was as Alessandro wrote it on the board.

"I've got a drawing of a button," said Rosalina.

Alessandro clicked his fingers. "Remember? We found a brass

button in Wade's things." Alessandro reached for his laptop, and after a couple of seconds, he glanced over the top. "Box number twenty-three." His eyes fell to the boxes, presumably looking at the numbers Alessandro had written on the lids. "Not here. Of course, it's not here." He strode off, and Archer assumed he was going to the Moreton room where the rest of the boxes were stacked up.

Archer flicked over the page in his book to reveal a chart. At the top were three large Cs. The first column had a list of names, none of them he recognized. The first one was Allnatt, and beneath each column headed with a C, Wade had written 101, yellow, cushion. The next one was Beau then 34, colorless and pear. The list went on and on, and Archer had no idea what it meant until the line that had Blue Heart, 103, blue, brilliant. That was when he realized he was looking at a list of famous diamonds. The Cs at the top were carat, color, and cut.

Alessandro returned, carrying box number twenty-three. He lowered it to the floor and began removing the items from the carton and placing them around him on the carpet. "Here it is." He held up the button as if presenting a precious artifact.

"What does it mean?" Ginger grinned like a bride on her wedding night.

"I don't know." Alessandro's shoulders sagged as he studied the button. "Hey Ginger, this looks like a Japanese symbol." He handed her the button.

"It is," Ginger's eyes gleamed. "It's Awa Maru."

Archer glanced at his mother. "Mom, do you remember where Dad found this button?"

"Of course I do." She rolled her eyes with exaggeration. "The Solomon Islands. He dragged me into the jungle to see a museum." She scrunched up her nose. "It wasn't really a museum, but this fellow had been collecting bits and pieces he'd been finding in the dense vegetation around him for decades. He had plane parts, rusted machine guns, ammunition, helmets, dog tags, bottles. . ." She sighed. "Everything you'd expect to find in the aftermath of war." Her voice was slow. Every word was measured. "That's where Wade found the button. I remember he was ridiculously excited when he saw it." She shook her head. "I can't remember why though."

"I'm guessing the button belonged to the only survivor of the Awa Maru's sinking, Kimoda Yukimura."

Alessandro was at his whiteboard again. "Which means that Kimoda made it back to the Solomon Islands after the war."

"And there's only one plausible reason why he'd return there rather than his homeland," Archer said. "Treasure."

Alessandro wrote button in big letters on the board.

"My turn," Ginger said. "I've got a woman with lots of red hair and a ghost."

"What?" Archer chuckled. "Show me."

She turned the book towards them and sure enough, there was a woman drawn in pencil, but a red pen had been used to give her an exaggerated head of red hair. Beside her was a floating sheet with eyes, like the type of ghost a child would draw. After some thought, Archer gave up trying to work out what these two could mean. In the end, he shrugged them off as one of his father's decoys.

Jimmy strode into the room. The poor bugger looked completely exhausted. His eyes were puffy and his hair scrambled in all directions. It wasn't surprising, considering between the two of them they'd been alternating eight-hour shifts for twelve days. "Hey boss. We're pulling into port now."

Archer rose to his feet and put his book on the chair. "Pack up, guys, just in case someone needs to come on board."

He made his way to the bridge and the first thing he noticed was the glorious ocean surrounding them. Its intense turquoise color indicated it was fairly shallow with a sandy bottom and so very clean. Islands were dotted all around, and the temptation to pull up anchor at any one of them was overwhelming. But Archer needed to focus on the job at hand before they settled in for some down time.

The previous day, he'd forwarded all necessary information to the Maldives Port Authority and they were expecting *Evangeline* to arrive. So, their first stop was to show themselves at the port and register arrival. After that, it was refueling via the fuel barge, and then stocking up on fresh food and gas supplies.

It was nearly three in the afternoon when Archer found the nice secluded island he'd pre-determined as ideal and nestled *Evangeline* in a convenient horseshoe-shaped bay. He dropped anchor, turned off engines that deserved a good rest, and went in search of Rosalina.

He found her in the galley, cleaning out the fridge, and he snuck up behind her and wrapped his arms around her waist. "Hey gorgeous. Want to come for a walk along the beach?"

She beamed when she turned to face him. "Oh, I'd love that."

"Get your bikini on then. We have to swim there." He turned her away from the kitchen and gave her a light smack on the bottom. "Meet me at the dive deck."

Archer plucked the fins, snorkels and masks off their hooks in the equipment cupboard and laid them out on the deck. Rosalina arrived in a blue string bikini that showed off her flawless olive skin and her womanly curves. She'd overlaid the bikini with a white cotton shirt that she'd tied at her hips. Her hair caught in the sunlight, shimmering shades of auburn and expensive brandy. It cascaded over her shoulders to nudge her delicious bulging breasts. Just the sight of her took his breath away.

"This is gorgeous." Her eyes were hidden behind her sunglasses, yet she shielded them from the sun with her hand and took in the view.

"I know. It's incredible. Give me your things."

He placed her shirt and sunglasses into a water-tight bag, along with his glasses, and sealed it up. Working simultaneously, they tugged their masks to their necks and with their fins in their hands, they jumped in. The water was just the right temperature. . . not too hot that it was like a bath tub, and not too cold to produce goose pimples. They tugged their masks and fins into place, and then Archer reached for her hand and together they kicked towards the shore.

Beneath the water was a diver's fantasy land. Coral gardens of all shapes and sizes created a colorful landscape as far as he could see. Fish were in abundance. Black and white striped fish the size of his hand were having a party in and around white spikey coral. A school of orange and yellow Damsel fish with a black dot on their tailfins hid within the tentacles of giant purple coral balls with green fingers that wafted in the current.

Rosalina pointed out a long banana-yellow Trumpetfish that was reversing into a narrow hole in the coral. Below it, nestled within the sand was a stingray, only its eyes were visible. As they neared, it popped up and scooted along with its tail drifting behind it. A giant school of blue fin trevally parted ways as the couple swam into their enormous school.

Archer tugged on Rosalina's hand to point it out a black tip reef shark cruising along in the distance. They stopped kicking and drifted as the shark glided with elegant swings of its tail towards them. Behind the shark were four more, each one seemingly oblivious to their existence. The first shark came within seven feet of them but glided on past and kept on going. The four others did the same, and once they'd completely disappeared, Rosalina and Archer resumed kicking towards the shore.

A small turtle, about the size of a dinner plate, led the way for them, gliding its fins through the water to propel himself along. At one point it stopped, hovering in the water to look around, and the lime green and gray platelet pattern on its fins was highlighted by the sun. It turned to them, blinked a few times, then, apparently deciding they were uninteresting, it moved on.

As soon as Archer's knees hit the sand, he tugged off his fins and hooked them over his wrist, then stood up. Water shimmered off Rosalina's body as she rose up beside him like a movie temptress.

"That was magic." She ran her hand through her wet hair.

"I agree." He reached for her fins and then held her hand so they could walk out of the water together. "Shall we walk along the beach?"

"Yes please."

He put their things in the shadow of a large palm tree and removed her shirt and their sunglasses from the waterproof bag. He also removed a white towel and his favorite Hawaiian shirt.

Rosalina giggled. "I can't believe you still have that shirt."

"What's wrong with it?"

"Nothing." She giggled again and then reached up to kiss him.

Their feet sank with each step they made into sand that was as white and as fine as sugar. He'd chosen this deserted island because it should take about an hour to walk around. The pure pleasure of the sand beneath his feet was almost as good as a full-body massage.

"I feel like I haven't had a good walk in months." Rosalina was doing her mind-reading trick again.

"Same." Hand in hand, they headed in the direction of the setting sun. "It's been a long time since I've seen that many fish."

"It was really wonderful. The water was so clear. . . what do you think, about fifty-yard visibility?"

"At least," he agreed.

The center of the island was thick with palm trees that grew out of the sand in long, straight poles. At the top, fronds swayed in the breeze. Many coconuts hung from the foliage and just as many dotted the sand beneath them.

Archer pointed at a bunch of coconuts surrounding the closest tree. "Hey, I don't suppose you could make your Choo Chee curry?"

"That's a great idea."

The first time Rosalina had made him that dish, he'd thought he'd died and gone to heaven. It was one of the first meals she'd made on the yacht, back when she was just an employee. But even way back then, he knew she was going to be so much more. Rosalina was the first woman he'd truly desired. She was alluring, sensual, confident and delightfully unaware of just how gorgeous she'd been. She still was.

Halfway around the island, where the shadows from the palms stretched to the shallow water, Archer removed his shirt and laid the towel on the sand, then he scooped Rosalina into his arms and lowered her onto it. When their eyes locked, he saw the look that always made him fall in love with her over and over.

She reached up, wove her fingers into his hair and pulled him down for a kiss. Her lips parted, and her tongue fluttered out to touch his. Their breaths whispered in and out. Citrus and vanilla, the scent that always captured him, drifted off her. Her nails trailed up and down his back, driving a tingling sensation over his skin. His pounding heart matched the throbbing in his loins, and he never ceased to be amazed at how quickly she aroused him.

Archer glided his hand beneath her neck, pulled the string and folded her bikini down her chest to release her breasts into his hands. He welcomed their full weight, and as he ran his tongue around her nipple the delicate bud firmed, and he obliged by teasing the tip.

She seemed extra sensitive to his touch today, and her moans of pleasure and shifting hips had a full-blown jackhammer pounding in his shorts. He stood, and as he undid the drawstring on his board shorts, she ran her tongue along her lips when her gaze fell to his groin.

Rosalina raised her hips, and he took it as a sign to remove her bikini bottoms. As he glided the fabric down her long legs, he devoured her with his eyes, taking in every naked curve of his beautiful fiancée.

Rosalina began to squirm, and he lowered to his knees onto his shirt at her side. He drew his finger over her lips, down the line of her exquisite neck and around the darker part of her nipple, gradually circling it until it grew as hard as a pebble. He continued the line down her flat stomach and over her very sexy navel. Seeking her hot zone, he skimmed over her small patch of dark hair and down between her legs.

A moan tumbled from the back of her throat, and her eyes rolled when he slipped his fingers into her warm oasis. He started slowly at first, reacting according to her movements. As she rode wave after wave of ecstasy his toes curled in the sand. Shivers rained through her body again and again. . . he'd watch the erotic show all afternoon if she'd let him.

It took all his concentration to take this slowly. Watching Rosalina fall over the edge like that had him as hard as a rock and ready to blast through the stratosphere. Rosalina reached for him and fireworks blazed through his veins.

"Oh Rosa, I've missed you."

"Make love to me, Archer." She said his name as a throaty whisper.

He didn't need to be asked twice. Archer eased between her knees, and with his toes buried deep in the sand he was taken to another world. The luscious heat was sensation overload that took him onto the exquisite knife-edge, teetering between mind-blowing arousal and ultimate release. United together, they moved as one, riding out the momentum like a perfect choreographed dance.

Pleasure, divine unparalleled pleasure, overwhelmed him, and he couldn't hold back a moment more. They climaxed together, coming alive in a thrilling avalanche of heavenly bliss. Archer fell to Rosalina's chest and she glided her fingers up and down his back until their breathing returned to normal.

He kissed her neck. "I love you."

"I love you, too."

Naked, they slipped into the water for a quick swim before they dressed again and continued their walk around the island. Rosalina's hand fit snuggly within his, and the only time she released it was to collect the odd shell along the beach.

Back on the sunny side of the island, *Evangeline* languished in the distance. He searched the shoreline, seeking out the surprise he'd organized for Rosalina.

He spied it just as she did.

"What's that?"

"That, my darling, is how our engagement party should've ended." It already seemed like years ago since their engagement party was ruined by Ignatius Montpellier and his helicopter.

Four poles had been secured in the sand with a large white sheet hooked up between them as a soft canopy. A table and two chairs were centered in the middle, and dozens of candles dotted around flickered white flames. "Your table awaits, madam."

"Oh Arch, this is wonderful. You're wonderful."

He led her to a seat and turned his attention to the bottle of champagne. The cork released with a pop and he filled their glasses.

"To my beautiful bride-to-be."

She chinked her glass against his. "To my future husband. I love you."

"I love you too."

The sun had completely set by the time they'd eaten the pork and shrimp san choy bow Ginger had prepared from one of Rosalina's handwritten recipes. They finished with a glass of Baileys Irish Cream and another box of Roberto Cattinari's fine chocolates.

Although Archer didn't want it to end, they were both yawning when he phoned Jimmy to request a pickup.

"Thank you for this." Rosalina's troubled gaze gave him a feeling she wanted to say something more.

"Are you okay, babe?"

Her lips drew into line. "Of course."

Archer waited.

She was on the verge of saying something else when the sound of a motor had him looking out to *Evangeline*. Jimmy was at the tiller of the small boat and Ginger was at the front with the high-powered flashlight, navigating the abundant coral.

Rosalina yawned again. "I think I'll be going straight to bed."

"Same." Since they'd left Italy, he hadn't had a sleep longer than five hours, and the idea of waking up to the sunrise rather than an alarm sure was a welcome thought.

The small tender was driven right up onto the beach and Archer helped Rosalina climb aboard.

They returned to *Evangeline* and within an hour they were both tucked up in bed.

Chapter Thirty-Two

Nox scooped the mushroom risotto into two large bowls, then tucked a bread roll into one pocket and a water bottle into the other. Then, juggling the two bowls, cutlery and his gun, he made his way to the medical room. He placed one of the bowls on the floor, and a quick glance through the small window confirmed Filippo was on his bed at the back of the room. With the gun pointed forward, he undid the latch, opened the door and gathered the bowl off the floor to enter the room.

"You're late," Filippo snarled. "And I'm starving."

"I went shopping. Well, not exactly shopping. More like scrounging."

Filippo scratched his rapidly thickening beard. "What do you mean scrounging?"

"No money means I have to. . ." Nox searched for the right words, "find food."

A look of disgust crawled across Filippo's face. "Is that mushroom risotto? Isn't that how you poisoned that man in the church?"

Nox laughed. "Yes. Yes, it is. But don't worry; I didn't harvest these mushrooms. I found them in the rubbish outside the *supermercato*. They're fine."

Filippo screwed his face up even more. "All the same, I'll wait until you eat some first."

Nox accepted the challenge and reached for the bowl nearest to him and ate four or five mouthfuls with the eyes of Filippo watching every bite.

Filippo then stepped forward. "I'll take that one." He reached for the bowl Nox had just eaten from and plucked the unused spoon from the other bowl.

"Don't you trust me?"

"No."

Nox huffed. He was itching to find out what Rosalina had told Filippo today but it pissed him off that Filippo had demanded food before he'd reveal anything. Nox was meant to be the one in charge. Filippo was getting more and more cocky each day and if he wasn't careful, Nox may consider preparing him a nasty meal to shut him up for a while.

Filippo returned to his bed and eased onto the mattress with the bowl of risotto.

"You have your food," Nox said, "now tell me what Rosalina said."

Filippo swallowed a mouthful. "They've arrived in the Maldives, so it's about another twelve days before they reach the Solomons."

"And?"

Filippo scooped a tentative spoonful into his mouth. "They have confirmation that Kimoda returned to the Solomons after the war."

Nox tried to establish the importance. "Why is that significant?"

"Because most people would go home at war's end. He didn't."

Nox contemplated this. Kimoda must have returned there for something important. "Do they know where in the Solomons he went?"

"She did say . . . it had something to do with a jungle museum where Archer's father found a clue."

"Do you believe her?"

Filippo cocked one eyebrow. "Why wouldn't I?"

"Because she knows you trade information for food. She saw you do it in the other room. Why would she tell you anything?"

Filippo lowered his eyes to the bowl and stirred the rice around. "That's the tragedy of love. To love someone, you have to trust them.

So, if she doesn't trust me with this information then she's basically saying that she doesn't love me. Rosalina thinks she's so pure that the whole fucking world should love her, including me." He ate a mouthful of food. "So, yes I believe her."

"She didn't look pure when she shot me with that spear."

"Exactly. She's a deceiving bitch." Filippo pointed at the risotto with his spoon. "This is good, Nox."

Nox chuckled. "It's my specialty."

Filippo huffed. "Now it's your turn, Nox. You need to tell me how you found out about the treasure."

"You told me."

"No, not the Awa Maru treasure. The other one."

"The Calimala treasure."

"Yes, that one. Hey, have you seen that ugly necklace Archer wears?"

Nox pictured the curved piece of gold dangling around the Australian's neck. "Yes, I've seen it."

"Apparently it's part of the treasure. His dad found it in the Greek Islands. Right before he got eaten by a shark. It's taken Archer twenty years to figure out where they were scuba diving when he found it. But once he figured it out, all he had to do was bring it up. All that gold. . ."

All my gold. Now at least he knew how Archer had found it. But how did his father find it? That treasure was stolen from the Church of St Apostoli seven hundred years ago. The details of that theft were written on a scroll, and he thought he was the only person in the world who could possibly know about the treasure. "How did Archer's father know so much?"

"How do you know so much?" Filippo shrugged half-heartedly. "I asked first."

Nox twisted the bulky antique ring around his finger as he eyed Filippo. The details on the scroll had been his leverage, anchoring him and only him to the vast wealth. "See this ring?" Nox said finally.

Filippo nodded. "Can hardly miss it."

"When I was a kid, I found this hidden in a statue of a baby holding a trumpet. I accidently knocked the statue over, shattering it to pieces, and this ring and what it secured fell out."

"What did it secure?"

213

"A seven-hundred-year-old confession written on animal parchment." Nox paused as he recalled the first time he'd unrolled the scroll. It had been curled tightly, refusing to lie flat, and it wasn't until Nox saw the date at the top of the parchment that he had realized why.

"What was the confession?"

Nox swallowed. His mind debated over whether or not to reveal the secret that had been driving him for three decades. Surely Filippo must know Nox couldn't let him live once he revealed the details. Could the man be that stupid?

Filippo sat with his hands around the bowl that rested on his thighs, like an eager child ready to listen to a bedtime story. Maybe, like Father Benedici had, he already knew his ultimate fate. Nox could accept that. He was a believer in destiny. Sitting here with Rosalina's brother and chatting about the Calimala treasure was a testament to his belief.

He let out a slow and steady breath. "The scroll was signed by Tommasello da Lucca, who was a priest at the Church of St Apostoli in 1348. That was the year the great plague ripped through Italy, killing millions of people."

"Huh. . . they say," Filippo licked his spoon," thirty-five per cent of the population died in Europe alone from the plague. Over twenty million people."

Nox raised his eyebrows at him.

"I went to school."

Nox couldn't remember ever learning about the plague in any class he attended, although he had skipped a majority of his school lessons. "They had no idea what caused the disease to spread."

"That's right, it wasn't until the 1900s that they worked out it was fleas on the rats that carried the disease."

"Exactly. In the 1300s, the people thought it was the wrath of God, punishing them for their sins. They were flocking to the churches with their valuables, begging to be absolved of their sins."

Filippo sat forward on his chair. "So, what was on that confession?"

Nox let out a slow breath. Then he recited the inscription he'd memorized on the scroll, word for word.

June 21st 1348

We are being punished for our sins. Black Death so vile and colossal has possessed our land. The sinners offer treasure in exchange for absolution because they believe a man of God will save them. But I cannot. They fall at my feet and I step away to watch them die from afar. I refuse the dying their last rites for fear of being struck down.

But I will be mankind's savior. I will use this wealth to create a church in a safe land. I have paid three men very well to keep my secret safe. They will captain three ships - The Flying Seahorse, Occhio del Vento and Aquila di Mare. We will sail to Egypt and pray it is free from God's poison.

I leave this confession with a diary of all I have taken. These possessions will be used to create a new home for those who outlive this wrath. Paradise awaits anyone who meets me there.

This is the end, but I give you a new beginning. I am your man and forever will be, by the grace of God, yours in safekeeping,

Tommasello da Lucca

NOX'S EYES SHIFTED FROM THE HOLD THEY'D HAD ON HIS ANTIQUE RING during the recital back to Filippo. "I've been looking for the diary he talks about ever since the day I found that scroll."

"You never found it?"

"No. But Archer did." Nox clenched his jaw.

Filippo's eyes widened. "Oh yes, Rosalina told me about it. It lists all the treasure. That was how they worked out that only one third of the treasure was on the Flying Seahorse."

"So, they know there were three ships?"

Filippo frowned. "I don't know about that."

"Did they know the ships were going to Egypt?"

"I don't know."

Nox squeezed his fist and glared at him. "You need to find out"

Filippo clenched his jaw, squaring out his bearded chin. "If you'd told me about this scroll days ago, I'd have known what to ask."

Nox hurled his bowl at Filippo. The prisoner ducked and the dish hit the tiles behind his head, shattering to pieces and tumbling onto the bed along with several blue tiles.

"What was that for?" Filippo wailed.

"You need to remember who's in charge."

"How can I forget? You're treating me like a caged animal."

"You're lucky I don't kill you."

"You can't kill me."

"Don't be so sure about that!"

"You need me, Nox. And you know it."

Nox turned and strode towards the door.

"Nox!" Filippo's stern voice bounced off the tiled walls. "I don't want food from rubbish bins."

Nox twisted to him. "You don't want the alternative. Believe me."

Filippo's squinted his eyes. "What's the alternative?"

"Nothing. Absolutely nothing for days on end."

"Fuck that. I'm talking about buying food. And decent food, too."

Nox cocked his head. "I don't have enough money. You get what you get."

"I have money. Release me, and I'll get it."

Chapter Thirty-Three

Alessandro watched their departure from the Maldives with a peaceful sense of melancholy. The scenery was magnificent from his view in the jacuzzi and its beauty affected him like no other. The Maldives was nature at its finest.

As the sun set into the pristine aquamarine waters, he and Ginger sat in the bubbling water and sipped her signature drink. . . the Cosmopolitan cocktail. After Archer pulled up anchor and they cruised away from the beautiful secluded beach, with its sugar white sand and waving palm trees, Alessandro made a promise to himself. . . he would return to the Maldives with Ginger very soon.

It was the perfect place to propose to her.

They'd been at sea one week already and would be cruising into Australian waters within a couple of days. Alessandro had never been to Australia; he'd never been outside Italy until he'd joined Archer's treasure-hunting expedition. He still couldn't believe he was doing it.

This experience was a world away from his real life.

It suddenly occurred to him that he may never want to go back to his job teaching uninterested students the glory of ancient history. He was surprised that the thought didn't worry him.

After several hours in the jacuzzi, he and Ginger settled inside to do their customary afternoon activity. . . scrutinize Wade's notes. As they refilled their cocktails several times over, each of them scanned a different book looking for something that made sense.

Jimmy was taking his turn at the bridge and Archer was sleeping. Rosalina, as usual, had the yacht filled with delicious aromas from the meal she was preparing for tonight.

"I wonder if we're looking at this all wrong." Ginger's hair cascaded in luscious blonde waves over her shoulders.

He fell into the blue pool of her eyes. "What do you mean?"

She pumped an elegant shoulder. "I don't know. It just seems weird that we've been staring at the books for weeks and got nowhere."

Alessandro huffed. "I know. It's infuriating. Wade certainly did a great job of encrypting things."

Ginger jolted. "Hey, will the Egyptian professor be back from New York yet?"

"Oh gosh." Alessandro glanced at the date on his computer. "Yes, he should be." He jumped up. "Rosalina, do you think Archer would mind if I used his office to make a call?"

"Of course not."

Ginger reached for Alessandro's hand and they strolled to the study together. He bent down and opened the safe door, then he put on his white cotton gloves to remove the blue cylinder. Ginger grabbed a red cushion off the lounge, and Alessandro centered the precious piece in the middle of it.

The Lapis Lazuli relic was exquisite. The intense blue shades of the stone appeared to radiate from within. Hints of fine gold veins weaving across the surface added to the luxurious tones. The gold caps at each end that replicated woven rope were in perfect condition. One of these caps had a gold ring attached to it. It too was decorated in Egyptian hieroglyphics.

Alessandro found it impossible to believe this piece could be thousands of years old.

Archer's diary was on the desk and Alessandro flicked to the day they'd taken the monkey statue to Accademia di Belle Arti. The professor's number was at the top of the page with several circles drawn around it.

He dialed the number and the professor answered almost immediately. "*Ciao Alessandro, dove sei stato.*"

"Sorry Professor, we had to leave on important business." Alessandro deliberately spoke in English so Ginger wouldn't be excluded from the conversation.

"Surely nothing is as important as this."

Alessandro put the phone on speaker so Ginger could hear. "I agree, but like you, it was something we couldn't miss. How did you go with the cylinder?" The professor had objected, to the point of insistence, at Alessandro not leaving the cylinder or the statue at the museum, but Alessandro had given his word to Archer that he would remain with the statue at all times. And he had every intention of doing just that. After the professor had calmed down, they'd taken dozens of photos, and Sezoine promised to work on deciphering the images until they could speak again.

"Do you have the cylinder with you?"

"Yes, we do."

"Okay, for this demonstration I'll call the gold ring the top."

"Yes, I understand." Alessandro pointed at the gold ring. It looked like the type of link that would allow a pendant to glide along a chain. Although this piece was much too big to be a pendant of any kind, so the significance of the ring was lost on him.

"Please maneuver the cylinder so you can look through the hole of the ring."

Alessandro understood and rolled the cylinder sideways. "Done."

"At the bottom do you see a circle with a man wearing a crown?"

Ginger pointed at it. "Yes, we see it."

"That, my friend, is King Ptolemy the Third."

Ginger sucked the air between her teeth as if she understood the significance of the name. Alessandro wrote the name down in Archer's diary and they grinned at each other.

"King Ptolemy the Third was a particularly aggressive king and he made it his business to march far and wide, claiming land and wealth as his own."

"Interesting."

"What is interesting," Sezoine continued, "is the man kneeling at the king's side."

Alessandro pointed at the engraved figure. It looked like the kneeling man was reaching out.

"That's a scribe. When can you return the cylinder to me, Alessandro?"

Alessandro cleared his throat. "We cannot be certain at the moment. Why?"

"I believe we'll find a scroll inside the cylinder."

"Let's open it," Ginger said.

"No!" Sezoine's voice was fearful.

"Why not?"

Sezoine let out a sigh. "Because the inscription on the outside also details the contents are protected. Only the rightful owner can open it."

"Meaning?" Alessandro let out a breath.

"Meaning another ambush could be waiting inside." The seriousness in the professor's voice was unmissable.

Ginger huffed.

"In that case, Professor, we shall have to wait until we return to Italy."

"Return? Where did you go?"

"We're treasure hunters, Professor Sezoine," Alessandro said. "We go where the clues take us." For the first time in his life, Alessandro liked that he was the man in charge.

After Alessandro said goodbye and hung up the phone, he opened his laptop and typed in King Ptolemy the Third. After half an hour of research, they went to find the others. The sounds of laughter had them walking towards the saloon where they found Jimmy and Archer. Rosalina was in the kitchen and by the look of the flour everywhere, she was making pastry.

"I'm so glad you're all here." Alessandro pulled out one of the bar stools along the kitchen counter for Ginger to sit. "We've just spoken to Professor Sezoine."

"Oh right, the blue cylinder," Rosalina said. "I forgot all about it."

"Yes, we nearly did too." Alessandro weaved his hand into Ginger's.

"What did he say?" Archer asked.

"He wants us to bring the cylinder back."

"I bet he does." Jimmy jutted his chin out. "Why?"

"He believes there's a scroll inside."

"Well let's open the bugger." Jimmy huffed.

"We can't. . . he thinks there'll be another booby trap," Ginger said.

"Pfft. Yeah right." Jimmy jabbed his stubby finger on the bar top. "He's just saying that."

"Maybe not, Jimmy. Since we nearly lost our heads the first time, I've done a little research. Over the years, scrolls have been completely destroyed by carelessness. What the ancient Egyptians did was put little vials inside the container with the scroll, and when the container is opened without the correct sequence, the vial shatters and liquid spills over the porous paper, ruining the parchment."

"Well that blows that idea then. It'll just have to wait until we get back," Archer said.

Alessandro nodded. "I've arranged to call Professor Sezoine the moment we return to Italy." He glanced at Wade's notebooks still dotted around the room and sighed. They were getting nowhere with all the information that was both painfully obvious and discreetly concealed in the notes. In a way, Wade had created his own booby traps. "Shall we have another review of Wade's notes?"

"Sure," Jimmy said. "Nothing like scrambling our brains before dinner."

Alessandro collected a notebook from the floor and flicked to the middle pages. Book number twenty-four. He turned to the front pages and noted the four countries. Australia. United Kingdom. Spain. Egypt. He flicked the pages through his fingers, allowing them to fall in a kaleidoscope of words and pictures. The book fell open at a page with a drawing of a man fishing and then a can, like the types of cans that contained tuna or salmon. Wade had even drawn a ring-pull on the top.

"Here it is again," Archer said, seeking Alessandro's attention. "This is the second time I've seen a reference to diamonds. The first one was a list of diamonds detailing their cut, color and carats. Here's a picture of a diamond ring."

"Remember, the Awa Maru not only carried gold bullion, it also carried diamonds. As well as ivory, jewels and antiques," Ginger said.

Alessandro sat forward. "That's right. What number book do you have?"

Archer flicked to the middle pages. "Sixteen."

"Okay, where are the books before it?"

Everyone called out their numbers, but none of them had the

preceding four books. Alessandro slipped off his chair and went through the books until he located them. Book thirteen had Solomon Islands listed as the third country down. "This confirms your book has Solomon Islands information in it." Out of curiosity, he checked the books prior to his. By coincidence, his book also had Solomon Islands in it.

"What's wrong, babe?" Ginger placed her hand on Alessandro's knee, and he glanced at her. "You're frowning."

He sighed. "I was just wondering what on earth this could mean. Wade's drawn a man fishing and a tin of tuna." It was infuriating to have more questions than answers.

Ginger's eyes bulged. "There was a fish in one of the books I had. It was on the second page." She launched off her stool and fell to her hands and knees to rummage through the books. It seemed like an eternity before she found it. "Here. Look." She presented the open book to him.

Wade had drawn a very basic fish and beside it was a crude drawing of a boat with giant poles protruding up from the tail end of it. Alessandro turned the drawing towards Archer and Jimmy. "What type of boat would this be?"

"A trawler," they both said in unison.

Alessandro frowned. "What do you think Wade was trying to tell us?"

"Something about tuna fishing?" Ginger volunteered.

Archer rubbed his chin and Alessandro heard the scratch on his stubble. "I wonder if Dad did tuna fishing or something in the Solomon Islands."

"Maybe there's a boat called the Tuna Fish," Rosalina suggested.

"I'll see what I can find." Alessandro opened his laptop on the table and Google searched for tuna fishing in the Solomon Islands. It was a long while before he hit a jackpot. "Oh my God."

"What?" Ginger said as everyone looked at him.

He smiled at Ginger. "Remember the drawing of the woman with red hair and the ghost?"

Ginger edged forward on her seat. "Yes."

"A boat loaded with a cargo of canned tuna was sunk by a bouncing bomb in May, 1945. The boat was called the Ranga Spirit."

Chapter Thirty-Four

Nox spent three days trying to extract Filippo's banking pin from him, but the stubborn Italian wouldn't divulge it. So, he had no choice. It was still weird though to be traveling the winding road that skirted the edge of the coastline with Filippo behind the wheel of Nurse Isabella's car, and Nox aiming a gun at Filippo's hip. Filippo had begun whistling almost from the moment they'd left the orphanage and gave the appearance he was completely at ease with the situation.

It was risky taking Filippo from the confines of the orphanage, potentially giving him the opportunity to escape. Strangely, he believed Filippo wouldn't try anything. He also believed Filippo was in this for the treasure as much as Nox was. Rosalina's brother seemed to have total faith in their partnership.

Nox nearly laughed aloud at the concept.

Filippo pulled into a parking lot at a strip of shops. Nox stepped out and raced to catch Filippo, who was striding to a banking machine.

"Don't try anything." Nox concealed the weapon beneath his shirt and nudged the gun into the small of Filippo's back.

"Calm down. I've told you already, I'm not going anywhere." True to his word, Filippo withdrew two hundred euro and handed half to Nox.

"Now. . ." Filippo cocked his head. "I'm hungry, and because I'm paying, I'll choose where." He glanced around at the dining options, and after only a brief pause, he headed towards the restaurant at the end of the strip of shops.

La Pasta Gialla had as many hanging plants as it had table settings, and the first impression Nox had was of walking into an overgrown backyard. Every table, decorated in red and white checkered cloths, took in the view over the ocean. A waiter was quick to greet them and to Nox's relief, they were directed to a table a decent distance from other diners in the restaurant.

Their water glasses were filled, menus were handed to them, the daily special was detailed with great flamboyance, cloth napkins were draped across their laps, and then their waiter waddled off to leave them to decide on their meals. Nox was bewildered by this strange scenario, but Filippo seemed completely oblivious to the absurdity of what they were doing.

Nox would've been happy with takeaway fish and chips. But with Filippo's offer to pay, he couldn't resist something more substantial. He took Filippo's lead and scanned the menu, but he couldn't go past *bistecca alla fiorentina*. If the T-bone steak was cooked half as good as it was described on the menu, then he'd be happy. He added a side of rosemary potatoes and buttery greens.

Once they'd placed their orders with the waiter, Nox glanced around the restaurant. It seemed that nobody in the café was interested in them. Not the elderly couple in the booth who hardly spoke two words to each other. Not the four young women who barely stopped speaking to breathe. And not the staff who served them with professional indifference.

It was like being invisible.

Nox had been invisible many times. The Church of St Apostoli, his home for decades, offered dozens of discreet nooks that had allowed him to watch and listen unnoticed. He'd learned many secrets, and just as many facts that way. Knowledge was power. And as he glared into the eyes of Rosalina's brother, he realized this fateful partnership was another avenue for obtaining knowledge.

When his two-inch thick steak arrived, lightly charred on the outside and still simmering on a hot stone, he was grateful Filippo was insistent on paying. It was cooked to perfection and so tender he could slice it with a butter knife. Blood seeped from the delicious meat as he cut into it.

"How's your steak?" Filippo asked with a mouthful.

It was like they were just a couple of friends sharing a lunch meeting, not the kidnapper and captive that they really were. Nox nodded. "It's good."

As he savored another slice of his rare steak, he leaned back on his chair and felt the gun tucked into his pants at his lower backbone. Although it now seemed unlikely Filippo would do anything, it was reassuring having the weapon at hand. He would have no hesitation to use it should the need arise, regardless of who was watching.

"So." Filippo reached for his wine glass and settled back on his chair. "Why don't you tell me about what happened in that room you have me locked up in?"

Nox leered at Filippo.

"What? You think I haven't noticed? Whenever you walk in, you look about the room as if expecting ghosts to crawl out of the cracks."

Filippo's insight was unsettling. Nox hadn't realized he was that easy to read.

"Did someone play doctors and nurses with you?" Filippo peered over his wine glass with a snide grin.

"No." Nox scanned the restaurant, ignoring Filippo's chuckle. Nobody was listening.

"No one cares, Nox." Filippo took a large gulp of wine. "Come on, tell me what. . ." he shrugged, ". . . business went on in there."

Business? That was an interesting term for it.

So far, as he'd recounted to Filippo how he'd killed people, Nox had kept it brief, brushing over the nitty-gritty. Then again, all the murders he'd talked about to this point had been done by relatively civilized means. The dentist though, the one who'd tortured him in that very room Filippo was sleeping in, had not received such gentle treatment.

Nox broke off a chunk of his bread roll and scooped up the blood on his plate, and as he ate the food, he went back to that horrible place in his memory. "I was nine years old when I was dragged into that room to see the dentist. I'd never seen one before and had no idea what to expect. The dentist, Doctor Igor Vleshor--"

"You remember his name?" Filippo interrupted.

"I never forget the names of my tormentors." Nox lowered his eyes and rolled his knife from side to side, catching the glint of the sun on the blade. "Igor made the nurses hold me down while he prized open my mouth and drilled out two of my teeth. At some point during the torture, I passed out. When I woke, I was in my dorm bed, covered in blood, writhing in agony and with a group of children standing around me."

"Ahh, geez. That's a rotten story." Filippo's facial features glided from disgust to intrigue. He leaned forward and propped his elbows on the table. "What'd you do to him?"

Once again, Nox was perplexed by both Filippo's insight and his eagerness to hear the gory details. "I was twenty-five when I finally tracked down Vleshor. He was still a practicing dentist." Nox nibbled on a long green buttery bean. "So, I made an appointment."

"Weren't you worried about being recognized?"

"Nobody recognizes me." It was true; his disease ensured most people couldn't wait to get away from him. They'd lower their eyes and scurry past as if just being in his presence risked their lives. Filippo was the first man he'd ever met who didn't seem to notice it. His beloved Ophelia was the only woman. As his mind drifted to the abundantly homely woman who'd saved him in so many ways, he wondered if he would ever share a meal with her just like this, two people chatting about old times.

"I'd recognize you."

Nox lurched back from his mental drifting and captured Filippo's dark eyes with his. Filippo seemed unconcerned that his statement was exactly the reason why Nox had to kill him, when the time was right.

"So, come on." Filippo waved his wine glass at a waiter in the distance. "What'd you do to this dentist?"

The waiter walked towards him with efficient briskness and plucked the red wine bottle from the side counter on the way. "*Volete più vino signore?*"

Filippo agreed to more wine, however Nox declined; his glass was still half full. As much as he'd like several drinks, he needed to keep his mind clear.

Nox refrained from smiling at the waiter; his dreadful teeth were one of his distinguishing features. Once the waiter filled Filippo's glass and moved out of earshot, he continued the conversation. "While the nurse was holding some tube in my mouth and the dentist was poking and prodding with one of his gadgets, I stabbed both of them with tranquilizers. Simultaneously, like this." Nox demonstrated by suddenly yanking his arms apart with balled fists representing the needles he'd jabbed into the dentist and his nurse. "I bound and gagged the nurse and locked her in the cupboard. Then I tied up Vleshor and waited for him to come around."

"What did you do?" By the look on Filippo's face, any glancing patron in the restaurant would get the impression Nox was telling a piece of juicy gossip rather than detailing a bloody murder. The waiter arrived to clear their plates, once again stalling their conversation.

As soon as the waiter waddled away, Filippo eased forward on his elbows. A slight nod indicated it was time for Nox to continue.

"I reminded Vleshor of my nine-year-old self who'd lost two teeth under his torturous techniques." Nox shrugged. "Then I pulled his teeth out one by one. So much blood. When I finished, I stuffed a blood-soaked rag into his mouth and pegged his nostrils. Vleshor will never torture anyone ever again."

Filippo put his hands together, and for a moment Nox thought he would clap. "What about the two nurses who held you down when you were a kid?"

Nox drank the last of his wine, then twirled the remaining droplets around the glass. "I missed one of them; she died before I got to her. The other though, Sister Teresa Constanza, looked right into my eyes as I squeezed the life out of her."

"Just like Shyain," Filippo said with a gleam in his eyes.

"Yes. Just like Shyain." Although Nox would always remember the name of his first victim, he was surprised Filippo had.

Chapter Thirty-Five

It was only four o'clock in the afternoon, and although Rosalina had done very little other than lounge around all day, she was exhausted. Their arrival and departure at Darwin two days ago was so swift she'd barely had time to replenish their supplies. Yet she wondered if she'd picked up a bug there, because she'd thrown up the following morning.

She went to the restroom and splashed water on her face. Her freckles seemed more prominent than usual, and dark shadows loomed beneath her eyes. Maybe the worry over Filippo was affecting her more than she realized. Tonight was to be their last night at sea before they arrived at the Solomon Islands, which meant that it was potentially their last chance to rest. Who knew what tomorrow would bring?

She pulled open the cupboards, seeking her face cream, and when she saw the small black packet at the side, she froze. The sight of Archer's box of condoms had her brain screaming. For years she'd been the one managing their contraception, but when they'd broken up, she went off the pill altogether. She squeezed her temples with her thumbs and glared at herself in the mirror. "Am I pregnant?" Just the thought of it threaded fear through her body. She didn't want children, never had.

She gripped the vanity basin as she processed what she did and didn't know. In the last few weeks she'd been nauseous, dizzy, tired, and having all sorts of reactions to food. But they could all be explained away to strange foods and extreme stress. Had they been careful? The answer was a resounding no. Once they became a couple again, she should have gone back on the pill, but their life had been so crazy she hadn't even put two thoughts into it.

"Oh God." She forced down the acid in the back of her throat as she lifted her dress to look at her stomach. Turning sideways, she examined her torso in the mirror. It didn't look any different. She couldn't be pregnant. Rosalina began to giggle. The idea that she was having a baby was ridiculous. She leaned on the sink and stared at her reflection in the mirror until she'd forced the worry from her face.

On impulse she slipped into her bikini, scooped her hair into a ponytail at the base of her neck and tugged on her large lemon-colored sun hat. She grabbed sunglasses and a white sarong, and as she tied the soft fabric up over one shoulder she went in search of Archer. She found him at the bridge with Jimmy. "Hey guys, I'm going for a dip in the jacuzzi. Who wants to join me?"

Archer blinked at her. His eyes dazzled in the light.

"Go on, mate." Jimmy slapped him on the shoulder.

"Are you sure?"

"Of course. I got this."

"Thanks, Jimmy." Archer reached for Rosalina's hand and she led him out the door. "What brought this on?"

"I figured tonight was probably our last lazy night before the craziness began again, so I thought we should enjoy it."

He let go of her hand, slid it down to her hip and tugged her to his side. "Great idea. I'll get changed and meet you up top." Archer left her side, and as she strolled through the yacht, for the first time ever she hoped she didn't run into any of the others. All she wanted was some quiet time with Archer. She felt like she was running the gauntlet as she strode the length of the yacht and climbed the stairs to the sun deck.

She sighed with relief when she discovered the teak-lined area vacant. On the way to the jacuzzi, she tugged a couple of towels from the linen cupboard and placed them on a deck chair along with her sarong. The sun was still an enormous fireball in the sky, casting its intense heat rays across the deck. Fortunately, half the water was bathed in the shadows from the helipad.

She climbed the three steps to the jacuzzi and pushed the start button, and as the warm water bubbled to life, she eased into it. A sigh released from her throat as she found a curved seat below the waterline where her body was in the shade and her legs could bask in the sun. She rolled her head from side to side and realized just how tense she was. Her first thoughts were that it was her worry over Filippo that was causing the knot in her stomach. But she quickly conceded she had so much more on her mind.

"Want a drink, babe?" Archer called to her from behind the bar.

Her instant reaction was to say yes, but she forced herself to be cautious. "Just a water, please."

"Oh, are you sure? I'm having a beer."

"Yes, I'm sure."

Archer grinned as he strode towards her with the drinks in his hands, and Rosalina admired every delectable inch of his skin. He was ruggedly sexy with muscles in all the right places. . . not too big to throw his body out of proportion, but just enough muscle to ensure she felt safe in his arms.

He slipped in beside her and when he leaned over to share a kiss, she inhaled the scent of his freshly applied cologne. It was all tropical sunsets on secluded beaches, and exactly how she liked her fiancé.

"This is the life, hey?" He said it like it was something new, and she chuckled.

That was another thing she adored about Archer. Despite his abundant wealth, he was still very grounded.

"Sure is, babe." This was how life was meant to be. Enjoyed. She placed her hand on Archer's leg and glided her fingers over the jagged scar below his knee. The scar was a terrible reminder of how Archer's father had died. Archer was just lucky the shark hadn't killed him too.

He sipped his beer, then leaned his head against the soft cushion, and when he swallowed, his Adam's apple bobbed up and down. His wavy hair tussled in the breeze, dancing about his ears. It was a bit longer now, curling at the base of his neck and flopping down over his brows. It complemented his carefree personality.

Rosalina twisted her engagement ring around her finger. She was still getting accustomed to wearing it. Ever since Archer had proposed, their life had been anything but normal. And now, as they cruised towards yet another potential treasure hunt, she wondered if their life would ever be normal again.

"What're you thinking about?" Archer opened his coffee-colored eyes and turned to her.

She shrugged. "Nothing?"

"I can feel you thinking. You're not relaxing."

"Oh." She hadn't realized she was emitting those vibes. "It's nothing."

"It's not nothing. We're alone together in the best place in the world, and you're as stiff as a surfboard."

"No, I'm not." She forced her shoulders to relax.

Archer glided his hand along her thigh, and when their hands met, he weaved his fingers into hers. "Tell me."

She let out a slow breath, trying to form the words in her brain. "I was just thinking how ever since we became engaged, nothing has been normal."

He lifted her hand from the water and kissed her engagement ring. "Normal is a difficult thing to define. One couple's idea of normal is nothing like another's."

"Okay, I agree with that. What I mean is, before we started chasing after this treasure, we had jobs and lives where we went to work during the day and came home to relax each night. Now we seem to bounce from crazy times where people are trying to kill us, to days on end where we float at sea doing nothing."

"What would you like to do?"

She huffed out a breath. "That's just it. I don't know. I just wonder if we're ever going to settle down."

"Settle down?" He frowned. "What, and have a family or something? Is that what you mean?" He chuckled.

Rosalina's answer trapped in her throat. His flippant response may have been expected. But now, she couldn't decide if it was the answer she wanted.

LESS THAN TWENTY-FOUR HOURS LATER, *EVANGELINE* WAS ANCHORED just off the wreck of the Kawasaki Ki-56 plane that they hoped belonged to Hiro Yukimura. Rosalina looked down at the plane from the dive platform. It was clearly visible about fifty feet below. The wreck sat upright. The wings were still intact, as was the tail, and two blades of the propeller were still fixed to the nose of the plane. She found it hard to believe that it'd been a crash landing. It looked more like it'd been carefully lowered into position on purpose.

"Looks fantastic," Archer said. "Can't wait to get down there and check it out."

"It doesn't look like it crashed at all."

"I agree. Ready for your gear?"

She nodded and as Archer lifted it with ease, she leaned forward, ready to counteract the weight of her air tank. Shouts in the distance made her look out across the water. Three children paddled towards them in a small wooden canoe. Their golden curly hair was a dramatic contrast to their dark chocolate-colored skin. Their broad smiles captured her interest the most though. Each of them looked blissfully happy.

"Hey fellas," Archer called out to them as he helped Rosalina clip her buoyancy vest into place.

"Hey mister. You diving down to the plane?"

Archer winked at Rosalina as he did the last clip, then he turned and smiled at the boys. "Sure am."

The kids paddled right up to the yacht, and all three of them reached out and clung onto the dive deck. "Need some help?" The boy who spoke had a wild frizzy mop of blond curls.

"No thanks, buddy, we'll be fine."

Archer turned his attention back to her. "You ready?"

She inflated her buoyancy vest, put her regulator into her mouth and inhaled, ensuring her air was working. "I'm good."

He glanced over her shoulder. "Ginger, are you ready?"

Ginger's fins slapped onto the deck as she waddled up to them with gangling strides. "Sure am."

Archer kissed Rosalina on the cheek. "Look out, boys," Archer said to the kids, "The ladies are about to jump in."

The boys pushed their canoe back as far as they could without releasing their hold on the yacht.

Rosalina nodded at Ginger and the two of them jumped off the deck into the water. They promptly bobbed to the surface, and as she gave the 'all clear' signal to Archer, Helen made her way down the steps to the dive platform. This was the first time Rosalina had seen her down there.

Rosalina had thought Helen wouldn't want to see them scuba dive, because surely, it'd remind her of how her husband had died. But Helen didn't look distressed at all; she actually looked thrilled to be there.

Archer jumped when he saw his mother beside him. "Hey Mom, you're awake. We're about to dive down to that plane; here, have a look." Archer hooked his arm beneath his mother's elbow, guided her to the edge of the dive platform and pointed into the water.

"Oh." Rosalina barely heard Helen's voice.

"Will you be okay here with Alessandro?"

Alessandro stepped up. "Of course she will be."

The three boys started singing and tapping out a rhythm on the side of their canoe and to Rosalina's amazement, Helen clapped along with them. Her hips moved too. Archer turned to Rosalina and thumbed at his mother; the grin on his face was pure elation.

Archer kissed his mom on her forehead. "See you in about forty minutes, Mom."

"Be careful," Helen said.

Archer and Jimmy jumped in together and then the four of them glided beneath the surface. The water was crystal clear, blue as far as Rosalina could see. Archer's bubbles drifted up over her as he led the way to the plane. The wreck had turned into a beautiful underwater museum. Every part of the metal was covered in colorful coral and plant life. Green, yellow and purple dominated. Small blue and black fish darted in and out of the metal garden.

Rosalina lowered to the sand at the front of the plane while the men swam straight to the tail fin. Using her beloved underwater camera, she took a series of photos, ensuring she captured the length of the plane in the shot. Only two blades remained on the propeller; the third had most likely snapped off in the crash. Nestled at the center of the two blades was a clam, and she giggled when the shell snapped shut at her slight touch.

Ginger, hovering over the center of the plane, waved Rosalina over, and when she began removing her fins Rosalina knew what she was planning to do. As Rosalina clung onto Ginger fins, Ginger eased herself into the plane's cockpit. It was a bit of a wriggle with the tank on her back but she made it, and then she grinned at Rosalina like a little kid. Rosalina took several photographs and after a series of hand signals, Rosalina realized Ginger wanted her to get the men. She did, and soon they all chuckled as they watched Ginger pretend to drive the plane as if it were a car.

After a few more photos, Rosalina turned her attention to the back of the plane. Every inch of the metal was covered in coral, and it was immediately apparent that it'd be impossible to find any identifying marks on the tail fin. Without that, she had no idea where they were going to go from there.

Rosalina jabbed at a few more clams and they snapped shut at her touch. Archer arrived at her side and gave her the thumbs down signal, confirming her assumption. She shrugged in response, and then took a photo of Archer. He removed his regulator to poke his tongue at her, and she photographed that too.

He indicated 'boat' with his hands and she agreed. They swam over to Jimmy and Ginger and then the four of them pushed off the sand and rose to fifteen feet below the surface. As fish of all colors and sizes dodged around them, Rosalina glanced down at the wreck and snapped a few more photos. She wondered if the pilot had survived the crash. The wreck seemed intact enough for that to be possible. The surface was only fifty feet away, and in addition, land also was within swimming distance. The nearest island was only one hundred or so yards from the wreck. Not too far for someone to swim, provided they didn't have any injuries, that was.

As a group, they glided to the surface, and the instant Rosalina was in the fresh air she heard children laughing. She looked over at the yacht and saw Alessandro and the kids all glistening wet.

"There they are." Helen pointed at them.

"Watch this." One of the boys yelled out and then all four of them, including Alessandro, ran across the dive deck and jumped into the water.

"Looks like you've been having fun, Mom," Archer said as he tossed his fins onto the deck.

"These boys are delightful. So much energy." She beamed.

Rosalina removed her buoyancy vest, floated it to Archer and he pushed it up onto the deck. She unclipped her fins and climbed up the ladder as the kids and Alessandro swam around to join them.

"Did you find anything?" Alessandro said, as he waited for his turn to climb up out of the water.

"No, it's covered in coral."

"What you looking for?" The same boy who'd spoken earlier asked the question. His wet curls dangled in his face and he shoved them from his eyes.

Archer lowered onto one knee so he was eye level with the kid. "We were hoping to find some writing on the plane, so we could identify it."

"Why?"

Archer stood and ruffled the boy's curls. "It's a long story, buddy."

"You should ask Barney."

Archer lowered down again and cocked his head at the boy. "Who's Barney?"

"He collects things. He knows everything about the stuff that went on in the war. We'll take you to him."

"Yeah, we'll take you." The other two boys joined in.

Archer looked at Rosalina and she shrugged. "Might as well."

"Let's go now, boss." Jimmy scratched at his graying chest hairs.

"All right boys, how about you tie your boat to us and we'll get down our boat." Archer pointed up at the crane on the sun deck.

"Yeah, yeah." The boys jumped up and down with abundant energy.

Within twenty minutes, Rosalina, Archer, Jimmy and the three boys were crammed into the tender and heading towards a jetty jutting out from the shore. The boys chatted the whole way, and it was obvious they'd never been taught stranger-danger warnings. The outspoken boy was Abraham, the other two were George and Samson.

At the jetty, Jimmy tied up the boat and then the smallest of the three boys, Samson, grabbed Rosalina's hand.

"Come on." He tugged her along the rickety planks.

She glanced behind her and burst out laughing at both Archer and Jimmy being dragged along by a boy each too. They stepped onto the sand and walked past several thatched huts on stilts. The thatch work was held together by strips of wood, giving the walls a pillowed effect. Rosalina couldn't see any windows or doors and assumed they were on the other side.

Soft sand gave way to thick grass and within minutes they were walking along a narrow path through dense jungle. The escalating temperature smothered her more with every step she took. Giant leaves as wide as elephant ears brushed at her shoulders, and thick vines that wove from one tree to another threatened to take her head off if she didn't watch where she was going.

"Are you sure this is the right way?" she asked Samson.

"Yep. It's not far." He stepped on jagged rocks and slippery tree roots in his bare feet with unerring certainty.

"How do you know Barney?"

"Everybody knows Barney. He pays us to bring him stuff we find."

"What kind of stuff?"

He shrugged. "Oh, you know, guns, helmets, knives. . . anything from the war."

Rosalina gasped. "Do you still find things?" She glanced about the jungle around her.

"All the time. The war was big here, you know."

"Archer?" She didn't want to look over her shoulder for the risk of falling over.

"I'm here." He sounded like he was right behind her.

"I think we're going to the jungle museum your mom talked about."

"I think you're right."

"Peter Joseph's WW2 museum, yes." The way Samson said it, Rosalina wondered if he knew what the W's stood for.

"I thought you said his name was Barney."

"It is." Samson giggled and she chuckled along with him.

Once again, a twist of fate was showing them the way.

The path reached a dirt road and they spread out to walk in a line. Jimmy hoisted George up onto his shoulders and the kid squealed like he was on a rollercoaster ride. Archer, of course, had to do the same for Abraham.

Rosalina wiped the sweat from her forehead as they stepped off the dirt road and onto a driveway that was just two tire tracks that stretched as far as she could see.

"See his tank?" Samson pointed towards the trees.

Her jaw dropped. In amongst the vegetation, covered in leaves and vines, was an army tank. A white fungus had made the metal its home and the tank was an interesting medley of furry white and gunmetal gray. The gun barrel was tilted downward to the side as if it were bowing out.

"It's hard to believe they left something like that behind," Rosalina said to no one in particular.

The driveway seemed to go on forever, and it was an eternity before they finally stepped into a clearing. In the far reach of the grassy expanse was a wooden home. It was a significant building compared to the other shacks they'd passed to get here. The wrap-around veranda, decked out with an abundance of furniture and other bits and pieces, looked like it received plenty of use.

"Here's the museum," Samson announced. The building at their left was a ramshackle hut with all manner of rusted war paraphernalia scattered around it. Samson dropped her hand and skipped to a row of fence posts topped with war helmets. He picked one up and stuck his finger through a hole in the front.

"See the bullet hole?" Grinning, he put the helmet on his head and rapped his knuckles upon it.

Rosalina walked to the front of the shed and scanned the collection. There was everything from weapons to personal items. She ran her fingers over an assortment of dog tags tied together with a metal chain. They jingled under her touch. She saw a pair of eye glasses with one of the lenses smashed, little pill boxes, and old-fashioned Coke bottles. At eye level was a selection of knives: cooking knives, pocket knives, machetes and rifles with knives protruding from the ends of the barrels. Her heart nearly stopped at the row of grenades nestled in a wooden ammunition box.

"Is Barney here?" Archer asked.

"We'll go get him." The boys giggled as they ran towards the house in the distance.

"This had to be where Dad went, don't you think?"

"I think so," she said. "Look at this stuff. There's so much here. Samson told me they find it out in the jungle and Barney pays them for it."

Archer picked up the collection of dog tags and flicked through them like they were a pack of cards. "Japanese, American, Australian."

The boys appeared again. "He's coming."

Archer ruffled Samson's blond curls. "Thanks, mate."

Rosalina spied a large glass cabinet and eased her way through the bits and pieces to get to it. The glass was covered in fingerprints. Inside was a huge collection of coins with both Japanese and English writing. "Hey look, Archer," she said. "Buttons." The entire top row of the cabinet was filled with buttons of all shapes, metals and sizes.

"Halo."

Rosalina turned to the deep voice and was greeted by a shirtless man with coffee-colored leathery skin. Most of his curly hair, as dark as his eyes, was contained in a Nike baseball cap.

"Hello." Archer offered his hand and the man took it with a smile. "I'm Archer. Are you Barney?"

"Yes, I am. What would you like to know?"

"You have quite a collection here. The kids said it was all found in the jungle."

"Correct. And on the beaches. Some in the water, too. It's everywhere still, even after sixty years."

"Hi, I'm Rosalina." She stepped forward and offered her hand. Barney gripped it within his calloused fingers and tapped his other palm on the back of her hand. "Why did you call this the Peter Joseph Museum?"

"I named it after the first dog tag I found. Mr. Peter Joseph Palatini, American soldier."

She nodded, acknowledging how respectful that was.

"There are so many things here," she said wistfully.

"They fought on this island for three years; over 38,000 people died. This battle was one of the turning points of the war because the Japanese retreated."

Rosalina covered her mouth at the horror of it.

"They abandoned nearly everything when it was over." Barney removed his cap, wiped sweat from his forehead and placed his hat back in place. "Do you know much about the war here?"

"Not really," Archer said. "But we'd love to know more."

"It'll cost you." Barney's cheesy grin lit up his whole face.

"Sure, how much?"

Barney waved his hand. "I don't want your money. How about you join me for a drink on the deck? I was just about to have one."

Archer's eyes dashed to hers and Rosalina nodded. "We'd love to, but we didn't bring anything."

He shrugged. "That's okay; if you give Samson some money, he can buy a few drinks."

Rosalina wanted to object that Samson was way too young to be purchasing liquor, but by the look that crossed between Samson and Barney this was an arrangement they'd had many times over.

Archer fished out a bundle of notes that he'd taken from the ATM machine when they'd first arrived at the port and handed a few notes to Samson. "Buy yourself a chocolate while you're there, and some for George and Abraham too."

"Gee, thanks." The boys dashed off giggling, and Barney turned and walked towards what Rosalina assumed was his home.

"Come on, Jimmy."

Rosalina looked over at Jimmy. He was investigating an enormous gun that was elevated above the ground by a three-pronged frame.

"Where we goin'?" Jimmy said.

"It's beer time."

"Right." Jimmy dropped his hands to his sides and strode forward. He caught up with them in no time.

"Excuse the mess." Barney directed them past the front door and straight onto the veranda. He indicated to a long wooden table and two bench chairs. "Sit. I'll be back in a sec." Barney disappeared through a doorway

Rosalina tried to make herself comfortable on the hard bench seat that looked to have been homemade with a chainsaw, hammer and nails. Barney returned with a pail containing four beers and a bowl of brown nuts.

"You're in luck; I had four beers left. The boys won't be long though." Barney opened the first beer.

"Thank you." Rosalina accepted the first beer he handed to her and Barney opened the remaining three beers and handed one to each of the men.

Barney sat opposite her and pointed the open bottle at her before he took a long swig.

Their conversation was easy, Barney had a lovely welcoming way about him, and every one of their questions was answered with Barney's own twist on the story.

"We dived on the plane wreck out in the lagoon today."

"The Kawasaki Ki-56."

"Yes, that one. It's in excellent condition, considering it crashed."

"The plan was hit with a round of bullets. But after he was hit, the pilot tried to limp back to the airstrip, so he was fairly low when it actually struck the water."

Archer's eyebrows shot up. "Did he survive?"

"Sure did."

Rosalina sat forward and put her elbows on the table. "What happened to him?"

"Not sure what happened to him after that."

The kids returned with beer and a block of fruit-and-nut chocolate, and by the amount of chocolate over their faces they'd devoured at least one of their own chocolate blocks on their journey back. Samson presented his shopping purchases and handed the change to Archer.

"You can keep it, buddy."

The boy's eyes bulged. "Really?"

"Sure, you've been a great help."

"Gee, thanks." Samson squealed and ran off with his two friends chasing after him.

Archer pushed the beers towards Barney. "We heard there was a tuna boat that was hit by a bouncing bomb near the end of the war."

"Yes, it's off the main port. The position she's in made her too hard to salvage. Not that anyone would, I suppose. She'd been in port for the day to offload the cargo and was due to go again the next day when she was hit, so there was nothing on-board worth salvaging anyway. She's probably got a hole in her the size of a tank. Lucky she only had a skeleton crew on board when she was hit; no one survived." He cocked his head. "Why you interested in that old rust bucket, anyway?" Barney finished off his beer and reached for one of Archer's.

Archer shrugged, and when he drank from his beer, Rosalina knew he was stalling until he'd formed his answer.

"We heard it was in really close to the shore and thought it might be excellent diving." Rosalina gave Barney a lingering smile.

He waved his hand. "You're getting it mixed up with the Kari Maru. It's farther away, north side of New Georgia. It's a Japanese freighter that was also hit with a bouncing bomb. That one listed sideways and sits in about fifty feet of water. It's really beaut diving. Covered in clams. The tuna boat though, it's sitting up on its tail like a rearing horse." He stiffened his hand and pointed his fingers at the table, demonstrating the boat's position in the water.

"I'm so glad we asked you." Rosalina took a timid sip of the bitter liquid.

"Ask me anything, I've been here my whole life. Know this place like I know the smells of my mama's cooking."

Rosalina giggled at that. She felt exactly the same with her Nonna's meals.

It was only once they'd finished all the beer that Archer readied to move. "We better get going." He eased his legs over the side of the bench seat. "Thanks for the chat." Archer tucked a few dollars beneath the ice pail and Barney looked away as if embarrassed.

"Drop in anytime, I'll be here." He reached across the table and shook hands with Rosalina, then Archer, then Jimmy.

Jimmy led the way across the clearing, and as soon as they reached the museum hut the three boys appeared again.

Samson slipped in to take Rosalina's hand. "We'll show you the way back."

"Thank you."

"Did you have fun looking at all the war stuff?"

"I did. There's so much there."

"Japanese are crazy."

Rosalina resisted a laugh. "Why do you say that?"

Samson shrugged. "That's what Mama says. Keep away from crazy Japanese man."

She did laugh at that. "Why does your mom think the Japanese are crazy?"

"Not all the Japanese," said Abraham. "Just the crazy Japanese man on Headhunter Island."

Puzzled, Rosalina looked at him to see if he was kidding. It was hard to tell; a cheeky grin was permanently etched on his face. "There's an island called Headhunter Island?"

"Yes, you can see it from our place. He has skulls there."

Archer spun around. "What did you say?"

"He does. That's what Mama says, anyway."

"Sounds fascinating," Rosalina felt the need to protect the boy from Archer's leering. "You'll have to show us the island."

"Sure." Samson let go of her hand and skipped ahead.

"You don't really think it's the Peking Man skulls, do you, Arch?" She stifled a giggle.

"Don't laugh. Any Japanese man rumored to be holding skulls would pique my interest."

Chapter Thirty-Six

J immy was in a hurry and Archer agreed with his impatience. It was like the taste of gold was right on the tip of his tongue. All the clues were beginning to add up. As soon as they pushed the three boys off in their little canoe, they informed Helen, Ginger and Alessandro of what they'd discovered.

"Do you really think the Japanese guy could be Hiro or Kimoda? That would make them. . . how old?" Ginger rolled her eyes to the ceiling as if it would help her calculate.

"He'd be at least ninety years old," Alessandro finished.

Archer held his hands apart. "It's not impossible."

"It would be a miracle," Rosalina volunteered.

Archer clasped the gold pendant around his neck. "Remember when my pendant opened up the secret compartment in that tomb? You said that was a miracle, too."

The silence hummed between them.

"I told you, Rosa, we are this close." He held his fingers an inch apart. Her eyes met his and by the look of her, she was a long way off convincing.

"Alessandro." The Italian's eyes darted from Ginger to him. "I need you to find out everything you can about the Ranga Spirit. Type of ship. Size. Weight. Pictures or diagrams. Anything."

"Okay. Why? What's going on?"

"Jimmy and I are diving it tonight, and the more information we have the better."

"What do you want me to do?" Ginger sat forward on her seat.

"Food please. 'Cause I don't know about you lot, but I'm starving."

Rosalina frowned at him, obviously wondering why he didn't ask her to cook. "Babe, I need you to help me get the dive gear ready while Jimmy cruises *Evangeline* over near the Ranga Spirit wreck."

"And me?" Helen said in the meekest of voices. "What shall I do?"

Archer masked his surprise by touching his mother's forearm. "Do you think you could go through Dad's cryptic notebooks? We're looking for any clues that would help with either the Ranga Spirit, the Awa Maru treasure or the Peking Man skulls."

Helen nodded. "I can do that."

Archer reached for Rosalina's hand and they made their way towards the dive deck. The sun was setting, and the sky had changed to an interesting dappled orange and mauve. As *Evangeline*'s engines rumbled to life, Archer unlocked the dive gear cupboard.

"Arch?" The tentativeness in Rosalina's voice was unmistakable.

"Yeah, babe?" He tugged his and Jimmy's fins from their hooks and handed them back to her.

"Are you going to penetrate the Ranga Spirit?"

He hooked Jimmy's tank up to the air compressor and turned it on. "Don't worry. We'll be fine." When the tank was full, he closed the valve and wrestled Jimmy's tank to beside Rosalina. "Jimmy and I have done heaps of wreck diving."

"None that have been bombed. You don't know how unstable it is."

"Honey, it's been sitting stable for decades. I think if anything was going to move, it would have by now." He stepped back into the cupboard and repeated the air-filling process with his own tank.

"You think there'll be treasure hidden somewhere in that thing, don't you?"

"Wouldn't that be nice?"

"This is serious, Arch. You're risking your life when there could be nothing but fifty-year-old tuna cans on board."

He manhandled his tank to beside Jimmy's and turned to her. He caught anger, resignation and maybe a touch of fear in her eyes. "What's wrong, babe?"

She lowered her lashes, and when she chewed on her lip, he knew there was something she wasn't telling him.

"Is Filippo okay?"

She blinked up at him in a way that made him believe that whatever was troubling her was a long way from Filippo. "He's fine. I just. . ." She sighed. "I need you to be safe."

He wrapped his arms around her and tugged her to his chest. "It'll be okay. Jimmy and I will go in to poke around a bit and then we'll be back up in time for dessert. Why don't you make us something yummy to have on the top deck afterwards?" Archer had learned a long time ago that cooking was Rosalina's form of therapy, and he thanked his lucky stars for that often.

Jimmy had them anchored off Munda wharf and as the sun glided into the distant ocean, the wharf lights came on and lit up the surrounding waters.

"Tell us what you've got, Alex." Archer leaned forward to bite into the homemade hamburger Ginger had made for dinner and a slice of beet slipped out and slapped onto his plate. He tried to ignore Rosalina smirking at him. Archer had yet to eat a burger without losing half the contents. It was a little joke between them.

Alessandro swallowed as he put his burger down and wiped his fingers on his napkin. He tapped a button on his laptop, positioned in front of him. "The Ranga Spirit is a hundred and ten-foot tuna fishing boat. The superstructure that contains the wheelhouse and accommodation is mid-ship."

Archer imagined the positioning of the superstructure in his mind as he took another bite of his burger.

"It arrived on shore on the morning of the 16th of May 1945, and the catch from the night before had all been unloaded when the boat was hit by a bouncing bomb in a completely unexpected raid by an American bomber. The bomb hit the hull below the wheelhouse, blasting a significant hole in the side. *Per fortuna*, there were only three people on board at the time, however they all perished in the incident."

"I wonder if either of the Yukimura brothers were amongst them," Archer said.

"No names were listed in the details I perused."

"Okay," Archer said. "What else have you got?"

"The boat sunk in seconds and slipped backwards. It's perched with the bow facing upwards just three feet below the surface. The stern sits on a narrow coral ledge; beyond that is a sheer drop-off."

Archer swallowed the last bite of his burger and wiped his fingers on a napkin. "So, if it's sitting upright like this." Archer demonstrated by pretending his hand was the tuna boat. He placed his wrist on the table and pointed his fingers upward. "Then the superstructure is say, here." He pointed at his knuckles. "This would mean it's at a depth of about sixty feet." That was good news. They had enough to worry about with the wreck itself without worrying about its depth.

"Did anyone try to salvage it?" Jimmy asked.

"It appears no salvage was ever attempted. It sunk near the end of the war and as you know, they left hundreds of boats and planes out there in the ocean. That's why this area has become a diving mecca." Alessandro dabbed his lips with his napkin. "Although, the Ranga Spirit isn't a popular dive site because the water is constantly stirred up by all the boats coming and going from the wharf."

Archer felt Rosalina's eyes on him. "Excellent. That means we'll have no company. Right, Jimmy?"

"Right," Jimmy said with a mouthful.

"I think I should come with you," Rosalina said. But the look on her face said exactly the opposite. And that was a dangerous way to dive.

"No need, honey. The two of us will be quicker."

Her shoulders sagged. "Okay."

She conceded quickly. Way too quickly. Rosalina was normally very stubborn.

After the meal, they left the table the way it was and went to the dive deck where the equipment was set up and ready to go.

"Ready, buddy?" Archer said to Jimmy.

Jimmy belched. "Yep." The big fella's eyes glinted in the distant wharf lights.

"No hero stuff down there. We've got no idea what to expect, so we stick together."

"Sure thing, boss."

Once they were geared up and ready to go, Archer turned to Rosalina. "Don't worry, babe. We'll be back in seventy minutes and not a moment later."

"You better be, or I'll go looking for you." She handed him his high-powered flashlight, and he brushed his lips to hers.

"Back soon." He shuffled to the edge of the deck so his fins dangled over. Jimmy joined him and they slipped into the water together.

They descended and kicked forward at the same time but closing the distance from *Evangeline* to the Ranga Spirit took some effort as the current was full on. They'd anchored downstream and knew the push to the wreck would be a tough one. Returning to *Evangeline*, though, would be a breeze.

Unlike the dive to the plane wreck earlier today, the visibility here was like swimming in slime that'd been stirred up with a blender. The water was swamp green, and all sorts of crap swirled before his flashlight beam. Archer retained his focus on his compass; it was pointless to look anywhere else. He assumed Jimmy was doing the same, because he couldn't see him even if he wanted to.

The water cleared marginally and the bow of the Ranga Spirit finally materialized out of the murkiness. Giant red plate coral had made the ship's hull its home, giving a splash of color to the green marine growth covering the metal skeleton. His flashlight beam caught the gaping wound in the ship's side. Barney's comment about the hole being the size of a tank was an understatement. The Ranga Spirit would've had no chance against a bomb blast like that. It was just lucky that she snagged on the coral shelf when she did, or she would've shot straight to the bottom of the ocean.

Jimmy pointed at the hole, and Archer gave him an okay signal. Penetrating through that massive hole was the obvious entry. His breathing was slow and steady, and he concentrated on the therapeutic sound as he approached the wrecked hull.

At the threshold, they paused. Archer played his flashlight around the mangled space. It was a mess of metal, giant poles, small poles, broken wiring, and other bits and pieces he couldn't decipher. Hundreds of fish had made the Ranga Spirit their home, as did many crabs, and several eels that slithered amongst the piles of junk.

His flashlight lit up a ladder at one end and a square manhole at the other. Archer pointed at the manhole and Jimmy nodded. The surfaces were covered in decades of silt, and the trick was to move smoothly without stirring it up any more than it already was. Archer hoped once they progressed beyond this open area the visibility would clear.

He pushed off and checked his dive watch; ten minutes had passed already.

The flashlight beam lit up a lone boot with the laces still intact. Archer's mind pictured them belonging to one of the Yukimura brothers. It was a ridiculous thought and highlighted just how desperate he was to be onto something.

Forcing the dreaming aside, he glided through the manhole into another much smaller room. He shoved a shredded collection of wires aside to pass through, making sure his tank didn't snag. Archer hung onto a piece of metal with his gloved hand and helped Jimmy through the wires. With Jimmy in the lead, they continued to descend down through the body of the ship.

The first room they entered was the control room. Two giant steering wheels were still fixed in position. Wires and tubes dangled in amongst hundreds of knobs, dials, valves and switches that covered an entire console. It was actually well preserved, considering how quickly it would've sunk and how long it'd been submerged.

They moved on from that room in search of the captain's quarters. It shouldn't be too hard. A ship like this was built for cargo, not passengers. Along a narrow corridor, they stopped at the first door, and Archer pushed it open slowly so as not to stir up the water. The angle of the ship meant the weight of the door forced it to close onto him. He passed through and held it open for Jimmy. Once his buddy was inside, he eased the door shut behind him.

Everything in the room had tumbled to the lowest point when the ship fell backwards. His flashlight highlighted a metal bedframe, an upturned table, what was left of a chair, and an old-fashioned phone with a handset on a cord and a ring dial. A mirror inlaid on a cupboard door was still intact, and an orange fungus had made the glass its home. Other than that, there was barely any other coral, plant or animal life in this room. The closed door had ensured the room's significant preservation.

Not seeing anything of interest, and not entirely sure what he was looking for, Archer decided he'd seen enough and tapped Jimmy on his shoulder. He wriggled his hand to indicate 'swim' and Jimmy nodded agreement.

They passed back through the door and swam along the pipe-lined corridor to the next room. The word "Captain" on the door made his heart thump in his ears. Again, they had to fight gravity to get into the room. With the door shut behind them, they scanned the space with their flashlights.

It was a much larger room than the last. A series of small cupboards that once contained glass doors ran the length of the opposite wall and were now vertical rather than horizontal. The glass shards and everything that'd been inside the cupboards were now piled up at the lowest end. Archer eased over to the jumbled mess, and his eyes fell on a small tuna can. It was a colorful mix of dark gray, silver and orange, and some of the label was still adhered to the middle. Amused, he picked it up to show Jimmy, and shook it. He couldn't believe his ears. The can jingled. His eyes bulged. Jimmy's eyes bulged.

"Holy shit!" Jimmy's voice was hardly muffled, even through the regulator.

Archer braced himself on the debris and unclipped his dive knife from his ankle, and Jimmy shone his flashlight on the can. With the tip of his blade aimed at the rim of the can, Archer hammered the butt of his knife with his palm. The knife sliced through the metal, and as he worked it around the rim, he had to force himself to breath.

Finally, he peeled back the lid. Light, color and fire burst from the can. A heavenly aura had been released. Archer could barely breathe as he twirled diamonds around with his gloved finger. His heart thundered in his ears. Jimmy's 'woohoo' did too. Never in a million years could he have predicted this. He handed the can to Jimmy and could've sworn Jimmy had tears in his eyes when he reached for it.

Chapter Thirty-Seven

Rosalina stopped twisting her engagement ring around her finger to check her watch for what seemed like the hundredth time. Finally, a series of bubbles burst on the surface of the water and looked over the side. The churning in her stomach settled when two flashlight beams rose towards the surface.

Archer spat his regulator out. "Holy shit, babe, you won't believe it." He tossed his fins onto the deck.

"We're fucking rich." Jimmy slapped the water with his hand. "Sorry, Rosa."

"What?" she squealed. "What?"

Alessandro and Ginger arrived at her side as Archer handed something to her. "Here." Archer passed his flashlight up. "Careful."

She shone light into the can and gasped as glittering stars bounced back at her.

"Diamonds," Ginger squealed. "Are they really diamonds?"

"I reckon they are, sweetheart." Jimmy tossed his fins up.

Archer climbed the ladder and wrapped his wet body around Rosalina and squeezed. "There's probably more down there too." He kissed her neck. "This calls for a celebration." Archer peeled out of his wetsuit.

"What you doin', man?" Jimmy huffed. "We're going back down."

Archer turned to Jimmy and put his hand on his shoulder. "No we're not, mate. We've done our quota of dives for today. You know we can't do anymore."

"But we know where to go."

"Exactly. And it will still be there tomorrow night."

Jimmy was a caged animal, furling and unfurling his fists. "Tomorrow night! What the fuck? I ain't waitin' that long."

"Jimmy. Listen to me. We're not diving any more tonight and we can't dive during the day while there's ferries and all sorts of boats passing along this channel. We'll spend tomorrow chilling out so we can do two dives once the sun goes down. Got it?"

Rosalina loved that Archer was at least thinking straight.

Jimmy threw his hands in the air. "You sure know how to ruin a man's party."

Archer slapped Jimmy's shoulder. "Oh, we're still going to party. Right ladies?"

"Sure are." Rosalina squeezed his hand.

"Come on, let's check these babies out."

At the dining table, Archer spilled the diamonds onto a white dinner plate. They tinkled from the corroded can onto the china, casting radiant color and light as they reflected the lights of the saloon. The diamonds were all brilliant cut and of similar sizes. Fire blazed from each one, casting hundreds of stars onto the ceiling.

Alessandro counted thirty-one diamonds.

"I bet there are hundreds more down there." Jimmy sounded like a proud leader before his hundred-strong army. His fingers, thick as Cuban cigars, twirled the jewels around the plate.

"I reckon you're right." Archer clapped his mate on his shoulder, and Rosalina saw the emotion that passed between them. It was moments like these that almost made up for all the horror. Almost.

Archer shuffled the diamonds into a drastically inadequate Tupperware dish. "I'll put these in the safe. Then I'm showering, so let's meet at the bar in ten minutes."

"Roger that." Jimmy's eyes were trained on the Tupperware, as if reluctant to miss a single second of the spectacle.

"We'll get the drinks ready." Ginger and Alessandro scooted towards the stairs.

"I'll try to call Filippo. Tell him the good news," Rosalina said.

"Okay, babe." Archer draped his arm over her shoulders. "Tell him about the diamonds, but don't tell him we're looking for more."

She frowned up at him. "Why?"

"Because the less he knows, the better. You never know what information Nox is getting out of him."

As she nodded, she pictured Nox kicking her brother.

"And don't tell him that we're heading back yet. He doesn't need to know that we're flying there. We'll keep that little surprise up our sleeve."

She blinked at him, trying to process what he'd said.

He cupped his hand to her chin. "It'll take too long to cruise back, so I'll hire a private plane to take us to Italy as soon as possible."

Her heart skipped a beat. "Oh Archer, really?"

"Sure." He carried the diamonds like a hard-fought trophy as they walked towards his office. "It'll be easier to get the diamonds back with a private plane too."

"Thank you." She managed a quick kiss on his cheek mid-stride. "Love you."

"Love you, too." He opened the door and went to the safe. She watched him place the jewels on the top shelf and close the door again. "I'll see you upstairs soon."

"Okay." Rosalina picked up the phone and dialed Filippo. The phone eventually rang out and she waited. Moments later, the phone rang from a number she didn't recognize and Nox's voice grounded out a hello. "Put Filippo on."

"Hello Rosalina." The sound of his voice was a rasp up her back.

"Put Filippo on," she repeated. It was a process she went through with every call.

"Hi Rosa." Filippo's weary voice broke her heart open.

"Hey. How are you going?"

"I'm okay."

She knew Filippo was putting on a brave front. Nox was a monster, capable of despicable things. She could vividly imagine what horrors Filippo was experiencing every day. "We've found the diamonds," she said, eager to brighten his day.

His breath hitched. "Already. How many?"

"Thirty-one.

"Thirty-one! Where'd you find them?"

She told him all about their lucky meeting with the three kids who'd introduced them to Barney. The more she spoke, the more he seemed to rise from the gloom that'd gripped him when he'd first answered the phone. She described in detail how they'd worked out Wade's notes and followed the clues to the Ranga Spirit.

By the time she'd finished with Filippo, she was floating on air as she made her way to the galley. Everything would be back to normal very soon.

Laughter drifted down from the sundeck as she transferred the dessert ingredients onto a tray and carried them to the upper deck. The men had already started their little party. Jimmy was in his customary position behind the bar as he and Archer told blow-by-blow descriptions of their dive on the Ranga Spirit.

Rosalina nestled the foil-wrapped crepes she'd cooked earlier on the corner of the barbeque plate to retain warmth while she prepared the citrus sauce. She added the orange zest and juice to the butter and sugar mix in the pan and set it to simmer. "Honey, can I have the Cointreau and brandy please?"

Archer slipped off his bar stool, and when he turned to walk towards her, the lightness in his step was unmistakable. He was still riding the high that was treasure hunting. It was in his bones. He lived for these exact moments of unearthing a slice of history from its hiding place. She herself had felt the thrill of holding something that hadn't felt a human touch in centuries. It occurred to her that having a baby may offer the same elation. The thought tumbled from nowhere, and she quickly cast it aside before it consumed her.

"So, what're we doing tomorrow?" Ginger flicked her ponytail around her hand.

"I'm going to organize a private charter plane," Archer said. "But other than that, nothing."

"We could talk to that crazy Japanese guy." Ginger shrugged. "See if he knows anything."

"Because," Alessandro said, "in addition to the diamonds, there were other precious items on the Awa Maru yet to be found."

"Remember, I speak Japanese," Ginger chimed in. The two of them bounced the idea between them like a practiced debate.

Archer turned to Rosalina and cocked his head, seeking her thoughts. His cheeky grin told her he was already keen on the idea.

Rosalina flicked her hand. "Sure, why not?"

It was past ten o'clock when Rosalina leaned into Archer's ear. "Want to meet me in the bedroom in ten minutes?"

"Sure." He squeezed her knee and tried but failed to wipe the smile from his face.

Rosalina stood. "Good night, everyone."

It had been a long time since she'd felt this relaxed. All the tension of the last four weeks had evaporated as soon as she'd told Filippo she was coming home. The relief had been instant. She tugged her hair into a knot on her head and showered quickly. Stepping from the shower, she towel-dried, applied her favorite moisturizer and brushed her teeth. Glancing at the door, she hoped Archer didn't ruin her surprise by entering early.

She opened her bottom drawer, removed a flat box she'd placed in there months ago, tugged on the silver ribbon and cast it aside to lift the lid. The full-length white satin negligee was decorated with sheer lace and studded with dozens of diamantes. . . a perfect choice after today's success.

She slipped it over her head, relishing the feel of the silky fabric against her skin. Underwear wasn't necessary; she imagined it would be off in a flash anyway. As she adjusted the spaghetti straps on her shoulder, she slipped into silver six-inch heels. Juggling the shoes on the plush carpet, she raced to her dresser and fished out the diamond necklace Archer had bought her for her twenty-seventh birthday. The exquisite piece should be kept in the safe, but she couldn't bear to keep such lovely jewelry locked up. She raised the lid on the red velvet box and sighed at its beauty.

Lifting the necklace from the box, she took a brief moment to admire the unique pear-shaped diamond. She clipped it around her neck and then positioned herself at the end of the bed, ready for Archer's entrance. Rosalina leaned back, placing her hand on the duvet cover, crossed her legs and twirled her engagement ring around her finger. As she kicked her stiletto casually back and forward, a wave of pleasure rippled through her.

Everything was perfect.

When Archer opened the door, perfect became a dizzy cloud that consumed her mind and body. His cheeks dimpled as he released a slow whistle and peeled off his clothes as he strode towards her. Desire turned his eyes to fire. She rolled her tongue over her lips as a wave of heat caressed her body, warming everything from her heart to her loins. His fingers were a feather-light touch as he cupped under her chin and raised her face to him. He bent down, and as their lips met, he glided his hand around the back of her neck, teasing her skin to life.

He lowered her left strap and trailed soft kisses down her neck and over her shoulder. She slipped into another glorious world. The weight of the diamantes had the satin fall off her shoulder to reveal her breast. He lifted the satin negligee up over her head and tossed it onto the pillow, and with his hand behind her neck, Archer eased her back onto the bed and suckled her nipple. The delicate strokes of his tongue were delicious torture.

His hand glided up her thigh, igniting blazes of desire, and she threaded her hands over his back, kneading every defined muscle beneath his skin. He spread her legs open and she relaxed even more, welcoming his touch. She met Archer's eyes and adored the love she saw in them. He slipped his fingers into her, and her vision shifted from his eyes to the stars as she crested one heavenly wave after another.

One second her body quivered to sensory overload, then it imploded in a release of sensitive firecrackers that melted every part of her being. The pleasure was so acute. So hot. So wonderful.

She arched her back so he could taste her. As she clawed at the satin sheets, he made her body sing over and over. She heard a moan and couldn't decide if it was Archer or herself. He lifted her hips and glided into her. She clutched him there and scraped his back as he took her body the brink of the world. The lovely motions had another climax shimmering through her like glittering diamonds.

ROSALINA WOKE TO THE SUN ON HER FACE. NEITHER OF THEM HAD thought to close the window shade before they'd drifted off to sleep in each other's arms. Archer was facing her, but his slow and steady breathing confirmed he was still fast asleep. Certain she'd wake him; she chose not to move. Instead, she studied the man she loved.

They'd showered after their love-making last night and the faint smell of his soap lingered. The deep, smoky, earthy aroma was from the handmade soap he'd purchased called Shipwreck Soap. His motivation for buying it was no doubt because of the name rather than the scent. She nearly giggled at the predictability of him. Archer knew what he liked and would often go out of his way to make a purchase.

A sudden wave of heat rose up through her. It was as quick as it was horrible, and in an instant, she was on the verge of throwing up. She stumbled from the bed, raced to the restroom and lifted the lid on the toilet. As she rode a wave of nausea, Archer appeared at her side.

"Are you okay, babe?"

His warm hands on her shoulder were of little comfort. Her stomach bucked and twisted as she shook her head. She heaved and couldn't rid the contents of her stomach quick enough. Archer stayed with her the whole time. When she had nothing left, she eased back and wanted to curl into a ball. Archer handed her a glass of water, and after a few tentative sips he gathered her into his arms and carried her back to bed. They were both still naked and when he slipped in beside her. The warmth of his skin against hers was the tonic she needed.

Archer glided her hair back from her face, and the worry in his eyes crushed her heart.

She swallowed. Hard. "Arch?"

"Yes, babe? What's wrong?"

"I'm sorry. But I. . . I think I'm pregnant." She blurted it out without any consideration to the timing of it.

He blinked. His jaw dropped. He failed to deliver words.

Rosalina's breath trapped in her throat. Her heart thundered in her ears, and her already churning stomach summersaulted as she scanned his features, waiting for the moment he spoke.

The jolt that had marred his features turned. Ever so gradually, his face transformed from shock to uncertainty. "Are you sure?"

"No. I'm not sure?" It took all her restraint not to slap him at the idiocy of his question. "We're in the middle of the friggin' ocean and the nearest pharmacy is a million miles away. So no, I'm not sure."

"Okay, calm down."

"Don't tell me to calm down." She clenched her jaw until her teeth ached.

She read the panic in his eyes. He was a trapped man, and she'd done it to him.

Her chin trembled; tears threatened to burst. She sucked in a huge breath and blurted out, "I'm so sorry. It's all my fault."

Great wracking sobs overwhelmed her and as Archer pulled her to his chest, dread twisted a knife in her stomach. Her head rolled to the crook of his shoulder and he held her there, smoothing down her hair. "Rosa, honey, this's so wonderful."

She gasped for breath, unsure if she'd heard correctly. Swallowing hard, she forced her brain to clear. "What?"

"You've made me the happiest man in the world."

She pulled back, wiping her nose and seeking truth in his eyes. What she saw had her heart aching and reminded her why she loved him so much. Archer was capable of showing love. Real, unadulterated love. "I. . . thought you'd be upset."

He jerked his head, frowning. "What? Why?"

She rolled her engagement ring around her finger as she searched for the reason. There had been so many, and yet now, none of them seemed reasonable. "I don't know. I guess because we don't have a home. We're not settled."

"Honey? *Evangeline* is our home and with it we can go wherever we want in the world."

She'd thought about this over and over and still couldn't imagine living permanently on a boat. Her childhood had been so different to Archer's. Did that make her childhood right? Or better? It suddenly dawned on her that where a child grew up wasn't as important as the parents that child had. Both of them had grown up without either a mother or father present. Their child was going to be the most loved boy or girl that was ever born. The idea made her glow from the inside.

"I can't wait to tell everyone."

She jolted. "No, Archer. No one must know yet. I don't even know if it's true."

"Are you kidding?"

"No. I'm serious. This is to be our secret until we can confirm either way." She reached up, placed her hand on his cheek and drew his eyes to her. "Okay?"

He rolled his eyes. "Well, that's going to be hard."

"I mean it. No treating me any different, or the others will wonder what's going on."

He cupped her cheek, wiping a stray tear with his thumb. "You're carrying precious cargo. Of course I'll treat you differently."

She chuckled. "We don't know that. It's just a hunch."

He smiled and the sunlight had the flecks of gold circling his irises positively dancing. "And what a beautiful hunch it is."

"Really?"

"Really? Are you kidding? It's the best present in the world." He drew her in for a kiss. "I love you."

Her heart swelled to bursting. "I love you, too."

Chapter Thirty-Eight

The thrill of yesterday's diamond find was still coursing through Alessandro's brain, and based on the energy at the breakfast table, everyone else felt the same. The discussion flitted from diamonds to creepy Japanese men with ease. Alessandro loved that Ginger was confident she could obtain vital information from the 'Crazy Japanese Man'. Alessandro looked forward to watching her work, although he wasn't as confident their discussion would be successful.

After all, it had been seventy years since the war, and if this man had actually been in World War II, then he had to be at least ninety years old. The chances of him being one of the Yukimura brothers was highly improbable. On top of that, even if he was one of them, the chance of him remembering any important details was even lesser still.

Alessandro was both shocked and perplexed when Archer and Rosalina decided to stay on board *Evangeline* while he, Ginger and Jimmy went to Headhunter Island. His curiosity was short-lived though as they were swept up in the planning.

Every other island they'd seen in the Solomons was surrounded by a sandy beach and looked as inviting as any romantic getaway brochure. Not this one. Headhunter Island rose from the water like a giant molar tooth. The towering columns of jagged rocks were topped with a jungle of plants like a mop of wild green hair. It actually looked like a giant head and, Alessandro mused, was hopefully how it had earned its unfortunate name.

As Jimmy steered the boat towards the island, Alessandro wondered if the young boys were right. It didn't seem possible that someone could live on this island. But just as he was about to voice that opinion, Ginger pointed forward.

"Look. There's stairs."

"Thank God," said Jimmy. "I was beginning to think we were in for some rock climbing."

The stairs magically clung to the rock wall and wove their way around the island from the top to the bottom. Jimmy followed the construction, seeking the stairs' lowest point.

"There's a little jetty." Alessandro pointed it out. Alongside the jetty was both a canoe and a small motor boat. Jimmy angled towards it and when they became close enough, Alessandro jumped out and caught the rope Ginger tossed to him. He secured their boat to the jetty and offered his hand to Ginger.

"It all looks a little creepy," she said, as she climbed out.

"*Sì*, I agree."

Jimmy joined them on the jetty. "I'll go first," he said. "Ginger, you stay between us."

Alessandro wanted to look up to see where they were going, but once he realized how rickety the steps were, he had to keep his eyes on his footing instead. The incline was steep, and it was impossible to believe an old man could manage these steps. It was looking more and more like their intentions for today had no chance of coming to fruition.

At the top of the stairs, as they all paused to catch their breath. Alessandro looked out across the ocean. *Evangeline* stood out like a majestic castle in an ocean of blue. He still found it hard to believe he was living on such a luxurious vessel. His life in Italy was worlds away and it surprised him how little he missed it.

So much had changed.

As Ginger eased in front of him to walk along the path, he admired her slender legs as she stepped over the vegetation with ease.

A rugged path wove its way through the jungle. It was slightly over-grown but still obvious. Jimmy pushed plants back and they alternated holding them until all three of them had passed through. They stepped over a fallen palm tree that, judging by the amount of moss covering it, had toppled a long time ago.

A loud crack exploded from the silence and in a blast of air and dried leaves, a giant net swept Jimmy off his feet and flung him through the trees.

"Ohhhh shit!" Jimmy roared.

Alessandro jumped in front of Ginger, protecting her from the invisible onslaught, and braced for an attack from every angle. His breath shot in and out as he scanned the dense jungle around them, seeking their attacker, but there was nothing but Jimmy, trapped in an enormous net, swinging backward and forward.

Another crack sounded, and as Jimmy's net reached the lowest point in the pendulum, the tree branch holding the rope snapped off and Jimmy plummeted to the ground.

Alessandro dodged the plants to get to him. Jimmy was on his back, groaning. His arms and legs were tangled in the knotted rope.

"Jesus Christ. What the hell was that?" Jimmy bellowed.

"Are you okay?" Alessandro stifled a laugh as he tried to untangle Jimmy from the net. Finally, he found the opening and tugged it apart. Ginger too was trying not to giggle as she helped. Soon the opening was big enough to peel over Jimmy.

Ginger knelt beside him. "You didn't break anything, did you?" She burst out laughing. "Sorry, I can't help it. That was funny."

"Not fucking funny." Jimmy clenched his teeth and shook his head. "I could've broken my neck." He rolled his head from side to side and lifted his arms, apparently testing for injuries.

Alessandro reached down to the net that looked like it'd been knotted together by hand. "I was beginning to think we were wasting our time today, but now I'm not so sure."

"Yeah? How so, Einstein?" Jimmy rolled to his hands and knees, and Alessandro shared a grin with Ginger.

"Well. . . why would anyone build a trap like that unless they were trying to protect something?"

Jimmy groaned as he stood up. "Okay then genius, you can go first from now on."

Alessandro looked about the dense vegetation, a sea of green and brown. All manner of traps could be concealed, primed and ready for release. It was impossible to believe anyone lived on this island. And yet, they'd already seen proof that someone did. Or at least they once had.

"Okay." Alessandro made his way back to the path, deciding that was the safest plan. But all the same, he took every step with measured caution, searching for anything unusual. Although it was an impossible ask, as everything looked unusual. He froze.

"Smell that? Smoke."

"Yes," Ginger whispered close behind him.

"Do you still think this is a good idea? Whoever lives on this island obviously doesn't want visitors."

"We've come this far, numbnuts, might as well keep going."

"Don't call me that."

Ginger placed her hand on his shoulder. "There's no harm in talking to the man."

"The crazy Japanese man." Alessandro reminded them of the children's nickname.

"They're just kids."

"Yes, but from what I've seen so far, I may support their theory."

"Oh, for Christ's sake." Jimmy pushed past both of them and stormed along the path.

Alessandro allowed Ginger to step in front again, and the two of them caught up to the striding Jimmy. He couldn't decide if Jimmy was either stupid or brave as he strode along without a cautious step. The jungle suddenly opened to a clearing where the grass was lush and neatly trimmed.

There was one hut centered in the middle of the clearing. It wasn't ramshackle like all the others he'd seen dotted along the islands; this one was made with obvious skill. The high-pitched roof had a distinct Japanese feel to it and the stumps holding the building about a couple of feet off the ground were intricately carved with Japanese symbols. A decent-sized veranda ran the full length along the front of the building and the posts securing the railing had wood-carved creations of Ch'i-t'zu, the happy fat Buddhist monk sitting on top of them. Whoever lived here took meticulous care with their property.

A path, worn through the grass lead to a set of three steps. "Here we go." Jimmy strode across the path with all the bravado of a marauding captain.

As the three of them walked towards the front steps, Alessandro's gaze followed the line of smoke that drifted from a pipe at the back of the building into the surrounding trees and vanished.

"Hello." Jimmy rapped his knuckles on the open front door.

They were met with silence. "Is anyone home?"

"*Konnichiha, dare demo ha ei desu ka?*" It was strange to hear Ginger speaking in Japanese.

Ginger stepped over the threshold and Alessandro stepped in behind her. The room was sparsely decorated with an exposed-beam roof. At one end, a bed had the covers neatly made, and it seemed everything had its place.

Alessandro turned to a creaking noise and froze. An old man sat in a rocking chair; his hands folded casually in his lap. It was as if he'd been expecting them. The man was bald except for a few lingering hairs that were as fine as wind-blown cotton. His eyes were almost covered in drooping folds of skin. His long gray beard sat on his chest and his mustache, twisted into long threads, looked like ivory horns. He rocked back and forward, but other than that he didn't move.

Ginger stepped forward and held out her hand. "Hello, my name's Ginger. Are you Mr. Yukimura?"

His hands snapped from his lap, and Ginger jumped when her fingers vanished within the old man's grasp.

"I wonder when you find me." His voice was stones in a blender.

The man dropped Ginger's hand and continued to rock backward and forward as if he wasn't surprised to see strangers in his room. In the bristling silence, the creaking chair was the only sound as Alessandro stepped forward.

"Hello. I'm Alessandro, and this is Jimmy. Can we take a moment of your time please?"

When their eyes met, Alessandro was struck by their eeriness. The old man's left eye had lost its battle against glaucoma a long time ago. His right eye, though, drilled right into Alessandro.

The Japanese man stopped rocking, placed his feet on the ground and eased forward, maintaining his glare at Alessandro. "You here about skulls, yes?"

Alessandro fought back his gasp and swallowed hard. "Yes." He stammered. "Yes, we are. What do you know about them?"

The man reached up and twirled the two long mustache ribbons. "I know they ruin my life." A tear spilled out of his clouded left eye, trickled down his cheek and tumbled into his white beard.

"Would you like to talk about it?" Ginger touched the old man's forearm, and his eyes traveled down to her touch.

"I do. That why you here, yes?"

"Yes, Mr. Yukimura, it is." Ginger was concise with her words yet gentle with her tone.

"You sit." Mr. Yukimura leaned back and once again rocked backward and forward to a groaning rhythm.

Alessandro looked about the room, wondering where they would sit. There was a small table in the corner but no other chairs. When Ginger slipped to the floor and sat cross-legged, Alessandro followed her lead. Jimmy remained standing and Alessandro eyeballed him until the stubborn bugger sat down too.

"Mr. Yukimura," Ginger said.

He raised his hand, stopping her. "My name is Hiro."

Alessandro raised his eyebrows. For some inexplicable reason, he'd thought this would be Kimoda.

Ginger smiled and he smiled back. He had no teeth.

Hiro placed his feet on the ground again and leaned towards them. "You long time to come."

"Yes. We're sorry." Ginger frowned at Alessandro and shrugged her shoulder. "Would you mind telling us how you did it?"

He twirled his mustache and resumed his rocking. "Kimoda and I, we a formidable team." His eyelids drooped. "Until he stole it all. He ran off and left me."

Alessandro frowned. Was it possible Hiro had no idea what happened to his brother? He glanced at Ginger, and when her eyes bulged, he assumed she'd arrived at the same conclusion.

"Mr. Yukimura. . . Hiro, I'm sorry to tell you this, but we think Kimoda died in 1945." Ginger's voice was a sympathetic melody.

Hiro's eyes snapped open and he blinked at her. "What you mean?"

"There was a tuna boat called the Ranga Spirit that was sunk by a bouncing bomb in 1945," Alessandro said. "It's possible Kimoda Yukimura was on the ship when it sunk."

"He die." Hiro's lips thinned. "I thought he abandoned me."

"Why would he have done that?" Alessandro asked.

He shook his head. "That what I never understand. We plan to buy a farm after war. But he never return. He beat death so many times." Hiro shook his head. "I never think he die."

Alessandro recalled how Kimoda had been the sole survivor of three sinking ships. It wouldn't be hard to consider him invincible. This time, when a tear spilled out of the old man's eye, he wiped it away.

"I'm sorry," Ginger said.

He shook his head. "I no deserve apology. We stole things. Punishment was inevitable."

By the look of him, Hiro had been punishing himself for half a century.

"So, you never left this island?" Alessandro said.

Hiro shook his head. "Kimoda say wait until he return. It long time before I knew he never coming back."

"What did you steal, Hiro?" Jimmy was as gentle as a starving ox.

Hiro twirled his mustache and let out a long, slow breath. "The small things. Diamonds. Jewels. Some antiques. The skulls."

"Couldn't fit the gold bullion in the plane, hey?" Jimmy huffed.

Hiro's hairless eyebrows shot up and he nodded, as if accepting his fate. "We never expect my plane be shot down. When I crash into ocean, I lucky to survive. This was island I swam to."

"What did you do then?" Ginger asked.

"I took gamble one night, when moon was full, I swam to mainland. Swam for long time. Rumble of fighter plane overhead. Fear of shark below."

Alessandro recalled the trips they'd made in the boat yesterday. It would've taken hours to swim that distance.

"Kimoda, he no believe his eyes when he saw me. He saw my plane shot down. He thought I dead."

"So how did you get the treasure?"

"We deserted our post." His already guilt-ridden features crumbled even more. "We stole small boat and return to island."

"But how did you get the treasure out of the plane?" Jimmy said.

265

His good eye lit up. "We lucky I crash in shallow water."

Ginger's eyes bulged. "You swam down to it?"

"Yes. It took many weeks to bring pieces up from plane. We hid it here. . . closest island."

Alessandro adjusted his position on the floor. "But wasn't the war still going on?"

"Yes. Each time we expect to be kill. But we had nothing else to live for."

"What about family?" Ginger asked.

"Our parents. Grandparents. Sister." Hiro shook his head and commenced rocking again. "They all die in war."

"Oh, I'm so sorry," Ginger said.

"So you got it here to the island, then what?" Jimmy demanded.

Hiro glanced ahead; his eyes still as if he was traveling back in time. "I stay here while Kimoda make plan. He plan fishing boat to take us to Honiara. Another boat then take us back to Japan. But he never return. I been waiting with the skulls all this time."

Alessandro frowned. "You have the skulls! Where?"

Hiro extended a long bony finger and pointed to an ammunition box in the corner with a pair of battered shoes resting on the top.

/

Chapter Thirty-Nine

"So, you go through life killing people and getting away with it." Filippo sat cross-legged on his bed, eating a bowl of pasta. "When does it end, Nox?"

Nox had never thought about that. "When people stop betraying me."

"How many people have you killed?"

Nox shrugged. "I've never tallied it up."

"Are there many more on your list?"

He nodded.

Filippo put his bowl aside, sat his elbows on his knees and cupped his chin. "Who?"

Nox contemplated not saying it but couldn't resist seeing Filippo's reaction. "Archer."

Filippo wiggled his head from side to side and seemed completely at ease with his answer.

"And Rosalina," Nox said, stone-faced.

Filippo nodded. "I thought as much. She did spear you, after all."

"True."

Filippo's phone rang in Nox's pocket, and he lifted it out. "Speak of the devil."

He pressed the green button. "We were just talking about you," he said into the phone.

As per every other call, she insisted he put Filippo on. He handed the phone over and watched as Filippo spoke to the sister Nox had just declared he was going to kill. If ever there was a chance for his plan to go awry, this was it.

"Hey Rosa." Filippo played the battered little brother too well. "Fantastic. When? You think you'll find more?" Filippo actually winked at Nox.

Nox cocked his head. They were looking for more. Excellent news.

"I'm okay. No, it's fine. I'll just be glad to get out of here."

It suddenly occurred to Nox that Filippo could actually kill someone. He seemed ruthless enough. He certainly took the news that Nox planned to kill his sister with a cold indifference.

Nox contemplated how he would do it. He'd wait until he had his hands on the treasure first. It would happen at the exchange. Once he had the diamonds secured. Was that when Filippo planned to attack, too? He listened to Filippo fake agony in his voice and wondered what else the Italian was faking.

Filippo hung up the phone and smiled at Nox. "They're diving again tonight to see if there are any more diamonds."

"How much more?"

"They don't know."

Nox ran his tongue over the gap in his teeth and assessed if Filippo was telling the truth. He decided he wasn't. There was a whole lot more treasure heading back to Italy and those gems were only the tip of the haul. "What do you plan to do with your share of the diamonds?"

Filippo's eyes darted to him and Nox was certain he saw loathing in them. "I'm going to get the hell away from Tuscany. Maybe Australia."

Australia was an interesting choice. Archer was from Australia. Maybe he and Archer were friendlier than Filippo was implying. "How will you change the diamonds to cash?"

Filippo shrugged. "No idea. How're you doing it?"

Nox had no idea either. "I have someone ready for the exchange." He lied.

"Well." Filippo spread his hands. "Maybe we could exchange them all together and then split it. Get a bulk discount." Filippo laughed, but Nox had no idea what he was laughing at.

Chapter Forty

"Here they come." Archer pointed to the tender in the distance, and Rosalina let out a sigh of relief. Ginger and the men had been gone a long time, hopefully their lengthy delay meant some kind of success. The instant Archer saw Alessandro's beaming grin, he knew they had.

"We found them," Alessandro yelled across the water.

"Who did they find?" Rosalina asked Archer.

"We're about to find out."

Jimmy grinned like a crazy man as he angled the boat alongside *Evangeline*. "You ain't gonna believe this."

Archer secured the tender, and Jimmy and Alessandro handed up a battered wooden ammunition box.

"What is it?" Rosalina asked.

"Open it," Alessandro said.

Archer flicked the metal clasps, lifted the lid and he and Rosalina gasped in unison. Inside, nestled within a bed of yellow straw, were two skulls. The bone was stained brown and little spider cracks all over the cranium made them look brittle. They weren't complete, as each were missing the lower jaw, however a couple of dirty cracked teeth still jutted out from the upper jaw at odd angles. These didn't look like any skulls he'd seen pictures of. The brow bones were very prominent and the eye sockets were large and out of proportion with the rest of the skull. Archer looked at Alessandro. "Are these--"

"The Peking Man skulls." Alessandro nodded. "I think so."

"Jesus. I wasn't expecting you to return with anything, let alone this."

As they headed towards the saloon with the precious cargo held by Jimmy, the three of them told Hiro's story. It was fascinating stuff.

"So, he didn't know his brother had died," Rosalina said. "That's sad."

"Yeah. For years he expected Kimoda to return."

"Hell of a story." Archer tried to ignore Alessandro's ridiculous grin. "What did he say when you told him you found the diamonds?"

Jimmy clapped him on the back. "We didn't."

Archer laughed. If it was Kimoda who'd hidden the diamonds in tuna cans, then there was a good chance there was more than just diamonds to be found in the Captain's cabin. He turned to Jimmy. "I guess we've got our work cut out for us tonight then if we're looking for more than just tuna cans."

"Ginger and I can help," Rosalina said.

"No." Archer snapped his eyes to her then caught himself. "It's too dangerous."

Rosalina puffed out her chest. "We'll be fine. Won't we, Ginger?"

"Sure will. I've done heaps of wreck dives."

"Not like this you haven't." He had no intention of continuing this discussion here.

LATER THAT AFTERNOON BEFORE THEY PREPARED TO DIVE THE RANGA Spirit again, Archer managed to catch Rosalina in the bedroom. He made her sit with him in the easy chair, and it was obvious by the rigidness in her back she was ready for a fight.

"You know what I want to talk about."

"I'm doing these dives, Archer."

"No, you're not." He kept his voice calm, avoiding an argument at all cost. "Now hear me out."

"There's nothing to talk about. I may not be pregnant, and until we know for sure I'm not changing my life."

"But what if you are pregnant? Are you willing to risk your life, our baby's life? Remember what happened to your mother."

"Don't you bring that up." She aimed a finger at him. "Every day of my life I think of my mother dying during childbirth. That's why I never wanted children."

Archer jolted. "What do you mean?"

"I don't want kids, and I always thought you were the same. Now look what's happened."

He scowled. "Why do you think I don't want children?"

"Because you're a businessman. You're willing to put your life on the line to chase some stupid treasure. That's not father material."

He glared at her. "My dad was the best father in the world."

"Yes, and he was eaten by a shark chasing gold. It ruined your life."

"It doesn't mean he wasn't a great dad."

She stood, and with her fists at her side she stomped the length of the room. When she turned, her eyes were a dark, stormy sea. The fear in them scared him.

"What is it, Rosa? You're scared. I see it in your eyes."

She dashed a tear from her cheek and he strode to her, wrapped his arms around her and squeezed her to his chest. It was a long time before her rigid body eased. "I'm scared of childbirth."

It tore him to shreds at how vehemently she said it. As much as she was scared, he was angry that she'd never shared this before. It was a bitter pill to swallow. Archer had squirrelled away his tormented secrets for years too. Both of them still had so much to learn about each other. "Honey." He ran his hand over her hair. "Medicine has improved dramatically since then."

"I'm even more scared of bringing a child into the world and then leaving them to fend for themselves when one or both of us dies."

"Oh, baby. Nothing's going to happen."

"It happened to both our parents."

He pulled back from her, cupped her chin and drew her troubled eyes to his. "We're both going to grow old and fat together. We're going to have kids and lots of grandkids and maybe even great-grandkids and we're all going to see the world."

Her chin dimpled. "I'm not going to get fat."

He chuckled and squeezed her to his chest. "Okay, you're not going to get fat." He smoothed her hair then bent down to kiss her, tasting the salty tears on her lips. She kissed him too. Her breath quickened as she clutched at his neck, drawing him down to her. She stunned him with her impassioned force. With his hands on Rosalina's bottom, he lifted her onto his hips. She wrapped her long legs around him, and as he carried her to bed, she planted kisses along his neck, over his ear.

He was blind to everything but Rosalina's savage urge to have him. She clawed at her clothing, tearing it off. He was weak to her demands, falling for the velvet huskiness in her voice, guided by her needy hands. Naked in an instant, he was on her, filling her with his manhood as she climaxed around him, squeezing her molten insides around him like a fist.

It was over in minutes, and yet he felt like he'd run a marathon. Their breathing was erratic as he rolled to her side. He raised his eyebrows at his seductive fiancée who had him dizzy with love.

She tugged her lip, and judging by the cheekiness in her eyes, she was trying not to laugh.

"Okay, madam, what was that about?"

"Do you complain?"

"Oh no, I no complain." He cupped her breast and wobbled the luscious flesh in his palm. "You can do that to me anytime."

She laughed, and at first it was a timid chuckle, but soon she kicked back her head and laughed so hard she was gasping for breath. Archer couldn't help himself and joined in. It was as if the final treads of tension that'd had Rosalina wound so tight for months had finally snapped. His beautiful Italian bride-to-be was back, and he couldn't be happier.

When she stopped to wipe the laughter tears from her eyes, Archer seized the moment to be serious.

"We don't know whether or not you're pregnant, honey. So, until we know for sure, you're not diving. Okay?"

She released a sigh and nodded. "Okay. But we have to make up some other excuse."

"Deal."

~

WHEN THEY RETURNED UPSTAIRS, ROSALINA TOLD EVERYONE SHE wasn't feeling one hundred per cent and thought it advisable not to dive.

"Ginger, you can stay up here too. It'll be quicker with just Jimmy and I," Archer said.

Ginger wore her disappointment in her eyes, but she didn't voice it.

Sunset came quickly and before they were plunged into complete darkness, Archer and Jimmy launched the tender with Ginger and Rosalina. "It'll be difficult holding it against this current," he said to Rosalina.

"We'll be fine." Archer noted the determination in Rosalina's voice. She was a confident woman; it was just another one of the many reasons why he loved her so much.

As they neared the Ranga Spirit wreck site, Archer leaned over to kiss Rosalina. "Be careful, baby."

"You too," she said.

"Always."

Archer put the regulator in his mouth, nodded at Jimmy, and the two of them flipped backwards together. As he slipped below the murky water, the engine roared and as Rosalina took the boat back to *Evangeline*, he turned his attention to his dive compass. In less than five minutes they'd returned to the captain's cabin on the Ranga Spirit, where they'd found the diamond-filled can.

Careful not to dislodge the sediment, they worked together to lift the pieces that had tumbled against one wall when the ship toppled backwards. The cans appeared again and again and each time, Jimmy yelled a muffled 'yes' through his mouthpiece as he tucked them into the net bag at his hip.

They found a small metal box, like an old tobacco tin, and decided to examine the contents later. A large metal cross, the size of a man's shoe, was hidden beneath an upturned chair. They also found a challis-style cup and several gold plates. Right in the corner Archer tried to move what looked like fabric, but the entire thing disintegrated in his hands. The water clouded with mush, and Archer wondered if it was the remains of a pillow. Once he'd fanned the debris away his flashlight lit up a collection of jewelry, all jumbled together and Jimmy's cheer was his loudest yet.

Time was up, and he and Jimmy headed towards the surface. They paused at their decompression stop, and when they surfaced, he blew his whistle and flashed his light to signal the ladies to pick them up.

Alessandro was like a kid in a candy store when they produced their findings. As was Jimmy. Once all the cans were opened, they counted a total of 691 diamonds. The exquisite stones were a variety of colors and sizes with the largest one being about the size of a macadamia nut.

By the end of the second dive, Archer and Jimmy were certain they'd found everything there was to find in that room and this dive produced very little in comparison to their first haul.

"What about the rest of the ship?" Ginger asked.

Archer pictured the Ranga Spirit in his head. The mid-ship consisted of just two rooms. They'd found nothing in the wheelhouse and nothing in the first room they'd searched. "Every item we found was in the captain's cabin. It didn't make sense that the person who stole the treasure would risk spreading the load out. I think we've got all there is."

The look of relief on Rosalina's face was unmistakable.

By the time they'd examined the collection and had the customary celebration afterwards, Archer was weary with exhaustion. He said goodnight and led his beautiful fiancée to bed. He showered and crawled into the sheets beside her. Dreams of cheeky little children and priceless diamonds guided him through the night to the break of dawn.

Archer hadn't told Jimmy yet that he needed him to stay with *Evangeline* while the rest of them flew back to Italy. He wasn't looking forward to that conversation and waited until after breakfast when Jimmy was at the bridge to tell him.

"How're we going, Captain?" he said, as he strode into the room.

Jimmy's eyebrows bounced together. "Here we go. What do you want this time?"

Archer was tempted to fake shock, but Jimmy was too good a friend to do that. "Sorry mate, but I need you to hire a crew and run *Evangeline* back to Italy."

"Ahhh, shit. What're you doing?"

"We're flying back."

"Why do I miss out on all the fun?"

"Not true. You've had plenty of fun over the last couple of days."

Jimmy rolled his eyes. "I'm talking about smashing Nox's head in."

Archer laughed. "Right. I'll make sure I put a boot in him for you."

"You better. Seriously though, are you giving him the diamonds?" The look on his face showed how devastated he was at the impending loss.

"Nox can have the diamonds, as long as we get Filippo back."

Jimmy's shoulders sagged.

"Just the first thirty-one diamonds he knows about." Archer grinned at his best mate.

Jimmy's face lit up. "Now we're talking."

They shared a quick hug and a slap on the back. "You take care."

"Always."

By three o'clock that afternoon, Rosalina, Alessandro and Ginger sat with Archer on the Gulfstream Galaxy plane that he'd privately chartered. The plane was slightly bigger than they needed, but he chose it because of the distance it could travel. With refueling stops in Singapore and Dubai, they should be in Florence within forty or so hours.

The cargo held a priceless fortune. Between the monkey statue, Peking Man skulls, the ancient lapis lazuli cylinder, a bundle of jewelry and hundreds of diamonds, it was mind-boggling to think what the value of the cargo would be. He just hoped he didn't have to explain any of it to nosy customs staff. It was another good reason to hire a private jet. It meant they should get priority processing at all the airports. He'd paid the pilots triple their standard price to do exactly that.

Chapter Forty-One

N ox felt the phone buzz in his pocket before he heard it ring, and he plucked it out. The sight of Archer's phone number set his pulse racing. This was the call he'd waited months for. Hell, it could be years. Decades even. A lifetime of work had led to this point. He deserved it. Every single piece of it.

"It's time to do business, Nox." Archer didn't waste breath on pleasantries.

"Do you have my diamonds?"

"Yes. Let me hear Filippo?"

"Say hello, Filippo." Nox held the phone to Filippo's ear.

"Hello. . . yes."

Nox took the phone back and barked into the receiver. "We'll do the exchange at the old Provenzia orphanage where I took Rosalina and Filippo. It's on Stada Statale One about thirty minutes south of Livorno; look it up, you'll find it. When will you be here?"

"About two hours."

Nox would make sure he was ready within one. "Don't be late." He clicked the call off and slipped the phone back into his pocket.

"I'll be back soon," he said to his prisoner.

He locked the door and made his way to the kitchen for one last meal in Provenzia. As he ate a bowl of cold pasta, he checked the gun for the tenth time. It only had two bullets. One for Archer. One for Rosalina. He'd better not miss. Filippo would have to be dealt with later. He clipped the cylinder closed after once again ensuring a bullet was in the firing chamber.

Rather than risk being trapped inside the orphanage it made sense to make the exchange outside where there was nothing to hide behind. It also made it easier to toss the bodies over the cliff. With a bit of luck, Archer and that bitch Rosalina would never be seen again. Just like the three little boys who'd tumbled over the edge decades ago.

He opened the door to Filippo's room for the last time. "Let's go."

"Are they here?" Filippo slipped off the cot bed.

"Soon." It would've made sense to keep Filippo trapped in there, but he assumed Archer would never reveal the diamonds without seeing Nox's captive first. "Come on. We're going outside."

"Why?" Filippo's calm indifference had him stroll past Nox and take the lead as if the two of them were heading for a walk in a park.

"So we can see them coming. And it makes it easier to dispose of the bodies."

Filippo simply nodded and Nox couldn't decide if Filippo was heartless or cold and calculating. It didn't matter either way; his end was near too.

Nox instructed Filippo out of the orphanage and down the front steps, and when they walked out from the protection of the derelict building the wind whipped in a frenzy, carrying salt and sea spray up from the ocean below. They stood with their backs to the ocean and a full view of the road into the orphanage at their front.

If Filippo was nervous with the gun pointed at his back, he showed no sign of it. Yet from what Nox had seen so far, Filippo was about to put on the show of his life.

Right on time, a black car eased along the overgrown driveway, and as it approached, Nox shuddered with pleasure. Even from behind the wheel, the strong, hard lines of Archer's jaw were unmissable. As was the terror on Rosalina's face. He was both surprised and relieved to see them alone.

"Remember, I'll threaten to kill you and toss you into the ocean if they don't hand over the diamonds."

"Okay. Got it." Filippo sounded excited.

Filippo waved his arms and the car steered off the driveway and along the spindly grass towards them. It pulled to a halt and Rosalina jumped out. The wind assaulted her, whipping her hair across her face and threatening to tear the clothes from her body.

"Rosalina!" Archer barked at her as he leapt from the car and she stopped in her tracks, barely three strides from Filippo.

As Nox glared at the bitch, the power of revenge blazed through him like a shot of adrenalin. His finger twitched on the trigger. He could put a bullet through her brain right now. It would be easy and quick. Too quick, though. He wanted to make her suffer. Needed to make her suffer. He couldn't wait to see her reaction when she discovered her own brother had double crossed her.

"Filippo, are you okay?" Rosalina's fingers strangled her hair. Her lips trembled and her eyes were wild with fear. She was the picture of a terrified sister.

Archer arrived at her side and tugged her back two paces. His hardened glare had the cockiness of a man who thought he was in charge.

"Yes, I'm okay," Filippo answered like a broken child.

Nox nudged the gun into his lower back.

"He has a gun." Filippo followed their script.

"Let him go, Nox, and you can have the diamonds." Archer's fist was clenched at his side, his dark eyes drilled like guided missiles.

"Give me the diamonds." Nox counted the waves crashing onto the rocks below as he waited for Archer to move. One. Two. Three. . .

Archer reached into his pants pocket and, fearful he might have a gun, Nox nudged behind Filippo. He swallowed hard when Archer removed a small velvet pouch. This was too easy, he thought. But the pouch in Archer's hand was small. Too small.

Archer took one step closer. "Here." He pegged the black bag across the distance. Filippo reached up and grabbed it, and despite the roaring wind, a sound like rattling glass was unmistakable.

"Give it to me," Nox demanded, and Filippo handed it over willingly.

"Come to us, Filippo," Archer ordered.

"No," Nox yelled. "I want to see them first." With anxious fingers and the gun in his hand, he struggled to undo the knot on the black drawstring securing the bag. Out of the corner of his eye, Filippo looked over his shoulder.

The string finally released, and he tipped the contents into his palm. They were beautiful, radiating the fire of the sun. He twirled them with the gun and did a rough count. About thirty diamonds.

"You got your diamonds, Nox. Now let Filippo go," Archer barked the demand.

Nox guided the stones back into the bag, folded over the top and pushed it into his pants pocket. Then he shoved the gun into the small of Filippo's back.

"We want the rest," Nox yelled.

The muscle in Archer's jaw bulged. "There is no more. That's all we found. We had a deal, Nox." Archer spoke through clenched teeth. "You got the diamonds, now let Filippo go."

"We changed our mind. Tell them, Filippo."

Filippo turned; his eyes fierce with confusion. "What're you doing?"

Nox held his stare. "You're a fool." Fate had dealt him a new deck of cards and for the first time in his life, Nox was holding all the aces.

Filippo lashed out for the gun, startling him with his speed. Nox launched backwards and brought the gun up to eye level. "Your brother and I are working together, Rosalina. He's told me everything. I know all about the statue and the blue cylinder. We're a team now. Tell her, Filippo."

Filippo stood, legs apart, hands balled at his sides, and the look of bewilderment on his face proved Filippo had honestly believed they were in a partnership together.

Damn fool deserved to die.

Rosalina took a tentative step forward. "What did you do, Filippo?" Her voice was a strangled panic.

Filippo twisted to her. "Shut up, Rosa."

"We did this for you."

A blaze of red flooded Filippo's cheeks. "Bullshit. You selfish fucking bitch. You never did anything for me."

Archer stood solid, his face a mask of defiance and fury. His eyes bounced from Nox to Filippo, to Rosalina, to the cliff. He was planning every step of his attack.

"Filippo, I love you." Rosalina fell to her knees, clutching her stomach as if trying to tear her guts out.

Archer fell in at her side, his arms around her.

"Family!" Nox said sarcastically. "Isn't it precious?"

Filippo spun to him so quick Nox was caught off-guard. His elbow came up fast and hard, ramming into Nox's ribs with the force of a sledgehammer.

Nox's breath punched out of him. He doubled over.

"Give me my fucking diamonds." Filippo went for his pocket and Nox cracked the gun over his head.

Screaming and clutching his temple, Filippo stumbled backwards.

Archer reached behind his back. A glint of steel flashed in the sunlight. Nox snapped his gaze to Filippo's blazing eyes. His heart launched to his throat.

Filippo charged like a raging rhino. Nox didn't even blink. He drew up the weapon and fired. Filippo barely broke stride as the bullet tore through his shoulder.

Nox thought it would stop him. Instead, the unthinkable happened.

They both went over the cliff. A gnarled tree jutting out from the rocks glanced off Nox's back, and the blow created enough momentum to roll him sideways, edging him above Filippo.

With a loud crack, Filippo hit solid rock first. Nox landed hard at his side.

The wind slammed out of him. Pain ripped up his spine and his back blazed with fire. His legs were alien, somehow removed from his body. The sun's inferno was behind his eyes, burning his eyeballs from within.

As he lay there, gasping, Rosalina's screams mingled with the crashing waves.

His body was broken, every bone shattered like fractured ice. A wave crashed over him and his head rolled to the side. When he blinked back the salty water, he saw diamonds.

His diamonds. . . dancing with the sunlight shimmering off the ocean.

He reached out and wrapped his fingers around a brilliant gemstone, and as he closed his eyes the pain washed away with the next wave.

Chapter Forty-Two

At the edge of the pier, Rosalina held both her Nonna's hand and Archer's hand as Jimmy guided *Evangeline* into her allocated berth at Marina Di San Vencenzo. The second the glass on the bridge moved out of the reflecting sun, Jimmy's grinning face beamed from behind the windshield. Archer jumped aboard as soon as he could, but Rosalina waited until the engines turned off before she helped Nonna on board.

"Watch your step, Nonna."

"Stop fussing. I'm okay."

Nonna's stubbornness always surprised Rosalina. Her grandmother might look frail, but there was one hell of a strong woman within that thin frame. Nonna mumbled signs of approval as Rosalina led her along the main deck. Archer embraced his mother when she found him in the saloon. Helen actually looked healthier than when they'd left her with Jimmy in the Solomon Islands.

Rosalina hugged Helen to her chest. "How are you?"

"Fantastic. We've had a grand time, haven't we, Jimmy?" Helen turned and grinned at Jimmy.

"Yeah." He thumped Archer in the shoulder. "You never told me your mom was a shark at the card table."

Rosalina cringed at Jimmy's choice of the word 'shark', but Archer's laughter saved her.

"I had no idea you played cards, Mom."

Helen grinned. "Your father and I played all the time. Didn't think I'd remember how." She shrugged. "Guess it's like riding a bike."

"Pfft, is that what you reckon?" Jimmy huffed. "I think she's been zipping off to Vegas in her spare time. You should see her poker face."

Leaving them to tussle it out, Rosalina tucked her arm beneath her grandmother's elbow and led her towards the galley. "Let me show you the kitchen."

Nonna refrained from displaying any emotion as she touched all the surfaces. She opened and closed cupboards and drawers. It wasn't until she walked into the pantry that a look of pleasure lit up her face.

When Nonna finally emerged, her eyes beamed. "I've been waiting years for you to show me your home. It doesn't disappoint."

Rosalina was taken aback. Her home was Villa Pandolfini, the seven-hundred-year-old villa that had raised four generations of the Calucci family. The home she was born in and lived in until the day she left to explore the world as a naïve twenty-two-year-old. That was eight years ago. She'd been living on *Evangeline* for just over seven years. It surprised her to calculate that it was more than one quarter of her life. Maybe it was time she called it home.

Alessandro and Ginger walked in, holding hands, and by the look on his face he was itching to tell them something. He paused to say hello to everyone first, and Rosalina took the opportunity to lead Nonna to the lounges. She helped Nonna to sit and Helen sat beside her.

Alessandro rubbed his hands together. "I'm so pleased you're all here." He reached for Ginger's hand, and Rosalina's breath hitched. Certain he was about to announce their engagement, she readied to cheer.

"We've spent the morning with Professor Sezoine."

"Beauty," Jimmy said. "What'd he say?"

"As we had hoped, the blue cylinder contained a scroll--"

"We were lucky we didn't open it," Ginger interrupted. "Because it had a vial of liquid in there that would've ruined the whole thing."

"Anyway," Alessandro continued. "The scroll details an exchange that was made seven hundred years ago."

"The Calimala treasure?" Archer cocked his head, and Rosalina agreed with the confusion etched across his face.

Alessandro clicked his fingers. "*Correcto*. We learned that the priest who stole the treasure from the Church of St Apostoli, Tommasello da Lucca, was concerned about pirates, so he arranged for the ships to separate. The scroll inside the monkey statue constituted the deal he made with the three captains. The plan was that once he'd built his new church in Rhodes, he would arrange for the transportation of the rest of the treasure."

Jimmy clapped his hands together with a loud crack. "But he never made it."

Alessandro pointed his finger at Jimmy. "*Correcto*. So, the treasure could still be hidden where it was buried centuries ago."

Jimmy swatted Alessandro across the shoulder. "Spit it out, Sherlock. Where'd they bury it?"

Alessandro's thick eyebrows bounced together. "Abu Simbel Temple in Egypt."

"Holy shit, that's fantastic." Jimmy clapped his enormous hands together with a loud crack.

Rosalina felt Archer looking at her, and she glanced in his direction. A shadow played across his eyes. He was torn. The excitement of yet another treasure hunt was right at his fingertips, but she'd already asked him for a break from treasure hunting for a while.

"But. . ." Alessandro caught her attention. "There's one problem."

Jimmy scrunched up his nose. "Let me guess. . . more bad guys."

Rosalina's mind drifted to the picture of Nox in the hospital bed that she'd seen on the news yesterday. His back was broken, they'd said, and he may never walk again. She felt no pity. He was a murderer, though not convicted yet. The trial would be months away as the police continued to piece together and gather evidence to the mounting atrocities he'd committed.

"Worse than bad buys." Ginger's comment dragged Rosalina from her mental drifting.

"I don't think that's possible." She joined in the conversation.

Alessandro's bushy eyebrows launched upwards, and he cleared his throat. "Abu Simbel temple was relocated in 1968 to save it from being submerged when they built the Aswan High Dam."

"Which means our treasure is somewhere beneath Lake Nasser," Ginger said it like she was announcing a party or something.

Archer's jaw dropped.

As did Jimmy's. "It's in a lake? In Egypt?"

"That's what we believe." Alessandro twisted his hands together.

Nonna clapped her hands together. "Oh, how exciting. The way you gather these clues together is *affascinante*. Are you going to look for it?"

Rosalina frowned at her. "Nonna?"

"What, Rosa? Hardly anyone lives the exciting life you have. I think it's wonderful."

"Me too." Jimmy beamed.

Rosalina shot Jimmy a look.

The smile slipped from his face. "What?" He shrugged.

Rosalina turned her knees towards her grandmother. "Nonna, these treasure hunts take me away from you." She owed it to her family to be there for them now. It didn't matter what Archer said, or the rest of her family. . . Filippo's death was her fault.

"*Ridicolo.*" Nonna scowled. "You phone me all the time. I speak to you more than I speak to all the family put together."

Rosalina looked deep into Nonna's dark eyes. "Really?"

"Yes, really. They're so busy with careers and bambini." She flicked her hand as if brushing away flies. "It is *importante* to me that you enjoy your life."

Rosalina swallowed and stood. She reached for Archer, and he strode to her side and draped his arm over her shoulder.

"Nonna." She glanced at all of them before she fixed her eyes on her grandmother. "We have some news. Archer and I are having a baby."

Nonna clapped, everybody cheered, and Archer kissed her temple. He then looked at his mother, beaming. "You're going to be a grandma, Mom."

Tears sprung to Helen's eyes. "Wonderful." Her chin dimpled. "Wonderful, wonderful."

Nonna tried to jump up but fell down again and Rosalina giggled as she lowered to her knees at her side and wrapped her arms around her frail old grandmother, the most important woman in the world to her. "This is why we can't go on any more treasure hunts, Nonna. We're going to be a family."

Nonna squeezed her then pulled back. She waved her hand in an arc, taking in the people surrounding them. "Darling, this is your family too. You've been together for many years and it's time you accepted this. Treasure hunting is what you do, and from what you've told me, you are very good." She raised one eyebrow. "Maybe I can come with you one day."

Rosalina felt her eyes bulge. "Really?"

"*Certamente!*" Nonna clasped Rosalina's hand within hers. "Rosa, every time you speak of what you do, you have gleaming in your eyes. You are living your dream. Not many *popolo* do."

"I'll drink to that." Jimmy held up an imaginary drink.

"I think we should all have a drink. Except you, Rosa." Ginger giggled and trotted off towards the bar with Alessandro following her.

They were soon swept up in an impromptu party, and it was several hours later when Rosalina was in the kitchen, checking on the savory scrolls Nonna had baked that Archer wrapped his arms around her stomach.

"Gotcha," he said. "How's my gorgeous baby-maker going?"

She snuggled into him. "You won't be able to do that soon." At twelve weeks, she was just beginning to show signs of her pregnancy. "I'm sorry I announced our pregnancy like that." She'd had trouble convincing Archer to keep it a secret, and they had previously agreed to make an occasion of their announcement.

He picked her up, placed her on the counter and nudged his hips between her knees. "Are you kidding? It couldn't have gone better if we'd planned it."

She pressed her forehead against his. "I'm sorry, babe."

"Why?"

"For being so selfish."

He pulled back. "You're not--"

She placed a finger on his lips, hushing him. "Our childhoods were very different. Our families were different. Our homes were different. And I'd always stubbornly believed mine was better. But I was wrong,

Arch. What we have here. . ." She glanced about the room. "This is the best home in the world. It's the perfect place to raise children."

He tilted his head and the kitchen lights caught the golden halo of flecks around his dark irises. "Are you sure, baby?"

"I'm more than sure. I'm convinced."

"What about the treasure hunting?"

It scared her to answer, not because she didn't believe it was right, for now. But neither of them had any comprehension of how their lives would change once their little baby came into the world. But even as the debate rolled around her head, she knew that with *Evangeline* as their home, and Archer as the father, this little baby would have the best of everything.

"I think we should do it quickly, before this baby takes over our lives."

"Are you serious? We're still treasure hunting?" His eyes searched hers, no doubt seeking truth.

She cupped his cheeks and drew him in for a lingering kiss. "Yes, we're still treasure hunting."

Authors Note

The Awa Maru was a Japanese ocean liner that was requisitioned by the Japanese Navy during World War Two. Whist the author has detailed some truth of the ship's history and its ultimate sinking near the end of the war, many details have also been fictionalized for the purpose of this story.

The Awa Maru was also rumored to be involved in billions of dollars' worth of missing treasure and the priceless Peking Man skulls. Some of these details have also been fictionalized for the purpose of this story.

∾

DEAR READER, THANK YOU FOR FOLLOWING ROSALINA AND CARTER AND the gang in their journey to find ancient treasure but not get killed along the way.

ARE YOU READY FOR ANOTHER ACTION-PACKED ADVENTURE?

. . .

KEEP TURNING THE PAGES FOR MORE THRILLING BOOKS BY KENDALL Talbot, including the stand-alone books in Kendall's Maximum Exposure series: Zero Escape, Deadly Twist and Extreme Limit.

P.S. FOR AUTHORS, REVIEWS ARE LIKE FINDING GOLD AFTER A LONG HARD treasure hunt. . . they're priceless. It doesn't need to be much, just a quick star rating and maybe a couple of words saying what you loved about my book.

THANK YOU AND HAPPY READING,
Kendall Talbot

Lost In Kakadu

Together, they survived the plane crash. Now the real danger begins.

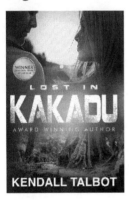

Socialite, Abigail Mulholland, has spent a lifetime surrounded in luxury… until her scenic flight plummets into the remote Australian wilderness. When rescue doesn't come, she finds herself thrust into a world of deadly snakes and primitive conditions in a landscape that is both brutal and beautiful. But trekking the wilds of Kakadu means fighting two wars—one against the elements, and the other against the magnetic pull she feels toward fellow survivor Mackenzie, a much younger man.

Mackenzie Steel had finally achieved his dreams of becoming a five-star chef when his much-anticipated joy flight turned each day into a waking nightmare. But years of pain and grief have left Mackenzie no stranger to a harsh life. As he battles his demons in the wild, he finds he has a new struggle on his hands: his growing feelings for Abigail, a woman who is as frustratingly naïve as she is funny.

Fate brought them together. Nature may tear them apart. But one thing is certain—love is as unpredictable as Kakadu, and survival is just the beginning…

Lost in Kakadu is a gripping action-adventure novel set deep in Australia's rugged Kakadu National Park. Winner of the Romantic Book of the Year in 2014, this full-length, stand-alone novel is an extraordinary story of endurance, grief, survival and undying love.

Extreme Limit

Two lovers frozen in ice. One dangerous expedition.

Holly Parmenter doesn't remember the helicopter crash that claimed the life of her fiancé and left her in a coma. The only details she does remember from that fateful day haunt her—two mysterious bodies sealed within the ice, dressed for dinner rather than a dangerous hike up the Canadian Rockies.

No one believes Holly's story about the couple encased deep in the icy crevasse. Instead, she's wrongly accused of murdering her fiancé for his million-dollar estate. Desperate to uncover the truth about the bodies and to prove her innocence, Holly resolves to climb the treacherous mountain and return to the crash site. But to do that she'll need the help of Oliver, a handsome rock-climbing specialist who has his own questions about Holly's motives.

When a documentary about an unsolved kidnapping offers clues as to the identity of the frozen bodies, it's no longer just Oliver and Holly heading to the dangerous mountaintop . . . there's also a killer, who'll stop at nothing to keep the case cold.

Will a harrowing trip to the icy crevasse bring Holly and Oliver the answers they seek? Or will disaster strike twice, claiming all Holly has left?

Extreme Limit is a thrilling, stand-alone, action-adventure novel with a dash of romance set high in the Canadian Rockies.

Deadly Twist

An ancient Mayan Temple. A dark family secret. A desperate fight for survival.

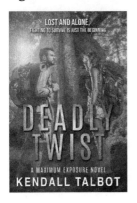

When a mysterious ancient Mayan temple is discovered by a team of explorers deep in the Yucatan jungle, the world is entranced. But Liliana Bennett is shocked by the images sweeping the headlines. She's seen the temple before, drawn in detail, in her late father's secret journal.

Now, the explorers at Agulinta aren't the only ones digging up secrets. Liliana is consumed by the mysteries surrounding her father's sketches and, refusing to believe she's out of her depth, she heads to Mexico, determined to see the temple for herself.

To reach the heart of the jungle, she'll have to join forces with Carter Logan, a nature photographer with a restless heart and secrets of his own. But a journey to Agulinta means battling crocodiles, lethal drug runners, and an unforgiving Mother Nature.

Lost and alone, they stumble upon something they should never have seen. Liliana's quest for answers becomes a desperate race to stay alive. Will Agulinta be the key to their survival? Or will Carter and Liliana become victims to the cruel relentless jungle and the evil men lurking within?

Deadly Twist is a gripping, stand-alone, action-adventure novel with a dash of romance, set deep in Mexico's Yucatan Jungle.

Zero Escape

To survive, Charlene must accept that her whole life was a lie.

For twenty years, Charlene Bailey has been living by the same mantra: pay in cash, keep only what you can carry, trust no one and always be ready to run. That is until her father is brutally murdered in New Orleans by a woman screaming a language Charlene doesn't understand. When police reveal the man she'd known all her life was not her biological father, Charlene is swept up in a riptide of dark secrets and deadly crimes.

The key to her true identity lies in a dangerous Cuban compound run by a lethal kingpin, but Charlene can't reach it alone. After a life of relying on herself, she'll have to trust Marshall Crow, a tough-as-nails ex-Navy man, to smuggle her into Havana.

The answers to Charlene's past are as dark as the waters she and Marshall must navigate, but a killer in the shadows will stop at nothing to drown the truth.

Zero Escape is a heart-pounding, stand-alone, action-adventure novel with a dash of romance that crosses from New Orleans to the back streets of Havana, Cuba.

Made in the USA
Middletown, DE
22 June 2021